the Unplanned Life of Josie Hale

STEPHANIE EDING

sourcebooks
casablanca

Copyright © 2022 by Stephanie Eding
Cover and internal design © 2022 by Sourcebooks
Cover illustration by Hannah Strassburger/Sourcebooks

Sourcebooks and the colophon are registered trademarks of Sourcebooks.

Published by Sourcebooks Casablanca, an imprint of Sourcebooks
P.O. Box 4410, Naperville, Illinois 60567-4410
(630) 961-3900
sourcebooks.com

Library of Congress Cataloging-in-Publication Data

Names: Eding, Stephanie, author.
Title: The unplanned life of Josie Hale / Stephanie Eding.
Description: Naperville, Illinois : Sourcebooks Casablanca, [2022]
Identifiers: LCCN 2021048842 (print) | LCCN 2021048843 (ebook)
Subjects: LCGFT: Domestic fiction. | Humorous fiction. | Novels.
Classification: LCC PS3605.D53 U57 2022 (print) | LCC PS3605.D53 (ebook)
 | DDC 813/.6--dc23/eng/20211008
LC record available at https://lccn.loc.gov/2021048842
LC ebook record available at https://lccn.loc.gov/2021048843

Printed and bound in the United States of America.
VP 10 9 8 7 6 5 4 3 2 1

1

Deep-Fried Emotional Support

ONLY A FEW MORE days until the county fair closed for another season, and Josie hadn't gotten her fried food fix yet. She could run into anybody there. Literally anybody: her grandmother, an ex-boyfriend, that one girl from the smoothie shop who already judged her for not sticking around to save her marriage...

The car engine shut off, and Josie breathed in the aroma of cow manure through the open car windows. She probably should have sought therapy at a time like this, but instead she opted for a corn dog.

She didn't want just any ole corn dog either. It had to come from the county fair, made in an overheated food truck, and deep-fried to a crisp. Twice. A funnel cake or elephant ear would suffice for dessert. After all, she was eating for two now. She was absolutely, un-questionably, dollar-store-test-certified pregnant as of an hour ago.

Despite the late August sun burning with the fury of hell, Josie trudged through the fairgrounds, tugging her jean shorts down between her sweaty thighs whenever the need arose.

She should be in her bed crying right now, making a plan. Surely, that's what the evening held in store for her: punching her pillow, doing some internet research, and crying some more. But cravings took precedence over common sense at the moment.

After she shoved a few corn dogs down her throat, she'd feel better. Her parents would be home from work soon, and she'd break the news to them. Not like she could hide a baby for long when she lived with them.

And Grant, the baby's father, deserved to know how their failed attempt to mend their marriage had resulted in new life.

That was some sucky irony right there. As if she hadn't longed to erase that drunken night a thousand times already. Josie bit hard on her knuckle and walked across the grassy excuse for a parking lot.

At the Lions Club booth, she examined the fair's layout and simultaneously scoped out her surroundings for anyone she knew. Fairs always brought the locals together. The idea of having an impromptu reunion with everyone in her hometown almost made her forget about lunch.

Almost.

After she got the corn dog, she'd be able to think more clearly. Deep-fried food made everything better. It was science.

Josie hit the dusty midway, and the golden mix of sand and earth powdered her sweaty legs. An earsplitting ring sounded when some guy hit the Skee-Ball jackpot. Distant carousel flutes sang their usual haunting ditty that always made her check over her shoulder to ensure no murderous clowns stalked about.

No bloody clowns, but the carnies definitely heckled harder than she remembered from high school. In their boredom, they pleaded for her to come and play.

Not today, Satan.

The setup had changed somewhat from the last time she'd visited. It seemed cruel to hide the food vendors from a preggo lady, but Clarkson, Illinois's biggest attractions remained a Pizza Hut and a half-dead mall. They couldn't afford anything close to a mega-fair for people to get lost in.

Josie rounded a corner and found rival schools set up with their food stands, attempting to earn money for their respective band programs. It was like gang territory for small-town folk. But even a turf war with flying baritones couldn't keep Josephine Hale from her goal.

She took longer strides up to the food stand, retrieved a few dollars from her pocket, and searched the menu. "Can I get a corn dog?"

"Ketchup?" The raspy-voiced vendor either smoked five packs of cigarettes a day or had taken a shot of boiling fryer grease at some point in his career.

"Yes, please." Josie leaned against the counter. Sort of. It came up to her shoulders, so more like she tucked herself underneath it. If she knew anybody at the fair, maybe they wouldn't look *below* the food truck. Even if they did, her position should give off enough don't-talk-to-me-vibes to keep them away.

After gathering her napkins and catching sight of the vinegar squirt bottle, she tapped on the glass window to add fries to the order. She'd nearly forgotten that most important of side dishes, and holy mother, did she need it.

She ground the heel of her flip-flop into the dirt and forced her focus onto the horse racetrack behind the food truck line. The midway began filling up quicker than Josie wanted now that school had let out. She willed the raspy man to fry a little faster. The longer she stood with nothing to do but wait on her food, the more she recognized faces: a teller from her bank, some guy that ran for office and had his mug plastered all over people's yard signs, her eighth-grade science teacher.

"Josie Claybrook?" A smooth, husky voice rose behind her.

Oh, no.

She clutched the countertop until her fingers threatened to snap off. The muscles in her shoulders seized, and her face contorted into what had to be all kinds of attractive. Nothing good came from a surprise guest who referred to her by her maiden name. She could not mentally deal with a blast from the past right now.

Her flip-flops squeaked under her feet as she made the agonizing pivot toward her company. With a deep breath, she lifted her head.

"It *is* you!" The last person she expected to see rushed forward to pull her into his arms.

It had been twelve years since she'd nearly suffocated in that bear hug. Twelve years since she went away to college with promises to keep in touch. Their late-night instant messaging sustained them for a few months, but even that died because adult life killed all things good and wonderful.

"Kevin?" Josie coughed into his chest when he squeezed her again. She sucked in her stomach as much as physically possible, trying not to make the pregnancy announcement that already felt like a neon exclamation point over her head.

Kevin smelled exactly the way she remembered, triggering a montage of flashbacks: cruising in circles around town, climbing onto the roof to listen to music, toilet-papering their enemies' houses on Saturday nights. He'd been her best friend once. The first guy she danced with at a school function. The one who'd call her at midnight just because he couldn't wait to tell her about a movie he watched. One of the few people who ever knew her deepest, darkest crush.

"You look great." He released her to reveal the same goofball smile he'd given her during sixth-period chemistry when the teacher made them select project partners. "I totally didn't expect to run into you today."

"Likewise. I mean, wow. It's been forever. How have you been?" She immediately regretted the question. When asked, people reciprocate.

The corn-dog man interrupted the exchange like an apron-wearing hero. Josie grabbed the goods and stepped to the side for the next person in line: Kevin, apparently.

"Can I get two dogs?" He held up two fingers, then turned to Josie, clearly not about to let her get away so easily.

He hadn't changed much since high school. He'd cut his sandy curls shorter, though he still had to shake them out of his face. His shoulders had broadened. He stood a full foot and a half taller than her but had now gained a bit of muscle definition to go with it. Turning thirty suited him so much more than it did her.

"You're smaller than I remember," Kevin teased as if they hadn't spent more than a decade away from each other. He used to love setting his lunch tray on top of her head in the cafeteria or squishing her up against the bus window to use her as a pillow on field trips.

"Maybe your head just got bigger." Josie eased her posture and popped a fry into her mouth. Not *too* much had changed. Their friendship had always been an easy one.

"That's my little JoJo. Just as I left you." When he reached out for a high five, Josie balanced her food in one arm to oblige, but he didn't let go of her hand right away. "Dude, wait until Ben sees you."

Josie's entire body tensed, the edges of her lips trembling from her forced smile. Did he mean Ben Romero?

The sun turned up the heat a hundred degrees.

No. Not that Ben.

Anyone but him.

People like Ben were exactly why she shouldn't have gone to the fair over a stupid craving. Her world already threatened to hurl her into outer space at any moment, yet she *had* to risk her last thread of dignity by chasing down a corn dog.

Josie searched the heavens as she prayed for a freak storm that would send everyone dashing for cover. If she could escape in time, it'd be like none of this had ever happened.

Except she was still pregnant. Rain couldn't wash that away.

"Ben," Kevin called off toward one of the band pavilions.

Josie examined the sky, but no storm brewed. Not a single clap of thunder or bolt of lightning offered to save her from coming face-to-face with Benjamin Anthony Dominic Romero.

That deepest, darkest crush from high school and, conveniently, Kevin's best friend.

She bit her lip and pinched her eyes shut.

"Josie? No way." A hand cupped her shoulder, gently turning her to the side to face him.

No other choice. She met his gaze.

"Hey, Ben." Josie leaned into his side hug. At sixteen, she'd have given her left boob for this guy to smile at her, let alone pull her into his arms. He just had to do it now, when she looked like she'd crawled out of a dumpster, rather than in high school when she wore clothes that fit and shaved her armpits regularly.

"What are you doing here?" Ben took a bite of his pulled pork sandwich, dark eyes wide and as intoxicating as ever. "Thought you moved away."

She had to get a grip.

"I'm home now. Just wanted a corn dog." Because that explained everything. "I mean, I moved home this summer and came here for lunch today. I think corn dogs are the only reason anyone comes to the fair, right?"

"Not this traitor." Kevin gestured to his friend and rolled his eyes. "He eats pork from the enemy."

Ben's sandwich must have come from their high school rival's band booth. A decade ago, he wouldn't have dared set foot in enemy territory, lest his fellow football teammates ridicule him mercilessly.

"Come on, girl." Kevin slipped an arm around her and guided her along the midway. "Let's grab elephant ears and catch up."

How could she ever shake these guys if they knew her every deep-fried weakness? She didn't have the strength.

"Great." Her heart jumped so fast she'd likely cough it up if she didn't force it back down with some food. She clutched the paper container holding her lunch. Second lunch, if she wanted to be honest with herself.

"Gotta hear about all that's happened since graduation," Kevin added.

Josie ripped the corn dog from the bag and bit it so hard she nearly broke the wooden stick. Next time her life fell apart, she'd remember to just cry about it instead.

2

The Corn Dog Pact

KEVIN CHOSE THE CLARKSON High School band pavilion as the venue for their little reunion. The tattered shelter provided adequate seating with picnic tables, shade from the scorching sun, and an audience to enjoy the awkward reconnection taking place between three old friends. The only thing that could make it truly perfect was if one of the birds in the rafters dropped a bomb on Josie's head and added a hint more embarrassment to her situation.

"Drinks on me, like old times." Kevin scrunched until his long legs fit under the picnic table, and he placed a tray of frosty root beers at its center.

Thank God he'd returned when he did. She and Ben may have choked on their silence if the glue that held them together all those years ago hadn't come back. While the three of them often spent Friday nights together in high school, Kevin could hardly take a bathroom break without Josie and Ben becoming the two most uncomfortable creatures on earth, staring at the TV in silence or trying to make conversation over essay due dates. Kind of like the last few months of her marriage, actually. Only not in the same dreamy teenage way one avoids making eye contact with a crush. More like the silence-is-better-than-fighting way people use to attempt to save themselves from divorce court. Lot of good that did.

"Old times? When have you ever bought drinks?" Ben side-eyed his friend and took a big bite of his sandwich.

Josie held up her corn dog like a pointing finger. "Well, there was that one time at the football game when he refilled my water bottle at the drinking fountain."

"See? Generous." Kevin shifted again, and his knees knocked on the underside of the table. "So, JoJo. What's been going on with you? Why you keep holding your stomach? You sick or pregnant or something?"

A piece of french fry caught in Josie's throat. She swallowed hard to push it down, reaching for her root beer for help.

Ben groaned and whacked his friend upside the head. At least Ben understood the basic rules for *not* asking women taboo questions. Kevin, however, threw his hands in the air as if completely confused by the unwarranted violence.

Josie twiddled her thumbs in her lap, trying to gather her thoughts enough to address this beautiful nightmare before her. "Um, what's been going on with me? Well, I graduated from UIC, got married, rented an apartment in Chicago, worked at Lincoln Regional High School as a history teacher for four years… And, yes, it turns out that I am, in fact, with child."

Saying it out loud felt like a lie. Like she played a role in someone else's life.

If her math was correct, and she'd never been particularly good at that subject, she was about three months along. If her last birth-control shot hadn't eliminated her periods, she might have gotten a heads-up sooner. Not like she could count on her shorts getting tighter as a legitimate indicator, considering how much she'd eaten lately.

Three months pregnant. Holy shit. It was like she had no baby in there at all, and then boom! One appears and it's the size of a plum. A whole flipping plum coming out of nowhere.

Which sounded weirdly delicious right now. Did the ag building still have those produce stands?

"That's awesome." Kevin extended his fist, ripe for the bumping. His need for hand-to-hand validation hadn't changed over the years.

Josie's shoulders drooped, and she stared at his closed hand, unable to return his enthusiasm. This was her Kevin. He'd hugged her when she hadn't made the track team. He had walked her home after late-night football games to make sure no one abducted her. He had seen her cry many times when relationships fell apart, when Ben hadn't asked her to prom, or when she and her BFF, Ella, had fought over something stupid...

She sucked in a deep breath and stared at the contents atop the picnic table. "I'm also in the process of getting divorced, which led to leaving my teaching job, moving out of Chicago, working part time at a smoothie shop, and living in my parents' spare bedroom. So that's great too."

Neither Kevin nor Ben spoke or indicated they'd even heard her. She should have sugar-coated it somehow instead of dropping a cringe-worthy bomb. Now everything would be awkward.

Er. Awkward-*er.*

"So, how are you guys?" Josie peeked up through the strands of hair that had fallen from her messy bun.

Ben examined his sandwich wrapper, barbecue sauce dripping down his hand. He did nothing to prevent the mess. Kevin, too, didn't seem to notice he'd dipped his corn dog in ketchup so many times the outer layer had fallen off.

"Wow, Josie," Kevin finally said.

She shook her head to force her brain to function. The appropriate thing to do would have been to shut up. This had to be the *baby-brain* phenomenon she'd heard so much about it. Not cool. "Yeah, can we pretend that didn't just happen?"

Kevin dropped his corn dog into the paper bowl and sat up

straighter. "Lots to unpack there. But if it makes you feel any better, we aren't exactly living the dream either."

Ben responded with nothing more than a huff.

"I've thoroughly embarrassed myself. You might as well take a turn." Her head throbbed in the raging heat of the band pavilion. Or maybe that came with making horrible confessions to people she had loved and lost and then found again.

This day had gotten out of control, and there was still so much of it left to go. If only she could melt under the table and die in the pile of straw wrappers and sweetener packets.

Ben pushed Josie's elephant ear across the table until it brushed her arm. "You ready for this? I quit college because I'd gotten my then-girlfriend pregnant and couldn't handle both. Never finished my degree like I planned. I've been working at a shitty factory with shitty pay for the last ten years. My daughter hates me. Her mother and I broke up right after she was born, and there hasn't been a moment of peace in that relationship since. I bought a house but can't afford furniture or, really, the house. And I'm pretty sure I'll be a hundred before I ever pay off my student loan on my one measly year of college because I defaulted for so long." Ben waved a hand to give his friend the floor. "Kevin?"

Kevin took a long sip of his root beer, belched, and leaned forward on his elbows. "I sell insurance for my dad and am set to inherit the company one day. I live with Ben and spend most of my free time playing video games and getting takeout because who wants to cook in this economy? I'm single but still go on dates. Oh, and I just had to get the air-conditioning fixed in my car because it went out."

"Yikes." Josie tore at her elephant ear, covering her fingers in sticky cinnamon sugar. Kevin had always made her smile when she hit one of those despair walls. In algebra, when she had failed her second test in a row, he'd offered to flash the teacher to get her a better grade. "You win, Kev. Hands down, your life is the worst."

"*That's* what you present when we bare our souls?" Ben shook his head and shifted toward Kevin. "I live with you. I know firsthand how pathetic your life is."

Kevin scoffed. "Okay, so sometimes I wear socks with sandals when I run errands or snore when I sleep on my back. You don't have to be a dick about it. Geesh."

Ben picked up Kevin's corn dog and shoved it into his friend's mouth. Kevin choked on a laugh—and, well, the corn dog—and punched Ben in the shoulder.

"In his lame attempt at solidarity, what Kevin meant to say is that he's completely broke due to mounting credit-card debt. He's dating around because he can't keep a girlfriend for more than a few days. The insurance job? He hates it with a passion and does not *want* to inherit the company." Ben tapped his finger against his chin when he regarded Kevin again. "And didn't your doctor tell you to watch your cholesterol?"

"Hearsay. It's all hearsay, Benjamin. You have no proof." Kevin finished his corn dog in one bite and reached for his elephant ear.

Josie giggled into her napkin. If only she attacked life the way Kevin did: deny it and move on like a boss. "Hearsay or not, I'm glad I'm not alone in the hell that is adulthood. Though socks with flip-flops, Kev? I mean, seriously. Get yourself together."

She tried to laugh with them, but hormones spiked her joy away like a front-row volleyball player. Tears pricked her eyes, and she couldn't take in the stuffy air. She covered her face with her hands, fighting in vain to make the emotions go away.

Faking a cough might work.

Her chest tightened. She could do nothing to stop it.

Behind her fingers, Josie cried like she had so many times since June 4 when her entire world fell apart. Sometimes, it came on with such force she had to lock herself in a bathroom until the moment passed. Other times, she found herself in a public place with no escape. Pregnancy would absolutely make that so much worse.

A large hand coiled around Josie's wrist, pulling her fingers away from her face far enough to slip a napkin into her palm.

"Let it out, kiddo," Kevin whispered across the table. "If anyone asks, I'll tell them Ben said something stupid."

Josie couldn't see them from behind the wadded napkin, but she heard a thump that could be Ben's reaction to Kevin's comment. Gosh, she'd missed them. She hadn't realized it until now, but she had.

After using the gritty paper to wipe away any trace of raccoon eyes, Josie dotted at her nose and finally let her hands fall away from her face. She glanced around the pavilion to dry her eyes and ensure nobody had noticed the disheveled lady weeping in the corner.

"Sorry." Josie ripped more of her elephant ear to shreds. "That keeps happening. Probably should have stayed home, but I had to have that damned corn dog."

"Can't resist the power of a corn dog. I get it." Kevin passed an extra napkin across the table when another tear trickled down Josie's cheek.

To think, she still had another seven months of these hormone-fueled outbursts to go. The Plum Baby had entirely too much power over her. "Thanks. I appreciate you not judging me. At least, not out loud."

"I'm used to Ben's crying. You're fine."

Ben's face scrunched like Popeye at yet another insult coming from his roommate. "What did I do to you?"

Kevin ignored him, leaning across the table toward Josie. "And if you hadn't come to the fair today, you wouldn't have run into us, and we wouldn't get to hate on our thirties together. So, that's not all that bad, right?"

"Gotta vent sometimes, I guess." Seeing these two men had become the one flicker of joy in the day from hell. The simplicities of their high school lives had long passed. To think, Ben had a kid of his own now. A broken relationship between father and daughter had to be like a knife twisting his insides.

And Kevin. Knowing he had to inherit an entire company and spend the rest of his life working a job he hated? Whether he admitted it or not, that really sucked. Their respective futures seemed awfully bleak in their current states.

A woman wearing a band shirt interrupted the trio to take their trash. The pavilion had grown fuller over the past half hour as suppertime arrived. Josie yawned, and her eyes grew heavy. Soon, she'd have to head home and eat yet another meal with her parents. Her news would inevitably slip out. Probably not subtly.

And there was the Grant situation.

It'd be best if she wrapped things up with the guys, went home, and got the hellishness over with. Then she could crawl under the sheets and play dead, since fatigue had hit her like a freight train.

Kevin clutched the edge of the picnic table and stretched backward. The crackling that ran down his spine echoed over the hum of the surrounding crowd. Yep, age had caught up with them.

"So, how do we fix it?" Kevin asked.

Josie rubbed at her eyes and tried to force some pep into her voice. "Fix what exactly?"

Kevin swirled his hands in front of him for effect. "This. All the crap going wrong with your lives."

"Kevin." Ben took a long swig of root beer to accompany his eye roll. "We can't just *fix* what's wrong with *our* lives."

"Sure you can. We just need to figure out how. Like Dad says at all our lame-ass board meetings, 'There's always a solution to every problem.'" Kevin smiled so wide his cheeks nearly swallowed his eyes. "I don't know why that was my only takeaway from a budget assessment, but whatever."

Josie kicked her leg over the picnic table bench to stand. "You're cute, Kev, but I'm with Ben. There's not a quick fix to my situation."

"I didn't say it had to be quick. You just need the proper motivation." Kevin snatched his cup and stood, too, elbowing Ben on his way up. "Like, you remember back in Mr. Clune's history class when he told us he'd bring in pizza if we all memorized the presidents in the correct order?"

Ben's arms went limp, and he groaned toward the ceiling. "I remember we didn't get that pizza party because you put Ronald Reagan on the list, like, six times. Mr. Clune bought us candy bars as a substitute because your sob story was so convincing. And then you made us swear that if any of us ever became president, we'd appoint you Secretary of Education and abolish school testing."

"Oh my gosh. I forgot about that!" A beautiful flashback was just the medicine she needed. "You were always forcing us into some kind of stupid promise or challenge."

If it wasn't a promise or challenge, it was a pact. They'd go to the spring fling together if they couldn't find real dates and perform the dance from *Naked Gun 2½*. They'd put one another's names in for homecoming attendant. They'd all complain to the cafeteria staff until they cut the pizza slices bigger.

She preferred the pacts over the challenges, honestly. No one wanted to eat twenty dollars' worth of Taco Bell at midnight, no matter how much trash talk they got from an opponent.

"Hey, my stupid challenges got shit done, didn't they? That's what you two need right now." Kevin launched his wadded trash into the receptacle like he was shooting a basketball. "You need a good ole-fashioned pact to motivate you toward change and a life worthy of Kevintude."

"Nope. I regret even bringing this up." Ben started around the table to meet up with Josie as they exited the pavilion. "Besides, if your pacts were so successful, you and Josie would be married by now, if I'm remembering correctly."

She'd almost forgotten about that one: a football game after-party pact that got a little silly. "That was if neither of us had married by twenty-eight. I was married." A lifetime of laughter with Kevin might have been preferable to what she'd had with Grant, even if they'd lacked the whole romantic attraction part.

Hindsight would have had her make that pact with Ben. She might have dropped out of college and locked herself in her room until she turned twenty-eight. He made thirty look pretty damn good with his stupid-cute dimples and spectacular muscle definition.

Not that she needed to daydream about an old crush mid-divorce.

"Well, you guys aren't married *now*. Just sayin'." Ben ducked out of the way in case anyone tried to whack him.

Kevin spun around to walk backward in front of his friends. "Ben, you're distracting us from the point here. I'm trying to get y'all to focus. I'm declaring it right here, right now. We're forming a pact to change our lives around."

"*You* are forming a pact." Josie laughed. "Let's be clear on that."

"One person can't make a pact, Josie. We're doing this." Kevin held up his hand for a high five and waited, nearly crashing into several people as he continued in reverse down the midway.

Ben tapped his hand to Kevin's. "I'm not getting a say in this since I live with you, am I?"

"None whatsoever." Kevin turned his outstretched hand to Josie. "How 'bout it? You need the kind of help only an expert like myself can give."

"*Ugh*. Whatever." Josie clapped her hand to his.

She only had one way to go from rock bottom anyway.

3

A Casserole of Confessions

JOSIE STEERED ONTO HER street and groaned at the sight of her mother's car already in the driveway. If her mom saw her looking so rough, she'd freak out and assume something horrible had happened, like a mugging, a car accident, or that Josie just missed Grant *that* much.

Her mom had already suggested group therapy for divorcees offered through the YWCA. She'd even produced multiple sticky notes full of prescription drugs advertised on daytime TV. If Josie couldn't pull it together, nothing would stop her mom from slipping pills in her pasta or dropping her off at some sad summer camp for lonely women.

Josie had already had to cancel several doctor's appointments her mother had scheduled for her at the gynecologist because Josie hadn't had a full exam in well over a year. As hard as cash had been to come by, she wasn't about to ditch work at the smoothie shop to appease her mother and spend a hundred-and-some bucks on the worst kind of medical exam.

The car spat its usual putter when Josie put it in park and killed the engine. She flipped the mirror down from the visor to check the damage, sighing at the dark circles under her eyes and frizzy hair sticking up like lightning had struck. This was the Josie she'd presented to Kevin and Ben. At least they seemed to understand a lot of her struggles, considering how their own lives hadn't quite gone according to plan. She still couldn't get over the fact that Ben had a daughter now. One could only assume the child was gorgeous, if she'd gotten any of her father's glorious genes. And she absolutely would have. Obviously.

Blerg. She needed to call her own baby daddy. Or text. What did a text of this magnitude look like? *Hey, Grant. It's Josie, your estranged wife. Listen, I know we're in the middle of a divorce, but you knocked me up. Surprise!*

Maybe take out an ad on a Chicago city bus?

Did Hallmark make cards for this?

She could pay her lawyer to take care of it.

Every nerve inside Josie's body tingled, and blood rushed to her head, threatening to knock her out against the steering wheel. If she didn't call Grant now, when would she do it? After breaking the news to her parents and hearing their opinions on the matter? In the middle of the night, during a full-blown panic attack? How about when she screamed through contractions and pushed out the evidence?

Her unsteady fingers tapped across the screen, hitting many wrong numbers before she found the correct ones. It didn't matter that she'd deleted his number two months ago. She'd always have it memorized. After all, she still accidentally wrote his social security number rather than her own when filling out documents.

The green Send seemed to prick her finger when she touched it, her hand slow to draw the phone up to her ear. The deafening ring set her nerves further on edge.

"Josie?" Grant answered in a gruff tone.

Her lips pasted together as her name echoed through the phone. She should have waited until she had a better plan for what to say.

"Josie, you there?" He probably thought she'd butt-dialed him.

"Yes, hi." The last time they'd spoken, she'd had an armload of clothes and photos and shouted at him to stay away from her forever. Her lawyer handled any other contact with him these days.

Grant paused on the other end, then cleared his throat. "Why are you calling? Are you okay?"

"No. I mean, yes. I'm fine. But...I have to tell you something."

He used to be so easy to talk to. They'd stay up for hours, laughing as they planned their future. She wanted a house in the suburbs, two kids, one cat, and a teaching career with summers off. He wanted to become a full-fledged veterinarian, adopt two giant dogs, no kids please, but the suburban house was fine.

No kids. He hadn't wanted them.

The only thing they had in common was a love for reality ghost shows—not enough to sustain a marriage, apparently.

"What's up?" His apprehension oozed through the phone.

She pictured him scratching through his shaggy, chestnut waves the way he always did when he fretted over something out of his control.

"I'm pregnant."

Suddenly, none of it felt real. Maybe she'd dreamed the positive pregnancy test, or it had produced a false result. She had gotten the stick at the dollar store. The quality couldn't be that amazing. Had she seriously called the last person on earth she wanted to talk to and dumped information on him with no legitimate proof? Starting with a doctor's appointment might have been a good idea here.

"You're pregnant," Grant deadpanned.

"I think so." Sweat pasted the phone to the side of her face.

He let out a breathy laugh. "You can't be serious. It's...*mine?*"

"Yes, I'm serious, and it's definitely yours." The insecurity melted away like snow in the desert. Did he think she'd called to prank him with something like this?

Grant cursed. "That's... I'm kind of at work right now. Can I call you later? I need to process this."

"Sure." She should have known he'd dodge the topic or worm his way out of this conversation somehow. Hell, if she even needed help unloading groceries, he'd find some excuse to hold him up until she'd done it all herself.

Grant ended the call before Josie could come up with something smart to say in response.

Air pushed out between her lips like a deflating balloon. The phone fell from her grasp, bounced off her leg, and landed somewhere in the center console. She reclined her seat all the way and tried to catch her breath. At least the tears had completely dried up with the newfound desire to reach through the phone and strangle her ex.

That part was over. Now she had to tell her parents.

When she sat up, she almost screamed at the sight of her mother standing in front of the car, hand hovering over her eyes to block out the evening sun.

"What are you doing?" her mom called out.

Josie stared, everything but that phone call now a total blur in her mind. She unfolded herself from the car, gathered her misplaced phone and purse, and tugged her tank top down over her belly. Weird to think all the bloating she experienced in the past few weeks was actually a human being and not a side effect of massive sugar consumption. Another month or so and she'd have to use a hair tie to fasten the button on her jean shorts and figure out a way to keep her tank top from rolling up like a projector screen.

She needed a cold shower to wash away the fair grossness so she could retreat to bed for a Netflix marathon and ice cream. Anything to distract her.

"You're home late. Where ya been?" her mother asked as they walked up the winding path to the front door. She still wore her doctor's office scrubs, with the addition of a worn oven mitt on her left hand.

"Got lunch at the fair." Once through the door, Josie tossed her bag in the corner and kicked off her dusty flip-flops. Dirt lines painted both her feet.

"Lunch? It's almost six. What time did you eat?" Her mother returned to the kitchen, pots and pans clamoring the moment she was out of sight.

Josie ignored the question. Not that she could remember what time she'd eaten second lunch during a wild day like today.

"And fair food?" Her mother reappeared so Josie could see her judgmental expression. "Is that good for the baby?"

"I dunno, Mom. I… Wait. What?" Josie's blood ran cold when she met her mother's gaze. "How do you know about that?"

"Come help me set the table."

Josie took a few slow steps forward to catch up to her mind-reading mother. "Mom?"

This was too weird.

Her mother's balled fist pressed against her waist. "I've suspected for a while, Josephine. You ate all my Tums, you fall asleep every time we put on a movie, and you've gotten extremely forgetful. For example, you left the positive pregnancy test on the bathroom floor."

Josie's eyes sprang wide open.

"Why do you think I've been trying to get you an appointment these past few weeks?" Her mom threw her hands in the air. "You keep canceling them."

"I didn't think it was all that suspicious since you work there, but I couldn't go because of *my* work." The words coming from her mouth seemed ridiculous given the circumstances. "Does Dad know?"

"Yes. I told him a few weeks ago and confirmed it when I found the test. I'll get you on Dr. Mallory's schedule for later in the week, and you're going this time." Her mother rounded the island counter and retrieved some salad toppings from the fridge. "Is the baby Grant's?"

"Yes, it's *Grant's*." Josie closed her eyes and wished away this moment.

"You said things weren't going well with him, but apparently they went well enough to make a baby?" Her mother slid the salad bowl down the counter and raised an eyebrow at her daughter. "Help me understand all this, because Diana hasn't been—"

"Mom, not now. *Please.*" Josie's mouth went dry. Over the past year, she'd come home for long weekends at a time without Grant, solely to get away for a bit. Her mother told her it was a phase. Lots of married people went through it. If they'd work on it, it'd be fine.

And they tried. Hence, how the baby came to be. And then, less than twenty-four hours later, she had caught him with someone else. There was no trying after that.

If only she could bring herself to tell her mother that part. Unfortunately, Josie's mother and Grant's mother, Diana, had struck up a wildly close friendship when first introduced. They even wore matching mother's dresses to the wedding and thought it was the best thing ever. The mothers still talked on the phone, trying to figure out what went wrong with their kids. Her mother swore up and down Diana had been acting strange lately and had been ignoring her texts and calls, but Josie wasn't about to investigate the reason why—or throw a shock like a pregnancy announcement into the mix of drama.

A lump the size of Montana formed in Josie's throat again. She had to get out of there. "I just need to go to bed right now, Mom."

"No, hang on. I'm making dinner." Her mother gestured to the spread of food with her mitted hand.

"I'm not hungry." Not after a heap of fair food, a brief but gut-wrenching conversation with Grant, and the promise of her mother's ongoing interrogation.

Her mom clicked her tongue and tossed her oven mitt onto the counter. "You can still sit with us and talk. I'm worried about you."

"I'm fine." Josie slid off her stool, ready to run.

"That's not…" Her mother hummed a frustrated tune. "What I mean to say is that your father and I wanted to talk to you about something tonight anyway, because it's going to directly affect you. It's not ideal timing, considering your circumstances, but it's a necessary conversation."

After the day she'd been through, the cryptic language had to stop. "What is it?"

Her mom circled around the island and sat on the stool opposite Josie. Turned out, they didn't need to wait on her father for this discussion after all. If present, he'd most likely sit quietly while his wife gave the lecture. He rarely got an opinion on matters after thirty-six years of marriage.

"Your father and I have decided to downsize." She paused and flattened her hands on the tops of her thighs. "We talked to the real estate agent this morning."

"You're selling the house?" Of all the bombs her mother could have dropped, Josie hadn't expected that one.

"We're hoping to move into something smaller by year's end, so we have it all wrapped up before Christmas. We're looking at one of those condos near the lake." Her mother reached across the counter and sprinkled more cheese into the salad bowl. "We didn't want to say anything until we knew for sure, but this house is bigger than we need since we're…empty nesters."

Josie examined the strokes of marbling on the countertop as she tried to process this. Her parents weren't empty nesters. They still had a daughter at home with them. Unless this was their way of ensuring they *didn't* have a daughter at home.

"Don't you go thinking we're kicking you out on purpose." Her mother placed a warm hand on top of Josie's knee. "We'd hoped to do this after you and Will went to college, but things got delayed when Grandpa Claybrook got sick. Since everything's calmed down now, we want to try again, especially now that Will's getting married. It'll be nice to travel and see them without having to manage this property."

Her parents had come to Chicago to visit Josie maybe twice a year since she moved there after high school. Now that her older brother, Will, the obvious favorite, had moved to Indianapolis, they wanted to sell all their possessions and go see him every chance they got.

"But you *are* kicking me out." Where would she go? Her piss-poor income from the smoothie shop had ended a day ago when it shut down for the end of the summer season. They normally stayed open until Labor Day, but closed a week early since the fair took away their business. Josie's stellar luck had struck again.

Her substitute teaching gig wouldn't start until someone needed her to fill in. It's not like she could count on a steady paycheck doing that. Everything she'd tried to save over the summer went straight to food and initial lawyer bills.

"I'll help you look for apartments, and your father and I have agreed to help you pay your first month's rent if necessary. With a baby on the way, you should have your own safe place to settle in." She gave Josie's knee a squeeze. "You have a lot to think about now: getting steadier work, insurance, talking to Grant—"

"I called him already."

Her mom covered her heart with her hand. "Called him? That's how you broke the news?"

This wasn't happening. Not on top of everything else. "Should I throw him a parade with baby-shaped balloons?"

"Seriously, Josephine." Her mother slid off her chair to return to the kitchen. She snatched up her oven mitt and flung open the oven to retrieve something that smelled like chicken casserole.

The garage door hummed at the side of the house, announcing her father's arrival and damming up the possibility of any other lectures from her mother.

"I'm going to shower." Josie hopped down from her stool and hurried to her room before her mother protested. She sank onto her lavender comforter and stared at the short wall of boxes lining the room. Her half-unpacked state took away from the bedroom's coziness, but she could never bring herself to find places to put her stuff. That was probably a good thing now that her mother demanded she pack it all up again.

Josie lifted her shirt and rested both hands across her bare abdomen. She tried to imagine the tiniest of babies sleeping beneath her fingers—tried to imagine herself as a mother. The thought used to come to her so easily in her early days with Grant. Rocking a baby to sleep while she and Grant watched an evening movie. Playfully arguing over whose turn it was to change a diaper. Celebrating together as their baby said its first words. Those images faded away to nothing over the years as they struggled to make things work.

She would have this kid. There was no doubt in her mind about that. But her beautiful plan for motherhood had gotten all shot to hell. She couldn't afford any of this, was about to lose the roof over her head for the second time that year, and didn't have the slightest idea where to begin with fixing any of it.

Her phone beeped with a text message. She groaned when she sat up and felt her hair pasted to her sweaty neck. The need for a shower had become desperate. Josie swiped the screen to read the message and did a double take.

Kevin?

When he'd said he wanted to keep in touch, she hadn't expected to hear from him a few hours after reconnecting.

His message was simple: JoJo, u up for drinks tonight with me and Benny? Want to run somethin by u.

Seeing her nickname on the screen made her smile. He'd always called her that. It took her back in time to eating tacos in the rain, ridiculous dance moves when their favorite jams came on the car radio, and passing notes under the desk during study hall. It also kind of transported her to that very afternoon. She could still taste the cinnamon sugar from her tearstained elephant ear.

Curiosity dictated her reply on the keyboard. She was not about to drag her newly pregnant butt out to a bar, but she did have a hankering for a milkshake, and since cravings were kind of her thing now…

Josie: Make it McDonald's and you're on.

Kevin: Meet ya in 20.

Twenty *minutes?* Josie nearly fell over her feet on her way to the bathroom. The shower would have to wait, but she could at least wash her face and throw on a clean shirt. They might have seen her cry, but pit stains crossed the line.

With a fresh coat of mascara and deodorant, she snuck out the front door to run off like a wayward teen. She needed a distraction more than she needed air in her lungs right now. And how could she resist a mysterious proposition from old friends and a glorious ice cream treat to sweeten the deal?

4

Mulling at McDonald's

THE SETTING SUN CREATED a glare across the windshield so intense, Josie had to stomp her foot on the gas and hope no cars hit her when she sped into the McDonald's parking lot. She snatched the spot under the flashing neon sign advertising their newest sandwich creation and stretched in her seat to examine the other cars down the row. Not like she knew what cars Kevin and Ben drove all these years later. It would have been a miracle if they still rolled around in the same puke-green Bravada and paint-chipped S-10 they drove in high school.

The memory of an awaiting proposition and snacks propelled her out of the car and toward the restaurant entrance. She'd barely pushed open the heavy door when an enormous arm swept around her and dragged her into a hug. Her face crashed into Kevin's armpit, muffling her laugh at the bizarre way he held her. He either had taken the time to shower or used some seriously impressive antiperspirant.

"I hear ice cream is good for babies." Kevin released her and pointed toward the menu.

Josie straightened her crumpled shirt and smoothed the flyaways around her ears. "Well, hopefully *something* I do is good for this baby."

"What?"

"Nothing. Mom drama." She sighed.

"Enough said. This is on me tonight." He extended an arm for her to go ahead of him and place her order.

As much as she wanted to protest his sweet offer, especially since she'd just learned of his financial distress courtesy of Ben, she couldn't turn down free ice cream.

Josie glanced up at the backlit menu as if she hadn't already memorized it many times over. She requested the largest vanilla shake offered and stepped away from the counter to look around the restaurant. Ben sat alone at a corner table near the window, licking M&M's ice cream off an elongated spoon.

How had it only been mere hours since they'd found one another again and snapped into friend mode like no time had passed? She'd spent so many weeknights at this very McDonald's with them, eating off the Dollar Menu, whining about homework, plotting new ways to rebel against their parents.

Watching Ben lick ice cream off spoons...

She blinked the thought away and returned her attention to Kevin before the past took her to uncomfortable places where she should definitely not go tonight. "So, what did you want to run by me?"

"Did you want to sit down first?" Kevin laughed. "We've got all night. Unless you have a curfew or something."

"Don't even say that out loud. I'm sure that's up next for me, if Mom has it her way."

Kevin squinted at the overhead menu. "That bad, huh?"

"It's like I'm thirteen all over again, but with baggage. Heaps and heaps of baggage and way more problems than I feel are necessary." Life had beaten the crap out of her lately. It seemed unfair she couldn't retaliate.

Another worker set Josie's milkshake on the counter with a thud. Kevin snatched it up, passing it to her like a peace offering. At least he seemed to understand that food could suppress the pain of almost any wound.

"You sure you don't want to get two?" he asked.

Of course, she wanted two. Maybe one day when they weren't all drowning in debt. "That's okay. Thanks, though."

Once Kevin got his large fries, caramel sundae, and two apple pies, they made their way toward the table. Even with only a handful of other people in the entire restaurant, Ben still waved wildly as if they'd never find him otherwise.

"Hey, you." Ben shoved his spoon into his mouth and held his outstretched fist across the table.

"Well, hi." Josie touched her fist to his. Was she supposed to make a sound with that?

"Have a seat, Josephine." Kevin sat at the head of the table and folded his hands in front of him.

Josephine now, huh? She'd walked straight into a business meeting. Perhaps jean shorts and an overworked tank top weren't the best attire for this.

"Okay. Not weird at all." She mirrored Kevin's hand folding. "By the way, I was not expecting to see either of you this soon." She sucked down a long drag of the velvety vanilla treat.

"Yeah, well, people always say they'll keep in touch, then you never hear from them again. We are not those people," Ben said. "Well, not this time anyway. We won't let that happen *again*." He winked and shoved another heaping scoop of ice cream into his mouth.

He just *had* to seal it with a wink.

Josie took another long sip of her shake, trying to absorb the unusual moment. The two men had become a bit of a vacation in human form, transporting her to a simpler time when life's greatest stress involved getting her period during volleyball conditioning.

"So, you're killing me with this businessy stuff," she said. "Sure,

I've missed you and all that, but what in the world? I fell apart on you guys today and caused a scene. Why did you bring me out in public again?"

"Hey, no one is denying you're a hot mess." Kevin pointed at her, while Ben's eyebrows shot up when he stifled a laugh.

"Shut up." Josie didn't bother taking the straw out of her mouth or even attempt to deny their claim.

"Your disaster life is why we're here." This time, Kevin left out the teasing tone.

She should have gotten that second milkshake. "So it's an intervention. Lovely. Should have seen this coming."

"If this were an intervention, we'd have a banner and a cheese tray. Duh." Ben grinned, but the way he shifted in his seat didn't quite convince her of his easy manner.

"So, JoJo…" The normally smooth Kevin avoided eye contact this time, but he *had* gone back to using her nickname.

She swallowed hard.

Kevin cleared his throat and rested his elbows on the table. "We talked a lot after you left today. It sucks what you're going through."

"Ah, so it's a charity thing. That's equally fantastic." The cold ice cream made her head throb in time with the embarrassment.

"Hear me out. I will not accept questions or comments until the end of my speech." He straightened his nonexistent collar, but his cheeks flushed a little.

A million possibilities ran through Josie's head as she waited for them to come out with their proposition. None of them made any sense. *Kevin* made no sense.

He licked his lips. "As you know, I'm king of my dad's insurance company."

"You sure about that?" Josie clicked her tongue. "Because earlier this afternoon, you made it sound like you were being held prisoner there, forced to serve out a life sentence."

Kevin threw his head back and made a guttural sound that drew the attention of the table across the room. "Could you feed my ego for, like, ten seconds here?"

"Oh, Kevin." He'd always made terrible days better.

"You know what? I should let Ben take this one, since his life sucks, too, and he can relate to you on a personal level." Kevin pointed to his friend, giving him the floor. "Leaving off with Kevin being CEO of Lawrence & Son Insurance. And go, Ben."

Ben shook his head. "Leaving off at Kevin being a regular, miserable insurance agent at Lawrence Insurance. No '& Son.' Got it."

Kevin sighed dramatically and slumped in his seat.

At this rate, they'd attend their fiftieth class reunion before either of these guys spit out their proposition. "Just get on with it. Between indigestion, anticipation, and hormones, I am dying over here."

"Fine." Ben choked on an M&M before resuming his previous state of discomfort. "Um. Well, like Kev said, he owns a multibillion-dollar company."

"Thank you." Kevin slapped his hands against the sticky table.

"And I work ridiculous second-shift hours making electronics systems, which doesn't put the finest bacon on the table. If you know what I mean," Ben said.

Josie rested her cheek on her palm and swirled her straw. "Sure. Sure."

"But I guess what we talked about after you left was how we're all kind of in the same boat. I mean, not pregnant. We're not pregnant."

That word made her stomach flop. What should have been a day filled with joy over the news had been nothing but a dumpster fire. That phone call with Grant added more fuel for the burn.

"She knows we're not pregnant, moron. Keep going." Kevin threw a straw wrapper across the table.

"Right. I just… Never mind. We all agree thirty sucks. Not only being thirty, but all of life right now."

"Already established. Moving on," Kevin said.

Josie stared across the table at Ben. Her head would fall completely off her shoulders if she had to nod at one more thing.

"I'm recapping." Ben pounded his fist against the table to demand attention.

Kevin's fists pounded on the tabletop in time with his words. "Ask her already."

"Ask me what?"

What could he possibly want to ask her that would make him act so jittery and bizarre? It's not like he meant to propose or anything.

Josie gulped.

If he'd done that ten years ago, she could have avoided this whole mess. Kevin would still be an active part of their lives, and she'd come home every night to those teddy-bear brown eyes, that full bottom lip, and…

Whoa.

She had to reel it in and focus.

"Look," Ben started again with much more confidence. "You know I bought that house a couple months ago. It's not huge, but too big for just me. I only have Izzy every few weeks, because Noel… Well, I told you about Izzy's mom."

Josie nodded for the thousandth time.

"So, I moved in with him three weeks ago," Kevin interrupted. "Cuts the cost of living for both of us."

"Right." Ben stared at Kevin, an unspoken exchange occurring between the pair that ended with Kevin grunting some code to urge Ben on.

"You guys have only gotten stranger over time." Josie rocked side to side on her swiveling stool and patted her stomach. "My shake's almost gone, so you might want to come out with it before I leave you for Netflix and Tums."

"Move in with us," Ben blurted out.

Josie's eyes widened, her flip-flops suctioning to the sticky floor. "What?"

Ben leaned across the table. "We have an extra room upstairs, so it's not like it'd be weird, all sleeping in bunk beds in one room or something. You could pay a third of the mortgage and utilities and get out of your parents' house."

"I–I don't know if I can—"

"We thought it'd help all three of us out, and we agreed you can wait on rent till your new job starts." Kevin held up his hand. "Plus, with all three of us chipping in, it'll give you and Ben a chance to save for your futures like real adults."

Ben scoffed. "Excuse me?"

"We already covered this earlier." Kevin ignored his offended friend. "Or have you forgotten you both agreed to join me in another magnificent pact?"

"Do not start with that pact stuff again." Ben's palm connected with his forehead.

"Just wait. I came prepared." Kevin reached into his pocket to retrieve a folded sheet of notebook paper and flattened it on the table. Across the top of the page, he'd scrawled the words THE CORN DOG PACT.

Ben snatched up the paper and drew it closer to him. "You made an actual pact page? When did you even have time to do this?"

"While I was in the bathroom." Kevin shrugged.

"That's why you were in there so long?" Ben's voice carried across the restaurant. "Dude, I had to pee by the shed because of you. And there's only, like, three things on this list. It should not have taken that long."

Josie's giggling overtook her so much, she couldn't wrap her lips around her straw. Their house had to be one of the most entertaining places on earth if they acted like this all the time.

And they wanted her to join them there.

Kevin ripped the paper out of Ben's hand and placed it at the center of the table. "Ben, you are a savage, and you disgust me. But look at this list." He tapped hard on the page. "And, yes, I broke it into three parts. It's a three-part pact. Just read it and tell me it's not gold."

Curiosity won her over. Josie pushed her shake to the side and leaned across the oblong table, her head nearly colliding with the guys as they mimicked her movement.

The Corn Dog Pact

MONEY: Pay off your debts and build savings.
JOB: Pursue your dream careers.
LOVE: Find love. Get over your pasts. Do right by the littles that depend on you.

Ben sank into his seat as the chair swiveled and squeaked underneath his weight. "Great list, bud. Wishful thinking."

"We already high-fived and forged this pact into existence at the fair, d-bags. This is happening. By thirty-one, you guys will have your lives together. I'd better put that on the list." Kevin patted himself down until he found the pen he'd stashed. He scrawled the deadline "31" at the bottom of the page.

"*We*," Ben corrected and gestured to all three bodies around their table. "I'm not even going to remotely consider this unless you acknowledge that you need this as much as I do."

"You sassy thing." Kevin tore open his last apple pie box. "Fine. *We.* I'll do it with you, even though I'm definitely more of a moderator or awesome host in this thing. But whatever. We Corn Dog Pact from now until thirty-one. It sounds good, right?"

"We don't all turn thirty-one at the same time." In any other circumstance, Josie might have cramped up from laughing so hard at Kevin's comments, but she couldn't stop staring at the strange little list now. Those three simple-sounding categories summed up all her needs, yet there was nothing truly simple about any of it.

"So we go with the last birthday. Baby Ben over here. Newly thirty." Kevin shook his head. "Or we can speed up the process and be awesome by my birthday in February."

"I don't know," Josie said.

Nobody tried to convince her. They all sat in silence for a moment, staring at the sheet of paper, the tension thick enough to choke someone.

Her parents meant to sell their house, which didn't give her much time to find a place of her own. With no income, her chances of locking down an apartment might not be great, and she did *not* want her folks paying her rent. But she hadn't been around these guys in more than a decade. Could she make such a rash decision based on a few hours of interaction?

Three old friends thrown together with terrible relationship histories, crap jobs, a life pact, and loads of pregnancy hormones? It sounded more like a pitch for a sitcom than a real-life possibility.

"What about the baby?" She rolled her sticky straw between her fingers, unable to meet their gazes.

A hormonal woman would certainly cramp their bachelor vibes and throw off their friendship dynamic. Not to mention, she'd had a massive crush on Ben once upon a time, and still found him rather magnificent-looking. Then there was the fact that if she moved in and it didn't work, she couldn't return to her parents' house because there wouldn't be room for her. She'd be back at square one.

"The upstairs is pretty big. Plenty of room for both of you." Kevin hunched against the table, moving into Josie's line of sight. "It's not like we'll kick you out or bump your rent because you're going to produce another person. We can handle it."

"You want me to live with you," she repeated.

Ben kicked his leg up on the chair beside him and pushed his empty ice cream cup toward the center of the table. "We're *inviting* you to live with us. You don't have to if you don't want to. I know it's weird and random."

"My mother will not approve of this." Josie's mouth twitched at the evil thought.

"Probably as much as my mom hates me living with Kev." Ben stretched his arms high and tucked them behind his head. "Good Catholic boy like me should have married Noel and made something of myself, not be playing video games with my feral friend all night."

"All these years later and I'm still a terrible influence." Kevin's wide grin showed off his ornery side.

Some things changed over time: cell phone sizes, menu options, MTV. People grew, too, evolving into adults who busied themselves with boring responsibilities. Not this trio. They still sat around trying to think up ways to defy their parents.

But it was more than that this time. They'd thrown her a lifeline. These two guys had shown up out of nowhere and offered her a chance to gather the pieces of her broken life and put it back together at a fraction of the cost.

The path ahead still held so many speed bumps, but she knew one thing for sure: if she didn't say yes, she'd probably have to live in her car. That and she'd always wonder what might have happened if she'd agreed to their proposal.

Josie took one more look at the crumpled pact that called to her from the center of the table. "How soon can I move in?"

5

Surviving on Hope and Pop-Tarts

THE FRIDAY NIGHT AFTER meeting with her old friends, Josie finished eating the last meal she'd have as a live-in resident of her childhood home, grabbed her laptop and purse, and then headed out to her loaded car. She dropped her stuff into the back seat on top of the bonus box her dad had given her. His parting gift comprised toaster pastries, macaroni and cheese, a bottle of juice, tissues, and a roll of toilet paper. If only she had a flashlight, she could survive the apocalypse.

Not for the first time, she lamented the fact that everything she owned fit into an economy-sized vehicle. Someday, she might require a moving truck to get from one place to another, but that wouldn't be anytime soon.

When she'd left her home in Chicago, she'd forfeited most of her belongings. She couldn't stand the embarrassment of hauling out more than she could carry in a few trips or returning to the apartment for more later on. It had hurt badly enough gathering her things while Grant sat at the dining room table and watched, trying to convince her she'd blown things way out of proportion. Christa was a one-time thing. A mistake.

Josie couldn't stomach any more arguing and left Apartment C on Leo Street with her clothes, a few blankets, books, a nightstand, an air mattress, and a few decorations and pictures she kept on her special shelf.

Just over two months later, here she was, still waiting to hear back from Grant after announcing she carried his child. Since he'd failed to answer her texts, she went ahead and notified her lawyer. Maybe Karleen would have more luck getting through to him.

Josie's mother placed a plastic container of seven-layer salad in the passenger seat and shut the door. "I still don't think this is a good idea. But since when have you ever listened to my opinion? Those boys were crazy in high school, always trying to get you in trouble. What if they grew up to be ax murderers?"

"They aren't ax murderers. I'm not being lured to an untimely death."

Her father shifted away from the women to avoid revealing his smile, which would surely get him into trouble with his wife if he was caught.

"I want you safe." Her mother crossed her arms. "I just think you rushed into this decision without fully thinking it through. People can change a lot in twenty years."

Twelve years. Her mother was super great at math.

"I love you guys. Thanks for helping me load the car." Josie didn't have the energy to argue Kevin and Ben's morality or her own decision-making skills after an evening of packing and prepping to turn her life in a totally different direction.

"You sure you don't want help unloading?" Josie's dad leaned forward and kissed her cheek.

The simple gesture almost made her sad to think she wouldn't live under the same roof with him again. But not having to live there as an adult granted Josie so much more freedom. Freedom she desperately craved.

"I'm okay, Dad. Kevin and Ben will be there to help."

He winked, no doubt relieved not to miss the season premiere of *NCIS* at eight.

Josie hugged her parents goodbye and pulled out of the driveway without looking back. At the end of the road, she turned left instead of right. She knew where Ben lived, having driven past his house so many times in the last couple of days that the local police probably had her name on a special list of stalkers. Even so, she wandered farther into suburbia.

"New chapter. Time for change. Piece of cake," she repeated over the noise of the radio.

Her sweaty palms stuck to the steering wheel, and she cranked the AC higher.

Why was she so nervous about this? Kevin and Ben were, well, Kevin and Ben. They had been some of her best friends once upon a time.

She tapped the top of the wheel with her fist.

No matter what song came on the radio, she found no inspiration. Did nobody write songs about hope anymore? This current stuff wailed about love lost and the death of dreams. Where was Jimmy Eat World when she needed them?

The clock read 7:00 p.m., and she still had to unpack the car and set up her room. She'd at least have to dig out her face wash and contact lenses case before bed. Plus, she had to inflate the air mattress if she wanted to avoid sleeping on the floor. It might not hurt to make sure the bathroom had space for girl stuff too. That and there was the important matter of finding the ideal spot to store her macaroni and cheese in the kitchen cupboards.

So much to do.

When she rounded the last corner, the gleaming white house stood out like a beacon on a foggy sea. The porch light blazed as bright as the setting sun, the shutters fluttering on the breeze like eyelashes. The stone path curved around the gargantuan hedges up to the front doors.

Okay. So, it was a simple house on an average street, and the shutters didn't move at all. The hedges were knee-high shrubs at best. Her internal drama-meter always skyrocketed when anxiety came knocking.

She eased up the gravel driveway, hoping the kicked stone wouldn't alert the entire street to fresh blood. Today was not a good day to deal with overly friendly neighbors bringing her fruit salads.

With the car in park, she unbuckled her seat belt and pressed a hand to her belly. At least she didn't have to do this entirely alone.

"You ready for this?" Josie imagined a sunflower-seed-sized hand giving her a thumbs-up. "Yeah, let's do it."

She was reaching for the door handle when a figure cast a dark shadow over her window. Her backside rammed into the center console, and she swallowed her scream.

"You all right in there?"

Kevin. His voice seemed crazy loud from inside the car. She could only imagine the volume on the outside. So much for avoiding neighborly attention.

Josie tried to talk her heart into a normal rhythm as she cracked open the door. "You scared me half to death."

"Sorry about that." He gave a hearty laugh and pulled the door open the rest of the way, nearly tearing Josie out of the car with it. "You looked pained, and your hand was on your stomach. Thought you'd gone into labor."

Yeah, living here would definitely keep her entertained. "I'm only three months pregnant. I'd better not be going into labor anytime soon."

"Great. 'Cause I know nothing about delivering babies." He took hold of her arm and helped her out of the car like she was his grandmother and not a mildly expectant friend.

Josie patted his forearm. "That's why we have doctors."

"True statement." Kevin peered into the window, cupping his hands around his face for a better view. "You got more at your parents'?"

"Yeah, no. My entire life is in this car. Thought I would at least get to keep the spare bed, but apparently my aunt Cayla already claimed it when she found out my parents were downsizing." Josie rolled her eyes. "What you see is what you get with me, unfortunately."

"So, no furniture at all? You're going to fit in so well here. My stuff all belonged to my former apartment, so I came with nothing but an Xbox and some underwear." Kevin slapped his hand on the roof of the car. "Come on. I'll show you around, then we'll get your stuff."

Josie fell into his offered side hug. The falling part happened mostly because she'd tripped on her flip-flops, but Kevin didn't notice. She probably looked extra buddy-buddy or something from his point of view.

Kevin twisted the knob and thrust his hip into the door with a warning that it had a tendency to stick and proceeded with the tour. The side entrance split off two ways: one path went down to the basement, while a second door to her left opened into the kitchen.

Where she'd expected a simple, possibly outdated kitchen to match the completely ordinary-looking exterior of the home, she found a fully remodeled room with stainless-steel appliances. The dishwasher looked brand new, with a double sink large enough to wash her baby through toddlerhood, not just infancy. The oak cabinets brought enough storage room that she could stash a million bottles and formula containers.

"And this is where the magic happens." Kevin hopped onto the counter, his arms spread wide in presentation.

"I thought that's what people said about bedrooms." Josie chuckled as she ran her fingers across the cold surface of the refrigerator.

His eyebrows shot up as if he'd revealed a century-old secret. "Not in this house. I'm, of course, referring to nachos: the light of my life. You haven't loved until you've had Ben's nachos."

Ben's nachos. Like it was all as simple as some chips and cheese. Her high-school crush might make her dinner from time to time—because she lived with him now.

Her heart hammered against her rib cage. She'd just flippin' moved in with her high-school crush. She'd said yes to a living arrangement where she would see her actual first love every day. Sometimes in his pajamas.

It's not like she'd moved in to respark an old flame. And, honestly, how many men lined up to date pregnant, unemployed, divorce-in-progress train wrecks who brought a truckload of baggage and the potential for psychotic in-laws? Probably not many. Definitely not Ben.

Those days of writing *Josie Romero* all over her notebooks in study hall ended long ago. The wedding plans she'd sketched out during homeroom went in the trash can after graduation. She didn't remember all of it, but she could still see the wedding party, coral gowns, yellow flowers, and a Hawaiian honeymoon. Pretty standard stuff.

Those were Past Josie's feelings, not Present Josie's.

She pointed in Kevin's direction and tried to play it cool. "Noted. Good thing I'm here to experience such a delicacy."

"Best decision you've ever made."

"I can see that." She stood on her tiptoes to look past the bar top and into the rest of the house. "Where is Ben, by the way?"

"Work. He's on seconds."

"That's right. I forgot he said that."

"I'm out of here from eight to five every day. He's usually gone from two to ten. What's your schedule looking like?" he asked.

It took a minute for the question to register as she calculated she and Ben would hardly ever cross paths on opposite schedules. That might keep Past Josie from decorating another planner.

"Well, the smoothie shop is officially closed for the season, so

I'm just waiting on a sub gig. School hours will be around eight to three, I think. Sounds like I won't know if I'm working until the day of most of the time. May not even need me every day. The joys of substitute teaching, I guess."

Kevin's face twisted to reveal how much he'd hate that job. He'd always given their subs a hard time in high school. Hopefully, she'd never have to deal with any Kevin Lawrences in her career, but every school had one. Kevin's most notorious trick involved feigning the flu and requiring the young, attractive substitute teacher to help him down to the nurse's office. He was a total turd back then. No wonder he got so many detentions.

"What's that on the fridge?" Josie inched closer to get a better look at the purple magnetic notepad adorned with the picture of a squatting bull and the phrase "Bull Sheet" printed at the top. Someone else had scribbled something across the page. Up close, she made out the words: *Get milk, asshat.*

"Oh, that's where we leave each other notes. Or insults. Every home should have a focal piece, right?" Kevin jumped down from the counter. "Moving on. I'll show you the rest of the house." He waved her into the dining room devoid of nearly everything but a two-person, high-top patio table.

On the other side of that…

Josie's chin nearly dropped to the faux-wood laminate flooring when she saw more ash-colored walls offset with a big-screen TV longer than she was tall. Two beanbag chairs sat next to each other in the middle of the room, with an oversize saucer towering behind them. Surround-sound speakers hung in all four corners, and an impressive batch of cords led away from the makeshift TV stand where the guys displayed multiple gaming systems, a cable box, a Blu-ray player, and several cases of games.

"You game?" Kevin stared at the console collection like some men regarded their bride walking down the aisle.

Sudoku on her phone probably didn't count. "I can't say I play many video games, no."

"You'll learn."

Josie grinned at the image of the three of them parked on beanbag chairs, munching nachos, and shooting each other up on-screen. Her plate would fit on top of her stomach in a few months, so she'd have two free hands for the controller. What more could she ask for? Yesterday, she was a thirty-year-old damsel in distress. Today, a college frat boy.

"On with the tour," Kevin said with a flourish.

He presented the last three rooms, two bedrooms and a bathroom, and promised her a housewarming slushie after they got everything unpacked. Together, they unloaded her entire life into the small house, and Josie finally dumped every bag and box onto the floor of her bedroom. By the time her bed filled with air, she had a shiny silver key on her key chain, and her peach towel hung in the bathroom alongside a ratty brown one and a Chicago Bears one.

Josie let the icy lemon slushie slide down her throat and imagined the stress of life slipping away just as easily. With the stars shining brightly overhead, she clinked Styrofoam cups with her new roommate on the steps of 422 Leeson Avenue.

6

Just Say No to Swordfish

THERE HAD TO BE a logical explanation for why inflatable bed manufacturers put so many divots in their products. Maybe it made the beds hold air better, or it somehow mimicked the quilted patterns on real mattresses. Whatever the reason, the little bubbles from hell roughed Josie up during her first night in the new house.

Even worse? She couldn't move to the couch when she got uncomfortable. Because there was no couch. Her options included the devil mattress, the thinly carpeted floor, balling up in that saucer-chair thing, or draping herself across some beanbags.

She'd get a real mattress immediately when the paychecks started rolling in. Well, before that, she had to pay her portion of the rent, utilities, and get some groceries. But after that: bed.

Although, her sleeping difficulty could be in part due to Grant ghosting her while she carried his baby. Nothing sparked imaginary conversations with her soon-to-be-ex-husband like lying in bed in the dark, even though her lawyer promised to look into it on her behalf. Surely, there'd be an additional fee for that service too.

Her phone lit up with a message from her long-time best friend, Ella: My mom can't watch the kids. If you come here, I'll make coffee. PLEEEASE

Ella had had big plans for their summer-break activities until they both returned to school as teachers, Josie on one end of the building with the high schoolers and Ella at the other end with the elementary students. Unfortunately, life had gotten in the way, as it did. During those rare occasions when Ella had childcare for her four children, the girls would hit up a fancy coffee shop or gorge themselves on pizza. They required their Frappuccino fix while it was still warm out. Today, however, coffee on her best friend's couch sounded equally fantastic.

Josie slid off the edge of the bed and landed with a thud, opting to crawl across the floor to her clothes pile rather than get up and bend down all over again. As she dug through her wardrobe, she mentally reviewed what Kevin had said about work schedules. They'd somehow forgotten to discuss bathroom rotations. Did bachelors shower in the morning like normal people? Or was it more of a "Hey, it's three in the morning and the system's lagging. I guess I'll go rinse off this chicken-wing grease" kind of thing?

She had a lot to learn about these men, but first and most importantly, she needed breakfast. The pregnancy explained why she'd felt nauseous in the mornings if she didn't eat right away. She didn't want to take any chances that full-blown, pukey morning sickness would take over. Especially not now that she'd moved in with the guys.

Tying a messy bun on top of her head, Josie grabbed her glasses from the nightstand and wiggled into her bra without taking her shirt off: her greatest of talents.

The narrow stairs taunted her. They'd only get harder to navigate as her stomach grew and impaired her vision of each step. Somehow, she'd ascended them at least twice during the night on her half-awake, glasses-free bathroom runs. A brand-new talent to add to her impressive list.

At the bottom of the steps, her feet nearly slipped out from under her on the faux hardwood floor. She muffled a shriek while catching hold of the doorframe for support.

"Good morning, sunshine," a groggy voice said from around the corner. "Forgot to tell you the floors are slippery in this place."

She peeked into the living room, and her stomach dipped at the sight. Ben sat cross-legged on a blue beanbag chair with a controller in his hand. He paused the game to address her, his dark hair sticking up around his head in an unkempt mess.

Josie kept most of her body hidden behind the doorframe, suddenly feeling more naked than clothed in her fitted T-shirt and yoga shorts. At least she'd remembered the bra. "Did you just call me 'sunshine'?"

"Kevin likes it when I call him 'beautiful' first thing in the morning. Starts his day off right, you know?" Ben scratched at his head. "Thought I'd try it out on you. We can always go with something else, eh, tiger?"

If he wanted to call her beautiful, it'd *also* start her day out just right. "Going to have to ask you to keep thinking on that one."

Ben tugged at the front of his shirt and fell backward against the beanbag, repositioning the controller across his stomach.

Except for the gunshots coming from the TV and her overactive mind, the house remained silent. Kevin had gone to work, or he'd surely have joined his comrade in arms, blowing up zombies or aliens or whatever the hell those funky blue things were.

"Didn't think you'd be up yet." Josie grew less paranoid about her appearance when she realized how intensely Ben stared at his enemy, paying very little attention to her presence. She could have done any number of antics: danced like a spider monkey, faked labor, seduced him. He'd never notice.

"Normally, I'm not. Kevin said you seemed nervous last night and thought it'd be a good idea to be up to greet you. Make you feel all at home and crap."

She warmed at the thoughtfulness of the gesture, even if it came out a little silly. "Wow. That's supersweet of you."

"Right? Oh, and there's coffee out there. Not sure if you're allowed to have it."

"Allowed to have it?" Her foot slipped when she leaned against the wall, but she righted herself before he noticed. If she continued to live in this house, she should stop exfoliating her feet or invest in grippy granny socks to go with her granny panties.

"Yeah, Kevin was looking it up last night and said you might not be able to have coffee or something. Also, he said stay away from swordfish. I forget what else."

Josie tapped her hand against the doorframe. "Can't remember the last time I encountered a swordfish in central Illinois, but okay."

She caught the slightest grin from him before she headed toward the kitchen to ease her hunger. It hadn't occurred to her to avoid coffee. Well, caffeine was probably the real foe. The fact that Kevin had done more pregnancy research than she had didn't bode well for her parenting résumé. Maybe she needed these two guys more than she thought. Still, she ought to set up a date with Google later and catch up with Kevin's advanced pregnancy knowledge.

The kitchen smelled faintly of used K-Cups, but something else tainted the otherwise wonderful aroma. Old pizza, maybe? She had no intention of checking the trash to confirm.

On the fridge, a new note covered the bull-sheet pad: *Welcome home, JoJo!*

She grinned. *Home* had such a lovely ring to it.

Beside the notepad, Kevin had stuck his homemade pact up with a Drake's Hardware magnet in the shape of a hammer. The page appeared the same as it had when she'd seen it on the McDonald's table, except for Kevin's signature at the bottom.

Her smile broadened as she shook her head and moved on in search of breakfast and mugs. She opened the cabinet doors and gasped. Nothing. They had no cups or plates. No dishes or cereal boxes or anything. The only item in the entire three-shelved cupboard was a single can of soup. And not even one of the good kinds. Just store-brand mushroom, which everybody knew couldn't hold a candle to the name-brand stuff.

"Hey, Ben?"

A muffled acknowledgment came from the living room.

"The only thing in your cupboard is soup." This had to be one of Kevin's pranks.

"You can have it. I don't care," he said over the sounds of inhuman bloodcurdling screams.

For a moment, she stood dumbfounded, flat feet suctioned to the floor.

Thank goodness her dad had sent those toaster pastries. He must have had the wisdom to know what living with unattached men might entail, which concerned her on a new level when she thought about why he sent along the toilet paper.

Ben came around the corner so quickly that Josie jumped. One eyebrow shot up as he examined her, then moved toward the cabinet on the opposite side of the kitchen. "I forgot to show you where the cups are."

When he opened the designated cupboard, she held her breath in anticipation of what might be inside and had to swallow a chuckle when she saw it. The top shelf displayed an array of mismatched paper products and plastic utensils. In the middle, six different boxes of cereal and a container of coffee grounds sat stuffed together as if they fought to squeeze the others from their space. The bottom shelf had three assorted mugs and two plastic cups stolen from nearby restaurants.

"Help yourself to cereal. It's got tons of vitamins and minerals for your, uh, condition." He patted his stomach.

This would be a very interesting pregnancy in the company of her new roommates. "Thanks, Dr. Romero. I'm in good hands."

He flashed a quick thumbs-up. "I'm going back to bed. Shower's open, and you're on your own there. No tutorials." His face scrunched, and his cheeks flushed a little, though not nearly as much as Josie's did. "I have no idea why I said that. Make yourself at home, I guess. Oh, and Kevin wants us to sign the pact." He gestured to the fridge and picked up one of the pens on the counter. "He's only texted me about it seven times since he got up this morning."

Ben scrawled his name underneath Kevin's and held out the pen for Josie.

"So, we're really doing this, huh?" By signing the pact, she committed to making all the horrible things better. It wouldn't be easy, and she had zero idea where to begin.

Ben shrugged and stepped out of the way for Josie to sign her name. "Pretty sure we don't get a choice. We're going to have to be on our best behavior for at least one year or suffer Kevin's whining and/or harassment."

If Kevin had forged a pact, he would definitely harass his fellow pacters until completion. Ben was not wrong about that. Josie took the pen and approached the refrigerator. If she ever wanted to improve her life—for her, for her child—she had to keep moving forward. There was no going back.

She signed her name below Ben's. "It's a lovely thought. The money thing isn't bad. We can get jobs, sure. But why is there a love category? I'm not about to put my pregnant ass on Tinder."

His laugh came out louder than she expected. Then again, he was *closer* than she expected too. So close, his T-shirt sleeve tickled her shoulder. He smelled of sleep and candied pecans. Were the pregnancy hormones responsible for this too? Turning man scents into delicious foods?

"Kevin brings home a new girlfriend about every other weekend. If anyone needs to figure stuff out, it's him. You and I can focus on our kids, I guess." Ben ran his fingers through his hair and rested his elbow against the fridge, his muscle flexing in a way that made it hard for her not to stare.

Our kids. Not a phrase she thought she'd ever hear him say. Obviously, he didn't mean their kids *together*. That was stupid. But still. She, too, had a kid in the works. So strange.

Josie assumed Ben would leave after saying his piece. He didn't. He just stood there studying her as if waiting for something. She smiled, swaying on her feet and praying for the awkwardness to end.

"Good talk, Benjamin," she said.

Ben scrunched his nose and shook his head. "Yeah, sorry. It's weirding me out how little you've changed since high school. I feel like I'm in a *Twilight Zone* or something."

"I've changed a lot, actually. Notice the gray hairs? Beginning stages of crow's-feet and forehead wrinkles? Underarm fat?" Seriously, listing her flaws to the former love of her life had to be another pregnancy side effect. She needed that coffee in her system *right now.* Screw what the internet said about it.

"So, you're older." He waved off the thought and chuckled. "I don't mean your looks, but you act the same too."

"You think so?" She walked past him for a cup to slip under the Keurig. In what way did he think she acted the same? Painfully awkward? Adult fatigue had done a number on her personality for sure. "This is pretty weird for me too. I never would have thought we'd all be back together, let alone living under the same roof. Going to take some getting used to."

"Definitely." Ben yawned and thumped his fist against the kitchen counter. "Okay, well, I really am going to bed now. I stayed up late last night."

"All business?" He probably just played games until the wee hours, but she couldn't resist the urge to tease him.

"Oh, yeah. Business. Lots and lots of business." He grinned wide enough to show his dimples, which made Josie's breath hitch like it had a decade ago. "Hey, wait. Before I forget: I probably should have mentioned this earlier, but Izzy comes next weekend. She usually stays on the other side of the loft up there. Just wanted to give you a heads-up."

Josie froze.

Izzy didn't stay with him or have a bedroom of her own? Why was this the first time Josie heard about this? It's not like having an eleven-year-old roommate was an everyday occurrence for her.

She couldn't turn and face him, lest he see the extreme panic setting in.

"Like, she's sleeping in my *room* room?" Her voice squeaked despite her attempt at calm, and she took a deep breath as she faced him.

Ben cleared his throat. "Uh, yeah? I mean, maybe we could put up a shower curtain between the two sides or—"

"She doesn't stay in *your* room?" Josie clutched the mug handle harder, trying not to spill the freshly brewed coffee or shatter the ceramic material if she Hulked out too much. She had to play it cool. He'd already let her delay rent until her new job started. Neither guy had complained about *her* kid eventually sharing the space. She kind of owed him some leniency or something.

Ben's eyes widened even more. "I... No, she can't. It's part of the whole custody thing and her being a preteen, and... Are you mad at me?"

Josie held up a finger and took a long swig of her coffee, leaning against the sink for additional support. The straight black brew burned her throat and left a bitter aftertaste. She needed cream, but she needed caffeine more. "No. It's fine. It's totally fine. Kind of wish you'd mentioned the arrangement before I moved in. Given me some time to mentally prepare."

"Would it have changed your mind?" Ben took a few steps back as if she'd slapped him across the face.

Maybe? Probably not? A preteen for a few nights every couple of weeks wasn't the worst thing in the world. Better than living in an itty-bitty condo with her mother. Better than sleeping next to a cheating husband.

Josie took another long swig. Black coffee was disgusting, bitter, and acidic. It so suited this moment. "Nah, I'm good. Sorry. It's fine."

"Are you sure?" Ben took a couple more steps in reverse. He probably planned to run from the room before she fully freaked.

"Yes."

He bit his lip and made his way around the island. "You're the best."

"Sure." Josie reached into the cupboard and freed a box of off-brand Froot Loops that would not survive the morning.

"Okay. Good night, Josie." Ben fled to his basement bedroom.

Great. Not only did she have to share a room with a child she didn't know, but she'd oozed a bit of crazy on the first morning in her new home. Couldn't she have smiled and nodded when he'd asked her? *Sure, Benny. I'd love to bunk with your daughter for a weekend.*

Josie stuffed a handful of faux loops into her mouth and crunched down hard.

7

Some Toffee for Your Trauma

"YOU'RE SHARING A ROOM with his daughter? Are you nuts?" Ella readjusted a bald-headed baby Leland on her lap, while he spat bubbles of delight.

Josie groaned. "Not every night. Only on the weekends he has her, which doesn't sound like very often." She refocused her attention on stilling her palm for Petey to build his block tower in her hand.

"You do realize this will make you like her second mother, right?" Ella asked.

Their kids. The phrase still stuck in her head like construction paper to cement glue. "Oh, no it won't. Temp roommate. Not mother."

"Yeah. Jo, when a woman lives with a kid's dad, they see her as a mother figure. My students talk about it all the time." Ella's friendship meant the world to Josie, but her lectures and interrogation style could get a little overwhelming at times.

Josie's hand tower toppled. "Your students are first graders. Izzy's, like, eleven or something. It's so not the same situation. I'm Ben's friend. And Kevin's there, too, so it's not as shacky-uppy romance as you're implying."

"You'll see." Ella hugged Leland in to her. "And that's sad he doesn't get to see her much. I couldn't do it."

Leland grinned up at his mom, seeming to enjoy every bit of her affection.

How had Izzy's lack of desire to go see her father affected Ben? It's not like Josie had anything outside of his high school self to compare him to, and back then, parental rights weren't on any of their minds. It couldn't be easy on him, though. Josie certainly hadn't considered those feelings at eight in the morning when he'd dropped the bomb on her pre-coffee.

Sharing custody would suck. She'd barely come to understand her baby's existence and already couldn't bear the thought of sending him or her away for weekends at a time or spending months apart entirely. And Grant lived three hours north. Switching back and forth would be an epic pain in the butt.

Would Grant even want to see their kid? In their first year of marriage, she'd often tried to picture him holding their babies in his lap. Then everything went to shit and kind of ruined that dream. Now, she'd have to share Baby with Grant *and* Christa, or whoever he was with.

Ouch.

While she still hadn't spoken directly with Grant, her lawyer had assured her she'd receive child support upon the baby's arrival. The financial help sounded great on paper, but relying on Grant for anything nowadays left a sour taste in Josie's mouth.

"So, the first night went okay? I mean, you didn't see anyone in their underwear or win any belching contests?" Ella asked.

"Underwear," Petey and Gavin yelled in unison before breaking into a fit of giggles. At barely two years old, Gavin only thought it was funny because his brother did.

"No, nothing like that. It was weird to shower, though." All those musky smells that rose around her as she washed behind a clear curtain in a bathroom she only rented. "I felt strangely naked."

Ella side-eyed her friend. "You were naked, right? You didn't shower in your clothes?"

"No, I was definitely naked. It was just strange because it wasn't *my* shower."

Petey laughed again. "Naked."

"All right. Enough of that." Ella rubbed the bridge of her nose and returned her attention to Josie. "Sorry. It's a step up from poop jokes, but still."

"POOP!" the boys shouted together and began making fart sounds as they chased each other around the room.

"Nothing I can't handle. No worries." Josie wouldn't mind a little boy of her own. He'd fit in well with her new roommates.

Leland fussed and pawed at his mother, so she switched him to her other leg and gave him a rattle for entertainment. "I may have to pop over for a visit sometime. I'll admit I'm kind of dying to see what they look like after all this time. So crazy you live with them now. I still can't believe it."

Ella had known the guys from way back when, too, but she wasn't as close to them as Josie was. She'd already been dating Cory then, the man who would become her husband, and didn't do much outside of macking on him. Come to think of it, Kevin had kind of filled in as BFF when the smitten Ella got distracted. Funny how all that worked.

"And it's only for a year?" Ella asked. "Am I understanding this all correctly?"

"I guess. I don't know. I never signed a lease, just a handwritten pact hanging on the refrigerator. We didn't discuss the terms of our living arrangements, but I'm kind of wondering if Kevin will kick me out if I don't get remarried and fully fund my retirement by Ben's birthday." Josie chuckled at the idea of them pursuing the pact so intensely. "I probably should get out of there after the baby comes, though."

"Might want to clarify the terms of your agreement before you get too comfy."

"Right? And that Ben hasn't already set my stuff on the curb for being weird about his daughter sleeping in my room. *Our* room." She'd gone from living with one person, to two, to three. Her baby would make four.

Ella patted Josie's leg. "If he's any kind of friend, he'll understand you were surprised, pregnant, hungry, cranky—"

"Stop. I'm sure all of that crossed his mind. Moving on."

"Really, though, I kind of like this pact thing," Ella said.

Josie's brow furrowed. "Um, why?"

"It's cute. Take a year and get your life together. It's so Lifetime-movie of you. I want in." Ella held her mug high as if making a toast.

Of all the people who *didn't* need a life pact. "Your life is perfect. What could you possibly change?"

"Whoa, dude. My life is far from perfect. For starters, have you seen this belly pooch? I can't even walk to the bathroom without getting winded. And money-wise, we have one last student loan to pay off before we can replace Cory's junker car. Plus, I haven't dusted this house in, like, eight months. So, I should probably work on that too."

Josie half-heartedly held her mug up. "Whatever, Elles. I'm sure all you gotta do is sign our refrigerator, and you're in."

Ella snuggled into the couch cushions. "I can't wait to tell Cory we're in a pact to change our lives."

"He'll be thrilled, I'm sure." Josie could only hope her next husband—*if* she ever married again—would be as supportive of her as Cory was of Ella and all the crazy schemes she presented him with.

Ella pushed a pile of laundry over on the couch so she could sprawl out more. "Any word from Grant since 'the call'?"

"No. I texted him again the other night, but got nothing back. Mom thinks I should have gone up to tell him in person." It still made her want to hurl. Josie took a long whiff of the toffee creamer in her cup to soothe her.

Ella scoffed. "That wouldn't be horrible at all."

"Exactly. I wouldn't be surprised if she's already reached out to him somehow or called his mom to form a plan to make Grant and me get back together."

"Only because they don't know the truth." Ella's brow rose, and she took a long, condescending slurp of coffee.

Josie suddenly required something stronger to drink. "I'd rather keep it that way. Grant obviously hasn't told his mom what happened between us, so if *I* do, I'll either look like a liar or I'll destroy my mother's favorite friendship. Then again, Mom said Diana hasn't been terribly responsive lately. She must know *something*, but I'm not about to try and find out which part it is or tip off my mom."

"Honestly, Jo, I don't envy you on that one. It'd be nice if Grant would grow out of his moron-ness and take some responsibility here." Ella stood to put the cooing Leland in his Jumperoo, all while keeping her curious brown eyes focused on her friend. "Someday, he'll realize what a jerk he's been and what he's missing out on."

"It won't matter. I can't erase what I know. Or *saw*. There's no going back. No forgiveness."

That wretched Saturday had been the worst day of her entire life.

The morning after they'd unknowingly conceived a child, Josie had tried to keep the momentum going in their attempt to fix the relationship. Grant had gotten up early to take care of the boarded animals at the vet's office and administer medications in the hospital wing as he did every Saturday. Josie had thought it might be nice to surprise him with coffee and scones to help break up his morning.

With their breakfast set out in the break room, she began searching the clinic for her husband. Dogs barked in their kennels, and cats reached from their cages to grab hold of her sleeve as she went past. She couldn't hear any voices to indicate Grant's or anyone else's presence.

She found him in the medication room. He held onto the younger lab tech, Christa, as if she might float away on the wind, his hands wound into her hair. Josie couldn't find her voice, but the door alerted them to her presence. Grant pulled Christa even tighter against him like a shield when he realized his wife stood before him. He didn't even try to play it off.

All around her, Ella's living room took on an eerie silence. The young children couldn't possibly understand the magnitude of the conversation. They barely understood the plot to *PAW Patrol* at this age.

Ella returned to the couch and reached over to rub Josie's hint of a baby bump that, let's be honest, was mostly fat at this point. "How's my niece?"

"Your niece, huh?" Josie welcomed the topic change.

"Maddy can't be the only girl in our clan. She needs a little friend. Besides, you said you were nauseous, and you're super moody, so that all totally means girl." Ella clapped her hands together like a goofy seal.

Josie scrunched her nose. "Well, the astrological gender-prediction chart would disagree with you."

She may not have known to avoid swordfish, but she had looked up gender predictors and baby names. *So many* baby names. They whirled through her head with none of them sounding right for a child she'd get to take home from the hospital and raise as her own. What a weird, weird thing. Would she be the mother of Lila? Cadence? Ellie? Theodore had always been her favorite boy name, but would people associate it with chipmunks?

"Well, when you find out the gender, you call me first, okay? Don't call your mom. Don't call Ben. Call me," Ella said.

Josie sat upright so fast a few drops of coffee splashed over the edge of her cup. "Why would I call Ben first?"

"I don't know." Ella tossed a burp cloth Josie's way to wipe up the mess. "In case you two fall in love by then."

"Yeah, that's not going to happen." Josie's cheeks burned.

Ella's accusatory eyebrow rose even higher than it had before. "She says as she spills her coffee and turns a dark shade of raspberry."

"No." Josie covered her face with her hands. "We never got together in high school. We won't get together now. This is a temporary life solution to help us all out, not the final round of *The Bachelorette*."

Leland started fussing, so Ella got up to grab him again. Petey and Gavin stacked more blocks on their floor tower, and the distant sound of Maddy singing to her dolls up in her bedroom drifted down the stairwell.

In a matter of months, this would be her life. Minus a few kids. The chaos factor couldn't be too far off for her household, though.

"Well, regardless of your romantic intentions, I want to stay in the loop. Don't go denying stuff if it exists. You're free now," Ella said.

Josie ruffled Gavin's hair when he crawled over and handed her a small block person. She couldn't promise anything about Ben if he continued to sport those darling brown eyes and that untamed cowlick. Like he could even help that crap, the poor guy. "I'm not looking to start anything, regardless of number three on the Corn Dog Pact. Nor am I exactly marketable for love interests, what with my budding bump and traumatic history."

Ella shrugged. "Unless you come across an equally unmarketable guy with a daughter and loads of his own drama-filled backstory to match yours."

8

Nachos Fill the Cracks in the Heart

BY THE END OF the first week, Josie had found homes for the rest of her belongings, using the emptied boxes as makeshift tables and converting some laundry baskets into dressers. She did her best to keep things on her half of the loft so as not to cross into Izzy's territory when she finally arrived.

"Are you decent?" Ben shouted up the stairs.

Josie glared toward the stairwell at the man who dropped unpleasant surprises on his roommates. "Yes."

He bounded up the steps with an armload of bedding and dropped it in a heap on the carpet. The roar of the twin mattress inflating filled the space as Ben set to work opening the zippered seal on a set of My Little Pony bedding. Granted, Josie's child interaction mostly comprised time spent with high school students at Lincoln Regional and hanging out with Ella's little ones, but she was pretty sure My Little Pony didn't fit the preteen scene.

Josie watched from her seated position on her own air mattress as Ben fought with the fitted sheet continuously springing up at him. He growled and swore, but Josie was not about to offer any help. The image provided entirely too much entertainment, and she still kind of wanted to deck him for not mentioning she'd have to share the loft.

Ben wiped a bead of sweat from his forehead and plopped down on his finished product. A corner of the fitted sheet popped up with the pressure, and Ben collapsed over the edge of the bed and rolled to his hands and knees. He shot upward and scurried down the steps to outrun the mattress woes once and for all.

God love him. He may drop inconveniences of epic proportions and currently be on her shit list, but he was still a cute little son of a gun.

Josie wandered through the doorless entryway between the two halves of the loft to examine the My Little Pony setup. The room offered no comfort of any kind. Ben may have just moved into this house, but did he have nothing for his daughter from his previous home? Had she slept on an air mattress every time she'd visited him all these years?

The housemates of 422 Leeson Avenue definitely lacked adequate cushioning in the house, between the fake beds and the living room's eclectic beanbags. Kevin was the only one with a legitimate mattress, but even that sagged in the middle like it predated his birth. Ben apparently slept on a futon in the basement, though he hadn't invited Josie downstairs to find out for sure. Maybe he, too, had pony sheets, but she pegged him as more of a Ninja Turtles guy.

On the off chance Izzy did like My Little Pony, Josie could try to call up her knowledge of the eighties version she'd watched at her cousin's house as a kid. The two could become best friends, not mother figure and daughter figure as Ella seemed to think would be the case. They could paint each other's toenails and chat about boys. Or at least which boys Izzy liked, because Josie refused to explain her situation to an eleven-year-old. Or that she'd once had feelings for the girl's father.

She headed down the stairs, slightly less annoyed at having to share her space. The beanbag chair caught her when she fell into it beside Kevin, and she peeled away the wrapper on the Pop-Tart she'd snagged from her survival box.

"How much longer?" she asked over the blaring TV.

"No idea. I'm guessing not till supper." Kevin didn't look at her, too engrossed in an HGTV special about a couple hunting for their perfect upscale home.

Part of her wanted to tease him. Not many guys she knew binged on home decor shows, especially guys who lived in a house without a stitch of decoration. But she loved that show too much to risk him changing the channel.

"This woman is whining about the open concept. Who does that?" Kevin slapped his chest as he laughed and leaned over to snatch the second Pop-Tart out of Josie's wrapper.

"Hey." She tried to retrieve it but lost her balance and nearly fell off her beanbag. Folded in half like that, she could tell how her stomach had changed shape, firmed up on the inside. Bending wouldn't be all that easy after another month.

The door leading out of the basement slammed, and Ben stomped across the dining room to the front door, muttering the entire way and slamming that door behind him too.

"Well, he's having a great day." Josie's hand rested over her heart as if she could manually stop the throbbing inside her chest. Honestly, she'd expected her stress levels to go down living with these two as opposed to living with her mother. At least her mom didn't slam doors and trigger heart attacks.

"Noel. He senses her impending presence." Kevin didn't appear fazed at all. "How can you complain about having to mow grass when you have a two-million-dollar budget? Hire a damn gardener if you make that much money."

Some guys yelled at the TV when they watched sports. Apparently, HGTV was Kevin's Super Bowl.

"You'd think he'd be used to it after all these years." She and

Grant started butting heads a year into their marriage. The emotional roller coaster that had ensued had made her walk on eggshells around the apartment. She never knew if they'd spend the evening cuddled on the couch watching a movie or eating dinner in separate rooms because one of them had said the wrong thing.

Kevin readjusted until the beanbag chair became a pillow. "He always gets this way on visitation weekends, and this is the first time Noel will see the house since he bought it."

"Does he think she won't like it or what?"

Kevin's face scrunched. "She'll hate it. Almost certainly. Did you ever meet her?"

Josie shook her head. Sure, she'd seen Noel several times but couldn't say she'd actually *met* her. In fact, she'd avoided her like the worst sort of plague.

To think Ben and Noel had carried on in this tense state for twelve years made her head spin. If Grant stayed away, she might avoid all that. She'd already proven brave enough to get out of there rather than suffer another year of arguing; she might as well parent on her own.

"Ben's never been good enough for her or her husband, if you know what I mean. No doubt she'll hate everything about this house. She'll make sure he knows it too. Bet you ten bucks."

"I'm not betting on Ben's misfortune. Plus, I don't have ten bucks." Josie put her half-eaten Pop-Tart in her lap and nestled down to mirror Kevin. They had their own version of the Hot Mess Club in here. Soon, they'd need a live-in therapist to deal with all the junk they dragged around with them. "What about Izzy?"

"Izzy is…" Kevin did a sit-up to check the front door. "Izzy is a pain in the ass. I mean, she's cute and all, as far as kids go, but she's got attitude for days. Ben loves her, obviously, but there's not much he can do when she's only with him for a day or two at a time. Just wait. You'll see how she is. He's got a lot of work to do on the third pact point with that one."

So much for braiding each other's hair and discussing boy bands across the ages.

Kevin leaned in toward her, his green eyes turning to slivers with his awkward squint. "It might be best to stay out of the way when they get here."

Their lack of furniture made locating a decent hiding spot a little more challenging.

"Well, Noel doesn't know you." He shrugged, which wasn't at all reassuring. "And, guaranteed, Ben didn't mention a woman moving in here. It won't be pretty. Izzy told her Ben had a date a few months ago, and Noel freaked a bit. It was via text, but the rage was pungent."

"Like, you could *smell* the rage?" Josie took a slightly more aggressive bite from her Pop-Tart. Ben had a date a couple of months ago? Were they *still* dating? He mentioned nothing about a girlfriend. Then again, he obviously didn't like to dish out important facts about his life. Also, it shouldn't matter because she did not like Ben like that. "Should I get out of the house for the weekend? I don't want to cause more problems."

Kevin flipped the channel to another renovation show preset on his remote. "No need to leave the country or anything. It'll be fine. We can hide out until the coast is clear, then make some nachos. They soothe us in a time of crisis. You'll catch on."

"Oh, I'm with you. I fully support emotional eating." Josie held up her hands in mock surrender before a thump at the door sent her rolling onto her side. "What was that?"

"Warning knock." Kevin cursed and fumbled with the remote, punching the power button a few times until it cooperated. His other hand grasped Josie's shoulder when he used her body to help him stand. The distant sound of gravel kicking up in the driveway grew louder. He swore again at an absurd volume. "We gotta go."

He reached down to snatch her up, pulling so hard her feet came off the floor. Josie shrieked.

"Shut up. She'll hear you." He covered her mouth and wrapped a hulking arm around her shoulders like an emergency responder ushering a victim from a burning building.

They hurried into the dining room, Kevin stopping once to search the area for hiding places. Josie could feel his stomach muscles against the side of her face as they contracted with a suppressed chuckle. She, too, tried in vain to keep from blurting out her amusement, but his hand kept her somewhat silent.

Footsteps on the porch urged them along, and Kevin spun toward his bedroom. He shoved her inside and mostly closed the door behind him, leaving an inch of space for eavesdropping.

"Take cover," he whisper-yelled.

Josie looked around the room and gestured that he might be crazy. He flailed his arms in response.

"You suck at ninja stealth mode." He leapt over the bed, rolling off the side between the mattress and the wall.

"You are not seriously hiding under the bed," she whispered through her laughter.

"If you don't hide, it's your own fault. Every man for himself."

Josie quickly followed orders when the front door opened.

Kevin's room was dark for the morning hour, thanks to the blankets he had pinned to the two windows like makeshift curtains. Josie only saw enough to make out Kevin's wave urging her to hide with him.

Suddenly, Josie was five again and building forts with her brother, taking commands and giggling at all their silly games. She hadn't truly played since then.

When she got to the other side of the bed, she realized she'd never fit in there with Kevin's oversize frame, and they couldn't *snuggle*. She instead made a beeline for his closet, praying it wouldn't smell like sweaty sneakers and gym shorts.

Her hands shook as she tried to hold back the laughter. Something about all this seemed both odd and wrong, and yet hilarious at the same time.

From behind so many half-closed doors, Josie barely heard what the former couple said to each other in the living room. She tried to hold her breath and listen.

"And you weren't planning to tell me that?" a woman's voice huffed.

Ben only mumbled, too softly for Josie to make out his words. Noel, however, spoke with plenty of force and volume.

"Are you ever going to grow up? Izzy needs a father, not a man-child. And you wonder why she doesn't want to come over more often!"

The stairs above Josie's head thumped as someone stomped up them. Izzy, most likely.

Josie bit into her finger as guilt crept through her. They may have been hiding, but spying? They shouldn't hear this conversation.

"You think I want her influenced by someone like Kevin?" Noel guffawed on the other side of the door.

Josie peered around the corner to see if she could spot Kevin across the room. And there he was, a shadow of a figure, only eyes above the mattress line. He shook his head, and Josie froze at the intensity in his gaze aimed at Noel on the other side of the door. Would he give up his location for a chance to take down the enemy?

As quickly as she'd come, the door banged shut, signaling Noel's departure, and a heavy sigh carried in from the dining room.

Josie emerged from between the clothes, tripping on some of Kevin's gigantic shoes. The bedroom door burst open, and she nearly fell backward into the closet once more.

"Are you both hiding in here?" Ben stood in the threshold, and Josie and Kevin peeked out from their positions.

"Yeah." Kevin grabbed his pillow and chucked it against the wall behind him. "We're not stupid." He flopped on the bed again and rolled across to the other side in an instant replay of how he'd gotten back there.

Josie inched the rest of the way out of the closet, avoiding eye contact with Ben in case he chastised them for eavesdropping. They shouldn't have been in there. She'd die if anyone witnessed a conversation between her and Grant when they were at their worst. What had seemed like childlike play with Kevin a few moments before felt child*ish* now that it was over.

When she finally braved a look at Ben, his half smirk set her at ease. If she had to guess, this wasn't the first time he'd caught Kevin in hiding, and Kevin peer-pressuring Josie into doing the same clearly didn't surprise him.

Ben ran his fingers through his hair, tugging on the ends until they stood straight up. "Is it too early to start drinking?"

Josie offered a sympathetic smile. At least she wouldn't have custody battles and arguments at every visitation if Grant kept away. But what was better for a child? Two parents who hated each other and couldn't be in the same room, or one parent who ignored the child's existence while the other did everything for them?

Ben laced his fingers behind his head and turned to leave the room. "I'll start cooking."

Yes. She needed comfort food so badly right now.

9

Hot Fudge and Wi-Fi, a Love Affair

EVERY TIME JOSIE GLANCED over at Ben, he had the same strained expression on his face. He didn't say much through the evening movie, other than asking Izzy if she needed anything—just about every few minutes. Izzy had four juice boxes, a plate of nachos, and a bowl of ice cream, but Ben acted as if the child might still starve to death. Hopefully Noel added some fruits and vegetables into her diet when she was home.

"This movie is so dumb," Kevin whispered.

He'd sacrificed his beanbag for Josie, though he continued to lean against it, invading all her personal space. Ben took up the other bag, and Izzy slurped her juice in the corner saucer while tapping away on her tablet.

Josie elbowed Kevin in the shoulder. "We're bonding. This is important to Ben."

"It's important to *me* I don't die of boredom while watching a bunch of kids singing nonsense."

Ben threw a chip at Kevin, having heard everything. Kevin promptly picked it up and put it in his mouth.

"Oh, Kevin," Josie said.

"I'm going out." He stood and patted down the front of his pants, checking for his wallet and simultaneously brushing off tortilla-chip crumbs. "Izzy, good to see you." He bowed for some reason, but Izzy didn't look up. "Yup. You're on your own with the third pact point, kids. I'm out."

Before Josie could protest his abandoning her with the father-daughter combo from two different planets, Kevin shot out the door like a rocket.

"He lasted longer than I thought he would," Ben mumbled.

Josie leaned in closer without actually touching him. "Should I leave? I don't want to interfere—"

"No." Ben snatched hold of Josie's wrist. Izzy *did* notice that, so Ben upped his volume to suit both ladies in the room. "It's almost bedtime, and the movie's about done."

Izzy returned to her tablet and popped her headphones into her ears, hugging the pillow to her that she'd brought from her mom's. Josie still couldn't tell if the picture on the front of it was a super-fat dolphin or a beluga whale.

Ben watched his daughter for a brief moment, then pulled Josie's hand against his chest. "Please don't leave me."

Her balled-up fingers froze in place against his T-shirt. The light from the TV reflected in his pleading brown eyes. Her stomach flipped wildly. Did she feel the baby move for the first time or did Ben do that to her?

"I will owe you forever. Just please stay. I don't know what I'm doing." He eased into his beanbag, and her fingers slipped from his grasp, dragging across his rib cage until she got ahold of herself enough to retract her arm.

Maybe it was a good thing they hadn't gotten together in high school. If he'd begged her with those puppy-dog eyes all those years ago, she'd have gotten into all kinds of trouble. That could be *her* kid in the corner.

Kids. Plural.

If she'd ended up with Ben, they probably would have reproduced like rabbits.

It took a moment to find her voice. "Dude. I don't know what I'm doing either. You've been a parent longer than I have." She checked over her shoulder to ensure Izzy stayed occupied with her tablet. Izzy's fingers flew across the screen, eyes alight with whatever game she played.

Ben nestled farther down and gestured for Josie to follow. He tugged at the side of her shirt, urging her to eliminate the gap between them.

She sank lower until she lay beside him, her head barely on the beanbag, body pressed into Ben's chest. Her heart throbbed. He'd either hear or feel that soon enough if he brought her any closer. Ben put his hand up like a barricade between his mouth and his daughter on the other side of the room.

"I don't need you to do anything. Just stay with me for moral support," he whispered.

How would she keep her brain in the friend zone if Ben continued to whisper into her ear in the romantic glow of the television? And why could she only stare at him like a deer about to get pulverized by a semi?

Like a gift from heaven, the movie ended.

"Izzy, you want to brush your teeth and get ready for bed?" Ben forced his sweetest voice and sat up. Izzy continued with her game, oblivious to anyone else's presence. He must have noticed she still had the earbuds in, because he repeated the question much, much louder.

"No." She gathered her tablet and left the room.

The moment she rounded the corner to the stairs, Ben dipped his head into his hands and groaned. "She hates me. How am I supposed to make this better after all these years?"

Josie didn't budge.

"Every time, we go through this. I've tried getting her favorite foods, renting movies. I let her play on that dumb tablet as much as she wants, but nothing works." His limp arms fell across his lap. "I'm pretty sure she's been talking to her mom on that thing the whole time she's been here. Probably telling her what a loser her dad is and how much she wants to go home."

"You're not a loser." Josie couldn't imagine her baby preferring Grant, or their child not wanting to visit her at all.

Ben didn't speak. She should say more, give him something to hang onto in this tough moment.

"Eleven is a hard age, so don't give up, okay? It's probably extra hard when she has two different families to make work, and everything's new here right now." Josie understood the nerves that came with *new*. But as a child? And when your parents only interacted by fighting?

Ben nodded slowly. Did he see her point? Hate the advice? If he'd at least do something besides nodding and furrowing his brow, she might get an inclination.

At last he said, "Will you do me one more giant favor?"

She gulped.

"Will you go upstairs with me while I say good night?"

Oh boy. That sounded…awkward.

"Yeah. I mean, I'll probably hit the hay soon, too, so…" Yep. He totally could have talked her into anything. He could talk her into anything *now*.

Josie hadn't really taken notice of Ben until sophomore year of high school. His quick wit always made her laugh during class, which probably wasn't the best timing. She'd watched Ben the whole period, waiting for him to do something silly. The longer she watched him, the more she liked him. And those feelings apparently ran pretty damn deep.

Ben scrambled up from his beanbag and immediately reached down to offer Josie a hand. She hesitated for a split second, still battling with the mindset of her much younger self who could barely get Ben to talk to her outside the classroom, let alone reach for her hand twice in one night. Her fingers tingled from his warmth when she slipped her hand inside his.

Once she made it to her feet, he didn't let go right away, brushing his thumb over her knuckles. His intense gaze sent goose bumps down her arms.

"Thank you. Seriously," he said in a hushed voice.

"You're welcome." Like an idiot, she shook his hand. She actually *shook* his hand as if they'd completed a business transaction.

Ben breathed a laugh and ran his fingers through his hair. He headed toward the stairwell, checking to ensure Josie followed close behind.

The short stairway appeared infinite before her, but she made it to the top in Ben's wake. Izzy sat on her bed in her pajamas, the blue light of her screen still illuminating her face.

"Hey, Iz," Ben started. "You have everything you need up here?"

"I guess." Izzy didn't look up.

Ben blinked more than necessary. "Okay. Well, if you think of something, you can ask me or Josie. She'll be—"

"Is she your girlfriend?" Izzy's dark eyebrows weaved together behind her screen.

Ben coughed like his tongue had gotten caught in his throat. "No, she's, um, Josie is my friend. She's living here with us for a while."

Izzy's head tilted, her body contorting with all sorts of preteen attitude as she observed Josie clutching the doorframe. "Kevin said you're pregnant."

Now Ben didn't move. They *clearly* made an excellent team for these confrontations. No wonder they required a pact on the refrigerator to remind them to get it together.

"Yes, I'm pregnant," Josie spoke up. If they had to tag-team giving this child the birds and the bees talk, God help them. "I'm due in March, so the baby's only as big as peach now. Still a long way to go."

Because she totally needed to quote her pregnancy app at this kid like the most awkward human on earth.

"Is it a boy or a girl?" Izzy let the tablet fall into her lap.

Ben's gaze flickered between his flustered roommate and his inquisitive daughter.

"Um, I don't know yet." Josie rested her hand on the archway. "It's still too early to tell."

Izzy curled a thin leg underneath her, the tablet resting in her lap as she studied Josie with a look of uncertainty.

"I think it's a girl," Izzy said matter-of-factly.

That took a better turn than Josie had expected. "Really?"

Izzy shrugged. "Mom said she knew I was a girl because her hair and skin were so bad when she was pregnant with me."

"Isabel." Ben's hands flew to the railing behind him. "Holy shh—crap. Josie, I'm sorry. You look fine. Izzy, go to sleep *now*."

The air in Josie's chest deflated like a balloon. This kid could really dish the insults, and Josie couldn't send them right back as a grown-ass adult who had been trained in letting these sorts of comments roll off her back. Though her raging hormones begged her to ignore all she'd learned in the last four years of teaching and fire away. She wouldn't. For Ben's sake.

"Bet I'm right about the baby." Izzy smiled for the first time since she'd arrived at the house.

Since confirming her pregnancy, Josie had only wanted a healthy baby like any other mother would. But at that moment, oh she wanted a boy. "I'm sure your dad will let you know, but it's bedtime now."

Ben hurried to help Izzy under the covers. "Please stop," he whispered to his daughter.

"Good night, Ben," Izzy sneered.

Instead of retreating to her side of the loft, Josie hurried down the stairs, pausing at the landing.

Parenting might be the hardest job in the world. No wonder Ben struggled so much. Did Josie even have what it took to deal with a kid like that—or any age or stage of child development for that matter? She'd worked with a room full of inner-city Chicago teenagers during her student teaching. That had to count for something in the parenting department.

Josie smoothed her *horrible* hair and ran her hands along her bloated stomach. Suddenly, six months until the baby's arrival didn't seem like enough time to prepare.

Ben's footsteps padded down the stairs behind her, and she rushed toward the door to grab her purse and check for her keys.

"What are you doing?" Ben froze at the bottom of the steps as if Josie held an active bomb in her hands and not a set of car keys.

If she had any chance of surviving motherhood, she needed resources. McDonald's offered both hot fudge sundaes *and* Wi-Fi. She couldn't go wrong there. "I'm going out."

"I'm so sorry about—"

"It's fine. Don't worry about it." She held up a hand to stop him and reached for the front door. "I'll see you later."

10

Friends Don't Flirt over French Fries

SOMETHING ABOUT ENTERING THE fourth month of pregnancy knocked Josie down hard. Fatigue kept her from doing much more than napping and watching movies. Almost everything she put in her stomach came up again. For a week, she kept to her room as much as possible and texted her roommates to let them know she hadn't died.

Today, she woke up feeling much more like herself. As usual, the air mattress had deflated some during the night, and it took a few extra heaves to roll off the bed. As she landed on her hands and knees, her middle-of-the-night shenanigans shuffled through her mind while she crunched over muffin wrappers and granola-bar crumbs. Her appetite had returned with a vengeance, it would seem. The lemon-sized fetus blossoming in her stomach must require extra sustenance in preparation for this second trimester.

Damn. Why hadn't she thought to grab a lemon shake-up before the fair ended?

Her last check from Berry Sweet Smoothies finally graced her bank account. Late, like always. It wasn't much, but it paid her portion of the rent and utilities and gave her enough to spend on gas and groceries.

It occurred to her midway through her vomit-filled week that maybe her name hadn't appeared on the sub list yet. Many subs had signed on earlier than she had, and sometimes districts didn't send the updated lists to the school offices right away. She should call the principal and make sure they had her down, so she didn't continue thinking she had a job if she really didn't.

Josie hit the call button on the listed phone number for Principal Gale Abnor. Her fingers drummed her thighs as she waited.

"Clarkson High School. How can I help you?" the cheery voice greeted.

Josie cleared her throat. "Yes, hi. My name is Josephine Hale, and I'm on the substitute-teaching list. I wondered if you knew of any planned absences coming up? Or, I guess, I should ask if my name made it on the subbing list. I signed up late this summer, so I wanted to check. I'm a licensed teacher, formerly of Chicago."

Oh. My. Goodness. Could she stop rambling and be a real person for, like, ten seconds?

"Hi, Josephine." The secretary's pep spiked to a new level. "You're definitely on the list. I know because you went to school with my daughter, Melody, and I always loved your name, so it jumped right out at me on the page."

"Oh, yes. Melody was such a nice girl."

She most certainly was not. Josie had resorted to brownnosing the school secretary for work. What was next? Bribery? With desperation setting in, she'd do almost anything to get that job.

The secretary, whose last name must be Gabriel but whose first name remained a mystery, squealed with laughter on the other end. "Isn't she? She's married now, three kids. Lives in Tennessee. Can you believe that? Time just flies."

"It sure does." If Ms. Gabriel could keep quiet about Josie's life story when she talked to Melody with three kids, a husband, and a Tennessee driver's license, that'd be great. "But, hey, I'm wondering about sub openings. Do you have any information on that, or can I speak with Ms. Abnor about—"

"Oh, I'm sorry, honey. Gale's in meetings most of the day, but I can tell you we haven't needed a sub yet. It's been a healthy month so far, knock on wood."

"Oh, okay. I guess that's good, right? Thank—"

"Let me tell you what I'll do." Secretary Gabriel's humming filled Josie's ear. "I'll make a note for Gale and have her bump your name to the top of the list. Okay, sweetie?"

Melody's mother probably still pictured Josie as the ten-year-old kid playing peewee basketball. "Thank you so much. I appreciate that a lot."

"My pleasure. We'll see you real soon, and I'll tell Melody you said hi."

"Please do. Thanks again." So long as Melody didn't send her a friend request, the phone call might not have been entirely unproductive.

Josie ended the call and flipped over to her favorite job-search board. Since she hadn't visited it in twenty-four hours, it was high time she checked available positions around Clarkson in case the subbing gig fell through.

The first opening in her area popped up on the screen like a virus. "No. No, no, no, no, no."

Women's Health Alliance, Drs. Steinman, Richcreek, and Mallory—Receptionist.

Of all the opportunities in the world, why did her ob-gyn have to be hiring? As if it wouldn't already be awkward enough to work in an office where half the staff had seen her hoo-ha, her closest coworker would be her mother at the other end of the desk.

If her mom knew about the opening, she'd surely get on Josie's case. The job came with an hourly wage, insurance, and a 401(k), something mothers desperately wanted for their daughters.

Josie groaned and closed the app. Enough job hunting for the day. If she didn't hear from the school in another week or so, she'd reconsider. God help her if it came down to *that.*

With an armload of snack trash, she pattered down the steps, pausing at the landing to ensure no one would be there to judge her. But the house was still. She'd barely laid eyes on Ben and Kevin in the past week and almost dreaded running into them now. They'd invited a total bum to live with them. She didn't have a job, couldn't pay the rent, and slept most of the day.

Josie wrestled with Kevin's fancy Keurig, pushing every button on the front until it whirred to life and spat coffee into her cup. Eventually, she'd get the hang of it. Or finally make enough money to buy a cheapo pot like the one she used to own. She missed that thing. Why hadn't she thought to grab it in her rush to leave the apartment? Grant didn't even drink coffee. He'd probably trashed it the moment she'd left.

The scent of the roasted beans marinating inside the coffee maker revived her a little more. Once she showered and rinsed away the grogginess, she could at least pick up around the house and make herself useful.

In fact, she knew right where to start, since Ben had left a note on the bull sheet that read:

Someone put the laundry in the dryer, or I'm not wearing pants the rest of the week.

To spare some embarrassment all around, Josie changed the laundry and headed to the shower. She had barely gotten out and wrapped the towel all the way around her when her phone rang on the vanity top. Little puddles dotted the floor with every step, but she somehow stayed on her feet as she snatched up the phone before it went to voicemail.

"Josie?" Ben sang on the other end. "You're alive!"

"I am. Finally. What's up?" She clutched the towel against her naked frame. Though it wasn't like he could *see* her.

"I'm just finishing up errands. Wondered if you wanted lunch before I had to be at work. I heard you moving around last night and figured you might be feeling better."

Josie's cheeks warmed. Stupid cheeks. Ben simply asked if she wanted to eat, which was something everyone did to survive. "I am quite starving. Thank you."

He laughed. "You got it. Be there in about twenty minutes, depending on how long it takes at the bank."

Twenty minutes till lunch meant finding clothes and getting ready a little faster than she'd planned. Dressed in her only pair of maternity shorts and a tank top that proved every bit the "flexible fit" claimed by the brand, Josie knotted her damp hair into a messy ponytail. She brushed on a bit of blush and mascara to look less like death and pinned up the flyaway hairs at her neckline. The sound of Ben's engine revving when he pulled into the driveway sent her scurrying for her flip-flops so she could meet him on the porch.

"You need help?" she yelled down the driveway.

Ben shook his head. "Nope. I got it."

He had his hands full: a drink carrier in his right and two white paper bags in his left. How many people had he gotten lunch for?

"You are an angel, Benjamin. I feel like my stomach's trying to make up for the last week of not eating." Josie rubbed her hands together as he padded up the steps.

Ben spun around on the first step and plopped down, balancing the bags and drink carrier, then motioned for her to join him. "I'm glad you're feeling better. We were getting worried."

Worried. Not accusing her of slackerhood. Hopefully that was the actual truth and not merely Ben being polite.

Josie offered a shy smile and scooted into place beside him. The space between the deck railing and edge of the house couldn't have been over four feet wide, which made for some comfy quarters. "Yeah, I'm sorry I've pretty much been a dud around the house. I'll make up for it, I promise. And I'll get you some food money after we—"

"No, no. This is on me. It's the final day of the season for the root beer stand, and I've been waiting for you to feel better so I could make amends after all that went down with Izzy last weekend. I brought you a corn dog, among other things."

He opened the first bag and pulled out a foam cup overflowing with fries. The aroma of salt and vinegar hung on the breezy September air.

The mention of Izzy, however, drew out an uncomfortable laugh. "Really, it's okay. She said nothing that wasn't totally true."

Ben shoved a bunch of fries in his mouth and reached in the bag to retrieve a bouquet of corn dogs.

Josie hadn't exactly meant to trap him like that, but he'd made the right choice to stuff his face and avoid an awkward reply. That made her smile. She, too, grabbed a handful of the french fries, so warm they burned her palm—just the way she liked them. "But I still plan to earn my keep here. I swear."

"You don't have to 'earn your keep.' This isn't a pirate ship." Ben wiggled a Styrofoam cup from the holder and handed her a drink. "Here. Kinda ticked they don't have frosted mugs to go, but this'll have to do."

"Thanks. And any root beer from the root beer stand is good enough for me." Josie swirled her straw around the cup. The foam clung to the lid, and her mouth watered at the sweet smell that reminded her of being sixteen, with Ben at her side and a root beer in hand. Well, a sixteen-year-old version of herself, plus twenty-some pounds and new fun pressure on her pelvic bone.

"So, how did the rest of the weekend go with Izzy? When do you have her next?" After her late-night McDonald's research extravaganza, Josie had opted to sleep in the next day. By the time she'd finally come downstairs, Izzy was gone.

His lip curled, and he finished chewing his bite. "It went like it always does. Silence. Tension. Calling her mom to come get her before breakfast ended. She really does hate me. I have no idea when she'll be back. Probably not for another couple of weeks."

Defeat echoed off his every word.

"She doesn't hate you." Josie tried to sound convincing.

"Oh yeah, she does. Her mom hates me; therefore, Izzy hates me." Ben crushed a fry between his fingers. "I don't know how to undo the cycle, either, because it's damn near impossible to get along with Noel. Our relationship was never all that solid."

Josie squirted a ketchup packet onto her corn dog but didn't take a bite. It didn't feel right to stuff the thing into her mouth while Ben bared his soul like this. "It had to have been okay in the beginning, though, right?"

Ben's shoulders tensed. "Well, yeah, I guess. I met her at the homecoming basketball game, and she seemed pretty fun. It was that summer after graduation when we realized we had literally nothing in common. We'd only been together about six months when she got pregnant, and by the time she found out, we were about to break up. We stayed together until Izzy was born but fought constantly."

"Oh." That game was when he'd met Noel for the first time? Josie remembered that night vividly, the way Ben kept looking into the other team's stand and eventually excused himself from their group to go get a snack. She wanted to go with him to try to get him alone. The excitement of the game and having all their friends together had her feeling brave. Instead of chasing after him to ask him out, she'd stayed behind and decided to wait until they went back to Kev's house after the game. But when Ben came back, he had Noel with him.

"Yeah, I dunno. It's one of those things where you think about mistakes you made, but if I hadn't met Noel, we wouldn't have Izzy. And I love that kid. She's all fire and sass, but I wouldn't trade her for anything, ya know?"

The way he smiled from the side of his mouth when he talked about his daughter, even after how rudely she treated him last weekend, warmed Josie's insides. That something as terrible as a toxic relationship could lead to the creation of a beautiful human being was like music to her ears.

"I get it. Grant and I fought a lot too. For a while, I wondered if our lives might have been better if we hadn't met. He could have gone to vet school and been a successful doctor. I could be a hermit on a farm with a big garden and plum trees. I've always wanted to grow my own fruit. But, yeah, if Grant and I hadn't happened, I wouldn't have this little peanut." She tapped a greasy finger to her stomach.

"Least we survived and got a consolation prize from it. Even if mine might be demon-possessed and you haven't even met yours yet."

"Right." Who would have thought she'd one day be sitting on the steps with Benjamin Romero, eating junk food, talking exes, and swooning over their children that they definitely did not have together. Not quite the future she'd had in mind for the two of them when she watched him shooting hoops in Kevin's driveway and imagined him carrying her off into the sunset.

Josie tore the rest of the corn dog off its stick, savoring the last bite she'd have until next year when either the root beer stand reopened or the fair returned—or until she bought a box of the frozen kind. "So, speaking of exes and children, have you done anything to appease Kevin regarding the pact?"

Ben smacked his fist into his forehead. "Gah, that's the other reason I'm glad you're healed. He has been nonstop harassing me this week about that stupid pact. Apparently, he's watched some TED Talk on envelope-system budgeting and bought an ugly-ass briefcase to carry to work. Pretty sure he only has, like, two pens and a candy bar inside it. Now that you're feeling better, he can bother you with his enthusiasm, and I can go back to living my life."

"Uh, no. I am so not taking over on this one. His intensity will scare me into early labor…which he'd probably like. I'd be ahead of schedule with marking things off my to-do list."

Ben laughed and nudged her with his elbow. She pushed back before she realized what she'd done. Their shoulders touched now.

He didn't move away. Where they could fit three people side by side in the space at the top of the steps, they sat pressed against each other. In her head, she counted slowly, as if the seconds ticking away meant something. If he moved first, she'd have her answer. *She* didn't plan to move at all.

"Well, don't say I didn't warn you. He's going like a freight train on this, so you'd better get motivated." Ben leaned over enough to nudge her again, slower this time.

What exactly was happening right now?

His body warmth surpassed the heat of the sun in that moment, setting her skin on fire. "Right. I'll be a huge disappointment to him, for sure."

"You and me both. We can probably fake it. Tell him we paid off our debts, we've fallen in love with our jobs, and we'll get married soon."

Josie coughed against her straw when the root beer shot down the wrong pipe. This finally made her move away from Ben and crash into the deck rail. The last thing she wanted was to throw up root beer when she'd come to the closest level of flirting she'd done since first meeting Grant almost eight years ago.

The giggles wouldn't let up.

"Not to each other. I didn't mean it like that." Ben slapped his knee when he laughed and spilled the rest of his fries down the steps. "But geez. I'm not that repulsive, am I?"

She wiped the tears from her eyes and cleared her throat of the fizzy bubbles still trying to choke her. "I never said that."

"I am smoking hot, Josie." He pressed his lips together to keep a straight face.

"Absolutely." She reached for a napkin from the takeout bag to dab at her eyes and hide her blushing. If only he knew how much she agreed.

Ben brushed the french-fry crumbs and salt from his lap. "But for real, though, he better not take points away from us if we don't 'find love.' I'm barely hanging on with the two women already in my life. Not counting you, of course. You're sorta in my life now, too, I guess."

Well, that dialed down the flirtatious fun real fast. She'd reentered his life as a roommate, someone who would come and go with their life changes. "Yeah, well, I think that's why Kevin made the pact in the first place. None of us knows what we're doing."

"True. I've had enough failed relationships to figure that out." Ben wadded up his corn-dog wrapper and licked the dripping ketchup from his fist.

Josie gathered her trash and stuffed it into the paper bag. "We learn from those, I guess. Maybe we'll get it right next time. I mean, just because you've had some bad relationships doesn't mean the right one—"

"I'm gonna stop you right there because you're starting to sound like my mom." Ben's face scrunched, but he kept his eyes low.

Nothing sexier than sounding like a guy's mother.

"Yikes. I do not want to sound like a mom." Not a grown man's mother, anyway. Josie kicked a stray stone when she stood from her seat. As much as she'd enjoyed their spontaneous lunch on the front steps, she kind of wanted to get out of there at rocket speed now.

"Well, you're about to be one, so…" Ben breathed a laugh and ran his hand through his hair as he stood. He still wouldn't look at her. "I didn't mean that in a bad way. I'll just shut up now."

"No worries." Yeah, him seeing her as a mother figure definitely didn't equal romantic love unless she wanted to get into some weird Oedipus complex stuff. She had no hope of undoing any of that either. The fact remained she had a child growing inside her. A.k.a: boyfriend repellent.

Ben squinted at the yard before them. A couple of cars passed by, doing nothing to break the awkward silence. Josie rocked on her feet and bit into her cheek. They continued to stand still on the porch, each with a bag of food trash in one hand.

So much for the easy way they'd spoken to each other only moments before.

"Well, I'd better get ready for work," Ben said at last.

It was high school all over again. They'd hang out, laugh together, have fun all evening, and then nothing. Each time she thought maybe he felt something in return, he'd end up with another girlfriend. Josie could never be quite enough for him no matter the life stage.

Ben gave a half-hearted thumbs-up and paused when he put his hand on the door. "Oh, hey. I also wanted to thank you. About what you said last weekend with Izzy and this new house and all the switching. It made sense. I picked up some new bedroom stuff to make it feel more homey for when she comes next time. There's even a picture of a whale that matches that pillow she's always carrying around to hang over the bed. So, thanks."

"I'm glad it helped."

There had to be a reason Kevin put love as the *third* pact point. They needed to tackle the other things before they worried about their silly ole hearts. In fact, if she wanted to protect her heart *and* her baby, she probably should make sure her lawyer was on board, too, before she plunged forward with the pact plans to reclaim her life. Even if that meant putting aside her potential future with Ben… that was definitely not going to happen.

Josie sank down to the steps, picked a french fry off the concrete, and popped it into her mouth.

11

Equitable Division of Animal Crackers

THE LAWYER RAN HER tongue across her red-polished lips. "That threw a bit of a wrench into things, didn't it?"

Josie sank a little lower into the plush leather chair as the powerhouse of a woman typed away on her computer. Her knee bounced as the anxiety of sitting in that office crept through her, causing the nameplate that read KARLEEN VANLANDINGHAM to tremble on top of the marble desk.

She needed something strong to take the edge off. However, most options weren't exactly pregnancy-approved. Except for animal crackers. For some reason, probably because she'd spent the drive here mentally packing her future diaper bag, she really wanted those dang cookies. The little nutmeggy nuggets would definitely soothe her now. Karleen should keep them on the desk for these instances. Surely, Josie wasn't the only pregnant divorcee in need of snacks. She'd make sure to drop her suggestion off with the receptionist on her way out.

"And you're positive there's no chance it's anyone else's but his?" Karleen asked.

Josie instinctively wiped the sweat from her brow, although sweating in a building that cranked their AC to arctic levels didn't really make sense. "It's one thousand percent his. He's my one and only." Her jaw hurt from clenching her teeth so tightly throughout the meeting. "*Was*, I mean. Was my one and only."

Karleen peeked over her glasses and gave a small, sympathetic smile. "I'm sorry. I have to ask that for legal reasons. I know this isn't easy for you."

"Not even a little bit."

"There's been no indication that he's actively trying to contest this yet, but if he does, we can request a paternity test. I sent all of this information to his new lawyer, but I'm waiting to hear back. I'll call again this afternoon."

Josie stiffened in her chair. "New lawyer?"

Karleen sighed through her words. "Yes, he's apparently switched his case to a new law office in the past week. Unfortunately, that mixed with the baby development will slow your case down. The previous firm was particularly unresponsive."

Like Grant.

Not that Josie needed an expedited divorce. She had no plans of running off to get married and do this crap all over again. But there also wasn't any chance for reconciliation. Might as well get it over with as soon as possible.

The clock ticked away on the wall behind her. It took all of Josie's focus to concentrate on the task at hand and not count every second she had to spend inside the icy room.

"And what is your plan for this pregnancy?" Karleen asked.

At nearly four months pregnant, she had made most of her decisions already. But what answer did Karleen want here? "I'm going to have the baby and raise it."

That didn't sound totally awkward at all. Her nerves always got the better of her in this place. She might as well just sing some "Papa Don't Preach" lines, rather than try to answer a super-intimidating professional lawyer who seemed to have Josie's fate in her hands.

"Well, I'll make sure it's crystal clear in my communication that he'll be paying his state-ordered child support. His lawyer should have already let him know about this too." Karleen hit a few more keys on her open laptop. "My fear is that if he's not responding to you, maybe he's not acknowledging the pregnancy—which could mean he wants to fight it. He won't win, I assure you. But that never stops men from trying."

"Oh goody." Leave it to Grant to make everything more difficult.

Josie had hoped to start this day with some clarity and direction. In six months, she'd have a baby to take care of. She also had to figure out how to take care of *herself* within that time frame. And it didn't look like she'd get any help from Grant. She checked her phone often to see if he'd come around with a response.

Nothing.

Which was still totally fine. In fact, if she could erase him from the equation completely, she'd be even happier. Stupid laws.

Karleen shuffled some paperwork in front of her. "I know this seems pretty bleak right now, but you'll be okay in the end. I've seen this more than I'd like. The beginning is always the hardest."

Josie nodded at her lawyer-turned-therapist. Karleen probably had these kinds of speeches at the ready for whenever her clients fell apart in front of her. At least Josie hadn't cried yet like she had the past couple of times in this office. Now that the shock of Grant's infidelity had finally worn off, she could breathe. She had a new future on the horizon. A second chance.

Unless Grant tried to take everything away from her again.

She leaned forward in her chair, pressing her hands against her knees to keep her feet from bouncing. "What can I do to make sure I keep all rights with the baby?"

"Well, I'm sure Grant's lawyer will talk with him about his own rights, but to prove yourself in front of a judge, you'll want to have a solid job for sure. By showing you can securely provide for your child, you'll be leaps and bounds ahead of the game."

Steady work. Substitute teaching hardly counted as steady, but the pay wouldn't be too bad if she got a long-term gig. Berry Sweet Smoothies had invited all their employees to return next summer when they reopened in May. The two jobs could give her enough income until she found work as a full-time teacher.

The ob-gyn receptionist job would give her something even *steadier*, though. She'd work year-round with the same hours every day, no matter the season. If she had to do it to keep her child, she would.

Karleen folded her hands in front of her. "Get insurance in place for once the baby is born, have a secure living environment. It may not look great on paper moving three times this year, but if you're still in your current place of residence when the baby arrives, that will give you a solid six months of stability. That's better than nothing."

It had never occurred to Josie that her frequent moves might look bad in front of a judge. It's not like she could have done anything to prevent them. When she left Grant, she lost her home. In retrospect, she might have opted to kick *him* out. But everything in Chicago made her think of the life they'd built together. In that sickening wave of misery and embarrassment over finding him with someone else, getting away had mattered more than anything else.

Karleen made everything sound so simple, almost like a checklist. Josie could go home, make an Excel spreadsheet with goals and steps to take life from zero to awesome, and that'd do the trick.

Actually, that sounded exactly like a detailed version of the Corn Dog Pact. That silly little piece of paper on the refrigerator might be more important than she'd thought. Accomplishing Kevin's three pact points could give her a leg up in court when it came to both her child and divorce proceedings.

She had to think about this. To form a more detailed plan.

Next week, she'd walk in that school building and introduce herself to the principal. She'd fill out an application with the ob-gyn and have it at the ready if necessary. *Or* scour the job-site pages again for literally anything else.

Josie stood and shook Karleen's hand. "Thank you so much for all your help through this."

"My pleasure," Karleen said, but Josie figured that must be lawyer code for *That's why you pay me.*

The heavy door thumped shut behind her when she exited the building.

If she could get a job nailed down, she'd need to think about what to do with her baby while she worked. Ella could probably help suggest sitter options, so she'd get that in place. Changing her driver's license to the new address might make the residency appear more permanent, though she had no idea how "permanent" living in Ben's house might be.

But she could do this. She could handle all of this chaos and rein it in to prove herself. With a deep breath, she climbed into her car, ready to head home and fight for her baby.

12

Will Work for Pizza

JOSIE INSPECTED ALL FOUR ceiling corners as she sat on the kitchen counter, her feet crossed and swinging below her on that late September morning. She'd done a bang-up job of knocking out cobwebs with the help of a dustrag tied to the broom handle. After writing out a budget and downloading some grocery apps, she'd run off to the DMV to get a brand-new license with 422 Leeson Avenue printed under her name. Her WIC application was in *pending* status, and she'd scoured the house to clear her thoughts and release heaps of pent-up energy.

It also made her feel like she had at least contributed somehow to their home while she continued to wait on employment. She'd subscribed to several pregnancy vlogs and finally felt like she had a good understanding of what to expect over the next few months. Her knowledge had to have surpassed Kevin's by now.

She coiled her fingers around her hot mug of coffee. The mornings grew cooler as the month progressed, requiring the addition of her silky-soft Victoria's Secret robe in the mornings. She didn't hate the dropping temperatures. The more pregnant she got, the more body heat she produced.

"Mornin', sweet cheeks." Kevin rounded the bar top into the kitchen, threw open the refrigerator door, and took a long swig of orange juice straight from the jug.

"You know you guys don't have to give me a pet name, right? That can be your little bromance thing."

Kevin scoffed and shoved the juice into the fridge. "Where's Benny?"

"Probably still sleeping. Haven't seen him yet." She had learned to work around Ben's morning schedule. As a second-shifter, he slept later than she and Kevin did. They only had a few hours that intersected during the day and would pass each other from time to time when going to the bathroom or kitchen. Mostly, Ben spent a good deal of his home life downstairs playing video games.

"I'm gonna go wake him up. You stay there." Kevin made his way to the door leading to the basement and flung it open much like he'd done to the refrigerator a moment before.

"Why?" Josie pulled her legs all the way onto the counter and folded them crisscross.

Kevin stormed into the basement without giving her an answer. She never knew what to expect with that guy. He might gather his roommates for a grand announcement or simply inquire if anyone else wanted frozen toaster pastries.

She took another sip of her coffee and tried not to spit it out when Kevin shouted, "Put your pants on, and get up here!"

Josie's face warmed as she shook her head. Ben and his pantslessness.

Kevin flew up the steps and waved dramatically toward the two-person table at the front of the house. "Go sit at the table, JoJo. I'll make us breakfast."

She uncoiled her legs and scooted to the edge of the counter. "You don't need to do that. I can—"

"I said sit. We're having a family meeting."

"A what?" Josie hopped down, but Kevin didn't stop pointing until she made it all the way to the table.

Ben pushed open the door to the basement, scowling as he observed his friend.

"Table. Both of you." Kevin's commands only got harsher sounding with each repetition.

Ben's head dropped forward like that of a pouting toddler, but he followed orders and plopped his body weight onto the seat across from Josie. "I don't want to have a family meeting."

They'd lived with Kevin long enough to know they had no power over him or his wonky rule. Ben's whining wouldn't get him anywhere. He drummed his fingers on the table, gaze drifting across Josie before he averted his eyes and let out a long, slow breath.

She looked down at herself, suddenly remembering the silky robe she'd thrown on that morning. While she had on shorts and a tank top underneath the robe, it probably didn't look that way from the other side of the table.

Kevin dropped a paper plate of unwrapped cereal bars between his companions.

"Wow, Kev, you outdid yourself." Ben snatched up the bar closest to him and took an unnecessarily large bite.

"Shut it, Benjamin." Kevin grabbed a cereal bar as well and used it to point back and forth between Ben and Josie. "We're having a meeting because I'm disappointed in the two of you."

"Why? What'd we do?" Josie pulled her hand from the breakfast plate.

Kevin sighed. "We are roommates, friends, *family*. We pride ourselves on our integrity and working together to make our lives and home better."

"What's your point, dude?" Ben asked through a mouthful of breakfast.

"I'm talking about what's missing from the fridge." Kevin's empty hand hit the table like a lawyer trying to prove a point in court.

Josie stretched to inspect the refrigerator. She'd seen the bullsheet note he'd posted about having a Karate Kid marathon, but nothing seemed amiss.

"The Bagel Bites, dimwits. They're gone." Kevin paced in front of their table with no place to sit. "We had that giant bag, and now there's nothing left."

Josie pinched the bridge of her nose. Her head had been swimming with ideas for getting her life on solid ground, and Kevin had called them around for an official meeting over some missing frozen food? "You ate the rest of them last night. Remember? You asked if we wanted some, then rescinded your offer because there wasn't enough to share."

Kevin paused and scratched at his chin.

"This is not a good enough reason to make me put on pants." Ben swung around on his stool to rest his elbows atop his thighs.

Josie pointed to Ben. "Agreed. If we're going to have a household meeting, it should be about something like reconfiguring mortgage rates, establishing a chore chart, or checking in on our pact progress."

Kevin seemed to consider Josie's words and nodded. "I think you might be right about the Bagel Bites. But I don't know what configurating mortgages means, dibs on *not* cleaning toilets for the chore chart, and I'm def winning the pact thing. Not that anyone's surprised, considering the lead I had on y'all when we started."

"Denial's not a good color on you, Kev." Josie had a hard time imagining a man who misplaced snack food so easily being at the top of their leader board or someone who had his life together in any way, really.

He huffed as if her comment was the most insulting thing she'd ever said. "I have fifty-six dollars in my savings envelope, wear a tie to work, bought a briefcase, and I haven't been on a date in four days. I'm saving myself for *the one*, obviously. But you two have done nothing. You're still sitting down there at rock bottom, looking up at me, and wishing you could be awesome. It's sad, Josie. So, so sad."

Kevin booped her nose, and she swatted him away, nearly toppling from the high chair to do it.

"Wrong-o, chief. I may not have a fancy briefcase, but I have a shiny new driver's license, a list of day-care providers in the area, and I have pinned at least fifty healthy recipes on Pinterest. And then some." She crossed her arms and lifted her chin. A meager start, but a start no less.

Kevin clapped his approval, while Ben slid off his stool.

"I don't want to play this game," Ben said.

"Why? 'Cause you're *losing?*" Kevin puffed out his chest and knocked into his friend.

"Har-har." Ben headed toward the kitchen. "Put me down for doing nothing toward pact progress."

Josie jumped from her chair to intercept him, a wave of bravery overtaking her. "Wait." She pressed her hands to Ben's chest, then pulled them back again as if his shirt were lava. "You got Izzy all that stuff for her room."

"So? What does that have to do with anything?" His brow furrowed. He looked from Josie's outstretched hands to her face.

"You *are* making progress." The words came out almost as a whisper, the adrenaline surge she'd had a moment ago waning. "You've given your daughter a cozy space all of her own and added some touches that show you *know* her. That's definitely a big step on pact point three."

"Doesn't feel like it."

Kevin paced in a circle around his friends. "I'll send you some Ted Talks, bud. Maybe that'll help you reach my level of awesome."

"Kevin, sit *down.*" Josie gave him a friendly shove toward the table and returned her attention to Ben. He didn't move, seemingly frozen in place in front of her. "You sit too."

"Are you commandeering my meeting?" Kevin slumped in his seat and grasped his heart.

That's exactly what she was doing. The three of them had hardly been in the same room together lately, let alone discussed their Corn

Dog Pact triumphs and failures. She'd played along with Kevin in the beginning, but now she *needed* that pact. "Look. I just met with my lawyer yesterday, and I need to get my life together to ensure I get full custody of my baby. Now, I've done a few things, but I need to know the two of you are on my side too. If we're going to do this, let's do it well."

Ben stiffened in his seat. "Of course we're on your side."

"There's a chance they could take the baby?" Kevin's eyes grew wide.

"No, not like that. I mean, I have to prove I'm a strong, independent adult so I look good in court just in case Grant challenges me on anything. I have to crush this pact. If I crush it, it gets me one step closer to not having to worry about this anymore." Her hand instinctively fell over her stomach.

"Fine." Kevin slammed his fist on the table, rattling the metal legs against the nuts and bolts. "Then we gotta step it up to a level above briefcases and Pinterest pages."

Ben laughed. "I'm here for moral support, Josie, but I really can't think of what else to do."

Kevin stuck his pointer finger in his friend's face. "What do you want to be when you grow up?"

Ben's nose scrunched. "Not broke."

"Your job, douche canoe." Kevin snatched up the last cereal bar, snapped it in half, and shoved one part into his mouth.

Ben closed his eyes and collapsed dramatically against the table. "It's too early for this, no matter how motivational you two think you are."

"I recall you wanted to be a train engineer of some kind?" Kevin asked.

"When I was eight…"

Josie covered her mouth to hide the giggle. "Maybe the better question is how do you think you can improve your job?"

"I put in for first shift. Does that count?" Ben shrugged.

"It's a start." Kevin rolled his eyes and shoved the other half of the cereal bar into his mouth. Poor Ben had to put on pants, eat stale cereal bars, and withstand the most unorganized motivational talk ever. The world had yet to make coffee strong enough for these kinds of mornings.

Josie lowered her voice as she shifted toward Ben. "You said you never got a chance to finish college. Would you ever go back?"

She prayed the suggestion wouldn't come out as offensive or pushy. Ben didn't *have* to change for her. The camaraderie and accountability that came with their joint pact was great, sure. But he at least *had* a job, unlike her at the moment. Technically, he already had his life more together than she did.

"Haven't really thought about it." Ben examined the empty paper plate in front of him as if it held all the answers to the universe.

He hadn't yelled at her, which allowed her a moment to breathe again.

Kevin made a series of shushing and spitting sounds. "I think I know what our problem is. It's that whole Schrödinger's cat thing. You need proper motivation and reinforcement to meet your goals. Like, obviously, we gotta raise the stakes."

Across the table, Ben shook his head slowly, trying not to laugh out loud. It seemed to pain him somewhat.

"Please tell me it's not part of your plan to pursue a career in psychology," Josie said.

"Are you crazy? Dealing with people like the two of you all day would kill me. Why don't we have another chair for this table? Josie, sit down. I'll go get a beanbag. This is ridiculous." While Ben and Josie couldn't get enough coffee in their system, Kevin had apparently consumed too much. His energy levels compared to that of a toddler on Mountain Dew and Pixy Stix.

Kevin huffed into the living room and dragged a beanbag chair with him, dropping his full body weight into it…well below their eye level.

Josie sighed and climbed onto the chair again. "I like this raising-the-stakes thing, but my stakes are kind of huge already, if you know what I mean."

"Right." Kevin rubbed his hands together like he was ready to place a bet on the races. "It's the motivation we need, a little pep in our step. And I'd never turn down a friendly competition."

Ben stretched his arms over his head. "No competition is ever friendly with you."

"Yeah, I have some concerns…" Josie readjusted her robe around her. "But keep going. I'm ready to get this thing started."

Kevin flung upward out of his chair. "Get this: pact winner gets free Saturday night pizza for a month. The losers have to pay for it."

"The winner of the *Corn Dog* Pact gets *pizza*?" Josie tapped her index finger to her chin.

Ben offered Josie an amused smile, then tilted his head in Kevin's direction. "So what determines a win?"

Kevin scratched at his stubbly sideburns. "Whoever accomplishes the most in those three pact goals as determined by the other housemates."

"Not gonna lie. That sounds rigged." Ben folded his arms in front of him.

"Not rigged." Kevin spoke much louder than necessary in the tiny room and fell backward into his beanbag. "But I *am* the official judge of this, so that we're clear."

"Oh geez." Who had put Kevin in charge of making all the rules to this thing? Still, free pizza for a month wasn't a bad addition to proving herself worthy in court.

"I'm not buying you pizza for a month." Ben grabbed the empty cereal-bar plate and walked it to the kitchen.

"But you're in, though, right?" Kevin hung backward over the beanbag to watch him go.

Ben spun around to flick the piece of paper hanging from the hardware magnet. "I have no choice, according to this official document, which I signed."

"Damn straight."

Josie hopped down from her seat. "I'd say our meeting was a success, boys. But let it be known that neither of you is going to beat me at something like adulting. Not even in your imagination, *Kevin*. You'd better start an envelope for pizza money." She kicked the edge of the beanbag when she walked past.

"Atta girl." Kevin tried to swat her leg as she made her way toward the stairwell but missed.

"And can we conclude this meeting by officially acknowledging that Kevin was the one who ate the Bagel Bites?" Ben leaned against the kitchen counter and awaited their response.

"Hear. Hear," Josie called out.

Kevin growled as he rolled off his beanbag, then kicked it toward the living room. "Whatever. Go do your adult stuff."

Josie blew him a kiss on her way up to her room to gather clothes and tackle this new day. In six months, these guys would buy her pizza for at least four weekends in a row. And they'd better be ready to dish out some breadsticks, too, because there was no way she would lose this thing.

13

An Ultrasound of an Onion

WITH THE WEEKEND OUT of the way, Josie could tackle her life head-on. The paper cloth crumpled under her every movement. Her feet dangled off the exam table, unable to touch the step she'd used to climb up. She stared at the dish of cotton swabs and tongue depressors, thankful she'd gotten to keep her clothes on for this appointment.

She'd already gotten a thumbs-up on her urine specimen. Now, she just had to wait for the doctor to check her over and the ultrasound technician to cover her belly in toothpaste and reveal the gender of her baby, now roughly the size of an onion. Because onion sizes were *super* consistent and gave her so much clarity about her child's proportions.

After today, Josie could cut her baby name options in half, which felt like one step in the right direction. Would she have an Elias or an Adelie?

She used to love making up baby-name lists, even before she settled down with Grant. Once he came along, she had to keep it a little more hushed, as he thought the idea rather stupid, considering they weren't having kids anyway. Plus, he hated every name she loved, especially Theodore. It meant "divine gift" which seemed so perfect and fitting for a tiny baby. He thought it sounded like an old man, but that didn't quell her love for the name.

They never agreed about their stance on gender-reveal parties either, which often resulted in a nonsensical argument.

"Why waste money on something everybody will find out in a few months?" he'd told her repeatedly.

Josie, however, dreamed of balloons or colored cakes, surrounded by their family and friends as they all found out the surprise together. Late at night, she'd look through her Pinterest boards for ideas on fun announcements in case it ever came to that point for them.

Now, sitting alone in the doctor's office, with Grant long gone, she could reveal her baby's sex however the hell she wanted. Alas, hosting a big party at this point in her life sounded more like torture than the glorious event Pinterest had promised.

The sitting-alone part still sucked. Grant should have been there. Not the Grant that cheated on her and refused to call her back after the pregnancy announcement. The version of Grant that had vowed to be her husband for better or worse. The Grant that would love their child unconditionally and cry with his wife when they watched the tiny fetal movements on the ultrasound machine. The Grant that didn't exist.

Josie rubbed at the tightening muscles in her neck. When this was all over, she deserved a gender-reveal party cake all to herself.

The door opened simultaneously with the knock, and Dr. Mallory walked in with her laptop.

"Hi, Josie." The doctor's long white coat swished as she spun around to greet her patient with a smile. "We're at that halfway point. How are you feeling so far?"

Josie readjusted on the exam table to keep the paper from scratching the backs of her legs. "Fine, I guess. Hungry, a little nauseous sometimes, stressed, and mildly irritable."

"Sounds about right." Dr. Mallory sat and scooted her rolling chair closer to take Josie's wrist in her hand. After a few seconds, she let go and rolled toward her computer. "Everything's looking pretty good here, but your blood pressure is a little higher than what we want in our mamas. Not dangerously so, but I know you've got a lot going on. Make sure you're not overdoing things and getting plenty of rest."

Adding naps to her daily to-do list sounded kind of awesome. She couldn't exactly argue with doctor's orders…

Dr. Mallory returned to her computer and clicked away some more. "To help stay calm and healthy, make sure you're getting some sunshine. Try to move around as much as you can to get the blood flowing without anything too strenuous. Take walks. Try yoga. Work on your nutritional intake. Cut back on sugar, caffeine, and processed foods."

So what *could* she eat? This doctor seriously expected her patients to remain calm without good food. Sure, Josie had pinned all those healthy recipes, but she'd kind of hoped she didn't have to actually *make* them.

"If you don't have any questions, I can send you down the hall, and Sonia will get you going on the ultrasound, okay?" Dr. Mallory offered a tender smile, patted Josie's knee, and left.

Good thing Josie didn't have questions. That's what the internet was for.

The paper crinkled as she hopped down to the built-in step stool. She took a right and headed toward the last room at the end of the hallway. The freshly painted mauve walls took away from the usual scent of latex and rubbing alcohol.

Could she take her good doctor's report home to tell the guys? Get bonus pact points for a perfect baby and dynamite urine specimen?

She rounded the corner to an exact replica of the room she just left, except for the rolling cart carrying the ultrasound machine. Repeating the same process she had in the other exam room, she climbed aboard the table and plopped down on the white paper top. In mere moments, she'd get to see her baby. Find out if she needed a pink or blue blanket. Start shopping with intention.

Her heart fluttered in a way she'd never experienced. This was a whole new kind of love.

The clock ticked louder on the wall with each passing minute. Josie tried to refocus on literally anything other than the anticipation, which only led to her contemplating the possible flavors of the tongue depressors inside the glass jar on the counter.

She pulled her phone from her pocket to check for messages.

Ella: I AM DYING TO KNOW!

Kevin had sent two screenshots, both of someone named Mandy's Facebook profile. One indicated he'd sent her a friend request, and on the other, he'd circled her relationship status "single" several times. The only included text had been two heart-eyes emojis, one mind-blown face, an angel, and a bomb.

Ben: Bought Bagel Bites in bulk to shut Kev up.

Kevin: Giiiiiiiirrrrrrrrlllll

A knock sounded at the door, and Josie shoved the phone back into her pocket. A short-statured, dark-haired woman in scrubs walked in, followed closely by the receptionist.

"Mom?" Josie sat up straighter.

Her mother beamed. "They let me come back with you for the big reveal."

Josie refocused on the tongue depressors. Why hadn't she thought to invite anyone to take Grant's place today? Ella had to teach, or she definitely would have come. Kevin or Ben standing at her side didn't seem right for this one.

At least her mom had thought ahead to this, though Josie couldn't always rely on her mother stepping in. Josie was on her own now. A single mom. Totally new territory. But she had a plan in place to deal with all that.

"That's okay, right?" her mom asked when Josie forgot to respond.

"Oh, yeah. I'm glad you came back. I didn't know they let you do that."

Her mother waved her arm like the thought made no sense. "They're super flexible here. It's a great place to work. Lots of benefits."

Oh, no. Would she bring up the job now, of all places to do it? Josie had promised herself one more week of waiting on a subbing call before she sent in an application for the receptionist job. She didn't want to have to speed up that time frame. It already came too quickly.

The technician, Sonia, washed her hands with extra bubbles. Josie's mother settled into the rolling chair and inched her way closer to the table, taking Josie's hand in hers. "I'm so excited to find out. Your dad thinks it's a boy, but I know it's a girl. You're already carrying high. What do you think it is, Jo?"

Yes, the baby. Her heart pounded wildly all over again.

"I haven't let myself guess." Baby was her "little peanut." Truth be told, she didn't envision herself being the mother to a boy *or* a girl.

She tried to picture herself standing in front of a mirror, braiding pigtails and talking Barbies. She thought about building with Legos or throwing a ball around in the backyard. Neither seemed possible. Josie was pregnant. With a baby. That's all she knew.

"I'm gonna have you lie back on the table, Josie." Sonia pushed a button, and the table hummed to life, lowering to a reclined angle.

Josie adjusted, the paper table cover crunching like footsteps on snow in the icy winter. Sonia's fingers echoed the chill when they wriggled Josie's shirt up, tucking it under her bra. Sonia squirted the frosty toothpaste gel all over Josie's abdomen.

All routine. Sonia did this every day of the week, used this machine to give expectant mothers a window into their womb. Did every awaiting mom have trouble controlling her breathing the way Josie did? She hadn't been this nervous since move-in night at Ben's.

Sonia rolled the ultrasound machine closer and tilted the screen for Josie to see. So far, only blackness appeared while Sonia typed away on the keyboard. Josie's mother squeezed her fingers, leaning closer with every breath.

It had been over a month since Josie had seen her child at her first OB appointment. With her pregnancy only at thirteen weeks, she might as well have watched an image of a wiggly bean with a heartbeat. But, oh, the sound of that faint little thumping. She hadn't truly believed the pregnancy tests until she'd heard those speedy little beats.

"Let's see what we've got here." Sonia touched the device to Josie's belly. A sea of black and white fuzz overtook the screen, then a little round head appeared. Sonia pushed harder for better focus, and the baby's full facial profile appeared.

Everything inside Josie stilled. The room went silent, and everyone else disappeared in that moment. The little black and white face yawned, tiny fists rubbing against its chin.

She fought the urge to wrap her hands around her bare stomach and give her little peanut a snuggle, but her mother held one hand, and with the other, she gripped the table hard enough that her knuckles had turned white. Five more months. Five more months and she could hold him or her and kiss those pudgy little cheeks, count the itty-bitty fingers on that balled fist, feel the warmth of her child's skin next to hers.

"So precious," Josie's mother whispered.

"Yeah," was all Josie could say.

Sonia took a few screenshots and measurements before inching the monitor over. "Everything looks great so far. Let's take a listen to that heart."

At first, the sound muffled, then echoed loud and clear. *Thump. Thump. Thump. Thump.*

Josie smiled.

"That's a strong heart rate: 160," Sonia said and took another couple of screenshots.

Her mother squealed. "That's what your heart rate was. A girl would be perfect because I bought you the cutest pink penguin pajamas—"

"You bought clothes before we knew for sure?" Josie opened her fists to encourage blood flow after clutching the table.

Her mother swatted Josie's arm with her free hand and chuckled. "It was on clearance. I couldn't resist."

"You're positive you want to find out the sex?" Sonia asked. "I can always turn the screen away if you want the surprise."

Josie squeezed her mother's hand without will. "I want to know."

Sonia wriggled the monitor around on Josie's belly until an image appeared on the screen. No one had to say anything.

The tears slipped down Josie's cheek one after the other. "A boy?"

"It's a boy," Sonia confirmed.

"Oh my." Josie's mother sniffled and pulled a tissue from her pocket to dab at her nose. "I have a grandson."

Josie's tears fell faster.

She had a son.

"I hope you kept those receipts, Suzanne." Sonia laughed as she took a few more screenshots and printed a strip of ultrasound photos.

"I can always save them for the next one." Josie's mother stood and clapped her hands together. "Oh, I wish Grant could be here to see this."

Josie's lip quivered, and she pressed her eyes shut to force away her reaction to such a comment. Grant *should* be there, but he'd chosen not to be a part of this.

Sonia wiped away the goop across Josie's belly with a brown paper towel and handed over the long black-and-white strip of photographs. Josie sat upright and wiped her eyes with her palm, trying to ignore her mom entirely and focus everything on her perfect little boy.

"He would be so proud." Her mother gave Josie's arm a squeeze as if referring to Grant like the dearly departed and not an estranged ex-husband. "Do you think Diana would answer if I called? I think she'd want to know about this. Have you heard any—"

"No." Of course her mother would immediately think to call Grant's mother and turn this into yet another opportunity to see if Josie had any new information on why their friendship had suffered some mysterious setback. If divorce court split everything in half, her mother might opt to go with Grant's side.

"I was just asking." Her mother huffed.

Sonia helped Josie step down from the table, and Josie reached for a tissue on the counter.

Her mother snatched the photos from Josie's hand to review once more. "You know, Josephine, we have some wonderful names on our side of the family. There's always 'Brian' after your dad, or we can call him 'Garrett' after my father. Oooh. Brian Garrett."

It had suddenly gotten harder to breathe inside that little ultrasound room. "Mom, I'm not exactly ready to pin down a name yet."

"Oh, I know that, but it's fun to think them up. You know it'd mean so much to your dad if you named the baby after him." Her mother linked arms with Josie and walked her to the front desk. "There're great-grandparents too. You can have the name we picked out if we ever had a third child."

"Which was?" Josie felt all power slipping away. If she mentioned how much she loved the name Theodore, would her mother race her to the birth certificate and fill in a different name? Josie took the photos and clutched them to her chest. Her mother had already decided on a penguin nursery theme the week Josie got the positive test. She'd gifted her daughter with a penguin lamp and penguin mobile to set up.

"You'll love this. It'll fit right in with all those hipster names your generation keeps calling their babies." She held her hands up as if preparing for the dramatic reveal. "Franklin Clement."

Oh geez. "That sounds like a president eating an orange."

"What? Those were the names of my great-grandfather and your dad's uncle Frank."

"No, I get that. I'm just saying—"

"Think on it, Josie. You've got plenty of time." Her mother waved her away.

Which Josie knew was Mom code for *You'll come around.*

"What was Grant's uncle's name I liked?" Her mother paused, searching the air for an answer.

In no way would she name her child after Grant's side of the family. As far as she cared, they no longer existed in her life or her child's. "No idea, Mom."

"If I can get ahold of Diana, I'll remember to ask her."

Josie was expecting a son. The baby was a boy. Nothing else mattered.

What her mother said *didn't matter.*

They reached the front desk, and her mother began typing away on her computer and proceeded with the checkout process. She shook her head as she keyed in the information and clicked her tongue. "You know this Medicaid system is a mess, Josie. I'll be so glad when you're off that."

Not this too. The last thing Josie wanted was to listen to her mother rant about her government assistance. She couldn't imagine trying to pay hospital bills on top of barely surviving.

"Mom, please. Can you—"

"I know. I know. It's just that you had such great insurance in Chicago…" Her mother typed harder on the keys and looked up at her younger child. "Something to think about: I've already talked with my office manager about this. We're hiring for a position up front here, and she'd be happy to have you come in for an interview. Regular workday hours. 401(k) options. *Real* insurance—"

"No." Josie pounded a fist against the counter, the images of her yawning baby still clutched to her chest with the opposite hand. "I don't want to work here."

The check-in receptionist across the way leaned in her chair to observe the situation, probably with one finger on the panic button in case she needed to call the cops on an unruly patient.

"Hear me out," her mother said.

"No. I know what you're going to say. I know you don't think I can handle this without Grant or my former life, but I can. I don't need him. I don't need a job *here*. And I don't need any help naming my son."

Josie's fingers trembled against the photographs in her grasp as she flung open the front door on her way to the car.

14

The Cereal Daters

JOSIE ROLLED ONTO A hamburger wrapper and let her arm fall over her face. She'd gone back to hiding out in her room ever since the little doctor's office incident the day before. Her mom had tried calling every few hours since, but Josie let the calls go to voicemail. She opted instead to text her mom and blame her outburst on hormones.

Then she could sleep. That one moment of standing up to her mother had taken way too much out of her. Kevin and Ben had it way too easy. They didn't deal with the exhaustion that came from creating life in their wombs or a meddling mother who insisted she knew best.

Josie hadn't even told them she found out the baby's gender. It seemed an odd thing to spring on them. Did guys care about that stuff? If Grant didn't, maybe Kevin and Ben wouldn't either. She could always call a meeting Kevin-style and shout the news at them like a drill sergeant.

The clock on her phone read 6:30 a.m. She'd only eaten a box of cereal the day before, and the hollow container now lay flattened beside her bed. She sat up and rubbed her eyes with the hem of her T-shirt, the dark residue reminding her she hadn't bothered to take off her makeup before crawling into bed yesterday. It probably smeared all over the place by now.

Her phone vibrated beside her pillow with an incoming call, and she wanted to ignore it until she read the number across the screen.

"This is Josie." Her hands shook as she waited for an answer on the other end of the phone.

"Josie, hi. This is Gale Abnor at Clarkson High."

Josie let out a sigh. She may not have to go back on her word about working at the ob-gyn after all. "Good morning, Ms. Abnor. How are you today?"

"I'm fine, but I find myself in need of a substitute teacher. Are you available? Barb Gabriel left me a note to call you first if I needed someone."

Wow. Melody's mom had come through.

Josie tried not to shout into the phone. "Of course. I'll be there."

"Thank you so much. Meet me in the office at seven forty, and I'll show you to the classroom. We've got about four teachers out with food poisoning. Can you believe that?"

"Oh, no. That's definitely not good." For *them*. For *her*, it was freakin' fantastic.

Ms. Abnor said goodbye, and Josie tumbled from her air mattress. She crossed her legs to keep from peeing herself as she picked out the most professional outfit she owned.

As quietly as she could, she slipped down the steps and tiptoed into the bathroom. She had a job today, which meant a paycheck would soon follow. Once work started coming in more steadily, she wouldn't have to sweat rent payments and could buy more things for the baby. Visions of silky blue blankets and onesies with "Mommy's Little Man" printed across the chest danced through her mind and made her heart sing.

The bathroom vent fan roared overhead and sucked the steam from the room until her naked image appeared in the vanity mirror. Where had these boobs come from? Her innie belly button wasn't quite as "in" these days. Her thighs more than touched; they clung together with great passion.

No time for self-evaluation before coffee.

Wearing her black maternity dress pants and a loose-fitting black top she'd found at the local thrift store, she slid her feet into the first closed-toe shoes she'd worn since summer began. She twisted her hair into a loose, messy bun at the base of her neck and brushed on some eyeliner and mascara.

In her teacher attire, she slipped back in time. Any moment, Grant would knock on the bathroom door to wish her a good day and let her know he had to leave early.

Josie's reflection grimaced.

When she flung open the bathroom door, the strong scent of freshly brewed coffee met her. That brought her to the present and out of her old life. Grant never made coffee in the morning.

"Hey, JoJo, I didn't think you'd be up and ready this early. You workin'?" Kevin lifted his cup from its place on the kitchen counter. His blond hair tangled like a bird's nest, and his antique T-shirt appeared slightly more comfortable than condemned.

"Thanks. Yeah, I finally got a call, so I guess it's off to work for me." She tried to keep the squeal out of her voice as she pointed to the second pact point on the fridge. "I'm on my way with this bad boy."

"All right, working girl. I'll put another coffee on."

Before she could object, Kevin had already hopped off the counter and grabbed a K-Cup out of the box. With the Keurig gurgling to life, he bent down to retrieve two bowls and a paper sack from the kitchen cabinet.

"You have to eat before you go. There's three kinds of cereal. I thought we had four, but I can't find the other one."

Josie bit down on her lip, debating whether or not to confess to the disappearance of the fourth box.

Kevin held up the paper sack. "And do you pack your lunch?"

Would he pack it for her in addition to making her breakfast? He'd already put a spoon in the bowl and lined up the cereal boxes so she could choose her favorite.

"I haven't packed my lunch in so long." Josie took her cup of coffee from the machine, catching sight of the K-Cup box with the word *decaf* marked on the top.

"Well, we've got peanut butter and jelly. There's bologna, butter, eggs, and maybe a can of soup."

Josie held up her finger. "Honestly, I'm pretty fond of school lunches. I'll grab something there."

"Suit yourself. Dibs on the bologna." Kevin shrugged and blew into the paper sack.

He threw open the double doors to the fridge, though he took nothing out from the freezer side. Josie squeezed underneath him to grab the creamer from the lower shelf. It had been so funny to Kevin to store her groceries at the bottom, since she was the shortest roommate.

"How much time you got?" He kicked the doors shut behind him and stuffed the entire package of bologna into his lunch pail.

Josie checked the clock on the oven. "I need to leave in twenty minutes."

She'd never gotten ready that early for school before. Normally, she grabbed a granola bar on her way out and rolled a few stop signs to make it in time.

"Perfect." Kevin returned to the fridge for the gallon of milk and tucked two of the three boxes of cereal under his arm. "Get the bowls, JoJo."

Josie set her coffee and their bowls down, then climbed into the tall chair with more effort than it used to take. "I can't remember the last time I sat around a table for breakfast."

Kevin wrestled with his cereal box, spilling several pieces on the floor before he got any inside his bowl. "Really? I haven't in this house yet. Ben and I have a truce that we will never sip our coffee at this table at the same time. This is for date use only."

"Is this a date? Have I totally misread the signals?" Josie puckered her lips and batted her eyes.

Kevin winked and tilted his head in his best Joey Tribbiani impression. "It's the most romantic kind of date. Just you, me, and this leprechaun. Not weird at all."

"No. Definitely not." Josie reached over and snatched the box. "A cartoon leprechaun is actually a big step up for me."

While Kevin remained much more like a brother than a potential love interest, this had been the kind of morning she'd always hoped to have with a significant other. Sitting around the table, having coffee, discussing the day's plans, and filling each other's souls, or some such garbage.

Milk splashed over the edge of Kevin's bowl when his spoon plunged in for a first bite. "Aw. Poor Josie-Jo. We need to get you back out there. Time to reel in all those fish in the sea."

"I don't plan to do any fishing in the near future. Thank you. I'll focus my love on my baby for now, and you'd better still count that as a pact win because I am not buying you pizza for a whole month." Josie used her spoon to point at him.

Kevin made a goofy face and waved her off. "Why not branch out farther than the baby? You're single, cute, funny…in a rude sort of way."

Josie reached into her bowl and threw a marshmallow at him.

"I rest my case," he said.

She shifted to the side to show off her plumping stomach, courtesy of an onion-sized human. "I'm sure this is a total turn-on. Do you see men lined up at the door to get a piece of this? I didn't think so."

"You're not gonna be pregnant forever. I'm just saying."

"Thanks, Dr. Love. I appreciate the reminder." She cleared her throat and rested her back against the wall behind her. "Did you want to finally tell me who this single Mandy-Facebook-person is from your text the other day?"

He rested his elbows on the table and smiled. "She's my ex-girlfriend and possibly the sweetest, nicest person in the world. She's a nurse over at the hospital now. We dated for maybe two months a couple years ago, but I dunno. I got kind of freaked out by how well it was going and jumped ship."

"You broke up with her because things were going *well?*"

Kevin's spoon clanked against the edge of his bowl. "I've had a lot of girlfriends. I'm not used to it going good for that long."

"That's maybe the craziest thing I've heard someone say." He definitely had a full dating history, but Josie had never met anyone who dumped someone for *that* reason.

Kevin's head sank on his shoulders. "I'm already locked in at my job since the company will be in my name one day. That's not a bad thing, but it's a lot of pressure, you know?"

Josie hunched over her cereal bowl and stirred the remaining marshmallows around the milk. "Did you tell Mandy that?"

"No." He answered as if she'd asked him if he'd murdered someone. "Girls don't take that 'I can't do commitment 'cause I'm a coward' line very well in my experience."

"Yeah, that one sends up red flags for us…" Yet he somehow thought breaking up with them would go over better. "And you thought wearing socks with sandals was your biggest growth area in this pact."

He stuffed a spoonful of breakfast into his mouth and kept going. "I'm not saying these things are unrelated. Domino effect. Poor footwear equals poor relationships. But I did really like her. I tried texting her a few months later, but she never responded."

Josie watched her sad friend stuff another large spoonful of cereal into his mouth and crunch away. "Do you *still* like her?"

"Never stopped." He slurped up some milk from his bowl. "I went out to get my flu shot at the hospital 'cause they had them on sale, and she was talking to someone at the reception desk. I couldn't breathe, JoJo. I just waved like an idiot when she looked over at me. She waved back but didn't come say hi or anything."

"And did she accept your friend request?" Josie peeked over the rim of her mug.

"Not yet. I'm hoping it's just because she doesn't get on Facebook much and not because of *me*." He stared into his cereal. "Can't stop thinking about her. I'm going to make her my Number Three pact point. I want to be better and win her back, ya know?"

Josie watched Kevin somberly eat his cereal for a long moment. They all had something much bigger than pizza at stake if the pact didn't work out. "Even if it means settling down?"

Kevin looked up from across the table, a slight grin playing at the side of his mouth. "Especially then. Forever's a long time, whether or not we're together. I'd rather have that time *with* her than without her."

"Then I can't wait to meet her someday." Josie's heart swelled as she watched her friend flush with such an honest admission. She only wished she could have been there for him during that ten-year void to help sort things out sooner and save a lot of heartbreak. "Have I told you how much I've missed you?"

"I've missed you too. I'm super glad you're here." He reached an arm across the table and bumped his fist to hers. "I think Ben kind of likes having you here too."

Across from her, Kevin took an obnoxious sip of his coffee and averted his eyes.

Oh no. He hadn't forgotten about her crush.

She took a long drink of her coffee, using her mug to shield her face.

"What was it you used to call him?" Kevin leaned on the table.

"Just stop." She nearly choked on her own spit.

Kevin laughed and stood to take his dishes to the kitchen. "Was it Hottie Romero or Total Ten Ben?"

"Shut your freakin' face. I hate you so much right now." Her cheeks warmed beyond all control, and she followed Kevin to the kitchen to put away breakfast. She said a silent prayer that Ben still slept soundly on the floor below and hadn't heard this conversation through the air vents.

Kevin picked up his lunch sack, still chuckling to himself as he added a few more side dishes to the pack of bologna. "He could be *your* Number Three, ya know?"

Josie loaded her bowl into the dishwasher. "Don't you have some cholesterol to watch or something?"

"My breakfast cereal did that for me. Says so on the label. I have nothing to do now but tease you." He kissed the air between them.

Josie groaned on the way to grab her purse and keys. "Well, just know that if marrying Ben means the two of us beat you in the Corn Dog Pact, we will form that alliance to take you down. You are warned."

Kevin picked up his new briefcase and tucked it under his arm, the couple of pens inside rattling around the otherwise empty container. "Or maybe I created this entire challenge to bring you two together once and for all. You'll never know." His laugh became comically sinister, and his fingers danced together like an old-timey cartoon villain. "Good day, Josie. Good day, indeed."

15

No Substitute for Wine

TEACHERS HUSTLED IN AND out of the front office, the hum of the copier and the scent of dark-roast coffee filling the air. Josie sat in her chair and drummed her fingers on her knee.

The inside of a principal's office still intimidated her after all these years, even if she'd now crossed over to the teacher's side of things. It seemed an eternity ago she'd taught at Lincoln Regional. Teaching had come easy to her after those first few years, but now it was like she couldn't remember anything. Her fingers trembled in her lap, and her mind couldn't form a single classroom plan.

"One more form, and we'll get you to your room." Ms. Abnor spun in her chair and slid a paper across the desk. "You've got multiple addresses on file here. Which is correct?"

It had never occurred to her to change her substitute teaching license info. At least she got everything right on the current paperwork. She hoped, anyway. "The Leeson Avenue one is my current address."

So long as she didn't have to explain the transition. *After my life fell apart in Chicago, I mooched off my parents for a few months, then moved in with two random guys from my past after they lured me in with ice cream.* It'd almost be amusing if it wasn't entirely true.

Ms. Abnor swiveled in her chair to view her computer screen.

She'd probably wondered why she called in such an unstable woman to oversee her students. Great role model. Here, kids, don't worry about getting jobs. Move in with strangers, have babies, and eat Pop-Tarts three meals a day.

"Alrighty. Let's get you down to your room. Have you been here before?" Ms. Abnor asked.

"I went to high school here." A million years ago.

Ms. Abnor clicked her pen and swiveled in her chair. "Oh, wonderful. Not much has changed, I'm sure. I've only been here four years, though."

"I graduated twelve years ago." Life had come full circle in some rather weird ways. She still dined with the same friends. Still got unsolicited advice from her mother. Still had a bit of a thing for the same guy, though she would never admit that to Kevin, no matter what teasing torture he put her through.

"Oh, nice. You were a teacher in…" She looked over her notes. "Chicago. Then our motley crew shouldn't be too tough for you. You'll be down in Room 216, second floor, third door on the left. It's a humanities class."

Humanities. How different could it be from the history classes she'd taught at her old school? Granted, she'd taken two semesters of humanities in college and still didn't know what the purpose of the class was. But perhaps she could BS it enough to get by for a day?

"Thank you so much," Josie said.

"I'll check in with you later to make sure everything is going okay." Ms. Abnor reached over and shook Josie's hand, then ushered her to the door.

With her heavy purse over her shoulder, weighted by snacks and bottles of water, Josie walked to the stairwell. On the second level, students chattered in front of their lockers, and she examined each of their faces as she passed. She tried to keep a low profile as she sized them all up.

Substitutes often got the worst of student behavior. Her own subs had left many notes stating how much grief the kids gave them. Why did she think this was a good idea again?

She'd lost her mind. Simple as that.

Near the end of the hall, she found "216" labeled in faded red paint over the door. More than a dozen students already sat in their seats, a few more trickling in.

Her first-period history classes had always been tricky. Participation lacked as brains hadn't fully woken up, and the expressions of I-don't-want-to-be-here lingered. By second period, most students had accepted their fate and perked up a bit. But first-period humanities? Josie could barely read tweets at this early hour, let alone explore the human race.

"Good morning," she said over the talkative crew.

A few students faced her, while others kept chatting.

"Good morning." She spoke louder. Butterflies fluttered in her stomach in hordes.

The students shifted in their seats, all flashing that questionable glare she knew too well.

"My name is Ms. Hale. I'll be standing in for your teacher today." She scooted the chair out from behind the desk to pull out the drawer and glanced over the contents. No lesson plans in sight. The regular teacher obviously hadn't anticipated needing a sub any time soon. "I used to teach history at Lincoln Regional High School in Chicago, but Clarkson is my hometown."

A shaggy-haired boy in the front row raised his hand, and Josie pointed at him. He smirked. "Are you pregnant?"

The class erupted in laughter.

Josie folded her arms and readjusted her posture, waiting for the group to settle. What had she done in the past? She'd had a plethora of tactics for dealing with unruly students, but for the life of her, she couldn't think of a single one. The parenting books she'd read on strong-willed children mentioned positive reinforcement and giving choices. Those tips targeted parents raising toddlers, but they may work for high schoolers.

She could handle this. Well, she had to. She was the teacher.

The tops of her thighs bumped the instigator's desk when she approached him, her glare set.

Intimidation might work too.

In her head, she counted to nearly a full minute. She'd won almost every single staring contest against her brother as a kid. A sixteen-year-old adolescent in a vintage Pink Floyd shirt didn't stand a chance.

When the silence reached an adequate level of complete awkwardness throughout the room, Josie crossed her arms. "Your name is?"

His eyes narrowed. "Kade."

"Hi, Kade. I like your name." *Boom: positively reinforced.* She tilted her head and refocused her unwavering eye contact. Thank goodness she'd worn all black today and remembered eyeliner. That helped her pull off the creepy vibes.

"Kade, could you please tell me what you're doing in this class right now?"

She held her breath for the response Kevin had always given the sub. He would turn every single thing anyone said to him in high school into a "your mom" joke. Hopefully that had died with her generation.

He slid a purple, pink, and blue book out from underneath his notebook. "Maya Angelou poetry."

Not what she expected from humanities, but okay. "Kade, why don't you read the first ten poems in there for us."

"Ten? But we've already cover—"

"When you're ready, Kade." Josie maintained her stance as best as she could through her nervousness.

"Maybe I don't want to." Kade didn't open his book.

A few other students giggled around him. That ob-gyn receptionist job didn't sound as horrible now, even if it meant submitting to her mother.

Her Chicago students had known what to expect from her, but she was the "new kid" here. If she didn't put her foot down, they'd walk all over her every time she worked. Subs hardly ever attained that level of respect from students.

In that moment, Josie's mind was fixed on that weird show she'd watched on pecking order in the animal kingdom where giraffes banged their necks against one another to assert dominance. Of all the things to focus on. Not exactly student-teacher appropriate behavior or socially acceptable in any realm.

It was much better to stick with human-toddler discipline. She'd forgotten to give Kade choices after the positive reinforcement. That had to be why it hadn't worked. "You can read it for me now, or you can read it for Principal Abnor in two minutes. Because I am, in fact, pregnant, and pregnant women have zero patience for students who can't get their act together. Choose wisely."

Kade flashed an eerie smile and opened his book. In a voice much too loud for the small classroom, he began to read. He also forced some sort of bizarre accent into his phrasing. The students loved it.

But her method still worked. Kind of. Intimidation plus toddler parenting strategies had won the battle for her this round. If she survived this day, she'd need to get some more solid strategies.

Josie returned to the desk and took a seat. She didn't have her own copy of the book to follow along in. Who knew if what Kade said was even correct? Hardly any other students flipped the pages in time with his words either. They just watched him.

In the last row of students, a redheaded girl with a button nose and pink-polished lips peeked up from her book to observe the new teacher. Unlike the others, this girl simply smiled when she caught Josie's eye. Then she went back to her open book, her finger moving down the page in time with Kade's ludicrous speech pattern.

At least someone paid attention.

If she meant to get anybody else to straighten up and listen when she came to teach, she'd have to bring up some trick plays. She could always take a page out of Lincoln Regional's algebra teacher's playbook. Mr. Mandel's famous move involved waltzing into the classroom on the first day all cheery and happy, and when the first student spoke out of turn, he threw his notebook across the room in a rage. He rarely had trouble with students during the school year.

Josie coughed into her arm to avoid laughing at the image of herself throwing a notebook at the whiteboard. At this point in her sad life, she probably shouldn't jeopardize her only job with a mock tantrum.

The next thirty-five minutes of first period revolved around asking the class questions about the poetry reading and receiving almost no participation, except for the redheaded girl in the corner. Seven periods after that followed a similar pattern, minus a sympathetic redhead.

When the last bell rang for the day, Josie collapsed in her rolling chair. Principal Abnor rounded the corner, which sent Josie upright again.

"So, how'd the first day go?" Ms. Abnor asked.

"Pretty well," Josie lied. If she told even a smidgeon of the truth, she might never be invited back. She used to love teaching, but substitute teaching was a job from the seventh layer of hell. Thinking about sticking it out for a year or two while waiting for a permanent job opening made her cringe.

Ms. Abnor's face lit up. "Great! I talked with Meg Lamb. She's still feeling rotten and wants to take the rest of the week off. Would you mind covering that?"

Josie's heart sank when it should have soared. "Absolutely, I'd love to."

Oh boy.

16

Don't Bet on Lettuce

OVER THE NEXT WEEK, Josie got the hang of substitute teaching, working steadily in different classrooms throughout the high school. Her bank account stayed in the black, and she'd reached fifty dollars in her savings envelope.

Kevin could suck on that.

She waddled up the driveway, keeping her knees pinched together as she enacted her new after-work regimen, one she imagined would be a going theme over the next few months. She dropped the takeout on the kitchen counter, rushed to the bathroom to pee, then ran up the steps to change into her spaghetti-strap top and pink plaid pajama pants.

"Better now?" Kevin said from a living room beanbag. "And hi, by the way."

"Hi," she answered with a half wave at the bottom of the steps.

Kevin had already grabbed the food off the counter and started divvying it up. She may not have a solid lifestyle, but at least Josie had someone to bring food home for, even if he tended to steal her fries. Ben would join them shortly. With extended weekday hours during the fall, he got to enjoy half days on Fridays.

She didn't hate it.

"Lay off my fries, Captain Cholesterol. I brought you a salad." She wiggled into the bag next to him and snatched up her milkshake.

"Like hell you did. Ben'll eat it," he said.

Josie rolled her eyes and growled against her straw. "I'm trying to help you."

"Geesh. Rough day? There's no need to take it out on me with a…salad." Kevin made the gagging sign with his middle finger.

"You try being trapped in a room with teenagers all day and tell me how your patience holds up."

He laughed. "That job would be hell. You couldn't pay me enough to do that. I don't know how my little five-foot-tall Josie can get anything done there."

"I'm five two, thank you ever so much, and I am terrifying. They have to listen or I unleash my inner beast."

"Whatever you say, beast woman." He tore into his burger and reclined farther. "You remember how awful we were to our subs in high school?"

"I remember how awful *you* were to subs, yes. Kids haven't changed much all these years later. At least, so far, none of them have switched identities to try to confuse me when I take roll…"

Kevin slapped his knee and choked on his bite. "Ah, I forgot about that. Mrs. Markowitz thought Ben was me, and I was him. That was fantastic."

"You're terrible." Josie shook her head and laughed.

"Yeah, well, she personified crotchety. And as I recall, you went right along with it."

"Oh, please. I would never do such a thing."

Kevin sighed through a mouthful of fries. "I miss those days."

"Me too. Life seemed so stressful then. I wish I had those struggles now." In her younger years, a night out with her friends could fix almost anything. Nowadays, she *lived* with her friends and even that didn't do the trick. As much as she tried to make things better, she still felt as if she was running a marathon in molasses.

"Same. I'd rather only work summers as a busboy, drive a car my parents paid for, and sleep till noon every weekend."

Josie's face scrunched as she observed him. "You still do that last part."

"Yeah, but it's out of necessity now and not just pure laziness." Kevin crumpled his empty sandwich wrapper and reached for another. Ben really would have to eat the salad at this rate.

Josie took another long slurp of her shake and crossed her arms over her stomach. "One thing's for sure… This little dude is going to have to work to pay for his own car when he gets older. He's not getting a free ride, but I'm definitely making sure he starts out better than me."

Kevin didn't answer. Josie placed her cup on the floor in front of her and reached for the fry container. When Kevin's silence got a little uncomfortable, she looked up to see him staring at her, a single french fry hanging from his lips as he gaped.

"It's a boy?" he squeaked.

She cringed. How had she gotten so caught up in work and planning the *how* of telling them that she'd forgotten to do it? "Yes?"

Kevin flew off his beanbag and tackle-hugged her, sending fries into the air when they fell backward. "This is so cool!"

Josie laughed at the massive body crushing every part of her on the floor, while somehow sucking in his entire middle to protect her belly. Her doctors had never warned her about tackle-hugs, but, luckily, her budding bosom acted like an airbag in these instances.

He rolled over, keeping his hand on her arm and taking up most of her beanbag chair. "Have you told Ben? He guessed boy."

"He did?" The thought of Ben and Kevin passing around guesses amused her to no end. "No, I haven't told him yet. I meant to break this to you both very differently."

Kevin rotated again until he lay flat on his back. "Ah, you have to tell him ASAP. But damn if I don't owe him ten bucks."

"You bet on my baby's gender?" Now, she laughed even harder. "Sorry for your loss, I guess."

"Yeah, well. We looked up all these prediction things one night. Don't ask. Some drinking may have been involved. I was so sure it was a girl because of your Pop-Tart consumption." He scooted to his own beanbag and took a long sip of his Coke.

"Um…"

"Apparently sweet cravings mean a girl. Duh, Josie. Don't you know anything about pregnancy? Do you even know how you got into this situation?" His eyebrow rose higher than anyone's should.

"Don't remind me." She laughed so hard her eyes welled with tears. "And why did Ben think it was a boy?"

"'Cause girls 'steal your beauty.'" Kevin flexed his fingers in air quotes and rolled his eyes.

Josie smiled for a split second until the comment sank in. Girls steal your beauty. Ben had guessed boy. Ben Romero had bet ten whole dollars that she was having a boy because a baby boy hadn't stolen her beauty. Implying beauty existed in the first place.

"I figured you'd like that." Kevin folded his hands under his chin and batted his blond eyelashes at her.

"I don't know what you're talking about." She fumbled around for her drink, which took entirely too long.

Kevin reclined on his beanbag. "Yep, he def thinks you're beautiful."

In no way could she run with that right now unless she wanted to invite a whole new wave of Kevin teasing. She twisted her face into one of sorrow and anguish and punched her friend in the arm. "So, does that mean you *don't* think I'm beautiful?"

"Oh, whatever. I'm almost out of fries to throw at you, loser. I based my guess solely on Pop-Tarts. It's science."

Oh, brother. Josie needed to find a way to break the news to Ben before Kevin did. Somehow, she'd have to figure out how to look him in the eye and not think about this conversation. She'd surely giggle like a schoolgirl and out herself as completely incapable of maturity.

Besides, she kind of sucked at breaking big news anyway, like when she'd gotten engaged to Grant and blurted it out at her great-uncle's wake.

No, Ben definitely deserved something less awkward than that or a simple text.

Kevin tossed his next burger wrapper into the empty bag. "Well, I have some news too."

"Mandy news?" Josie asked.

"I wish. She still hasn't accepted my friend request. You think I should resend it?" He waited for Josie to acknowledge the question with a shrug, then continued. "No, the news is that I applied for a different job at work."

"Outside of insurance?" Could he do that when he worked for his own father?

"No, still for Dad, but it'd be in the mailroom instead of sales."

Josie shifted toward him, her hamburger just about to her lips. "Isn't that a rung down the corporate ladder?"

"And a pay cut. Which my dad made sure to point out. He's not thrilled about this, but I convinced him it'd help me get to know every aspect of our company better than sitting in a cubicle all day," Kevin said.

"But if it's a demotion, it doesn't count as advancing your life per the Corn Dog Pact, right? Do you *want* to buy me pizza?" Josie nestled into her beanbag and stretched her legs out in front of her.

Kevin rolled onto his side to face her. "Whoa now. I will not be buying you any pizza. Have you seen the pen collection in my briefcase? I am crushing my end of the pact, JoJo. I also put my entire last paycheck toward my credit-card debt. Thanks so much."

Josie tilted her head and held out her open hands, awaiting his reply. "Then why choose a pay cut?"

"I *want* to work in the mailroom. I am so sick of listening to whiney people call in and make demands for stuff I have almost no control over. I used to work down there after high school, and it was so much more relaxed. The only phone calls I had to take were interoffice calls. I got to run errands and joke around with my coworkers. Even now, I go there to hang out on my breaks. Yeah, it's less pay than the agents get, but I'd rather be happy in my work than fake it with my sweet briefcase and awesome-looking tie. Which is why, dear Josie, this still counts as a win for Kevin." He belched and reached for the remote control.

Josie patted him on the arm. It probably *did* count as a win if he chose a job because it made him happy more than it made him money, even if money played a significant part in their pact.

The front door sprang open, and Ben's keys jingled when he looped them to the hook by the front window. "You got food, right? I'm starving, but I've gotta get out of these jeans first."

Ben rushed to the basement door without waiting for an answer.

Josie sat up and propped her back against the beanbag. "Oh, he's gonna be so mad at you," she said to Kevin.

"Me? You're the one who ordered a salad as if anyone in this house would eat that." Kevin gagged again.

Ben returned, still tying the drawstrings on his sweatpants. He wore a plush Bears blanket around his shoulders to keep warm since nobody wanted to turn the heat on in October. Josie, however, hardly noticed the chill. Hormones kept her nice and sweaty most of the time. As did Ben's mere presence. Especially tonight.

"Scootch." Ben plopped down next to her, using part of her beanbag as a backrest, his hips pushing her into Kevin.

His intense closeness cemented her in place, her eyes locked on the TV screen ahead. Josie had somehow become the beef in these guys' bromance sandwich, which would have made for a lovely thought if she wasn't completely flustered.

Ben stretched forward to grab the food bag and pulled out...the salad. "Oh, this is not cool." When he angled it toward his companions, he smashed Josie more.

"Kevin did it," Josie said without a moment's hesitation.

Kevin responded with a nasty look, then upped the volume on the TV. Nothing topped cheap food and a *House Hunters* marathon on a Friday night with her "husbands." She may have lost one spouse that year, but she'd gotten two in his place.

"I figured," Ben said.

"Here." Josie held up the rest of her fries, though she couldn't fully pass them to him as her arm stayed pinned between their bodies.

Ben didn't take them from her, just let her keep holding the container while he helped himself. With his other hand, he snatched up the milkshake she'd brought him and slurped away. Each time he reached for a handful of fries, his body weight pressed against her, his Bears blanket practically covering half her body. She watched his every movement out of the corner of her eye.

Kevin nudged her and leaned in. "Tell him."

She squinted at Kevin, trying to figure out what he meant.

"The baby," Kevin added.

Ben thought she was beautiful. The baby hadn't stolen her beauty.

"Hey, Ben." Josie shifted in a way that tucked her under his arm. When he moved to regard her, his face came within inches of hers. She startled backward into Kevin.

"What's up?" Ben asked.

Kevin nudged her forward. "Josie has some news."

She cleared her throat. "Kevin owes you ten bucks. I'm having a boy."

Ben lowered his fist full of fries and smiled big enough to show his dimples. "This totally makes up for the salad."

"I admit my defeat, Benjamin," Kevin said. "You were right. The baby didn't steal her beauty."

Ben's eyes grew wide as he slowly pivoted from Josie to give his full attention to the TV. Josie's fingers wrapped around the parts of Ben's blanket that had fallen into her lap. She fought the urge to pull them up to her face and hide.

Oh, she would so kill Kevin later, if Ben didn't get to him first.

17

Powdered Sugar-Coated Heroes

AFTER WAITING FOR HER phone to ring—for nearly an hour—Josie had drifted off to sleep again. When Gale Abnor called in a wild panic at seven fifteen, Josie struggled to form a sentence coherent enough to accept the job.

Stumbling down the steps, she clung to the railing with one hand to keep upright, a wad of clothing stuffed under her opposite arm. She prayed Kevin had finished up in the bathroom so she didn't have to wait. One bathroom proved difficult enough in any household, but one bathroom with a pregnant woman who had to pee all the time?

As hoped, Kevin had already shut himself in his room to get ready, the scent of his body spray still wafting from the bathroom in great waves. Josie held her breath as she entered, anxious to get the shower running and overtake the odor with her own coconut body wash. She'd be so glad when normal smells stopped nauseating her, especially if she continued to live with such intensely scented men.

She had no time to wash her hair and opted instead for a quick rinse off to ensure she woke up enough to tackle the day. With clothes on, makeup swiped across her face, and hair in a messy ponytail on top of her head, she checked the time. She had to leave in five minutes to get to the school by the first bell. That left no time for breakfast, a drink, or much of anything. She couldn't *not* eat.

Josie shoved her phone in her pocket and nearly fell out of the bathroom. Why had she eaten the last of the Pop-Tarts? One would have made the perfect on-the-go breakfast.

She rushed to the fridge for a bottle of water to get her by when she noticed a six-pack of orange juice on the top shelf. On the kitchen counter, a bag of powdered doughnuts sat ripe for the taking.

She paused and turned toward the fridge to read the newest bull-sheet note.

Put an extra two hundred dollars on my student loan payment, suckas! Breakfast is on me. I prefer sausage on my pizza. Love, Ben

If she lost to anyone in the pact, it'd better be Ben. If Kevin had written such a note, it'd mean war.

Josie surveyed the house around her. Since she'd started working most weekdays, her meticulous housecleaning had come to an end, and so had the clean house. But today, someone had taken out the trash, emptied the dishwasher, and cleared off all countertops. The floors appeared freshly swept too.

Kevin couldn't have done it. They'd gone to bed at the same time the night before, and the place had still been a wreck. Had Ben done this? Brought home fun groceries and stayed up late to clean?

She stuffed a doughnut into her mouth. After school, she'd have to come up with a plan for how to step up her game. If Ben had resorted to buying them breakfast and paying down student loans, she had a long way to go to level up on the pact. Were mail-order husbands a thing? That'd put her in first place easily enough.

❧

Ms. Abnor walked Josie directly to her new classroom: biology lab. The only thing Josie hated more than math was science, but luckily the regular teacher displayed anal-retentive tendencies when it came to organization. Her color-coded lesson plans decorated the large calendar on the desktop, with a sticky note indicating the "emergency sub plans" hidden in the bottom desk drawer.

Just a couple of worksheets. She could handle passing out busywork, so long as she didn't have to teach them any actual biology. Josie had barely squeaked by in her high school science classes, receiving all F's for pig dissection, which she straight up refused to participate in.

During her free midmorning period, Josie took a few pages out of the regular teacher's book—borrowing sticky notes, construction paper, and highlighters—and made a list. On one sheet, she wrote down the baby necessities she still needed before the end of February. On another, she tried to mentally calculate her remaining debt. Thank God for those student loan forgiveness programs for inner-city teachers. If those hadn't come through for her, she'd be totally screwed.

Ben seemed to have made some progress on his own debt, according to the bull-sheet note. Then again, he'd been out of college for eleven years.

Would he tell her something so personal?

Considering Ben had once asked her if his armpits stank, and Kevin knew how much she weighed, she might as well *ask*. He never had to know her ulterior motives on this one.

She pulled her phone from her purse and sent the message: Thanks for breakfast, and nice job on the student loan payment. How much do you have left on those anyway?

Josie bit her thumbnail and reread her message. Maybe she shouldn't have asked. He may have thought her beautiful at one point, but her intrusiveness might take away from that.

Her phone vibrated in her palms, and she nearly dropped it when she scrolled over to read the text.

Ben had responded: $2,400-something. Why? You wanna make a contribution?

Well, he didn't sound offended. She typed away: Hard pass. Just needed to make sure you wouldn't lap me in pact progress. :-P

Ben: I'm sure you've still got me beat. It's a 10-year loan, but I was in default for the first 8. ;)

Josie shook her head. They so needed to get it together. At least she didn't have any students in the room to judge the stupid smile plastered on her face. This wasn't a romantic conversation to warrant idiot grinning.

The phone buzzed again.

Ben: PS. Talked to Noel. We planned a visitation schedule for the next 3 months. I'll show u later so u can prepare for Izzy time.

They talked? And planned? Ben had advanced so much further than his bull-sheet note let on. His success with his daughter also meant she had to share her bedroom more. She hadn't thought that far ahead on this one.

She texted back: That's awesome!

That's all she could come up with?

Immediately, she had another message from him: Work. Talk later.

Josie typed her goodbye, but he probably wouldn't get it until he went on dinner break.

The rest of the day passed by in silence as students did their busywork and Josie's lists got longer and more decorative out of pure boredom. In her second-to-last class of the day, she walked the aisles to hand out papers, catching the eye of the redheaded girl from the humanities class she'd subbed for during the Great Food Poisoning Epidemic. The girl returned Josie's smile, but the darkness under her eyes made her look tired, not quite the bright-eyed girl Josie took notice of a few weeks ago.

Josie kept watch of her throughout the entire class period, abandoning her lists and no longer checking for any more responses from Ben. It took the girl nearly twice as long to complete the worksheet as the rest of her classmates, and she often paused to stare at the ceiling tiles, bite her pencil eraser, or tap her fingernails on the desk. She might have had too much caffeine at lunch or struggled with focus issues in school. In her school days, Josie had taken longer than others to complete assignments too. It meant nothing.

The bell rang, and the students filed out in groups, dropping their papers in a messy pile on the desk corner. As Josie reached to straighten the pile, a lingering figure caught her attention in the back of the room: the redhead. Josie searched her roster for a name, but without an assigned seating chart, she couldn't narrow it down.

"Do you need any help... I'm sorry. I don't remember your name."

"Hadley." The girl drummed her pencil on the top of the page. "No, I'm okay. Just have one more question. Is it okay if I get a pass for English next?"

Josie checked the clock. The busywork didn't seem important enough to take time out of the next class to finish, but Hadley's expression begged her. Since the color-coded desk showed biology lab didn't have a final class of the day, it wouldn't be a problem anyway. "Yeah, I can do that."

The girl rolled her eraser across her lips as she read, then scratched at her chin. Finally, she jotted something down.

Josie looked over the stack of papers in her hands and scanned the assignment. The work contained a few essay questions about hypotheses, a multiple-choice section, and graphing data, nothing too difficult.

The girl gathered her books slowly and walked to the desk. Her head hung to keep her eyes shielded with her flowing hair when she set her worksheet on the desk corner.

"Sorry I took so long," she said.

"Not a problem at all, Hadley. Is everything okay today?" Josie didn't want to mention she'd noticed a difference in the girl's demeanor since they barely knew each other.

"Yeah. I'm fine." Her eyes misted, but she blinked the wetness away as she glanced up at the clock. "Ms. Hale?"

"What's up?" Josie stood, crept around the corner of her desk, and tried to lean casually on the edge. She didn't like speaking with students while she sat and they stood. It gave her a weird authority complex.

"Are you married?" she asked.

Not what Josie expected at all. "No, I'm not married. Not anymore."

"But you were? How long ago?"

"Um. Well, my husband and I broke up in June. Turns out, not all men are the Prince Charmings we want them to be." She paused for a moment, studying her student. "Why do you ask?"

"I just… I dunno. I admire you, I guess." Hadley placed her books on the edge of the desk and rested her hands on top of them for support.

"Admire me?" No one had told Josie that before. She'd spent most of her adult life playing catch-up to other people, not standing on any pedestals. "Why?"

"The way you kind of took control that first day with Kade was pretty awesome. Those guys always give our subs so much crap. Most of them don't come back."

Josie smiled at that. "Well, thank you."

"And you'll be a single mom, but you're still working and taking care of everything. That's pretty cool, I guess."

Josie couldn't, or *shouldn't*, admit how not together her life really was. After a buildup like that, she felt like an imposter.

"Well, I'm trying anyway," Josie said.

Hadley's brow furrowed. "Is it hard? Doing all that on your own?"

That seemed an understatement. "Yeah. Every day is hard, and my baby isn't even here yet. But I want to make a great life for him when he finally arrives."

"It's a boy?" Hadley's expression softened.

"It's a boy," Josie repeated.

Hadley shook her head and readjusted her backpack. "Sorry to ask so many questions. I was...curious. Thanks. I promise I'm not weird."

Josie laughed and took out a brightly colored notepad to excuse her student from being late for English. "No worries."

"Well, have a good day." Hadley gave a shy wave and headed toward the door.

"You too, Hadley." Josie let the girl get almost out the door before she thought to add, "If there's anything I can help you with, please let me know."

Hadley nodded and disappeared around the corner.

18

Heartstrings and Buffalo Wings

1:00 A.M.

Two pillows propped Josie's head to keep her upright. She'd already consumed two glasses of milk, but the heartburn raged. If the school called in the morning, she might have to warn them to expect a zombie in her place. Or worse, she'd have to turn down the work and forfeit the pay.

Why couldn't her stomach turn against her in another few days when they went on Thanksgiving break?

She should have listened to her doctor. If she'd eaten a nutritious meal that evening, rather than buffalo chicken wings, she might have rested without issue, especially since she had slept on an actual bed for once.

Well, calling it a real bed gave it way too much credit. Her new bed had shown up on the FedEx truck, rolled snugly in an airtight package and unrolled to reveal a mattress only about four inches thick. She laid it across the floor in place of the air monstrosity.

Josie crawled out of bed and tiptoed down the stairwell. Hopefully, the bathroom cupboards held something stronger than Tums. Nothing proved more inconvenient than trying to puke silently in a bathroom with paper-thin walls so her roommates didn't hear how disgusting she was.

Staying downstairs until the symptoms dissipated was her only hope now. That way she could get to the bathroom faster if she needed it. No use lying in bed and interrupting her Pinterest-board-organizing to run downstairs in a panic.

The house creaked with the gentle breeze outside, and the refrigerator hummed in the kitchen. Normally, the TV blared, or someone rustled somewhere in the house, but not tonight. Not at this hour.

Josie shut herself in the bathroom. Surely all the vomiting had ceased, but she'd hang out in there a bit to make sure. Being up and moving around provoked the nausea, but she managed to brush her teeth and wash her face with cool water.

Her hair frayed in its ponytail and stuck out at odd angles. She smoothed it down with water, but it wiggled right out again. With pale cheeks and sunken eyes, she appeared every bit the part of Death's bride. Her wrinkled tank top hugged her curvy belly, and her shorts had bunched and twisted. Stunning.

After a good ten minutes of not throwing up, Josie braved the world outside the bathroom. She could always watch something on low volume until her stomach calmed down enough to let her sleep.

She opened the door and clutched her chest to quell the heart attack that threatened to take her down. There, standing stone-still in the middle of the dining room was Ben.

Josie gasped. "You scared me to death."

He held up a hand. "Sorry. I just came up to get a drink. Couldn't decide if I should announce myself or not. Hindsight says an announcement might have been best."

Josie chuckled and walked over to the kitchen counter. Her stomach roiled again when Ben reached into the fridge for a beer. Not much sounded worse than that right now. Luckily, she couldn't have one anyway.

Ben popped the cap on the counter, his gaze flickering up to her. "You look a little bit like hell. You feeling okay?"

"At least it's not all the way like hell, right?" So much for him thinking the baby hadn't stolen her beauty.

"Eh. Solid forty percent." He winked. "What's up?"

She eased onto the barstool and propped her chin in her hands. "Heartburn, nausea, all the fun pregnant things."

"You take anything?"

"Some antacids." Josie tried again to smooth her hair. Not that she could really do anything with it in this state, but his intense gaze and her nauseous stomach made her more paranoid than usual.

"Nothing else?" He took a long swig from his bottle.

She averted her eyes to keep from imaging the awful taste but hummed to the affirmative. "I'm thinking about watching some TV for a bit until I feel better. Unless you were watching something?"

He had a TV in the basement, but it seemed the polite thing to ask.

"Care if I join you?"

Josie gripped harder on the edge of the counter. "No, not at all. As long as you don't mind my forty-percent hell face."

Ben grinned. "I was just messin' with you. You go pick a show, and I'll be in in a sec."

She flashed him a cheesy thumbs-up she'd probably regret in the morning and hobbled into the living room. The beanbag chair grew flatter every time she sat in it, but Josie wriggled her way in and flipped through the options on TV.

After a few minutes, she settled on a hoarding show. They always made her feel like she had her life together. In some areas, at least.

Ben rustled around in the kitchen for a while longer, then headed to the basement. Had he changed his mind about joining her? His downstairs cave had to be comfier than sitting scrunched up next to her on the floor, but she kinda *did* want his company tonight, even if his presence enhanced her stomach issues.

Just in time for the first hoarding cleanup day, the basement door squeaked again, and Ben's bare feet pattered across the dining room floor. He strode into the living room with his beer in one hand, a large cup of something else in the opposite hand, and a massive pillow tucked under his arm. He certainly came prepared for something. At least he came back.

With a glance at the television and a nod of approval, he knelt on the floor between Josie and the second beanbag chair. "Here. Vanilla milkshakes can help with nausea."

Josie sat forward to look into the cup. Sure enough, the hand-mixed vanilla shake came equipped with a pink bendy straw and spoon for scooping. Unlike the beer, the shake begged her consumption.

"This is for your back." Ben set his drink down and inched his way behind her, motioning for her to lean forward enough for him to prop the pillow between her and the beanbag.

His knuckles brushed over her sides as he positioned the bedding. Suddenly, her thin tank-top might as well have been lingerie. His breath on her neck became the greatest level of intimacy she'd experienced since her son's conception.

"Better?" he asked.

She waited until she could inhale actual oxygen and *not* his pecan scent; then she wriggled into place on the pillow. The goose bumps on her arms slowly subsided without his touch, and she could hear the TV again.

"Actually, yes." Not being as balled up in the beanbag helped. "Thank you."

He fell into the chair, kicking his legs out in front of him and tucking an arm behind his head.

When Josie had come downstairs, she certainly hadn't expected to get any sort of pampering, especially from Ben. At this late hour, he should have been winding down from work or getting ready for bed. Instead, he'd chosen to take care of her.

The icy drink chilled her throat and stomach, the smooth texture quelling the nausea almost instantaneously.

Josie moaned. "You are a saint, Benjamin Romero."

"Good stuff?"

"Heavenly. I'm already feeling better."

"I knew that'd work. Noel drank those all the time when she got sick with Izzy. I had to get good at making them. I know she talked about propping her bed up with books to stop the heartburn too."

Huh. She'd try that later. "I'm glad I'm living with a professional."

"Uh, hardly."

"But seriously, thanks. I hope I'm not taking you away from anything. I'm sure you're tired from work."

"I was doing this in my room. I might as well do it with you." His face scrunched. "But, you know, in a less awkward-sounding way."

Josie took a long sip through her straw to put out the fire sweeping across her face. "Well, I appreciate it. Good to have the company."

She rested a hand over her stomach, the cold drink waking up her little buddy, who kicked and wiggled inside her. She smiled and swirled her hand around to chase the movements.

"Baby awake?" Ben asked.

"Yeah. He must like ice cream as much as I do."

Ben watched Josie's hand move pointedly on her belly. "You're naming him Ben, right?"

"You already got ten bucks from Kevin. You don't get naming rights too." To think of crushing on Ben for so long, only to marry someone else, deliver that man's baby, and name the child after Ben because they lived under the same roof? Life was clearly drunk.

He clicked his tongue as if he knew deep down she'd go along with it in the end. "Kevin told me you made him godfather."

Josie sat forward, nearly spilling the rest of her milkshake. "He told you he's the godfather?"

"Yeah, he texted me that this afternoon."

Josie rubbed her forehead. "He's such a dork. I'm not even Catholic. I don't have to appoint a godfather or anything. And if I did, I'm not sure Kevin would be my first choice."

Ben's grin grew sinister. "I'm gonna mess with him."

"Of course you are." She shook her head. Just then, her son kicked her hard in the belly button. One of the hardest movements she'd felt yet. Something about reaching the size of a tart grapefruit had turned this kid into a fighter. His grapefruity self took another swing. "Oh my gosh. Feel this."

Without giving it any thought, she reached for Ben's hand and pressed his fingers against her stomach. She paused, waiting for another kick…until she slowly realized she held Ben's hand.

Ben barely moved. His chest pressed against her arm, his gaze not moving from their hands folded together on her abdomen. This time, when the baby kicked, she couldn't tell if it was him or if butterflies waged some kind of war inside her.

"Wow," was all he said. His hand flattened under hers, and he looked up to meet her gaze. She stared into his big brown eyes, her breath hitching. Their hands slid together to Josie's side.

The door down the hallway squeaked, and Kevin poked his head around the corner. "What kind of party is this and why wasn't I invited?"

Ben rolled away quick as lightning and sat up to grab his beer bottle. "Uh, this is a Josie-is-pregnant-and-sick party. You're welcome to stay and hold her hair."

He'd been so close to her, closer than ever before. Their fingers had almost fully intertwined. How many beers had Ben had? He must not have been in his right mind.

Kevin's nose scrunched. "Pass. I'll pee and go back to bed, thanks."

"Probably for the best. It's brutal out here," Josie added, her heart thrumming a wretched rhythm inside her chest.

Kevin headed to the bathroom.

Ben exhaled and snatched up his beer again, tipping back the bottle and finishing the rest of his drink in a couple of long gulps. Josie stared at the TV, watching as heaps of trash flew into the dumpster and an older lady dove in after her broken end table.

The toilet flushed, and Kevin threw open the bathroom door again. He waved a hand at his roommates as he dragged his feet across the floor on his way to bed. "Sorry if I interrupted your make-out sesh."

When the bedroom door shut behind him, Josie buried her face in her hands. It probably had looked like they'd been kissing.

They almost *did*.

She probably read way too far into their shared look, the way Ben's hand had moved under hers across her waist. It was entirely too far past her bedtime to think clearly about any of it.

Ben groaned beside her. "Sorry. He's being a dick 'cause he knows I had a thing for you in high school. Surprise, I guess."

Josie released an awkward chuckle…then his words sank in. "Um, excuse me. What?"

He rubbed at his forehead and held up his empty bottle. "I need another one of these."

She could not have heard him correctly.

"Not right now you don't." She grabbed his wrist to keep him in place. "Tell me what you just said."

Ben swore and laughed as he lay back and let his arm drape over his eyes. "In high school, I had a crush on you, okay? I know, way to make it weird and all—"

In one swift move, Josie yanked the pillow out from behind her and whapped Ben across the chest.

"What was that for?" He caught the pillow in his hands and sat up. "I can't retaliate against a pregnant woman. You've got an unfair advantage."

"You had a crush on me in high school, and you never did anything about it?" It took all she had not to shout the words at him, which would only bring Kevin back into the room to gloat and be a total turd about it.

Ben kept the pillow up between them like a barrier. "Well, I'm kind of glad I didn't if you would be all violent with me."

"No, it's not that. It's just…" Oh, she was really going to do this. "I had a crush on *you* in high school." She bit the edge of her lip as she watched him take in this new information. "Like, the whole time."

The hoarding psychologist on TV explained that hoarders often use their belongings to build up a wall to protect themselves from certain feelings, but who cared?

"No, you didn't." Ben's right eye twitched when he spoke.

"Uh, yah. You can't possibly tell me you had no idea. I'm fairly certain I wasn't the most discreet teenage girl in the world."

She let him win when they went bowling, asked to wear his jersey on football Fridays, and practically stared at him every time he entered a room. Somehow, he'd missed all of that.

Ben dropped the pillow on top of her beanbag again and shifted to better face her. "Well, I had no clue, okay? Why didn't *you* say something?"

"Yeah, Ben. How was that supposed to go? You were always dating someone else." She smooshed the pillow down to re-form it to her back. The nausea returned, but in a very different way. "I was going to ask you out that night at the basketball game. The one where you conveniently met Noel."

He ran his hand down his face hard, warping his skin until she could no longer read his expression. "You have got to be kidding me." He studied his empty bottle for a moment, then cocked his head in her direction. "As I recall, *you* were always dating someone else too. We were never single at the same time." With a scoff, he shifted toward the hoarding intervention, his brow still knit tightly together.

He wasn't wrong. Though he had her beat on the number of dates he'd had in high school. The fact that she'd wanted *him* had caused her other relationships to suffer a bit.

Josie dropped against the pillow, her arms folding over her chest as she refocused on the screen. The psychologist and organizational specialist freed the hoarder from her despair and helped her forgive her past hurts as her possessions disappeared and a clean house reappeared.

Ben took a loud breath. "Do you think it would have been weird? If we dated? Back then, I mean."

He didn't look at her.

"Why would it have been weird?" She always saw the girls he dated in school as so much prettier than her, more athletic, outgoing, everything. Maybe he would have been embarrassed by her. In the time she spent daydreaming about being with him, *weird* never crossed her mind.

He shrugged. "I dunno. Kevin probably would have made it weird. He's good at that. Or maybe you'd have ended up in Noel's position instead."

Good grief, she might projectile vomit all over the living room if he kept messing with her emotions like this.

"Well, we're living together, and I'm pregnant now, so…" Josie threw her hands in the air, because all his fears seemed to have come true no matter how much he tried to avoid it.

Ben turned enough for her to see his half smirk.

The hoarding show ended, and Ben's face sobered. "I would have hated to mess up our friendship. I think that's why I didn't tell you. You know, in case we didn't work out. I liked hanging out with you."

In her head, them not working out had never once crossed her mind. She'd planned their wedding in study hall, for Pete's sake. In excruciating detail. That part would not come out in this conversation, however.

Her mind rushed back in time to their daily interactions, but the present moment overshadowed all their run-ins by the locker, their conversations in the lunch line, or strolls across the parking lot to find their cars.

"Right," she said. Because she had to say something rather than simply sit there and overthink the past twelve-plus years of her life.

"And I guess it's good I didn't drag you through hell with me. You know how messy my life has gotten." He still didn't look at her, his arms hugging his knees as he sat a few feet ahead.

She tried to force a laugh, but it didn't work. "Yes, because my life has been smooth sailing, and you would have wrecked it."

The sarcasm tasted bitter on her lips. He'd already resolved they wouldn't work out, that she was better off without him.

Ben shifted onto his knees and finally looked at her in the dim TV light. He offered a small smile. "I'm glad you're feeling better. But now that I've thoroughly embarrassed myself, I'm going to bed."

"Ben, you—"

"It's cool, Sorry. I just suddenly feel kind of shitty, I guess? You should probably get some rest too." He nodded once and grabbed his empty bottle as he stood and headed to the basement. "G'night, Josie."

19

Thankful for Pity Pie

MARCHING BANDS TOOTED THEIR horns and musical numbers wailed away as the Macy's Thanksgiving Day Parade played on TV. Josie kept to the kitchen, pulling the last of the rolls out of the oven. Her mother had put her in charge of bread, and luckily, she found frozen ready-made dinner rolls at a discounted price with her grocery app.

But "cooking" wasn't the only reason she kept out of the living room where her roommates commented on the ridiculousness of the balloon selection.

Ben hadn't said three words to her since their middle-of-the-night confession a week ago. In fact, she'd barely seen him lately, certain he was avoiding her on purpose. He had, however, left a charming note for her and Kevin on the bull-sheet pad: *I'm thankful for you a-holes.*

She leaned against the kitchen counter and read over the Corn Dog Pact fastened to the fridge for the millionth time. She's gotten Number One under control. She'd paid rent a few days early this month, had saved a couple hundred dollars, and finally grocery shopped at the discount store without stressing that her account would bounce. Thanks to WIC, she could live on peanut butter, fruit juice, eggs, and cheese for a good while. It seemed a solid start, but she still had so far to go to appease the court and prove herself a worthy adult.

Number Two fell stagnant with her job on an as-needed basis. None of the schools within forty miles needed a full-time teacher, according to their websites. But subbing worked. The kids had gotten used to seeing her around enough now that she had formed some bonds, and they listened to her most of the time. She was slowly remembering why she loved teaching.

But that damn Number Three…

Her phone pinged with a text from Ella: Happy Thanksgiving! Good luck today. Let me know how it goes.

Ah, Ella. She understood the dread that came with family dinners during the holidays. She did not, however, understand the Ben situation. Ella already had a three-hour drive to her in-laws ahead of her today. Josie preferred to skip the texts that might come from Ella heckling her for the entirety of the trip if she disclosed her roommate drama.

Josie typed back: Will do. Give the kids big hugs for me and drive safely.

She set her phone on the counter and piled the rolls in an aluminum pan. Technically, her parents had invited her to come to the new condo at any time, but she didn't particularly want to be there any longer than she had to. A full afternoon spent listening to her mother fawn all over her brother Will's success went best with a shot of very strong whiskey. Which her doctor frowned upon.

Will's model-esque fiancée, Emily, wouldn't help Josie's low self-esteem either. And as a fun bonus, her parents had only *just* moved into their new place. No matter how many times Josie— and her father—argued with her mother that she didn't *need* to host Thanksgiving this year, her mother had insisted. The day held its fair share of absolute chaos for the Claybrook family.

❧

Brian Claybrook wrapped his daughter in a hug the moment she stepped into the condo. A man of few words, her father may not speak the rest of the day, but at least he made her entrance much less dreadful. He helped her with her coat and offered to carry the rolls to the kitchen. Alas, Josie knew not to approach her mother empty-handed.

In front of the stove, her mom tinkered away with food preparation while chatting incessantly with Will and Emily about wedding plans. Josie needed a Ben milkshake for this fresh wave of nausea. Although, the thought of him didn't help her stomach feel a whole lot better…

Emily smiled from her chair but said nothing, while Will came around the island to give his younger sister a hug.

"You're looking good, Josie," he said. "Mom told me I'm getting a nephew."

Well, there went her only topic of conversation.

"Yep, it's a boy." She should probably elaborate or something. "Everything's going well so far, just a little nauseous and—"

"Josephine, grab these hot pads and take them to the table, will you?" her mother asked.

Will jumped on the task, leaving Josie in the center of the room without much of a leg to stand on. If Josie didn't get a marching order, she'd have to make conversation, and there wasn't much in the world she sucked at more than small talk with her family. The only prayer she had was that Emily might bring out a board game to entertain them after the meal, so no one had to *talk*.

"How are you, Emily?" Josie pulled out the barstool next to her future sister-in-law and tried to smile brightly. The only thing the two of them ever seemed to have in common was that they both knew Will.

Emily straightened and brushed her thick blond hair over her shoulder. "Oh, good. Tired. Wrapping up my residency at the hospital has me working crazy hours, but Will has been great helping around the house and bringing me lots of coffee."

Josie tried to force her face into a look of empathy over Emily's tough schedule, but it didn't come easily. Emily was training for a prestigious job that had apparently exhausted her on many levels, and yet her fingernails remained beautifully manicured. Josie couldn't find her nail clippers most days, let alone get on the right path to a fancy career.

"We're trying to get the last wedding details in order." Emily shook her head. "Can you believe there's only three months left?"

Actually, Josie could. Of all the wonderfully timed life events, her baby was due a few weeks after the wedding date. As excited as her brother and his doctor-fiancée were about their wedding weekend, Josie loathed the idea of riding in a car for five hours up to a resort in Michigan, stuffing herself into a dress that would most likely resemble a tent, and spending the entire weekend wondering if her water might break. She'd begged her mom to let her stay home. However, her mother insisted Josie would be fine. They'd have the doctor make a thorough inspection before they left, and, besides, "They planned their wedding before you got pregnant."

Right.

"Sit down, everyone. The turkey's coming out of the oven. I hope you're hungry." Her mother whistled to herself as she retrieved the oversize bird and made her way to the table.

Everyone gathered around, and Josie snatched the seat closest to her father. She had Emily on the other side of her and a direct line of sight to her mother: perhaps the most unsafe spot in the room.

Josie and her mother had never quite made up after the outburst in the doctor's office. With any tiff, they simply resumed life as usual.

"Pass your plates," her mother said with her singsong voice. She loved serving home-cooked meals, especially when Will came to visit. Apparently, graduating with honors, becoming a big fancy architect, and preparing to marry way out of his league had solidified his place as her mother's favorite. Josie'd never catch up to that.

After she'd handed over her plate, Josie angled toward Emily. "So, have you decided on a honeymoon location?"

Why did she even ask? Last time they'd talked, the honeymoon options had made Josie want to cry with envy. She and Grant had gone to Florida for two nights. It'd been tropical and romantic enough for them on such a tight budget, but she would have loved to go away for longer. Emily and Will, on the other hand, had a combined doctor and architect salary. As a result, the decision between Paris, Spain, or Aruba had been *so stressful* for them. How would they know which location offered the most endearing weather for that time of year?

Josie fought against the surfacing eye roll. The measly mental check marks she'd made on her life pact progress seemed so piddly next to this couple's average, everyday existence.

"We've decided on Belize." Emily clapped her hands together, while Will beamed at his bride. "It worked out perfectly because that's when my residency officially ends, so I'll have the extra time off. With it being a slower season for Will, we'll get to go for two weeks instead of one."

Will jumped in. "You would not believe this place we found. It's this tiny hut you have to walk out on this long pier to get to. There's a big glass plate in the floor so you see the fish right under your feet, and you can jump off the bedroom porch into the water."

"Oh, Will, that sounds unbelievable," their mother cooed.

"I hope there aren't sharks," Josie deadpanned.

Her mom shoved the basket of bread across the table to her daughter with a warning look. "The rolls look delicious, Josephine. Have one."

Josie almost wished she didn't want to stuff her face with carbs. Unfortunately, bread always shut her right up. She took a piece and tore into it with her teeth, maintaining eye contact with her angry mother.

Will cleared his throat. "Have you booked your room for the wedding weekend yet?"

Their dad gestured to his wife because Lord knew he had no idea.

"I'm planning to call this week," their mother said.

Will threw his head back and let out a huff. "Mom, I told you to do it months ago. They only let us reserve thirty rooms, and it's first-come, first-served with the hotel. We don't have any say over who gets the rooms."

"Oh, I know." Their mother waved the thought away.

Will pointed at his sister. "Are you staying with them or getting your own room?"

Why would he assume she'd stay with them? As if she couldn't afford her own room or be separated from her parents for a weekend?

"Yeah, I'm staying with them." Josie shoved the last bite of her bread into her mouth to quell her annoyance.

Emily pushed her salad around on the plate. Had she taken a bite yet? "Are you bringing a date?"

Josie laughed, but Emily's eyes narrowed.

"No, I'm not."

Emily stiffened. "Oh. Your RSVP said two, so I wanted to make sure for the reception seating arrangements."

"I sent that RSVP six months ago. I was still married then, but I don't particularly want to bring him anymore."

"Josephine," her mother mumbled under her breath.

Josie reached across the table and snatched another piece of bread from the basket before her mother forced one down her throat.

They acted as if the wedding was the event of the century or the only big occasion in a person's life. Having a baby was a big deal too. If she went into labor before the wedding, would she have to send an emergency RSVP in for the baby, or would Emily ban the child from her picture-perfect reception hall because he didn't make the deadline?

"Aren't you living with someone, though?" Will asked.

Oh, yes. This topic would go over splendidly. "Uh-huh. Two men."

Emily coughed and wiped her mouth with her napkin. "Two?"

Josie's mother set her fork down and folded her hands across the table. "Josephine has moved in with some friends from high school, against my advisement."

"I sure did," Josie agreed. "Just me and two single guys living it up."

She leaned back in her chair and patted her stomach. Beside her, she could see how hard her father fought to keep his grin at bay. That always made her want to try harder to get the belly laugh, but her mother's gaze shot daggers across the table. Josie should have sat next to her. Then she could have avoided eye contact and would have had easier access to the stuffing.

"What's for dessert?" Josie asked.

She still had half a plate of food to eat, but the sooner they got dessert over with, the sooner she could either fall asleep on the couch during a football game or escape back to her house.

"Pie." Will showed off his unnaturally white teeth when he smiled. "Mom said you're substitute teaching?"

Great. Josie could not wait to discuss *that* either. "Yep. Sounds pretty promising I'll get something full-time there soon."

They'd totally buy that, right? A girl could dream.

"Oh, that's good. At least it's in your field." Will swirled his mashed potatoes around on his plate, a smirk playing at the corner of his lips. "These guys you're living with… Are they teachers too?"

Emily tilted her head toward Will, which appeared less like a don't-pick-on-your-sister look and more of a you're-making-this-dinner-hell look. At least, that's how Josie interpreted it.

"No, not teachers. Insurance and tech-factory something or another," Josie answered.

Her mom cleared her throat as she scooped a large helping of sweet potato casserole onto her husband's plate without his asking. Fattening everyone up seemed to be her mother's coping mechanism in times of discomfort.

How could Josie resist pushing a little bit more? "Ben works second shift so I don't see him very often." She swallowed hard to keep going with a straight face. "He makes excellent milkshakes and has an eleven-year-old daughter who stays with us sometimes. Kevin works in the mailroom at Lawrence Insurance and enjoys coupons and not eating salad."

Emily hummed to herself. "They sound very nice."

"You're not romantically involved with either of them?" Will folded his hands under his chin and rested his elbows in front of his plate. The way he jerked to the side indicated his mother must have nudged, or possibly kicked, him from under the table.

"Not yet. Still trying to decide who gets that final rose, ya know?" Josie stabbed into the butter and retrieved a large hunk to slather across the half-eaten roll in her hand. Beside her, her father coughed into his napkin, his shoulders shaking with the giggles he had no hope of hiding.

Their mother pinched the bridge of her nose. "Will, stop encouraging this. Brian, this is not funny. She is still a married woman."

Josie bit her bottom lip. Her mother hadn't said that for Will's benefit. Not at all.

Suzanne Claybrook was not a particularly religious woman, nor all that conservative in nature, but the moment her daughter had gotten knocked up, left her husband, and moved in with two single guys, all hell had broken loose in the upstanding morals department. If anything, she still expected Josie to run back home to Grant and make everything right again.

Maybe once the baby came, Josie could pack up her little hussy heinie and move far, far away. Away from the judging eyes, memories, and the guilt that suffocated her every time she stepped into her mother's presence.

Yep, her life had become a cornucopia of chaos and confusion. She needed that pie.

20

Leftover Love

Josie had no choice but to resume obsessive cleaning. The week off school for the holiday break proved a bit too much for her mental health. She had coffee with Ella in the mornings, but when the kids napped in the afternoon, she had to return to her house—and her roommates.

Her stomach brushed against the windowsill as she wiped the glass. The entire room smelled of cleaning product and pumpkin vanilla candles. The gray autumn sky made for quaint mood lighting with little to no inside lights necessary. City of the Sun played softly from her phone on the kitchen counter.

It would have been the perfect relaxing environment, if Ben hadn't been sitting at the table typing away on his laptop. She strained often to see what he was doing over there, but couldn't get close enough without making her snooping totally obvious.

Kevin passed through the room with a laundry bag slung over his shoulder. "We still have leftovers for lunch?"

"Yup." The three of them had accumulated enough Thanksgiving foods from their families that they wouldn't need to grocery shop for a week.

"Sweet. I'm starved." Kevin proceeded toward the laundry room near the basement landing.

"Me too. I'll start heating it up. Ben, do you..." Her words took on a robotic tone. It should not be that hard to speak to him. "Do you want some lunch?"

Ben rubbed hard at his eyes. "Please."

Josie got to work, setting out the containers of food, thankful to have something to do that didn't involve dusting for the second time in the past two days.

Kevin returned empty-handed and set to work at Josie's side, spearing turkey pieces onto a microwavable plate.

Across the room, Ben groaned. "Kevin, I kind of hate you these days."

"Why now?" he answered.

"Because of your stupid pact, I'm looking up online associate degrees. It's stressing me out." He shut his laptop a little more intensely than he usually did.

"Degree in what?" Josie couldn't keep from asking. She missed speaking freely to him with no weirdness.

Ben sauntered up to the bar top and dropped his head in his folded arms without looking at her. "Electrical technology. It'd get me a hell of a promotion at work. Plus, I wouldn't have to work on a line anymore, and I'd make about twice as much."

"Get that dream job, Benny." Kevin used his fork to point to the pact hanging behind them.

"Yeah, except I don't want to go back to school. I'm thirty, dude. School should be over forever." He stretched across the counter to snatch up a dinner roll. "Izzy thinks it's funny, at least. She said we can do homework together."

Ben smiled then and took a big bite of bread.

Josie spilled a spoonful of corn over the edge of the bowl as she watched him and quickly tried to clean it up before anyone realized. Ben rounded the corner to grab his cup off the sink ledge. He squeezed in between his two roommates, but Josie zigged when she should have zagged and stepped backward onto his foot.

Ben's hand moved to her waist to keep her from tripping, her shoulder all but crashing into his chest.

"Sorry," she said.

He pulled his hand away like it might catch fire if he touched her for too long and hurried to the microwave. "Sorry."

She reached into the microwave to retrieve a plate of warmed food, forcing it into Ben's hands. If she fed him, he might leave the room so she could breathe again.

"Thanks." He offered a small smile and retreated to the living room where he promptly switched on the TV.

Josie watched him until he sat on the beanbag, then she grabbed a second plate to stuff in the microwave, slammed the door, and pushed Start. As she stared at the plate going round in circles, two large arms wrapped around her shoulders and a stubbly face pressed against the side of her head.

"You wanna tell me what the hell is going on between the two of you?" Kevin whispered against her ear, but that didn't stop Josie from frantically searching the room as if Ben might walk in at any second.

She frowned and inched her way into the corner by the cabinets, the farthest place away from Ben's ears.

"Nothing is going on between us," Josie whisper-yelled. "Also, I'm kind of hating you, too, these days."

"What'd I do?" His voice rose too high for comfort, and she drew her finger to her lips to shush him.

The microwave chimed, and she pulled her shirtsleeves over her hands to retrieve the hot plate and pass it to Kevin. He nearly dropped it on the counter when it burned his fingers.

"Must be something bad if you're trying to scorch me as punishment," he added.

Josie pushed her own plate into the microwave and punched at the numbers. "Why didn't you tell me he had a thing for me in high school?"

A Grinch-like smile took over Kevin's face. "So Benny confessed, eh?"

What kitchen gadget could she murder him with? "Kevin Andrew Lawrence."

"This explains so much. Y'all are being awkward as hell." His laugh let her know just how much this pleased him.

Josie reached into the nearest drawer and grabbed the first thing she found: a whisk. She pressed the springy tool into Kevin's chest. "Why. Didn't. You. Tell. Me?"

"That the Whisk of Truth? What's happening?" He karate-chopped it away and placed one hand on her shoulder to bring her closer. "I didn't tell you 'cause Bro Code says that ain't cool. Just like I didn't break our Bro Code, sista."

"But wasn't there some sort of conflict of interest or—"

"Bro Code!" Kevin shouted.

She absolutely could have murdered him with that whisk in a very creative way. "Shut up," she mouthed.

"You guys coming?" Ben called from the living room, but he didn't bother getting up to check out the cause of the outburst. He'd lived with Kevin long enough that he probably expected those sorts of things.

Kevin put his hands on his hips. "I think we're focusing on the wrong question here, JoJo. Instead of why didn't I do something when we were eighteen, why aren't the two of you doing anything about it at thirty?"

"I'm not divorced yet. I'm pregnant. I... Ben doesn't even... I don't know, Kevin. There has been no declaration of love on either side of this." Words tumbled out of Josie's mouth faster than her brain processed.

Kevin leaned forward to study her.

She couldn't stop herself. "Besides. If a confession as old as high school made him shut down on me this much, then it's safe to say there's not much hope of a future here."

No hope. That thought stung. They'd lived under the same roof for nearly three months, yet she still couldn't sort out if the way she felt about Ben was a present feeling or a past feeling resurfacing. Was there a difference? Did it matter? What'd she do with her plate?

Josie stormed over to the microwave and flung open the door. She retrieved her lukewarm food and shoved a fistful of turkey into her mouth. Maybe the tryptophan would knock her to sleep and out of her misery.

Kevin came up behind her and rested his elbow high on the refrigerator, leaning down so she could hear his hushed words. "Did you know Ben had lunch with Noel this week?"

The pile of stuffing in the middle of her plate wobbled when she tried to steady it in front of her. "I know he talked to her about visitation—"

"No, not that talk. A different one. Like, they actually got together to have lunch without Izzy." Kevin took the plate from her, set it on the countertop, then took both of her hands in his. "I can't read this face you're making right now, but it's looking like you might start foaming at the mouth. I need you to get it together. Okay, hon? They aren't getting back together or anything."

"They're not," Josie repeated. She knew that. Deep down, she really did. Noel was married. Ben *seemed* uninterested in reconnecting with her.

"This might actually break Bro Code protocol, but since he never told me not to tell you this, I'm making an exception." Kevin leaned to ensure Ben stayed put on the living room floor. When his attention returned to Josie, his face softened. "He talked to Noel because of you."

"Me?"

Kevin clutched tighter onto her fingers. "He said he got to feel the baby kick, which I'm a little pissed he got to do first and he's not even the godfather. But he said it made him think of when Noel had

Izzy. They tried hard to make it work but couldn't. They grew further apart as time went on, but they still had the kid between them. And here you are, and your baby daddy's gone, which sucks. Ben doesn't want to be like Grant. He wants to make amends with Noel, so she knows she isn't doing this alone anymore. He wants a bigger part in his kid's life. Does that make sense?"

Yes? Ben hated the thought of Noel parenting on her own for so long because he had a front-row seat for watching *her*. If Grant reached out to her in this way, it might help. It couldn't have been easy for Ben to do, like it wouldn't be easy for Grant after all this time either. Though, she had a hard time comparing the two men. Ben was sweet, and Grant cheated on her and ruined their marriage beyond repair.

Kevin picked up his plate, which couldn't possibly be warm anymore, and turned to head toward the living room. "He may be awkward as all heck, but he's working through a lot of stuff in that tiny mind of his. So, try to get your weird self together 'cause it's an Izzy weekend, and I'm pretty sure that kid will smell tension from a mile away. You do not want to sit through that questioning. Am I right?" At the edge of the bar, he stopped. "Oh, and in case we haven't made it clear enough: As long as we're around, you aren't going to go through any of this alone either. Got it?"

He winked and went in to take over the other beanbag chair next to Ben.

Josie stood frozen in place for a moment. With a deep breath, she reached for her plate and headed to the living room. She plopped down next to Ben and his beanbag chair, pushing her hips into his to move him.

"Scootch," she said in a way that mimicked his approach to her a few weeks before.

Ben readjusted from his near topple and smiled. If he meant to make such leaps and bounds on pact progress and do something as beautiful as reaching out to make amends with an ex, Josie would do as Kevin had asked too. She'd get her weird self together.

She reached across to Ben's plate and snatched up a roasted carrot to pop in her mouth. Ben side-eyed her and retaliated by taking a piece of her turkey. And just like that, the ice between them shattered, their shoulders pressing together as they watched the latest episode of *Love It or List It*.

Josie had most definitely decided to love it.

21

A Savior Bearing Cinnamon Rolls

Izzy huffed and puffed her way through the bedroom. She folded up the comforter as small as possible and shoved it into its original plastic casing. When the bag refused to zip all the way, she growled and moved on to spreading a blue zebra-print blanket over her new mattress.

"Troubles?" Josie asked from her position on the floor where she scrolled from one online account to another, trying to make sense of it all.

"Goodwill can fold it if they want it to stay in that bag." Izzy threw herself on top of the bed, wrinkling the blanket she'd meticulously smoothed out moments ago. She snatched her tablet from the neon-green nightstand Ben had purchased to go along with the matching headboard. She kicked her legs up against the wall beside the beluga whale painting and propped the matching pillow behind her head.

Relaxing in Izzy's fashionable preteen-dream-loft wasn't such a bad way to spend a Saturday. It would have been better if Josie didn't have to balance her sad bank account and figure out how to access her teacher retirement fund.

"Are *you* having troubles?" Izzy's head hung over the edge of the mattress as she regarded her upstairs roommate.

"Be thankful your parents pay all your bills, kid." Josie popped another Tums and took a long sip of her warm milk with honey, one of the many random heartburn home remedies she'd discovered on some pregnancy blog. It helped with the heartburn some, though she may be beyond help when it came to dealing with 401(k) crap.

Izzy's hair cascaded over the mattress's edge like a shiny black drape. "Ben sent my mom some gift cards to take me shopping for school clothes. He let me choose the bedding colors too. I don't have to look at that My Little Pony crap ever again now that I've got my whales."

"Hey, now. Your dad tried with those ponies. He really did." Josie pushed around the papers at her feet, tucking the retirement stuff underneath the insurance bill. Out of sight, out of mind?

Izzy readjusted on the bed and tapped at the screen. "I know, but I like these ones way better."

"I'm jealous. I'll admit it." Josie smiled. She still couldn't believe Izzy chose to hang out with her while Ben made cinnamon rolls downstairs. At least Josie got to enjoy their father-daughter breakfast adventures by hanging around on their visitation weekends.

Josie took up her phone to check her email. She had heard nothing new from her lawyer in a while. She wanted it to end: every interaction in the law office, marriage purgatory, not knowing what might happen next. Why did it matter if the baby was biologically Grant's if he wanted nothing to do with their son anyway? The one and only interaction she'd had with her soon-to-be ex-husband was a thumbs-up emoji when she informed him the baby was a boy. Nothing else.

"Who you texting?" Izzy asked.

Josie closed the home screen and dropped her phone on the carpet. "Oh, no one. Just checking emails and stuff."

"Do you always frown at your emails?" Izzy's eyebrow rose as she watched Josie from across the room.

These days?

Josie had zero plans of admitting her adulthood defeat, divulging just how close she was to a full mental breakdown, or confessing the weird conflicting feelings she felt for Izzy's father. "Only when the emails make me cranky."

Izzy rolled over and propped her chin against her fist. "What kind of emails?"

Geesh. Kevin hadn't been wrong about Izzy's epic interrogation style.

"Adult stuff." Josie began stacking the papers to put on her nightstand. Nothing else productive could possibly happen today.

"That's what my mom says when she's mad at my stepdad." Izzy returned to scrolling through the page on her tablet. "They fight a lot. Least I don't have to listen to them this weekend."

The scent of cinnamon rolls wafted up the stairwell. Josie watched the girl tap at her screen as she tucked a pillow under her chest and wiggled her pink-painted toes in the air.

Did Ben know he'd become a respite for his daughter? "Well, I'm glad you get a bit of a break here then."

"And cinnamon rolls. They smell soooo good."

Josie picked up her phone again and texted Ella: Spending my morning having milk and chatting with Izzy. What world am I living in?

Mere moments later, her phone dinged with a reply: Can't wait to hear, Mama #2 ;)

Josie: NOOOOOO

"Did you name the baby yet?" Izzy asked.

Josie flipped the phone over in her hands to keep grounded in the conversation without her mind roaming off toward another to-do list or stress factor. "Not yet. Any suggestions?"

"Just don't name him after Kevin. He is so weird."

That helped keep her grounded. "That's an understatement."

Izzy sat up on the edge of her bed again and held her tablet out in front of her. "Okay. What about these? Beckett, Fenton, Luca? *Ugh.* Monty? No. And who would name their kid Zeus? That's a dog's name."

"Those are certainly interesting, and possibly hipster enough for my mother. I'll keep them in mind."

Izzy's smile took over her whole face. "There's a boy in my grade named Creed."

"Like from *The Office?*" Josie wiggled onto her hands and knees to stand.

Izzy's face scrunched. "What office?"

Thirty suddenly felt like the new ninety. "I have a girl in one of my classes named Alaska. I could name my baby Wyoming or something."

"Or Hawaii." The younger girl giggled behind her tablet screen. "Were you a teacher where you used to live too?"

The scent of brown sugar and cinnamon begged Josie to come downstairs in case Ben forgot to let them know breakfast was ready.

"Yeah. I taught high school history."

"Was your husband a teacher?" Izzy asked.

"Uh, no. He works at a veterinary clinic." How much had Ben told her about her former life?

"That sounds more fun than being a teacher." Izzy folded her arms, her head tilting as though trying to see through Josie to the real reason she'd ever choose a job as stupid as teaching.

"It probably is." Josie leaned toward the stairwell and yelled at the top of her lungs, "How much longer, Benjamin?"

After a moment's pause, he responded. "Five minutes. Don't get your panties in a bunch."

Five whole minutes. It wouldn't kill them to go downstairs now, though...

"I want to work with animals, too, when I grow up. I'll be a marine biologist probably. Did you have a lot of pets since your husband worked at a vet?" Izzy's question kept Josie from getting her foot onto the first step. "I have an axolotl and a bunch of neon tetras at home."

It wouldn't be easy to keep her past from the girl if she kept asking questions. Josie needed to steer things in another direction. "No. We didn't have any pets at all. Grant liked to keep work at work, I guess. What do you and your dad have planned for today?"

"So, you had a baby instead?" Izzy tossed her tablet to the foot of the bed, completely ignoring Josie's question.

Josie had avoided the birds and bees conversation of how her child came to be once, but this time it almost seemed inevitable. To answer such a question, she either had to explain an unplanned pregnancy or come across as a freak who opted to get knocked up because childbirth sounded easier than potty-training a dachshund.

"No…" That didn't work. She was, in fact, pregnant. "I mean, yes-ish? The baby is not in place of a pet, though. I always wanted a baby and hope to one day have a cat or something, but it definitely has nothing to do with Grant working at the vet. We just happened to have a baby at this particular time in our lives, and then the marriage didn't work out so—"

"Can we come eat now?" Izzy's voice roared through the upstairs to reach her father's ears, her eyes wide as she stared at her company.

Josie leaned against the wall behind her. In retrospect, she should have said yes. They had a baby because they didn't want a dog. Izzy already thought she was crazy. That statement would not make it worse.

From downstairs, Ben growled loudly, "Just come on."

Josie tripped over her own feet racing down the steps, nearly falling into Ben's outstretched arms.

"There a fire up there or what?" Ben steadied Josie with his hands on her elbows so she didn't slide any farther on the slick faux wood.

She clutched his forearms until she had her grounding. Though, being this close to him kind of made her knees weak anyway. "I may have started one, yes."

Ben shook his head and glanced upstairs. "What'd you do?"

She shrugged and walked in reverse toward the kitchen. "Never tell your daughter you got her instead of a puppy. It'll be fine. I'm gonna take my roll to go. Okay?"

With Izzy in the house, and knowing what Josie did about Ben now, she wanted to stay away and give the father-daughter duo a chance to connect. Kevin had to help his parents paint their dining room, and Ella was still away on a museum trip with her kids, leaving Josie to plan a solo adventure for this lovely Saturday.

She'd gathered a few coupons for Baby, Baby at the mall and reviewed her to-get list. After Ella had insisted on throwing Josie a baby shower, and Josie refused because of the extreme embarrassment such an event would bring at this phase in life, shower cards began to arrive in the mail. Each one held a gift card to Baby, Baby. Ella always found a way where she had a will—and what a strong will it was.

Izzy leapt off the last step with a thud. "You gonna play Mario Kart with us today? Winner gets pizza."

They really needed to get more creative on stakes in their household.

Josie started toward the kitchen. "I appreciate the invite, but I'm going out after breakfast."

"Where?" Izzy followed behind her, and Ben brought up the rear, watching the two women interact as if studying a foreign species.

"To Baby, Baby. There's some stuff I want to get for the little man." She patted her stomach.

"Can we go, Dad?" Izzy spun around and grabbed hold of the counter.

Ben stood dumbfounded. "Um…"

"Can we go with Josie to the baby store?" she repeated.

Josie, too, held perfectly still as if any movement might shatter this fragile moment. Izzy had called him "Dad." He had to be screaming on the inside.

"Please? Josie, can we go?" Izzy whined. "I don't want to stay here all day. After Mario Kart, we were gonna watch some dumb dog movie Dad rented."

"A *classic* dog movie." Ben now smiled from ear to ear despite his film tastes being critiqued.

Izzy folded her arms and looked from her dad to Josie. "I want to go to the mall. We can at least get ice cream after the baby place, right?"

Ooh dang. The child was extremely persuasive.

Josie leaned on the doorframe, a grin plastered to her face that wouldn't go away. She'd hoped for a stop at Starbucks for some strong decaf with marshmallow flavoring and a lazy stroll around Baby, Baby to daydream. She couldn't wait to finally make some purchases for her little guy. The day might lose an element of relaxation with an energetic preteen and a man who now knew she'd wanted him in high school.

Ben sighed through his goofy smile. "You care if we crash your party, Jo?"

"Fine by me." Like she could say no to that face. Besides, she doubted either of them would last long in a baby store. She'd probably lose both of them to the pet shop on the first level that drew kids in like a magnet.

"Go get dressed, then, and I'll get your cinnamon roll plated." Ben waved his daughter off. The moment she was out of sight, he ran around the kitchen island and dramatically fell on the floor. "She called me Dad! Josie, cross Number Three off the list. I just defeated that level."

Josie scooped some breakfast onto the plates and laughed. "Kevin would not be pleased if I tainted the pact, but that was totally awesome."

⌦⌧

When they'd eaten and made themselves presentable for the public, the three of them piled into Ben's car, and Josie stretched her legs in the front seat, thankful she at least didn't have to squeeze behind her own steering wheel with the two of them watching. The darn wheel got closer and closer to her stomach every time she got in.

They drove the twenty minutes in silence, with the exception of Izzy's mumblings over scenery and frequent requests to turn the music up louder. It didn't leave much room for conversation, not that she and Ben had much to say to each other as they played "house" with his daughter in tow.

Ben took full advantage of the stork parking option in the front row of the mall and rushed around to Josie's door to help her from the car as if to make a display of her "situation."

"You don't have to stay with me," Josie said to Ben when they walked through the main entrance. "I know this isn't very exciting. There's a pet store on the first floor."

"I want to stay with you," Izzy whined. "I want to look at the baby stuff."

"Seriously?" Josie examined the younger girl's expression, then shrugged.

"I haven't gotten to shop for baby stuff ever." Izzy crossed her arms and took the lead. She mumbled under her breath enough for the others to hear, "Mom won't give me a sister, and there's no hope for Dad."

"Heeey." Ben stuck out his tongue.

Josie laughed at the solid burn.

With a slight group detour for Josie's coffee, something she would not negotiate on, the trio entered the large children's store and froze at the sight of what had to be 600 baby departments. Bright colors battled for attention, while balloons of all shapes and sizes begged patrons to come explore the sales.

"So…" Ben paused and scratched his head, looking every bit the part of the adorable, clueless new father—even if he really wasn't. "What now?"

"Can we get clothes?" Izzy grabbed hold of Josie's arm and started dragging her toward the nearest rack of onesies.

"I do need clothes. And, like, fifty other things. Maybe it's a good thing you guys came along." About a zillion of the most adorable baby clothes Josie had ever seen stretched across this section of the store. As tiny as the zero-to-three-month onesies looked, she had trouble imaging her lettuce-sized infant fitting in any of them one day.

Izzy plucked outfit after outfit off the rack to show the mother-to-be. Josie hated saying no when Izzy offered so much enthusiasm. It was so nice to finally have an excited shopping buddy who wanted to fawn all over her unborn child, but after she hunted down the bigger ticket items with her gift cards, she wouldn't have much money left to get more than the bargain-bin favorites.

"Maybe we should start in the furniture department?" Josie waved her arms to direct the others and eventually got them to follow. "I need a portable bassinet, preferably with penguins."

"Penguins?" Izzy's face twisted. "Why penguins?"

Leave it to her mother to take an adorable arctic creature and turn it into an obnoxious decoration. "That's my nursery theme, apparently."

"Penguins it is." Ben patted Josie on the back and led the hunt. "You're keeping Baby in your room, right?"

"Nah, I was gonna put him in with you. You're the one up at all hours of the night." She nudged him with her elbow and winked.

"I don't remember that clause of your rental agreement…"

"What rental agreement? Our big roommate binding involved ice cream and a covenant to stop being terrible thirty-year-olds." Josie scanned the bassinet photos on each packaged box.

"Well, that part was implied. I'll make you milkshakes when

you're up for feedings, but you're on your own with diaper changes and whatnot," he added.

She loved having him back at her side and not just avoiding her or acting like a ghost around the house. Not to mention how much she'd missed his friendship, his quips, the closeness of sitting beside him.

Izzy squealed. "I found a penguin one."

"Oh, good." Josie walked ahead to check it out, while Ben stayed hot on her trail.

Ben examined the box in question. "We could always make Izzy share her part of the loft."

Izzy tried to scowl, but her face broke into a smile.

"True. Though, it's probably better if I find a place of my own after he's born and the divorce is finalized. I'd feel bad filling your trash with empty pizza boxes *and* dirty diapers." She hadn't applied anywhere yet, but a few low-income options might work out. The lawyer just said she had to stay put for the custody case, but living an entertaining life with Kevin and Ben couldn't go on forever when they had children to care for.

"You'd leave us?" Ben stiffened.

Did he not also see their living situation as temporary? She tilted toward him to send a telepathic answer. She didn't want to dive too deeply into this conversation now, especially in front of Izzy. "Ben…"

"Josie." He leaned in, touching his forehead to hers as he took hold of both her shoulders. "Why would you want to leave us?"

Izzy gagged loudly enough to draw the attention of nearby shoppers. "Could you guys just kiss and get it over with?"

Josie's cheeks caught fire. She held up a finger and stepped away from Ben. "The penguins. We have to get the penguins."

"Ah, the penguins." Ben reached forward and pulled the oblong box from the shelf, hoisting it onto his shoulders like a lumberjack might carry a small tree. "I'll go grab a cart."

Josie watched as Ben wandered to the end of the aisle and

searched his surroundings like he had no idea where to go next. Josie shook her head to force away the grin.

"Staaahp," Izzy cried and took Josie's hand to guide her into the car seat aisle.

Josie kept her head low to hide her expression. The last thing she needed was Izzy calling her out for crushing on her dad.

Izzy giggled and cooed over all the animal patterns, trying desperately to convince Josie to ditch the penguins for the tiny blue whales shooting water from their blowholes. "Maybe for my next baby in ten years," Josie would say each time to appease her.

Ben returned with a cart containing the penguin travel bassinet. "You disappeared."

"We literally went one aisle over. Calm your pits." She gave him a light punch in the ribs.

He held up his hands in surrender. "Pits calmed."

Izzy walked ahead of them, standing on tiptoe to see the designs higher on the shelves. Josie read weight requirements, having zero idea what all the numbers and measurements meant.

Suddenly, Ben's face appeared in her peripheral vision, growing closer and closer until his mouth almost touched her ear. "Why would you think you need to leave us, Josephine?"

Josie nearly fell into the display when his whispered words tickled her ear. "I'm leaving because my roommates are creepy, Benjamin."

He whined, and Josie saw immediately where Izzy had gotten it.

"And I dunno," Josie continued. "It's all this life-pact stuff and feeling like I need to break out on my own to truly experience adulthood and take care of myself in case Grant challenges me or something."

"Yeah, that's a stupid reason." Ben shook his head and pushed past her.

"What?" Josie followed him, grabbing hold of his arm to keep him from getting too far ahead.

He smiled smugly. "I said that's a stupid reason. Living alone isn't in our pact. Kev would agree here."

She tried to think of what category independent living fell under.

"You can be independent with us just as well as without us." Ben tapped Josie's nose.

She crossed her arms over her chest and glared at her roommate. "Uh-huh."

Izzy practically shouted. "Really, guys? It's like you're married. Can we move on to the ice cream part of this day now?"

Josie's mouth fell open as she examined Ben's daughter and cued up her best sarcastic voice. "Izzy, I had no idea you wanted me to be your stepmother so badly."

"Oh, gross." Izzy stuck her tongue out and gagged. "I didn't mean—"

"We could do each other's hair and talk about boys and cruise around the city listening to loud music while we run errands and—"

"Dad, make her stop." Izzy stepped back, but Josie reached forward and grabbed her by the shoulders, pulling her in for a big bear hug.

"My beautiful daughter," Josie shrieked.

Izzy laughed against Josie's chest, and Josie tickled her sides to keep the chuckles rolling.

When she finally released her captive, she turned back to Ben. A wide smile had overtaken his face as his gaze shifted between the two women before him.

"Huh." He scratched at the stubble on his chin.

Josie cocked her head, but Ben walked away without an explanation.

What was that all about?

22

He Who Makes the Breakfast Makes the Rules

THE GOVERNMENT NEEDED TO cast a vote about making every weekend three days long. Getting up on a Monday morning after the first full week at school post-Thanksgiving break proved hard enough for the average person, but for a preggo gal nearing the end of her second trimester, Monday became third-degree torture.

At least this week wouldn't come with any surprise calls in the wee hours for subbing. She'd finally landed a long-term gig covering for the English teacher's maternity leave. Job security was such a beautiful thing.

"The real stuff this time, Kevin." Josie shouted from the top of the stairs. She squirmed into her formfitting undershirt, trying to get the bottom to go over her bosom. After that, she had to tackle her stomach. She might as well try to cover a mountain ridge with plastic wrap.

"Sure thing," Kevin yelled.

"Don't try and fake me out again. I will kill you in your sleep." She stumbled into a wall and righted herself. Luckily, the topple helped set the shirt in place.

Kevin opened the door at the bottom of the steps. "Bring it on, little mama. I got all day."

He held his hands out to his sides to invite her attack. She stared at him from above. Fortunately, she'd gotten covered up enough that Kevin hadn't gotten a show. That'd be the last time she dressed on that end of the bedroom.

"Oh, whatever. Go pack your pound of bologna, and go to work." Josie tugged on her cardigan and began her waddling descent down the steps.

"Nope. Not till you're down here safely. You're not hurting my baby." Kevin reached up and took her free arm to help her with the final step.

Josie looked to the ceiling and grinned as she shook her head. "For the last time, this is not your baby. Stop saying that, especially in public places. You are not the godfather either." She shouldered him in the abs, and he tugged her in for a bear hug.

"You'll come around." He planted a loud kiss on top of her head before letting her go.

"Besides, I make this journey up and down the steps a hundred times a day without your help. Have you not noticed my killer glutes?" Josie headed toward the kitchen, smacking herself in the rear as she went.

Kevin chuckled and followed behind. "Coffee's on the counter, sexy ass."

She sighed and brought the travel mug up to her lips, inhaling the fresh aroma she desperately needed to perk her up for the day. With the first sip, she knew he'd duped her. "Oh, come on. I can taste the decaf all over this crap. I asked for the real stuff."

Kevin lifted his chin and walked toward the back door. "I make the coffee; I make the rules."

With a dramatic humph, he left.

Josie stood for a long moment with a lopsided grin on her face. Kevin was the world's best antidepressant.

She sipped her baby-friendly coffee and grabbed the bull sheet from the fridge. Ben had asked her to remind him to take his leftovers with him to work today. That was not a reminder she wanted to forget, as it would most likely lead to her having to smell the old burgers the next time she opened the fridge. At least his first-shift hours started soon, and they could all be on a normal eating schedule without having to save burgers overnight for lunch packing.

Her pen hovered above the page. All she needed was a simple "don't forget your burgers," but still, she tapped her pen against the paper without managing a single word.

Should the note be more personal than that? After all, she had spent two weekends in a row hanging out with Ben and his daughter.

Two weekends' worth of watching Ben in daddy mode had put her heart—and ovaries—on the brink of explosion. Sometimes, when he lay in the beanbag chair and picked dried cheese dip off his shirt, or threw a handful of popcorn at the television when the couple didn't choose his favorite of the three houses, Josie had a hard time imagining him with that level of adult responsibility. But the way he wrapped his arm around Izzy during movies, heckled her over a Wii bowling tournament, and kissed her forehead when he sent her off to bed at night…

Oh, Josie wanted that for herself *and* for her son.

Ben may not get to see Izzy every day or walk her to school in the mornings, but he had become an active part of her life. He loved her. And Josie wanted that kind of love for her child too.

Could Grant ever come around like that? He might reach out to make amends with her or ask to spend time getting to know his son better. Their little boy could still learn to throw a ball with his birth father and see him as an actual part of his life and not a sometimes parent.

Ben's note. She had to write his reminder note and get to school. She bit her lip and scribbled across the notepad:

Hey, Benny-Boo, get your nasty burgers out of the fridge before
we all die of salmonella. Sincerely, your penguin-loving coparent

⌒⌒⌒

Midway through the day, Josie got a burst of energy that counteract-
ed her defective coffee. Her spirits soared as the students took turns
reading the short stories they'd written over the weekend. While
the occasional plot went dark, most of the class took their stories
in a rather humorous direction. With a topic like "clown owls," two
words randomly drawn from a hat, she expected little else.

When the bell rang for last period to begin, Josie assigned the
first readers. They'd only be able to get through half the class in the
day, leaving the rest for their next period together. Josie plopped in
her rolling chair and reclined as far as it allowed, resisting the urge to
kick her feet up onto the desk. The first student spoke of "the majestic clown owls of the rainbow forest and the fire-breathing substitute
teacher that threatened both their joy and habitats."

Very funny, Kade.

As he read on, Josie scanned the classroom. A few of the students
got too rowdy over a certain part of the story, especially when the
fire-breathing substitute threw a notebook at the beautiful majestic
clown owl and destroyed his glorious rainbow nest.

It took Josie a little longer to find Hadley in the room. She remained focused on the desk in front of her, giving no attention to the
reader. Over the past few weeks, her grades had steadily gone down.
Occasionally, she missed assignments altogether. That could mean so
many things in high school.

Hadley brushed her hair from her face, her finger lingering near her
eye. Josie hardly noticed when the class applauded at the end of the story.

"Did you like that one, Ms. Hale?" Kade asked. "It's dedicated to
my favorite substitute teacher."

Josie cleared her throat, then examined her challenger. "That was lovely, Kade. I'll let Mr. Norris know all the sweet things you said about him."

Kade sat up as his classmates roared. "I didn't mean—"

"Brittney, you're up, slugger." Josie pointed to the dark-haired girl sitting behind Kade and raised her hands to settle the rest of the room.

Brittney read her story, followed by Jacelyn, Tony, Claire, Beckham, and Liam, but Josie couldn't take her eyes off Hadley.

The bell rang halfway through the last story, and Josie announced that "The Clown Owl Who Lost His Peep" would continue the following day. Students filed out of the room, whooping and hollering as they mocked one another's stories or bid their teacher farewell in the most animated manners they could muster.

Hadley tried to escape, but Josie followed her to the door, touching her arm gently to get her attention.

"What's going on today, Hadley? Are you all right?" Josie asked.

Hadley sniffled and tucked her hair behind her ears. "I'm fine."

Josie closed the classroom door as Hadley's tears fell freely. "Sit down, and take a minute, okay?"

She led her student to the desk and sat her in the teacher's chair. She situated herself against the desk's edge, leaning in to get a better look at Hadley.

"You're not riding the bus, are you? Do you need to call someone to come get you?"

"No." Hadley gasped for air and reached for a tissue on the corner of the desk. "I have my car. It's... I'm so sorry. I don't know why I'm crying. I promised myself I wouldn't."

"It's okay. No need to apologize for anything. I'm here if there's something you want to talk about."

Hadley's hands fell limp as she looked up at her teacher. Her voice squeaked out the smallest of whispers. "My parents are going to kill me."

Josie sat forward on the desk, trying desperately to search the girl's eyes for more. "What's going on?"

Hadley's voice cracked, and she squeezed the wadded-up tissue in her fist. "I'm pregnant."

It took every ounce of willpower Josie had not to reach up and cover her mouth. Students had dozens of reasons why they may fall behind in school, become emotional or distant. All of them held so much weight. This one would change Hadley's life forever.

"Oh, Hadley." Josie reached forward and took hold of the girl's hands.

"I suspected it for a while, but thought maybe I missed my period because of cross-country. It's happened before, so I…" Another wave of tears hit her, and Josie saw the immense exhaustion weighing on her.

Watching Hadley weep like this was like watching a younger redheaded version of herself from a few months ago. That shock and fear still seemed to sit right under the surface of Josie's heart. "How far along are you?"

"I haven't been to a doctor, but maybe a couple months?" Hadley pulled a hand out of Josie's clasp to wipe her nose. "I took the test over the weekend. I kept putting it off because I didn't want it to be real."

"Have you told your parents?" Josie didn't know what to ask. There had been pregnant students at Lincoln Regional when she'd taught there, but none of them had been in her classes or spoken with her about it. Should she send Hadley to the school counselor for this one?

"No. They're going to freak out. They're always telling me they're proud of me or that I'm a good girl, and they trust me, and…"

Her shoulders shook as she cried, and Josie squeezed her hand harder. "Hadley, you *are* a good girl, and you are absolutely someone to be proud of. I've suspected something was up with you for a while, but I've also seen how hard you're still trying."

Hadley's fingers tightened around Josie's, but she remained silent.

Josie continued. "I know it'll be awful to have to tell them. I can't imagine the weight on your shoulders right now."

She knelt in front of her student, still clutching one trembling hand as she looked into Hadley's desperate green eyes.

Hadley breathed the slightest hint of a laugh. "Can you go tell them for me while I move to Timbuktu?"

Josie laughed. "Full disclosure: my parents found out I was pregnant because I left the flippin' pregnancy test on the bathroom floor. You don't want my help in that area. Trust me." Josie reached for another tissue to pass along. "Does the father know?"

Was it another one of her students? She hadn't noticed anybody else sweating it out during class time.

Hadley rolled her eyes. "Yeah. We broke up a few weeks ago, but when I got the positive test, I went over to his house to tell him."

"And?"

"He pretty much told me it wasn't possible."

Josie shook her head. "Well, that is just precious, isn't it?"

Now Josie really wanted to know if it was one of her students so she could fail him.

"You have a plan?" she asked after a minute.

Hadley threw her hands up. "Crawl under a rock and die?"

That feeling sounded familiar too. Josie reached to retrieve her bag from the bottom desk drawer. Inside, she kept a couple of extra bottles of water to get her through the day. Thankfully, she hadn't consumed the last one, so she offered it to Hadley.

"Do you think this is something you need to talk to the counselor about? I mean, I don't know if I'm the best person to give advice when I'm clearly a mess." Josie pulled her cardigan apart to display her round belly.

Hadley shook her head and offered a quick smile. "I think I'd rather talk to you since you understand. Your guy left you knocked up too." She paused, then her eyes grew wide. "Can I say that to a teacher?"

"Well, when you put it that way…" Josie couldn't sit on the floor anymore. Her back already hurt from teaching all day. She got up and dragged her chair around to face Hadley.

"Where do I start with all this?" The teen looked so, so tired.

"That's a loaded question." Josie leaned sideways against the desk. "You're a tough cookie, kiddo. As bad as it sucks, I think you need to start by talking with your parents." What else could she say? She'd been in this same situation, only with thirteen years added to her age. What had she needed to hear when she found out she was pregnant? Kevin's voice echoed in the back of her mind: *You'll get through this, and no matter what happens, you won't have to do this alone.*

Josie's throat closed and cut off any further motivational speeches. In Hadley's position, encouragement would be hard to believe. But each day would get easier. She'd find that out eventually.

Hadley sat in silence, picking at the skin around her thumb.

Josie patted Hadley's knee and rolled her chair around to the desk. "I'm giving you my phone number. It's probably against the rules, but what are they going to do? Fire me? I'm not technically on the payroll."

Hadley breathed a small chuckle and reached to take the sticky note with Josie's number.

When Hadley stood, so did Josie, and they walked silently to the door. Before Hadley reached for the handle, she turned and fell into Josie's arms.

Her grandma used to tell her that everything happened for a reason. Had she gone through hell in her marriage, gotten pregnant, and moved to Clarkson simply to counsel this one sweet student from personal experience?

She squeezed Hadley a little tighter.

When the teen finally pulled away, her eyes shone with fresh tears. "Thanks, Ms. Hale. Seriously."

"Anytime. I mean that."

Hadley took a deep breath, then headed out to her locker. With the hallway emptied, no one would be there to judge her tearstained face or ask her why she'd had to stay after class. She was free. At least until she got home.

Josie returned to her desk and straightened things up, inspecting the room once more before heading out for the day. After putting on her coat, she gathered her purse and snack pail. She fumbled through her coat pocket to double-check for her keys, but the opposite pocket buzzed with a text.

Josie tapped on the message when she rounded the corner to the main hallway. The simple message from her mother screamed in all caps and stopped Josie short.

COME TO THE CONDO. NOW.

23

Using Cookies for Bait

JOSIE ROLLED THROUGH TWO stop signs on her way to her parents' condo but couldn't risk it with the stoplight-camera intersection. As she waited for it to turn green, she tapped her palms on the wheel.

"Come on," she begged.

What did that text mean? Her mom had never demanded she come to the house in such a way. Josie called the second she read the text, but her mom didn't pick up. Did something happen? Was it Dad?

She turned into the condo's parking lot, expecting to see the flashing red lights of an ambulance parked out front or flames shooting from the windows. As she drove up, she spotted her mom's car in its designated space and another car in the visitors' section.

A black car.

A black Chevy Cruze with a sunroof and a University of Illinois license plate frame.

A car she'd only ridden in a couple times between its purchase and the moment she'd left Chicago.

No, it couldn't be Grant. Not *here*.

Josie's heart sank to her swollen toes. Why had he come to her parents' place? Maybe Diana had borrowed her son's car. Regardless, Josie had no desire to visit with her soon-to-be ex-husband's mother, either, and it's not like Grant would ever let someone else drive his precious car.

The car puttered to a stop in the other visitor's space, and Josie slowly turned the key to kill the engine. She swallowed to encourage breathing. Once she'd wriggled out of her seat, she shut the door behind her as quietly as possible to keep her options open if she decided to turn and run without being noticed.

Her brain pleaded with her body to hightail it out of there. She felt like a lame gazelle walking directly into a lion's den to be devoured by her predator husband and imperious mother.

She'd take the pregnancy nausea and heartburn, the randomly popping hip sockets, and round ligament pain over this anxiety eruption. The slow elevator climb felt like a thrill ride right now.

With a long exhale, she turned down the hallway, stopping when she found the right unit.

The door opened under Josie's hand, and she raised her head. Her mother sat in a chair, Grant adjacent to her on the couch. They were… chatting. Each of them had a cup in hand, mugs from her mother's prized china set. A small plate of cookies decorated the end table between them. Upon her entry, both Grant and her mother stood.

"Josie." Grant forced a quick smile, his palms brushing against the sides of his pant legs. He looked her over, lingering on her budding belly.

Josie wanted to duck behind the curtains, run screaming from the complex, disappear from all existence—*anything*. She couldn't manage a simple hello.

"You really are pregnant," he murmured.

A plethora of sarcastic comments welled in Josie's mind, ready to break forth like a dam and drown her soon-to-be ex-husband in a sea of disgust and shame.

"Josephine?" Her mother lifted an eyebrow at her daughter, waiting for a response. It didn't matter if Josie was five or thirty, her mother required some manners and a response to the speaker.

"Why are you here?" Josie's gaze locked on her husband.

Grant took a step forward but stopped when his knee bumped the edge of the coffee table. "Your mother asked me to come."

Josie froze. Her fists clenched with the urge to flip the couch over, punch a hole through the recliner, or straight-up burn the condo down.

"*This* is what your text was about?" Josie seethed in her mother's direction.

Her mom rose from her chair and stood, blocking Josie's view of Grant. In a hushed voice, she tried to explain. "I'm sorry I didn't warn you, but I think you two should talk about things. I figured you wouldn't come if I told you why I wanted you here."

Had she finally spoken with Diana? Or was this her mother's attempt to make amends between Josie and her estranged ex-husband as a way to win his mother back as her best friend? Either way. Not cool.

Josie shifted her stance enough she could see Grant a few feet away. "You're right, Mother. I wouldn't have come if I'd known he was here."

Grant stepped around the coffee table, but Josie raised a finger to keep him from coming closer. He stopped and held his hands up in defense. "I'm sorry I didn't call or text you back. My new lawyer has been insisting he take care of everything. It's all been really intense, and I didn't know what to do."

Josie's mother linked her fingers in front of her. "Which is why this clarity is good. I'll leave you two to talk. There's coffee in the pot. I'll just take a little stroll around the grounds and—"

"In December?" Josie's teeth clenched as she tried to fight off the eruption bubbling in her mind.

"I'll go to the lounge then." Her mother pulled her sweater from the tree stand by the door. "Just talk. Everyone needs to *talk*."

With that, she left. Knowing her mother, she'd probably stand in the hallway with her ear pressed to the door while she texted Grant's mom with updates using entirely too many emojis in hopes of rekindling the relationship with this one *good deed*. But seriously, what kind of mother baited their daughter into coffee and cookies with an estranged husband? This would definitely affect the quality of her Christmas gift this year.

"Josie." The way Grant said her name drew her gaze to him.

She'd forgotten how smooth his voice sounded, the deep-blue hue of his eyes. She fully took in the sight of him now, remembering exactly how his arms had felt around her in the early days of their relationship when everything was fresh, new, full of hope. His lips hadn't met hers in almost six months, but she could taste him, smell the peppermint on his breath from his toothpaste, and hear his voice whisper in her ear as they curled up together in bed.

Damn him.

Grant dug his hands into his pockets. "I had no idea Suzanne didn't tell you about this. She made it sound like you were on board. In retrospect, I should have known better."

"Yeah, I probably should have too." Some part of her deep down wanted to laugh right now. Maybe it was the adrenaline crash after rushing to the house, expecting an emergency, and finding an ambush.

"Can I at least get you a cup of coffee?" He gestured toward the galley kitchen as if he'd been there a million times and knew where her mother stored everything.

Josie inched forward to examine the table in front of him. Did he have coffee in *his* cup? She flexed her hands at her sides to give them something to do that didn't include breaking anything nearby. "You drink coffee now?"

"I'm coming around to it. I kind of missed the smell in the mornings and started making it before work." His lip quirked in a half smirk. "It's not so bad with a bit of cream and sugar."

Josie closed her eyes and brought her fist to her forehead. "Haven't I been saying that for the past four years, you giant dumbass?"

Grant winced. "Okay. I probably deserved that."

That and more.

She stepped farther into the living room and grabbed a chocolate chip cookie from the plate. Her mom made the best cookies, half-baked and supersoft. Josie couldn't leave them sitting there while her entire world exploded around her.

With the cookie in hand, she plopped down in her mother's chair. A huge weight had settled between her shoulder blades.

"Tell me why you're here." She bit off a sizable chunk of cookie. Past Josie would have tried to impress him: eat more daintily, sit up straighter, smile, and laugh at his jokes. Present Josie wanted to flip him the bird and erase all memory of his existence.

He inched forward in his seat, his foot bouncing on the carpet. Josie had never seen him so nervous. "Well, Suzanne emailed me a picture of the ultrasound and some baby stats. She said she wanted to offer her living room as a place to talk because you're having a rough time going through this alone. I figured you didn't want me around, but she insisted you'd be here ready to talk. I didn't tell my lawyer I was coming. Or my mom."

The rest of her cookie crumpled in Josie's fist, and she let the crumbs crash to the new carpet below. "Your mom finally figured out what happened, I'm guessing?"

"She did."

That definitely explained the dead air between their mothers. Josie so hoped Diana had laid into Grant about it all too. He was her precious little boy, and he'd made a big mistake. Now there was a grandbaby involved.

"And am I understanding correctly that it took my mother emailing you an ultrasound photo for you to believe you really are this child's father?"

"No, that's not it. I knew it was mine, I just…" He lowered his head and growled under his breath before looking up at her again. "You didn't tell your mom what happened between us."

Josie's head fell back on her shoulders, and she released a pained groan. "No, I didn't. I'd hoped not to crush our mothers' friendship, for one, but that clearly didn't work. And as if it's not embarrassing enough to deal with on my own, the entire family on both sides would hear all about how I wasn't enough for you." Her voice broke. She sucked in her bottom lip to stop the trembling.

Silence enveloped the room. Grant couldn't argue her point, and she couldn't elaborate. She didn't want him to see her cry. Not again. She'd shed too many tears on his account already.

After a lengthy pause, Grant took a big breath. "So, this is definitely happening. We have a baby."

"You don't have to be involved, you know. I'm more than six months along. When you didn't respond, I kind of counted you out of the picture. Figured some kind of child support would appear in my account every so often, and Baby and I would go about our lives without you." Her mouth tightened when she thought of what her mother had told him in an email. "And despite what my mother says, I'm doing very well on my own."

"I'm sure you are, but I'm also not going to ignore the fact that we have a son." Grant swore under his breath. "Yes, I was delayed in accepting this fact or communicating directly with you about it, or whatever. But I have rights in this too. I'm going to want to see my kid."

"You said you didn't want kids," she whispered.

He shrugged. "No, but that doesn't mean I want nothing to do with the one we *have*."

Her hand covered her mouth as she fought a wave of emotion. Nothing prepared a person for a conversation like this.

"How am I supposed to share my baby with someone I don't trust?" She rocked up and out of her seat. Her shin smacked the coffee table, a welcome grounding in an unimaginable situation. "You cheated on me, and I'm supposed to do what, exactly? Send my son to your house while you and Christa—"

"Christa has a kid, too, Josie. She's two years old." He cleared his throat as if something got stuck there, then continued much quieter. "She lives at home with us, so it's not like we don't know what we're doing. Christa and I *both* want my son to be part of our family." He refused to look up.

Their *family*. Their *home*. Christa had not only taken Grant's heart, but slid in to take Josie's spot in their apartment too. And she'd brought her daughter along. Grant, the man who had adamantly denied Josie's desires to start a family, had already assumed the family life with someone else.

"Go home, Grant." She wiped her tears on the collar of her coat and pointed to the door.

Grant stood and reached out to her. "Josie, come on. Let's just talk. I'm sorry, okay? I'm sorry it's like this and—"

"I don't care." Josie backed away toward the door, her stare focused on the faux flames in the electronic fireplace across the room. She'd all but escaped him, had begun to move forward again. Now he wanted to be a part of her life—their baby's life—on a regular basis?

Unable to look at him, imagine him being a part of her for another minute, she turned toward the door and ran.

24

Ice Cream Meltdown

AFTER DRIVING ACROSS TOWN, heaving herself out of the car, and climbing the three steps to the front door, Josie lost all strength to turn the doorknob. She plopped down on the second step and cried into her gloves.

A car drove by and slowed, probably to gawk. Maybe they heard her sobs even with the windows up. It didn't matter. She'd seen Grant. He wanted her son to be part of his new life with Christa.

A second car slowed in the street and turned into their driveway. Great. Kevin was home from work, and she had no time to escape.

He parked and hurried up the driveway to the front of the house, a takeout bag in one hand and an empty travel mug in the other.

"What happened?" Kevin rushed to her side and sat down, dropping his things on the porch and pushing her hair out of her face to confirm her tears. "I haven't seen you this upset since you ate all the corn dogs."

Josie grimaced. "That's not why I cried that day, dork."

"Well, what happened?" He grasped his chest. "Is the baby—"

"Oh, no. The baby's fine. Sorry." Josie took a long breath and rested her gloved hand on Kevin's arm. "It's Grant. My mother arranged a surprise meeting for us at her house. I had to talk to him, and now I'm contemplating matricide."

"Oh. Oh hell. I'm sorry. That's… Damn, Josie." Kevin wrapped an arm around her shoulders. "I've got a chicken sandwich and fries in here, but you can have them if it'd help."

She laughed. "I'm not stealing your food. Don't think I can eat at the moment anyway."

Kevin opened his bag and took out some fries to snack on. "So, what'd he say? What did *you* say? What happened?"

Now that Josie could smell the grease and salt, she regretted passing on dinner. "Mom made us cookies and coffee so we could talk. Grant drinks coffee now, apparently."

Kevin made a fist. "That son of a—"

"I know, right?" Josie took another shuddering breath and sniffled. "He and Christa are living together now. She has a kid of her own who Grant's helping take care of."

Kevin stuffed another fry into his mouth. "I don't know what to say, JoJo. Should we call Ella? Do you need emergency ice cream?"

"I'll call her later, but thank you. Ice cream may help."

Kevin whipped his phone from his coat pocket and tapped away. "Ben'll get it."

"Where is he?" she asked.

"At Izzy's school meeting. Did you not sync to our family Google calendar? I sent you, like, six invites." The phone beeped when Kevin hit Send.

"I… What?"

"Family calendar. I'll do it for you tonight." His phone chimed, and he read the message. "He's on it. Be here soon." Kevin nearly threw his phone when he tried to stuff it into his pocket with a little extra style.

Oh, good. Now Ben would also get to see her in this disastrous state. Again.

Josie stared ahead at the road in front of their house. The icy air bit at the raw skin under her nose and eyes where she'd rubbed away the snot and tears. The afternoon replayed in her mind in slow motion, as though through a fog.

"I couldn't do it, Kev. I couldn't talk to him anymore. I don't know what happened. I just ran right out of the condo." She didn't budge from her trance.

Kevin shifted his body closer, wrapping his arm around her to pull her in. "It's okay. You were probably in shock."

She breathed a laugh. "He wants to be part of the baby's life. He and Christa both do." Josie pulled her coat tighter around her. Her ears went numb as the evening hours cooled the temperatures even more. "He never wanted kids before. Never. I prepared myself for that over the past few months, you know? To do this on my own. But now he wants to play house with someone else?" She growled and buried her forehead in his shoulder. "I'm dumping on you. I'm sorry."

"Don't be sorry. I want you to tell me this stuff," Kevin said. "I wish I had some kind of advice, but I don't. This is…out of my field of expertise."

He had to be cold. He didn't have any winter wear on but his dress coat from work. Josie hated that he'd stayed outside with her all this time just to listen to her cry when he'd come home with a hot meal, ready to unwind.

Kevin sat up a little straighter and patted her back. "Hey, here's someone who might be able to help more than I can."

Ben's car pulled into the driveway. A moment later, he walked around the corner of the house with two drink carriers: one with three ice cream sundaes and one with three hot drinks.

He examined the scene happening on their front steps, the way Josie wiped furiously at her eyes as he approached. "Who do we need to kill?"

"Her mom, I think." Kevin squeezed her arm. "Right? We're killing Mom? Or Grant? Two for one?"

Josie chuckled despite her coarse, dry throat. Her eyes must be so puffy by now, and no doubt her nose shined like Rudolph's.

"Ooh. That sounds like a terrible combination." Ben raised the drink carriers slightly. "I got hot chocolate. Didn't even know you were sitting on the steps when I got them either. You know we have perfectly good beanbag chairs in our warm living room, right?"

Kevin stood and took the drinks and ice cream from Ben. The pair of them exchanged a look Josie couldn't understand, though it held no judgment as far as she could tell. Sympathy, maybe.

Ben stretched out a hand to Josie to help her up. "You've got to be freezing. Let's go inside."

His hands warmed hers through her gloves. Ben pulled her in closer when she stood, his gaze locking on to hers. "You okay?"

"Not today," she said.

He bowed his head, his thumb brushing over her gloved knuckles as he guided her into the house, his opposite hand on her lower back. "Come on."

Once inside, Josie shrugged off her coat. Ben met her with a fleece blanket, wrapping both the blanket and his arms around her shoulders. She melted into him, his warmth stilling everything in her. She could have stayed that way forever, but his hands slid down her sides and fell away. "Go sit. I'll grab spoons."

Josie obeyed and curled up in the beanbag chair, tugging the edge of the blanket over her legs. The shivers had finally caught up with her, and she snatched a hot chocolate and chugged away, letting it burn her throat on the way down.

Ben sat in front of her this time, crisscrossing his legs as he handed out spoons for their ice cream. "So what's up?"

"Well, to sum up a horrible afternoon, my mom tricked me into a meeting with Grant at her house, and now he wants to be part of our baby's life—he *and* the new girlfriend who took my place." Josie scooped a large spoonful of ice cream into her mouth.

"Ah." Ben blew into the tiny hole in the top of his paper cup.

"I freaked and ran out," Josie mumbled.

Ben watched his lid with great focus. "What kind of parental rights is he hoping for?"

She shrugged and cradled her ice cream cup in her blanket-covered hands. "I don't know. I didn't stick around that long. I'm sure our mothers have something planned for that, though."

Of all the things her mother could do to her, she had resorted to emailing Grant baby pictures and arranging some sort of whack tea party for her daughter and soon-to-be ex-son-in-law.

"When are you going to talk to him about that?" Ben kept his voice low.

"Never? I don't know. Being around him today sucked. He didn't *want* to be a father six months ago. How am I supposed to entrust him and some strange woman with the most important thing in the world if he's going to be such an ass about everything?" The Corn Dog Pact had only told her to get over her past. It said nothing about welcoming the past back into her life. "Just when I thought I was moving in the right direction, he has to show up."

Ben let out some sort of squeak and looked to the ceiling. "I, uh, I know you don't want to talk to him, and this is the last thing you want to hear right now. But if you don't figure out an arrangement, the courts will do it for you. Been there. Done that. You don't want it."

Oh.

The lawyer mentioned the paternity test and divorce hold-up. Grant hadn't signed away any rights yet, so technically he *could* fight her in court. He could take the baby.

Grant had a good job with a steady income and a nice apartment he'd lived in for several years. He offered their child luxuries like insurance and stability.

God, what if Grant took the baby?

"He can't," she whispered, setting down her ice cream. Her hands covered her stomach to create a force field of protection around her son. The tears welled all over again.

Kevin caressed her back as he sat in silence. Ben leaned forward and put his hand on her ankle, urging her to look at him. "I know it sucks."

"I don't trust him, Ben." She searched his brown eyes for answers.

"I am not about to defend him. Cheating is unforgivable, and you deserve so much more than…" Ben blew out a breath and scratched at his neck. "What I'm trying to say is he's still the father. I didn't want to be a dad at nineteen. I had no idea what I was doing, but I would have lain down in traffic for that baby the moment I saw her."

Josie set her focus on his hand draped over her ankle. "What if he's just playing the part of doting father for *her*?"

"You can't really be sure on that one way or the other, and I know that's hard. I *know*. But it's better for the two of you to work out the details without the lawyers having to make decisions for you." Ben gave her ankle a squeeze.

Kevin pulled her in for a gentle side hug. "Told you he'd know more about this than me."

A deep fatigue set into her bones from all the tears she'd cried since leaving her parents' condo. She couldn't think about this anymore with a clear head.

"Does any of it make sense, though?" Ben asked.

Josie frowned. "Yes, but one problem remains. I don't want to see him again. Being with him brought everything up. All of it. I can't keep doing that." She bit hard on her lip as another tear rolled down her cheek.

"I wish you didn't have to," Ben whispered.

Have to.

So, no choice then. She *had* to talk to him. Why couldn't she hide with her baby in a protective bubble and shut out the rest of the world?

"I'm so tired," she said.

Kevin rose to his knees and began gathering their snack trash. "You should get some rest. You've had a hell of a day."

She thought of Hadley and all they'd discussed that afternoon. This day really had gone on forever.

"You think you can sleep?" Ben asked.

"I hope so. I don't have school tomorrow 'cause of my OB appointment." She grimaced. "Guess that means I won't be able to avoid my mother for long."

Kevin took Josie's elbow to help her stand. "Uh, yeah. Good luck with that."

"Thanks for listening to me whine. I'll try not to be this big of a mess tomorrow when you get home, I promise."

"Hey, if you are, we'll get more ice cream. No worries." Kevin winked and headed to the kitchen with the trash.

Ben offered her a shy smile and held the door open to the stairwell. "Rest will help."

"Thank you." She started up the first few steps but slowed when she heard him coming up behind her. Her feet carried her on when her mind fell blank as to why he followed.

As they rounded the corner into her room, she turned, unsure of what to say or do when he paused in the doorway.

Ben stepped into her side of the room for the first time and reached forward to pull the blanket around her shoulders a little tighter. "I wanted to tell you…" He kept his gaze down and released a heavy sigh. "I mean, I wanted to come up here and let you know that if you ever needed somebody to talk to who's been there, done that, I'm here. I know dealing with exes and kids can get kinda murky, I guess, and Kevin doesn't totally get that, so…"

Josie's eyes had completely dried now as she looked up into Ben's sullen face. As much as she loved the way Kevin cared for her and lent an ear when she was down, Ben had been in a similar place to hers. And he cared.

He kept a small piece of her blanket pinched between his fingers. "I, uh. I just wanted you to know that. I'll let you sleep."

The blanket fell from his grasp, and Josie reached out to take hold of his arm. Without any more hesitation, she wound her arms around his waist, drawing herself fully against him, baby bump and all. Her head rested on his collarbone, and she could feel the way his muscles stiffened under her touch. She exhaled her nerves and breathed in the scent of candied pecans that seemed to follow him around.

He wrapped his arms around her too, his chin sinking down against her hair. In that one fragile moment, her mind eased, and she relished the new sense of calm.

25

A Little Too Salty

Dr. Mallory's fingers hovered over the keyboard as she read Josie's chart. Her lips pursed, and her eyes narrowed.

Josie wiggled her feet as they hung limply from the table. The paper drape covering her nether region crumpled with every movement. She hated chatting with doctors and nurses when she didn't have any pants on. It felt…wrong.

"Have you been having any headaches or trouble breathing lately?" Dr. Mallory didn't look up from her computer as she scrolled to the next screen.

Of course, her head hurt. Her life had become a horrifying roller coaster, and pregnant women weren't supposed to ride those. "Yeah, I guess. The headaches come and go but aren't too bad. My chest gets tight, but mostly when I'm stressed out. Not like I can't breathe at all or anything."

"How often does that happen?" Dr. Mallory asked.

How often did she get stressed? "Maybe once a day?"

Or, like, a thousand.

Dr. Mallory got up from her rolling chair and took hold of the blood pressure cuff, but the nurse had already done that part when she first entered the room. "Have you been getting outside and exercising?"

If walking back and forth to her car counted. "I've been taking the stairs."

"How's your diet?" The doctor wrapped the cuff around Josie's arm and started pumping it up.

"Average?" Terrible.

Josie studied the picture on the wall of the fetal growth stages. Her rutabaga-sized son ate everything she ate, which meant she'd practically built her infant out of nachos and milkshakes.

"Are you taking your prenatal vitamins?" Dr. Mallory asked.

"Yes." That one was easy. She took them every morning with her breakfast, unless she forgot...like she had that morning.

The pressure cuff released with a hiss, and the Velcro crackled when Dr. Mallory ripped it apart. "Your blood pressure is still higher than I want it to be, higher than at your last checkup. One-forty over ninety-four. Lie back and let me listen to Baby Boy."

Josie walked her butt cheeks up the paper cloth to lie down. The doctor had told her she had high blood pressure at almost every visit, and she still felt fine. Maybe she had a speedy heart or something.

The cold stethoscope grazed her plump belly until it found its target. Dr. Mallory held stone-still, observing her watch. She made a clicking sound with her tongue as she placed the stethoscope around her neck.

"I'm getting about 192 on baby's heart rate. That's pretty high too. I'm going to send you down for a nonstress test to monitor this a little more. Okay? We'll see if we can't get that heart rate to settle a bit. If not, we'll talk about some options, but don't worry yet." Dr. Mallory patted Josie's knee hidden below the crinkled paper sheet. "Go ahead and get dressed, and Sonia will be down to get you set up with that."

The doctor exited, leaving Josie to sit in silence, her mouth parted with a host of unanswered questions. She got dressed in a daze and waited by the door until Sonia came and led her to the ultrasound room. There, Josie lay down on a reclining table, and Sonia hooked her up to a fetal heart-rate monitor, dimmed the lights, and told her to sit tight for a while.

Right.

Tears welled in her eyes now that she sat alone with her thoughts. Her baby had a high heart rate. How high was too high? Why hadn't Dr. Mallory given her a scale of normalcy so she knew when to panic and when to go along with procedure? Somehow they expected her to remain calm in a dark room, listening to the faint thumps of her son's heart that may or may not be healthy.

He shifted inside her, which made his heart beat faster on the monitor. Could she reach down and follow his little feet across her belly, or would that mess up the test results? They hadn't even explained the purpose of this test.

She could always google it while she waited, but WebMD might issue a diagnosis infinitely worse than anything she dreamed up. Her phone vibrated in her pocket, and she welcomed the sudden distraction of the multiple text message notifications awaiting her.

Kevin: I bought an Instant Pot! 30% off!

Ella: Text me after your appointment. Still on target???

Ben: Kevin thinks you can make frozen pizza in his new crock pot thing. Might wanna grab something to eat on your way home tonight.

Kevin: Do we need an automatic pan stirrer? Where are you???

Kevin: The calendar just told me you were at the Dr. My bad. I'll ask Ben.

Ben: On second thought, get something for me too. Kev got something called a taste-enhancing fork and I'm scared.

KEVIN: Found a sweet pack of baby-proofing gadgets. One even locks up the toilet! lol

Ella: Shouldn't you be done by now? Everything OK?

Ben: OMG. He won't stop. Should we evict him and save ourselves?

Josie's stomach wobbled up and down as she giggled at the

blessed diversion taking place in her texts. The monitor slid around on her belly, but she readjusted it to where she thought it went. She clicked Ella's message and sent a quick reply about the extra testing, trying to sound as casual as one could when one had zero idea what the heck was going on.

To Kevin, she asked if he could set up the family calendar app to remind him how counterproductive lunch-hour shopping was and that they definitely didn't want to seal the toilet when they only had one to begin with.

And to Ben…

Well, he'd offhandedly suggested they kick Kevin out and live together alone. That's how she interpreted it, anyway. She opted to send some laughing emojis because Lord knew words would not form for that one.

The minutes ticked away, and Sonia returned to unhook the machines. Dr. Mallory came in next and read the report on the computer screen.

"All right. Looks like his heart rate came down a little. He's in the 170s now." The doctor took a seat in the chair and crossed her legs. "You've still got thirteen weeks left, so I want you taking it easy. I have a feeling you'll see some bed rest the closer we get to the end. I also want you coming in every week to monitor that blood pressure. Start making notes of any other symptoms you notice or how you feel. If it's preeclampsia, we want to diagnose it as quickly as possible."

Josie tried to shuffle the information around in her mind. "Wait. You said bed rest? I might have to go on bed rest? What does that mean exactly? What's preeclampsia?"

"It's a fairly common complication that could indicate damage to your internal organs. It's something we want to monitor closely to ensure your health as well as your baby's." Dr. Mallory adjusted her coat underneath her stool and wheeled closer. "Basically, you'll want to start slowing down your activities now. If we decide you need full bed rest, you'll need to stay in bed and restrict your activities. In extreme cases, we may need to admit you to the hospital to monitor the remainder of the pregnancy, but we're not there yet, so don't worry too much until we know for sure."

"If I go on bed rest, I can't work." Josie could almost feel her blood pressure rising again at the very thought. "How do I pay my bills if I can't go to work?"

"Don't let that stress you out right now. You can ask these questions at Job and Family or file FMLA when the time comes. For now, I want you to relax, rest, and don't do anything too strenuous. I've got some informational packets I can get for you before you head out." Dr. Mallory said some other things, but Josie's mind had checked out.

She needed her job. Even if FMLA helped her make rent, she still needed to build her savings account and keep rapport with the school. Losing steady employment would reset everything she'd worked for. She'd only just started researching daycare options for him and lining up a plan, and things were falling apart.

At some point, Dr. Mallory dismissed her, and her feet instinctively carried her to checkout without her mind registering. Her mother sat in front of her, typing away on the computer. One minute, her baby's health was in question. The next, she may not be able to work and pay her bills.

"Some mail came to our address for you." Her mother passed a couple envelopes across the counter.

"Thanks," Josie said.

Her mom leaned back in her chair and observed the computer screen. "Oh my gosh! Your blood pressure, Josie. And you had an NST? What happened?"

The attention of those in the waiting room closed in on Josie at the counter. Maybe they assumed the receptionist made such comments when everyone checked out. Actually, she might. Josie had never witnessed her mom checking anyone else out.

"Yeah, the baby's heart rate was high, but it came down some. I have to rest more to get my BP lower and come back every week." Josie spoke softly to quell her mother's obvious HIPAA violation.

Her mom shook her head. "Why is your BP so high? Are you stressed?"

This question coming from the woman who had just arranged for her daughter to meet up with an ex by surprise?

"A little stressed, Mom." She tapped the mail on the counter and tried to ignore the tension in her neck and shoulders. "Can you just schedule my appointment so I can go home and lie down?"

Her mother rolled her eyes and clicked away some more. She printed out an appointment reminder, handing it to her daughter without bothering to confirm if that day and time worked.

"You going to tell me how it went with Grant?" Her mother kept her hand on the appointment paper to ensure Josie couldn't walk away with it. "It definitely didn't go how *I* thought it would. He told me he's been dating someone else, and that Diana isn't very happy with him for it. Did he tell you that? It's all way too soon for that if you ask me. I sent Diana a long text last night to tell her that you two met at my place and that I knew about his *girlfriend*. Blech. We'll see if she gets back to me since I'm sure that's why she's giving me the silent treatment. But I swear, Josie, I just wanted to help you two work through this, and then he goes and—"

"Mom." Josie's hands flattened on the counter. "It's nice of you to want to help me out, but can you let me handle things my way?" She could not work through this now on top of everything else the morning had brought. "Yes, I knew he was seeing someone else. She's blond and beautiful and works at the vet's office and has a two-year-old daughter. The woman's name is Christa." Josie sucked in a trembling breath. "I know all of this because he cheated on me with *her*."

The waiting room seemed to spin. A nurse opened the door to call another patient for her exam, and a small child ran a circle around his mother seated in the center row of chairs.

Josie's mom pressed her hand to her chest and sat forward in her seat. "He cheated on you?"

"That's why we split up. Yes, we had our differences, and things had been going downhill for a while. But we were working on it. At least, I *thought* we were. Then I caught him—" Her voice broke, and she swallowed hard to force away the tears.

Her mother reached across the counter and took hold of Josie's hand. "Why didn't you tell me?"

"Tell you one more way how I'm not good enough?" The rest of her explanation failed to come out.

The familiar shame she'd dragged around with her resurfaced all over again with the confession. Josie had never quite measured up to her brother in her mother's eyes. Will had found the perfect woman: wealthy, pretty, exciting. Josie's husband had pushed her aside for a better model.

"I'm so sorry, Jo." Her mother bowed her head, giving her daughter's hand a squeeze. "I'm sorry that happened. I'm sorry I made you feel like you couldn't tell me. I…"

Josie held tighter to her mother's hand as the rest of the conversation melted away between them. She hoped for a wave of relief to come over her after finally revealing the truth about her failed marriage, but the confession only drained her more.

Another patient rounded the corner to stand behind Josie in the checkout, giving her the out she needed. "I need to go home. We can talk more later."

With her appointment reminder and mail in hand, Josie lowered her head and hurried out of the office and away from the curious eyes in the waiting room.

The cold air slapped her in the face, bringing her back to the reality of what the doctor had said. She had to calm down. She had to figure out a way to eliminate stress in her life and settle her own heart so the baby's heart didn't go crazy too.

Josie sat numbly in her car, waiting for the heat to kick in. The mail her mother had passed along looked to be mostly junk: something about her car's extended warranty, a life insurance advertisement, a charity seeking money for the holidays, and something from a student loan company.

That last envelope made her pause. She had gotten nothing from a student loan company in years because of the loan forgiveness plan. Was this an end-of-year confirmation for taxes or something?

She dropped the rest of the mail into the passenger seat and tore into the envelope. She could only manage to read a sentence here and there as the magnitude of it all set in.

Regret to inform you…

Loan forgiveness plan denied…

Five years of teaching service incomplete…

Total amount to be repaid: $26,459.32

Payment plan effective immediately.

The letter slipped from her fingers to her lap. She'd only worked four years at Lincoln Regional. She hadn't completed the full five years of the loan forgiveness requirements. How had this totally slipped her mind when she'd walked out of her life in Chicago? One more year there and more than twenty-five grand would wash away forever.

The monthly payment amount nearly doubled that of her rent check. How could she possibly pay so much on such a small income, one that might diminish at any moment if her health didn't hold up?

Josie reclined her car seat and curled her legs into herself as much as her stomach allowed. She drew her coat up over her head and let the tears fall into her hood.

26

The Great Garlic Bread Incident

THE SCHOOL DAY DRAGGED on forever. Josie taught from her chair to force the doctor-ordered calm movements. Her voice came out hoarse from the amount of sobbing she'd done over the past couple of days. Not even Kevin's flavor forks could lift her out of despair.

Josie still hadn't seen Hadley in the hallway yet either. She'd missed the past two days of school. Now, last period approached, and Josie waited to find out if she'd miss a third.

When the final class of the day poured in the door, Josie spotted the red ponytail rounding the corner into the classroom. She searched Hadley's face for any indication of what might have happened over the past few days.

Josie stiffened in her seat. She stumbled through her lesson plans, ready to get the day over with and catch Hadley before she walked out the door. With the last of discussion questions discussed and the review page reviewed from the "comfort" of her rolling chair, Josie glanced up at the clock just in time for the bell to chime.

She ushered the students out with farewells and motivational reminders, all the while watching to make sure Hadley didn't slip out in the rush. As hoped, the girl remained, and Josie shut the door.

"What happened? Any updates?" Josie waved her student to the desk so the two of them could sit and keep their blood pressures nice and low.

Hadley grimaced and pressed her fingertips into her forehead. "Well, I told my parents Monday night after they got home from work. It was awful. We all cried. *A lot.*"

"Oh gosh. I know that wasn't easy." Telling Grant had damn near stopped her heart. She couldn't imagine being a teenager in a small town and having to deal with the rumors and whispers surrounding her situation.

"They aren't kicking me out at least." Hadley smiled shyly. "They're really disappointed. Like, super disappointed, and I'm pretty sure I'm never allowed out of the house ever again, especially if it involves a boy."

Josie clicked her tongue. "That sounds like parents."

"They took a few days off work to stay home with me and talk. They wanted to go to my ex's parents, but I said no. That would have been horrifying." Hadley shook her head. "I don't think I slept much the past few days. There's so much to think about."

Josie knew the feeling. She, too, had spent a tremendous amount of time trying to figure out this new budget app and how to live on a dime while simultaneously trying to maintain serenity. The FMLA assistance didn't sound promising for substitute teachers, but she'd be sure to fill it out anyway. The only thing that became clear was how much she had to keep working.

To further promote health, she'd taken lavender baths in the evening and survived on Instant Pot pizza rolls and rice, courtesy of her roommates. Kevin did his nightly stand-up routine, regaling Josie with tales of the mailroom and which middle-aged woman he'd lost to in arm wrestling that day. It helped, even if it didn't particularly solve any of her problems.

Josie tried to stretch her neck to relieve the tension headache without appearing bored with her student's company. "Did you go to the doctor or anything?"

"Yeah. I'm due at the end of May. Don't know what I'm having yet, though. It's too soon to tell," Hadley said.

The winter air rattled the windows. Christmas would soon shut everything down inside the school building for a solid two-week break, giving the pregnant women of Clarkson High a chance to rest and figure out how to keep going from one day to the next.

"So, do you have a plan?" Josie almost hated to ask, as if such a thing existed. Plans fell through; new plans had to be made. Hadley had only been home with her parents for a couple of days since breaking the news to them. Surely, she hadn't made too many life-altering decisions in such a short amount of time.

Hadley shrugged. "I really don't know. It's so embarrassing to say it out loud, but when I first suspected I was pregnant, I almost thought maybe my ex would come around and things would go back to how they were with us. Now that I say it, it just sounds stupid."

"I think anyone in a crisis goes through that, honestly. I know I did for a while. When my marriage started to decline, I wondered if getting pregnant would glue us back together." *Ugh*, so ridiculous.

"Yeah, that's pretty messed up. And relatable." Hadley laughed.

"There's not much of my story that isn't messed up." Josie thought back on all that had happened over the past few months that she hadn't voiced to her younger counterpart—or anyone in her life: her growing desire to jump on Ben or the tears she'd shed in the privacy of her car when Pizza Hut had only given her one slice of garlic bread instead of two. Josie scratched her eyebrow. "You going to the OB here in town?"

"Yeah. I saw Dr. Richcreek. He was nice, but I hated answering all those questions with my mom sitting next to me." Hadley's gaze fell into her lap. "He said he'd connect me with some families if I wanted to consider adoption."

"*Are* you considering?"

Hadley covered her face with her hands. "I don't know. Why do we have to make such huge decisions so fast? I haven't even looked at colleges because I thought I had a whole year left to think about it. Now, I've got college *and* a baby, and I don't even have a date to prom, let alone know if I'll fit into a stupid prom dress. What guy would want to take a pregnant date to the prom?"

Josie's heel tapped aggressively on the tiled floor. Would there ever come a time when they didn't have to deal with huge life-altering choices? The men in their lives didn't have to fight these kinds of battles. Grant could work as many hours as he wanted without having to arrange childcare. Hadley's ex could fit into his tux no matter how big Hadley's belly grew.

Josie dropped her elbows against the desk. "I weirdly get that too. My friend keeps telling me to start dating again, but I don't see too many guys lined up to date me and my lady lump here. Oh, plus there's college debt I didn't know I had because the forgiveness plans I signed up for fell through, which is probably Grant's fault. At least, I *want* to blame him. Part of me really wants to drag the divorce out even longer and make him pay even more for the loans since I'd still be at my old job if I hadn't caught him with someone else." *Seriously, life.* "And all the while, I'm supposed to keep calm and make sure my blood pressure stays down, and I don't get too excited and—"

"Ms. Hale?"

Josie looked up.

Her student sat wide-eyed across from her. "Are you okay?"

"I'm so sorry." She'd word-vomited all over the place. Her brain needed a cork. She didn't want Hadley to think Josie was trying to top her situation with a sadder story. "I didn't mean to dump that out. I'm here for you and want to support you however I can."

And she meant that. Josie was the grown-up. She had to be strong for her student.

Hadley smiled. "It's kind of nice to know I'm not the only one losing her mind right now. No offense."

That made Josie laugh. "None taken. We can walk this nutso journey together." She held her palm up for Hadley to high-five, yet another pact silently forming.

While they may be at wildly different stages in life, the feelings remained similar, their need for camaraderie at an all-time high.

"Thanks for letting me talk, Ms. Hale. I'm really glad you're here." Hadley stood and grabbed her bag from beside the seat. "I'd better get home before my parents think something happened."

"Probably a good idea." It neared four. The buses would have all left, the halls cleared from kids scurrying off to winter sports practices. "You get some rest and focus on your plans. When you're ready, we'll start working on getting your grades back to where they started."

"Okay. That will help." Hadley waved on her way out.

Josie grabbed her purse and shoved her chair under her desk. She'd go home, too, make a hot beverage, then figure out how to roundhouse kick her life into submission.

Calmly. Per doctor's orders.

27

A Cheesy Fling

JOSIE'S APP CHIMED WITH her newest update on her baby: less than two and a half months until the due date. Her acorn-squash-sized son could smile now and might experience extra bouts of hiccups. Josie might feel stronger kicks and develop varicose veins.

Oh, joy.

The app failed to mention she'd start having more trouble controlling her bladder, too, which wasn't terribly convenient when she lived with two comedians who liked to mess with her.

"I will murder you in front of your daughter." Josie used the snowman ornament to point at Ben. "This little sucker is made of clay, and it will be a very slow and messy death."

Izzy giggled into her hand as she hooked a small, green bulb onto the lowest branch of the Christmas tree.

"You gotta catch me first, Waddles." Ben tossed a string of garland from where he sat on the floor. It fell on top of the two girls.

With a dramatic groan, Josie shimmied out of the decorative rope. "I'm going to the bathroom."

"Good idea. Better than having you pee all over the living room floor."

Josie pushed Ben over as she walked out of the room, which made Izzy laugh harder.

From the kitchen, Kevin hummed monotone Christmas carols at the stove as he boiled water. Josie almost hated to have to take a bathroom break and miss the variety show going on around the house. Between Ben's horrible Christmas-themed jokes that tested the quality of her panty liners, Kevin's occasional operatic rendition of "O Holy Night," and Izzy's continuous giggles and confusing ornament configurations, she couldn't remember a better day.

"Josie," Kevin yelled the second she opened the bathroom door. "Marshmallows or whipped cream? Plain is also an option."

"Load that puppy up." Josie headed toward the kitchen to help him carry the toasty mugs of hot chocolate.

The fresh-from-the-oven cookies mixed with the chocolaty scent in the air and made Josie want to curl up and melt away in her joy. If there'd been a downside to the day at all, it was that she hadn't been able to eat the store-bought cookie dough before it had gone into the oven. Normally, she'd have no problem risking her life to a gooey salmonella death, but her child depended on her self-control now.

"Is it done?" Izzy squealed from the base of the tree and spun around to receive her steaming mug.

"Halfway filled with hot cocoa, halfway filled with toppings per your request." Kevin handed the girl her beverage and bowed with a flourish. He then turned toward Ben and rolled his eyes. "Same for you, douchebag."

"Language," Ben muttered.

"Oops." Kevin shrugged and winked at the giggly preteen.

Kevin had come a long way from hiding or running out the door when Ben's daughter arrived for the weekend. Maybe the Christmas spirit moved everyone to jolliness and better attitudes.

Josie reclined in her beanbag chair. "I used to love decorating for the holidays. Mom always made pie, and Dad would hold me up to put the star on top of the tree."

"You want us to hold you up there?" Ben nudged her foot. "We could build a pyramid."

Josie scrunched her nose. "My doctor would not recommend that. Besides, Izzy gets that honor this year."

When Izzy didn't respond, Josie stretched on her seat to observe the girl. From beside the tree, Izzy held her untouched hot chocolate in one hand and tapped away at her phone with the other. Her brow furrowed deeper with each word she typed.

Ben seemed to follow Josie's gaze. "What's wrong, Iz?"

Izzy shook her head. "Mom asked if I wanted to go skating in the morning."

"Ice-skating?" Ben lowered his mug to the carpet and leaned forward.

Kevin and Josie exchanged equally stricken looks from across the room. According to the new visitation agreement, Izzy got to spend the entire weekend with Ben. Did Noel want her home a full day early?

While the prospect of sharing her bedroom used to make Josie shudder, she'd grown to care about Izzy, to enjoy their conversations and teasing. When she came for visits, it brought new life into the house. On Izzy weekends, Ben and his daughter included her, made her part of their little family.

"Why tomorrow?" Ben's shoulders sank. "I mean, I guess you could always go and come back if your mom doesn't care."

Josie chewed her thumbnail as she watched Ben try to be diplomatic. His face couldn't hide his disappointment. He'd become practically giddy leading up to her visits now that their relationship had mended.

"She got a Groupon or something for tomorrow only. I asked if we could go later this week." Izzy brought her cup to her lips and licked the whipped topping.

The beanbag crumpled under Ben's weight when he spun around. "You did?"

"We're still watching *Elf* tonight, right?" Izzy picked at the marshmallows brimming her mug.

"Yeah, of course." Ben stood and paced the room as if searching for something he couldn't find.

Izzy took a large bite of cookie and shrugged. "I guess I'll stay and watch then."

Josie flashed Ben a thumbs-up from beside the beanbag chair. Kevin made wild gestures from the other side of the room every time Izzy looked away. They had to rejoice in every victory, and this one seemed pretty huge.

"I was thinking," Izzy began as she sifted through the remaining ornaments, "maybe we could run to the store and get Christmas stockings to decorate. We could make one for the baby."

Josie sat up in a way that would usually have been very difficult with her baby bump, but the Christmas spirit strengthened her destroyed abdominals. "I would love that."

Ben sank to the floor behind Josie and pinched the back of her shirt, tugging excitedly at the fabric so Izzy couldn't see them freaking out. She reached behind her and grabbed his fingers to acknowledge their double win for the night. His large hand fully enveloped hers and squeezed tighter. She wanted to fall back against him and relish in the magical moment unfolding in their living room, no matter how awkward it got for everyone else.

Izzy returned to slipping ornament hooks through bulbs to string on the tree, the rainbow-colored lights illuminating her smile. The scent of cocoa paired nicely with the love that filled the room.

This was what Josie wanted—to bring her son home to this environment she loved so much, one that had saved her in her time of need. She wanted to give her little boy a father who adored him above all else and looked at him the way Ben looked at Izzy.

She wanted Ben.

He'd make such a wonderful father for her son, be a great example and provide him with love and care. They'd become a family, and she'd finally be able to settle, to move forward without the risk of everything being taken away from her. She wanted him by her side more now than she ever had in high school.

Sometimes, when he smiled at her, she wondered if there might be the slightest inkling of returned affection. Other times, she worried she'd read too much into things, and Ben was just being a good friend. Maybe one day, when they truly had their lives together, and well after the baby was born, she could pursue him intentionally. If he rejected her attempt, she might at least be on her own two feet enough to run far, far away and avoid any embarrassing repercussions.

"Next year will be fun with the baby." Izzy sighed as she hung another ornament.

Ben raised his mug. "Kids always make Christmas better."

Izzy's cheeks flushed a shade of pink, and she let her dark hair topple over her shoulder to hide her face.

Next year. To think she'd still be here in this exact place celebrating the holidays with this same group of people, plus her own child, seemed both wonderful and impossible. Motherhood might exhaust her to the point she had no energy left to pursue Ben or any man. So many options whirled around in limbo. If only she could pick and choose her favorites.

Kevin bent to whisper something to Izzy, then lunged from his saucer chair. "It's getting late. If you guys want to start on supper, I'll take Iz to get those stockings."

"And glitter." Izzy jumped from her spot on the floor, nearly knocking the ornaments from the tree.

Ben got up too. "I can take her, Kev—"

Kevin's stern expression stopped Ben short. "No. You stay and make Christmas nachos. I suck at them. Josie sucks at them. My Instant Pot sucks at them. It's all up to you, bro. I've got the kid."

"Not a kid," Izzy added.

"I've got the young, sophisticated, independent woman," Kevin corrected.

Ben's eyebrow lifted as he regarded his daughter. "You good to go with Kevin…alone? I know I've told you to avoid creepy people…"

"Hey, it's not like I'm luring her out with candy or anything. You're gonna go passing all your judgments."

Izzy shifted her weight. "I thought you said I could pick out something from the checkout lane."

"Whose side are you on?" Kevin threw his arms in the air and flashed Izzy a comically dirty look.

"Whatever, weirdo. We'll be back soon, Dad. Promise." Izzy shrugged as if she and Kevin did everything together, and this wasn't at all out of the ordinary. "It's just down the road."

Ben moved out of the way for Izzy to run and grab her coat. Kevin stepped over Josie, pretending to trip on her legs until she stretched to kick him in the rear.

The unusual pair rushed out the door, leaving Josie on the living room floor and Ben in the window watching them go.

"What alternate universe is this?" Ben asked.

Josie laughed. "I have no idea. Maybe aliens inhabited his body."

"That's the only explanation for whatever the hell we just witnessed." He wandered into the living room. "You want to assist with nacho-makin' or you gonna do prenatal yoga with that hippie woman?"

"Hey, that hippie yoga is keeping my blood pressure low enough that I can avoid bed rest, so shut it. And I'll brown the meat." Josie tried to sit forward, but her stomach got in the way this time. A sound squeaked out of her mouth as she rolled to the side. At least it came out of her mouth and not the other end.

"You know I can help you, right? Pretty sure you're supposed to be taking it easy." Ben bent down and slid his hands up Josie's arms, grabbing her elbows to lift her.

"I feel like a house already, Ben," Josie whined. "Two more months of this, and I might actually explode."

Her long-time girlhood crush lifting her from the floor because she resembled a turtle on its back proved only slightly mortifying. This was not how one should woo a man.

"Poor Josie." He smirked and leaned down far enough that his head almost touched hers. "You smell like the beach, though, so it's not all bad, eh?"

"That's my shampoo."

He'd smelled her hair. On *purpose*. Goose bumps prickled up her arms, and she had to look away to keep from noticing how his eyes sparkled when they caught the fluorescent Christmas lights. She thought only Disney princes did that.

She followed him like a lost puppy into the kitchen.

Ben opened the fridge, tossed Josie the package of hamburger, and moved on to collecting the remaining ingredients. They hadn't had nachos in at least a month, and Josie had already taken some heartburn meds to prepare for the dinner treat.

Ben moved his cutting board next to the stove where she stirred the ground beef. "I'm still trying to wrap my head around the fact that Izzy chose me over ice-skating. Can you believe that?"

"That was kind of awesome." Josie's smile broadened. "She's been like a different kid lately. Not the same girl I met in September."

"Oh, I know." Ben's knife tapped away as he chopped the onions and sniffled when they started to get to him. "I don't know what it is. The house? Age?" He cleared his throat. "You?"

"Huh?" Josie shifted and grabbed the pan handle to keep from knocking it off the stove.

Ben's head tilted in her direction, his cheeks flushed a little darker than before. "Well, when I lived in my apartment alone, she never wanted to come over. We spent all our weekends watching TV. She'd mostly just play on her tablet or something. Once I moved here, she still didn't want to come, and she really didn't like Kevin."

"Well, you know. Kevin's a special brand."

Ben laughed. "Once you moved in, though, she warmed up more."

"Yeah, but that's also when the Corn Dog Pact took effect." Josie used her spatula to point toward the fridge.

"Could you please accept the credit so Kevin doesn't? You know it'll go right to his head if he thinks the pact did this."

"I'm fairly certain it doesn't matter. He'll take credit for whatever, no matter if he had a hand in it or not." Josie popped a hot bite of cooked hamburger into her mouth to test the flavor, then added a dash of onion salt. "But seriously, you've knocked it out of the park in the dad department lately. You're kind of at the top of the life-pact leader board right now."

"Eh, I dunno. I don't feel like I'm doing enough. I had Door Dash deliver her favorite ice cream the night before a big test she was freaking out over. Was that stupid? Sugar-loading before a test?"

Josie clasped her hands over her heart and stared at her roommate. "You sent her ice cream before a test? Benny, you can marry me if you want to."

He snorted, knocking a good portion of the chopped onion off the cutting board. "I'll keep that in mind." When she caught his eye, he whipped his head toward his project.

"Ice cream for a test is precious. Seriously. All props go to you for her wanting to be here more," Josie said.

"Well, I gotta give Noel some credit, too, even if she tried to lure her away with a Groupon this weekend. She *has* helped get Izzy on board with coming more often." Ben scooped his chopped toppings into a bowl.

"What do you mean?" she asked.

The large baking sheet clanged when Ben pulled it from the

cupboard and dropped it on the counter. "Well, like, I paid child support and saw Izzy whenever the stars aligned, but when I told Noel I wanted to do more, she seemed way more open to it than I thought. I apologized. Did I tell you that? Told her I felt bad about leaving her to raise Izzy pretty much by herself and told her I was trying to make things better. I dunno. We talked for a long time about it."

"That's so great." The pureness of his confession made her chest swell. She never smiled so much while pushing hamburger around a pan.

"We're not getting back together or anything," Ben added quickly.

Josie shifted to face him, eyes wide now. "I didn't say you were."

"I know. It was just in case you thought that."

"I, um. No. I mean, she's married, and… Why would you think I would think that?" She should shove the spoon in her mouth to shut herself up. Couldn't she simply nod and pass him the hamburger like a grown woman?

"I don't know." Ben spun toward the counter to shuffle some tortilla chips around on the cookie sheet.

Josie grabbed a hot pad and moved the skillet closer to Ben for him to assemble his famous dish.

"You know something funny?" He cleared his throat but kept his gaze down. "Izzy didn't believe us that night when she asked if you were my girlfriend."

The wooden spoon crashed against the edge of the frying pan. Josie snatched it up and tried to resume her posture. "She didn't?"

"Nope."

"She never asked me about it again after that." *Girlfriend* suddenly sounded like a forbidden word that made the hair on the back of her neck stand at attention each time he said it.

Ben shrugged and started chopping vegetables again, a little more intensely this time. "Yeah, she had some theories…"

Josie continued to stare at his back for a second. "Did she ask you about the baby? Is that why you're being weird right now?"

Ben chuckled into his shoulder.

"Benjamin?" She pointed her spoon at him and waited.

"She asked me about the baby, yes. Don't hit me."

Josie's eyes grew as big as the frying pan she cooked with. "And you said…?"

"Well, I told her it wasn't mine, but I didn't think it was right to explain your whole situation, since it's not my story to tell. So I told her it was, I dunno, like a magical thing."

"A magical thing? Ben, she's eleven. She knows where babies come from."

"Unless maybe that's why she likes you?" His ears grew redder as he chuckled and tried to hide his face. "She thinks you're some sort of magical pregnant wonder."

"Well, she's not wrong. But so help me, if she asks me about any of that, I will scar her for life and let you deal with the consequences."

"Fair enough." He reached past Josie to preheat the oven. One hand settled on her hip as if to guide her gently out of the way.

Josie watched as he pressed the buttons, then his hand fell away from her when he slid across the floor in his stocking feet for the bags of chips. His new haircut accentuated the mother of all cowlicks on his forehead.

"So, uh." Ben tore open the chip bag and dumped the contents onto the oversize baking sheet. "Speaking of where babies come from…"

Her bones froze her in place as she waited for whatever could come out next.

But he didn't continue.

She peeked slowly over her shoulder to see him wrestling with the tomato on the chopping block. "Dude, are you gonna finish that incredibly weird sentence start, or what?"

"Huh?" Ben's face twisted when he seemed to remember what he'd started saying. "Ah, yup. Probably a terrible place to pause. I was, um, trying to get this stem off."

The giggles set in. She did nothing to stop it and hoped her bladder held up.

Ben pushed the pico ingredients around on his cutting board and tried to regain his composure. "This is a very serious question. You had to make it all awkward."

She took a deep breath and leaned against the kitchen counter to see him better. "It was an alarming setup. I'm sorry."

Ben shifted from his work, and his tomato-juiced fingers took hold of her bare arms under her T-shirt cuff as he held her in place. "I was going to say: speaking about where babies come from, have you talked to your ex about his part in your baby's life?"

"Oh." Yeah, that took a turn she wanted to steer right the heck out of. "No."

"Why not? You've got, what, four more months?"

"Two."

He released her to return his attention on the needy tomatoes. Her skin grew colder in his absence.

"That's even less. You need to talk to him," he said.

"I just… I don't want to, if I'm being honest." Grant had done nothing to prove himself a good husband, let alone a good father.

Ben chopped away. "I'm sure Noel didn't want to deal with me all these years either."

"It is so not the same situation. You can't—"

"Josie." Ben peeked over his shoulder, which stopped everything inside her brain. "In ten years, are you going to be standing next to me in this kitchen chopping tomatoes and feeling glad you let your son's father into his life, or are you going to be like me and Noel, fighting every day until one of you forms a life pact and tries to make it right?"

"Uh." Josie stared at the faux-wood flooring, expecting to see her heart lying there in front of her. "There's a lot to unpack there."

Grant hadn't reached out again. Maybe he didn't want to be part of the baby's life after all. She didn't want to be like Noel and Ben. She wanted peace for both her and her child. But did Ben also imply a possibility of her standing at his side in this kitchen ten years from now?

"I've been thinking about it a lot, I guess. I know it's none of my business." Ben held a handful of cheese above the tray, his fist clenched tight without releasing any of it as he stared at her. "I also wanted to see where you stand on the whole moving-out thing. Are you still thinking about that? I get leaving your parents' as a step in the independent direction, or whatever, but we're all adults here. It's not like this is some nonstop party zone where we're unable to handle adult responsibilities. We have recycle bins and everything."

Ben threw the shredded cheese at the chips, missing most of the target and messing up a good portion of the kitchen counter. A few pieces stuck to his hand. He stepped forward and flicked the rest at Josie.

With a surprised squeal, she snatched his hand from the air. She plucked some cheese shreds from her hair and threw it back at him. His backside hit the counter, pushing the nacho tray against the wall with a crash. Ben grabbed another handful of cheddar blend from the bag and sent it flying her way.

As the cheese fight ensued, Josie kept hold of Ben's wrist, getting close enough to drop a small handful down his shirt. He yelped and spun her around until her back pressed into his chest. With one hand wrapped above the baby bump, he tried to drop his own handful down her tank top.

"You're gonna hurt my baby," Josie whined through her laughter.

Ben hardly paused. "It's dairy. It's good for him."

The doorknob turned, and Ben's hand fell away. Josie pivoted slowly toward the door to see Kevin entering in slow motion as he peered into the kitchen. He ushered his smaller companion inside, and Izzy held up their purchased stockings and rushed into the living room to craft.

"Looks like nachos are going well," Kevin said with a waggle of his eyebrows. "Maybe a little too well."

"Just a minor cheese incident," Ben said. "None of your damn business."

"Uh-huh." Kevin clicked his tongue and tried not to smile. "Josie, there's some cheese incident on your chest. Better work that out."

"Thanks." Josie's cheeks warmed when she looked down and saw how much of the shredded goodness had landed in her cleavage. With her back to Ben, she shook out what she could.

Ben cleared his throat, drawing her attention. "Yeah, I can clean this up if you want to go craft."

"I don't mind helping. I'll get—"

"No, it's okay. I'm sure Izzy will want your help with the stockings anyway." He readjusted the nacho tray and reached for the cheese bag once more. "Just think about what I said earlier."

Which part? He'd said so many things, then held her against his chest and filled her bra with cheese.

It had been a confusing night.

Ben winked over his shoulder as she slowly backed out of the room.

She definitely wanted to stand next to him in this kitchen ten years from now. He wanted her to fight for her future, and her son's, the way he'd fought for Izzy recently.

Her fingers brushed over her cheese-covered baby bump. So many things had gone horribly wrong on this journey toward improving her life. But many things had also gone right.

Josie plucked a cheese shred off her bosom and ate it as the Corn

Dog Pact taunted her from the fridge. The third point had always been her nemesis:

> 3. Love: Find love. Get over our pasts. Do right by the littles that depend on us.

Those last two pact lines came at a high cost, but everything did these days. She had to do right by her little, and the one she hoped to find love *with* had urged her on in that.

To move on from this point, she had to push past this daunting hurdle. It all came down to how much she'd risk for her son—and for Ben.

As she walked to the living room to glitterize stockings, she pulled her phone from her pocket and drafted a message to Grant.

28

New Year's Toast

"I KNOW WE SAID no gifts, but I couldn't resist." Kevin placed two poorly wrapped packages in front of his friends. The bow on top of Josie's toppled to the carpet when the paper clip holding it in place shifted.

After spending the holidays with their respective families, tending to adult responsibilities, and work for the guys, the three roommates finally carved out a special New Year's/Christmas party time just for them. They'd prepared a grand feast of frozen potato skins, shrimp cocktail, mozzarella sticks, and Josie's mother's recipe for cheesy sausage on tiny rye-bread slices, lovingly called "shit on a shingle."

Now, with full bellies that hurt from excess giggling over stupid jokes, the trio sat on their picnic blanket on the living room floor and waited for midnight when their Christmas celebration officially ended and the new year began.

"Yeah, we said no gifts. Hence why I didn't get you anything." Ben picked up the box and shook it like a curious child.

"It's not much, but I saw them during a late-night internet browse and thought of you. Consider these motivational expenses. Most likely tax-deductible on my part." Kevin urged them to get to opening, as he inched forward to see what they'd gotten, like he didn't already know.

Curiosity drove Josie to tear the crumpled snowman paper, but she couldn't keep her stink eye off Kevin. She hadn't gotten him a gift either. They really had agreed they wouldn't exchange gifts this year due to their financial crisis and attempt at bettering themselves. She should have known Kevin would break the rules. He'd never been good at following them in any capacity.

She lifted the lid on the tiny black cardboard box and pulled the square cotton sheet to the side to reveal maybe the last thing she would have expected.

"Are these corn dog earrings?" Josie laughed when she emptied them into her hand to study the jewelry. One itty-bitty corn dog had a streak of mustard down the front, and the other had ketchup. They looked exactly like the food, complete with wooden sticks poking out the bottom.

"The one has a little bite out of it. Isn't that hilarious?" Kevin slapped his knee.

Beside Josie, Ben held up a black T-shirt, decorated only with a single, giant corn dog.

"I'm sensing a theme," Ben said.

"You should be." Kevin reached for his eggnog—a sight that never ceased to make Josie gag a little. "I thought maybe if the two of you each had a little corn-dog-ish token, it might help you stay on the right track this year."

Of course Kevin had turned their holiday celebration into another one of his motivational speeches/family meetings. Another thing Josie should have seen coming.

Every year, she made a list of hopeful resolutions in her phone notes. And ironically, every year, she failed them. There didn't seem to be much point in making a separate list of goals for New Year's now when Kevin had already hung one on the refrigerator.

"Well, thanks," Josie said. "These are actually really cute."

Her students would definitely enjoy these quirky little trinkets if she ever wore them on a school day. It'd probably earn her some kind of a weird nickname she'd carry with her for the duration of her time with Clarkson High. Poor Mrs. Gillman used a cow-print background for a lesson at the beginning of the year, and not a day went by when a student didn't use some legend-dairy cow pun in her cowculus class.

"And inspirational." Kevin gestured to Ben's shirt. "Bet you'll ace your first test in that."

Ben groaned. "Don't remind me. I've already second-guessed this degree six hundred times, and I haven't even had my first class yet."

"Aw, Benny. It'll be great. Don't doubt yourself." For being the most reluctant participant in the Corn Dog Pact, Ben had taken some of the biggest leaps in the group. Josie envied him in so many ways for it. Every step forward she took seemed to come with a step back. "Did everything go okay for Christmas with Izzy?"

Kevin and Josie had opted to leave the house while Ben and his daughter celebrated the season for a few hours by themselves. Josie sure would have loved to be a fly on the wall, though. Ben had actually seemed nervous to host Izzy totally alone, even though their visits had gotten increasingly better with each weekend.

"It went really well." Ben's eyes lit with his growing smile. He had always loved his daughter, but his passion for fatherhood had really come to light lately. "She liked her gifts, but it's kind of hard with her birthday coming up in a couple weeks and having two gift-giving holidays so close together, you know? The pressure is up a notch."

"Yeah, that makes it tough, but I'm sure she won't care what you get her. She's seemed so much happier lately when she's here." Josie had come to enjoy her weekends with Izzy, too, even on those freaky mornings when she'd wake up to loud music on the other half of the loft and a nonchalant Izzy asking if Josie wanted to get breakfast with them *since she was up*.

Kevin shoved the empty shrimp platter out of his way to prop himself up on a beanbag chair. "So what are you going to get her? It's gotta be epic. She's turning twelve, Ben. *Twelve.*"

"Don't remind me. Nothing is going to prepare me for the teen years, I swear, and I need to make the most of this last year of *not-teen years.*" He wadded the shirt in his hands, face scrunching as he processed his thoughts aloud. "I'm thinking about taking her away for a weekend. Just the two of us. I'd have to talk to Noel about it, but Iz and I have never gone on a trip together. Maybe since things are going a little better, she might not totally hate it?"

Josie's mouth went dry enough to keep her from expressing her love for this idea. Watching Ben heal his relationship with Izzy had become medicine for Josie's soul. In the moments when life got her down or she didn't know how she might press on, she looked to Ben for inspiration. Even now, as he flashed a crooked grin in her direction, she felt peace in her heart—and a little ootz in her stomach.

"Can I come?" Kevin asked.

"On my one-on-one weekend away with my daughter? No." Ben's finger guns wounded Kevin deeply from the looks of it.

Josie laughed. "For real, though, I think that is a supersweet gift. I know Izzy will really love that."

"I won't plan it for *the* weekend, I promise. I'll just wait until after her birthday when I get a chance to celebrate with her."

At the mention of *the* weekend, the nausea increased. In less than a week, Josie and her cucumber-sized baby had a meeting with Grant. After she'd texted him and asked if they could try again and talk more civilly this time, he agreed. No mothers involved. No surprises. Just the two of them calmly sitting across from each other in a public coffee shop. She planned to *invite* him into their baby's life. The idea of it all still terrified her.

In the ultimate display of moral support, Ben had offered to drive her, and Kevin wouldn't be left behind on something so major.

With one of them on either side, making a run for it would be a whole lot harder.

"You ready for that little road trip, JoJo?" Kevin reached for the eggnog again. They should have just given him a straw to stick in the bottle because no one else wanted to touch that crap with a ten-foot pole.

"Nothing in the world can make me ready for that, Kev. We're going to wing it and hope I don't die of a heart attack in the process." Six days gave her entirely too much time to think of what she wanted to say and how much she wanted to back out. Sitting face-to-face with an estranged husband and agreeing to part with her son for days at a time was some next-level torture.

From the kitchen, Kevin's party mix played Pink's "Raise Your Glass" for the fourth time since they'd begun their celebration. It transported her back to the start of her college years, right before she met Grant and right after she'd parted with Kevin and Ben at graduation—a sad goodbye and an even sadder hello. She just didn't know it then.

"Trust me when I tell you you're going to feel better when this is over." Ben lay back on his elbows and flashed an adorable grin. "But, like, it is safe for us to make this drive, right? If we need to, we can force his ass to come to you."

Josie laughed. "No, that's fine. Thanks for the offer, though. Doc says I'm good to travel, so long as I'm not hopping on a plane or something. My BP has been better, luckily, and Little Dude is in good shape. I definitely prefer to go to Grant so it's easier to run away if I want to. Plus, a longish drive like this will be good practice for the upcoming wedding of the century." Another blessed event she just couldn't *wait* to go to.

"So much coming up. All hard but good stuff that chips away at the CDP." Kevin raised his plastic cup, then bolted upright. "We should toast this moment! I totally meant to do that tonight but almost forgot. Probably the eggnog's fault, am I right? Be right back."

Kevin stumbled a couple times on his way up and ran to the kitchen.

"I'm scared," Josie said.

"Same." Ben strained to see past the dining room and into the kitchen.

Their anticipation only lasted a few minutes before Kevin rounded the corner. Instead of glasses for toasting, he held a single paper plate. When he placed it in the middle of their huddle, Josie dropped her face into her hands.

"You made actual toast?" Ben snatched up a piece as if to double-check the claim.

Kevin took a slice too. "Well, Josie can't have champagne, so this seemed like the next best thing. Didn't want to leave her out of this."

"Couldn't do sparkling grape juice or literally any other liquid?" Josie's fingers shook from laughing, which sent crumbs spilling down the front of her ugly Christmas sweater.

"Obviously not. Just hoist the toast. Let's do this. I'll say all the words." Kevin held his toast higher than the others and cleared his throat. "To a new and better year. One where we destroy our pact goals, bring a new baby into the world, and present ourselves as legit adults in this cruel, cruel world."

Ben began lowering his arm. "So, do we take a bite or—"

"I'm not done. Shut up." Kevin sat up even taller. "May this be the year Mandy falls in love with me all over again, and we can live happily ever after and do double dates and stuff. Amen."

Double dates and stuff? Josie kept her gaze on the plain, unbuttered toast in her hand rather than risking eye contact with Ben. Drunk Kevin had better not elaborate, lest the rest of the evening get wildly uncomfortable.

"Um, amen," Josie repeated.

"Amen?" Ben's voice cracked. "Or cheers. Whatever."

Kevin dropped his partially eaten toast onto the paper plate and clapped his hands together. "Now, you two can arm wrestle to see who gets to kiss me at midnight."

29

A Latte Harder Than She Thought

THE CAR ROLLED INTO a parking spot outside the Coffee Bean and came to a stop. Rather than grabbing the handle to get out, Josie reclined her chair and laid herself flat, her headrest practically landing in Kevin's lap behind her. He reached forward and began massaging her shoulders the way a trainer might do for a boxer before a match.

"You got this, kiddo. You're gonna get in there. You're gonna be strong. You're gonna make shit happen."

In the driver's seat, Ben turned the radio off and leaned over on the center console. "Get yourself a pastry and something extra strong to drink. We'll stay here, and you can text an SOS if you need to."

"I feel bad you guys are going to be sitting out here. What if it takes a long time?" Josie dropped her arm across her face.

"It's Saturday. We have literally nowhere else to be, and we can stream *Flip or Flop* off the Wi-Fi," Kevin said.

They'd already driven almost three hours to deliver her to this coffee shop, and she hated asking more from them, especially when she didn't know what lay in store for her inside. "I don't want to go in."

Ben lifted Josie's arm and bent closer to meet her gaze. "Just go get it over with. It's like a Band-Aid; you gotta rip it right off. Then, when you're done, we'll go home, put on sweatpants, and make a blanket fort if we have to."

"Can we skip right to that?" Crawling into a blanket fort with Ben sounded infinitely better than sitting face-to-face with an ex and trying to arrange a plan for their unborn son.

Kevin laid his cheek against Josie's forehead, and Ben gave her wrist a squeeze.

"Trust me on this. Don't wait ten years." Ben spoke with the gravity of a man who'd made such a mistake himself.

Josie returned her seat to the upright position and grabbed her purse from the floor. She couldn't look at the guys as she left them. The tears sat too close to the surface.

She pulled her coat closed across her chest and entered the building. A warm gust of air and the fresh scent of brewed coffee swept over her. Before she searched for Grant, she headed straight to the counter to follow Ben's orders: asking the barista for a cherry Danish and a snickerdoodle latte.

When she finally held the treats in hand, she sucked in a deep breath and faced the patrons. In the far corner near the fireplace, Grant sat at a round metal table, his fingers grasping a paper coffee mug and his eyes locked on her.

Josie's feet moved as if stuck in wet cement, but she made it across the room and put her food on the table without spilling any of her latte. When was the last time she'd met Grant in an atmosphere like this? Seven or eight months ago, it would have been nothing to go to dinner with him. Now, her nerves practically ate her alive.

"Hey," he said.

"Hi," she answered. Off to an impressive start.

"How was the drive?" Grant's stiff voice matched his even stiffer shirt collar. He swirled the plastic stick around in his mug like a machine set on autopilot. "It snowed here this morning."

The pastry went down like a marble when she swallowed. They'd already resorted to talking about the weather. It really was all over for them, leaving Josie with a mix of both exhaustion and relief.

"The drive was fine." She took a long sip of her latte.

"Forgive your mom yet?" Grant tore off a piece of his bagel.

Now, that made her smile. "'Forgive' is a strong word, but we are speaking now. I told her she's still allowed to be with me during delivery, but that could change if she tries to surprise me like that again." She might need to get Ella on standby just in case her mother went rogue again. "Did your mom forgive *you*?"

His forehead creased. "Nope. Doubt she ever will."

"Good." Josie smirked and took another bite. If his mother still wanted to rub his face in what he did forever and ever, well then, so be it. At least the two moms were speaking to each other again. Whether they were as friendly as they were pre-divorce, Josie had no idea, but she definitely didn't feel like asking.

A television in the shop's corner played a morning talk show. Beside them, two girlfriends chatted about their week. Josie and Grant ate in silence, sipping their beverages and avoiding eye contact.

Josie glanced out the window to the parking lot. She found Ben's Malibu parked near the lamppost and tried to take strength from its presence. The two faces peeking out the rear window kind of threw her off, though.

Ben flashed a thumbs-up. He'd urged her not to wait ten years to make things right the way he had. Izzy needed her daddy. Her baby boy needed his too.

"Grant." She could do this. "I don't want to waste your time, but I asked you here for a very specific reason." Her throat went dry.

He set his bagel down on the plate and ran a napkin across his mouth. "Is it about the divorce?"

"No, everything is still moving forward with that." She'd signed all she needed to sign. They were almost done. Finished. Forever.

"Right. I told my lawyer you'd asked to meet with me today. He said a lot of women rescind divorce filings or draw things out when a baby is involved."

Yep, she wanted to flip the table.

"Well, you can tell your lawyer that's not why I'm here because we are never getting back together." She clenched her fist in her lap to keep from bursting out in a Taylor Swift song or elaborating on exactly how much she did not want their relationship to continue. The more time that passed between their marriage and separation, the more her eyes opened to what had happened between them and for how long that poison had seeped into their relationship. He'd spent more time on his phone than with her. He hadn't laughed at her jokes, hadn't asked about her day. He'd made her feel like she wasn't enough, all the while she continued to pull away from him, diving deeper into her work and spending more time than necessary at the gym/library/Target—wherever she knew he wouldn't be.

They both deserved better. He wanted to do life with someone else, and now so did she.

"Right." Grant tapped his plastic straw against the bottom of his iced coffee cup.

Knowing she felt this way about sharing their child and moving on in life was one thing; saying it out loud in front of him was a whole other. She should text Ben to fire up the car so she could jump in on the run and get away. Snatching up her baby and leaving the country with an alternate identity had to be easier than this.

"Look." Josie flattened her hands on the table and took a deep breath. "We obviously didn't end well, and we clearly aren't a fit for the future. But we have a child. Both of us. He'll be here in a month, so we have some decisions to make."

"I know you don't want us around him, but that's not—"

"Shut up, Grant. Let me finish." Her blood pressure couldn't possibly be in a good place today. She tore another chunk of pastry and shoved it in her mouth. Her gaze drifted off toward the Malibu to seek out her support system, but they weren't in the car.

Oh lordy. She couldn't search the coffee shop for them and make it obvious. She had to get this out and over with.

"I was mad. *Am* mad. But this baby comes first, and he needs his father." The words were burrs on her tongue. "I want you to be part of his life. I want him to know you and spend time with you."

Grant didn't speak for a long moment, his focus totally taken with a smudge of cream cheese on his plate, and then, "Wow. I was not expecting this."

"Is it what you want, though?"

He could always say no. Maybe he really didn't want to be a father, and she could keep her son safely under her wing for always. Maybe the only purpose of this conversation was to give her an outlet to prove her newfound strength and—

"Yes. I want that," he said.

Damn.

But also good. "I don't know if you want to hash out all the details now, but Karleen says if we can get a visitation schedule in writing, it'll make everything a lot smoother with the divorce."

The words seemed so harsh.

"My lawyer said the same thing, though he suggested I take you to court over custody."

"Well, I hope your lawyer gets hit by a bus."

Karleen had warned her of exactly that. If she hadn't made progress on the pact or reached out to Grant with an olive branch, she might have found herself in a nasty custody battle.

Grant chuckled, which was…new. "Yeah, he's kind of ruthless. I didn't want to do that. I know this whole thing is my fault, but I don't want to be left out of our kid's life forever, you know? I just didn't know how to bring it up…*nicely.*"

"Right." Thank God he hadn't just taken her to court over it. She'd pulled herself upright after he cheated, but if he'd forcibly come for their child? "Thanks for not doing that."

Grant wrapped his hand around his to-go cup and tapped it to the table once. "I really am sorry about all this. You know that, right? It is what it is, and there's nothing I can do now, but…" He shook his head. "You don't have to sit here with me and talk this all out. Just knowing the door's open to communication is enough for now."

She had nothing else to say. They used to spend hours talking on the phone in college, staying up all night to discuss their hopes and dreams. Now, a few sentences exchanged had exhausted her on every level. At least he understood that.

"Thank you." She covered the rest of her pastry in her napkin to take with her, not about to waste such a glorious, frosting-full treat; then she planned to casually make a run for it. "I'll send updates as we get closer to the due date, and we'll gather some ideas for an official visiting schedule."

"That would be nice." Grant stood and wiped his palms on his pants, looking his ex-in-progress-wife over.

What was the proper farewell in these instances? She refused to hug him. No cheek kisses. A handshake might be more awkward than anything else. High five?

He wet his lips and continued, "Um, well, I'm glad you came up here. I was nervous about today, but this means a lot, Josie. Seriously."

"I was also dreading this day passionately and contemplated bailing multiple times, but I'm glad I came too." Josie got up and looped her purse over her shoulder.

Grant glanced over the coffee shop and leaned in a little closer. "Can I walk you to your car?"

"Huh?" The abrupt question made her trip over the leg of her chair. She righted herself on the tabletop without causing too much of a scene.

His brow furrowed as he looked past her. "Not to freak you out, but there're these two creepy guys in the corner that have been staring at you nonstop since they came in. I want to make sure you get out of here safely."

Josie slapped her palm to her forehead. She pivoted slowly toward the direction of Grant's gaze and found Kevin and Ben flustered, maneuvering their table decor and holding up their drinks to appear as nonchalant as possible.

"Yeah, it won't do any good. I'm already going home with those weirdos. They're my roommates, and they drove me here since I barely fit behind a steering wheel anymore."

"Roommates?" Grant's eyes widened.

Josie smirked. "Old friends from high school. We moved in together to cut costs and fix our lives and yada-yada. You can thank the guy in the orange hoodie for talking me into coming here today. He's got a daughter and an ex all of his own."

"Oh." Grant offered a half-hearted salute in the guys' direction. "Okay then."

"Yep." Josie buttoned the top button on her coat—the only one that still fastened. "Well, I guess that's that."

"I'll be seeing you." He forced a quick smile and headed for the door, this time avoiding eye contact with the men in the opposite corner.

Like hawks swooping in for a meal, Kevin and Ben flanked her on either side, smooshing her in a hug.

"Don't squeeze the baby out," she mumbled between them.

Ben let go first but stayed close enough to whisper, "I'm proud of you." Those four words sent a tingle down her spine. The way he smiled erased the image of Grant sitting across from her and the reminder of all the hurt he'd caused every time she looked into his eyes. In Ben's gaze, she saw hope. Freedom.

"You're all grown up now, JoJo." Kevin pulled her toward the front of the coffee shop. "Now go hit the restroom before we blow this chicken coop. I don't want to stop fifty times like we did on the way here."

"It was three. Stop being so dramatic." Josie linked her arms through each of theirs. She'd try to put into words what their encouragement meant to her later. For now, she'd enjoy this brand-new feeling of tranquility.

30

A Whale of a Burrito

"How much longer?" Ben paced by the front door, pausing often to peek through the blinds.

"I don't know, dude. You made the plans." Josie added an extra dab of icing to the cake to cover the smudged spot where her stomach had bumped against it. Hopefully everybody understood the image was supposed to be a whale and not a burrito with a tail.

Ella's text tone chimed on the countertop: Is it a blue banana with eyes?

A whale! I even labeled the dang picture! That'd teach her to send photos of her baked goods in the future.

Ella: :-P Well, tell your daughter I said Happy Birthday. :D

This time, Josie just shook her head rather than denying her friend's claim. Izzy had become part of her family, even if in an unorthodox way. Treating her like a young friend—maybe daughter-like—didn't seem all that foreign anymore.

"They're two minutes late." The anxious father had barely managed to get the pizza rolls in the oven and the baking utensils in the dishwasher in the past half hour. Even though his relationship with Izzy had greatly improved over the past few months, the nerves still ran high. And today he meant to present his daughter with a mini vacation to celebrate turning the big one-two. Her last trip around the sun before the teen years. Josie loved getting to be a part of it.

"They're here." Ben bounced on his heels and pressed his cheek to the windowsill.

Footsteps tapped across the porch, but Ben threw open the door before anybody had to knock.

"My birthday girl," Ben exclaimed and reached forward to snatch Izzy into his arms.

"Dad, my birthday was on Tuesday." She giggled into his chest and tossed her bag into the house.

Ben released her and stepped aside so that both Izzy and her mother could enter. "I know, but I didn't get to see you Tuesday, so today is birthday two-point-o."

Noel smiled and readjusted her purse strap over her arm. Josie's entire body froze across the room, almost as though Noel might not see her if she held still enough. Somehow, she'd managed to avoid every other encounter with Ben's ex up to this point. Today, there was no dodging it.

"You're going to drop her off Sunday night, correct?" Noel spoke almost cryptically—which made sense. She knew about the surprise trip; Izzy didn't. "And she's got homework too. Don't let her forget about that."

"We'll get it done. No worries. And I'll call you when we're on our way back Sunday." Ben's attention focused on his daughter as she fumbled through her bag to gather another birthday gift she wanted to show him. That left the two women standing awkwardly a room's distance apart, avoiding eye contact until they had no other choice.

Noel smiled and offered a slight wave toward the kitchen, where Josie used the countertop to keep her balance.

"Hi." Josie took a few steps around the counter into the dining room. "I'm Josie. I don't think we've officially met in our adult lives." High school only gave them brief interactions, and Josie's jealousy had kept her from making any attempt to form a relationship with Noel.

"Noel. It's nice to meet you. I've heard good things." Noel nodded toward her daughter, but extended a hand for Josie to take.

It was weird. So much had changed in their situations. Yet, so much hadn't changed. Josie still found herself crushing on Ben. Noel was still insanely gorgeous. But the playing field had jumped to a whole new level.

"I've got a book report, Josie. I told Mom you could help me with it since you've been teaching English." Izzy gave her book bag a little kick with her foot to demonstrate her lack of enthusiasm over the project. "It's on *Treasure Island.*"

"You're in luck. Pirates are my specialty." Josie winked, her heart picking up speed. Somehow, she'd become an active part of this. Like Ben's live-in girlfriend or something—the kind that coparented with his daughter's real mother, did homework, made plans. Except the *girlfriend* part hadn't even happened. Though, it sure would be nice…

Noel reached forward and pulled Izzy into a hug. "Have fun this weekend. I'll see you Sunday. Love you."

"Love you too." Izzy hugged her mother back and waved goodbye as Noel bid the others farewell and left.

The night-and-day difference a few months had brought really rang strong in that moment. Nobody stomped up the stairs to avoid interaction. No one screamed or accused.

Ben rubbed his hands together and grinned even wider. "All right. We'll tackle the book report in a minute, but first things first!"

"We don't have to do homework *now*. We have all weekend. It's only Fri—"

"There's a reason we have to do it now. Hang on." Ben motioned for Josie to take her position, and she hustled back to the kitchen to light the candles on the whale cake.

Izzy squinted her skepticism as she waited in the dining room and shifted her gaze between Josie and her father. Nothing like a surprise party thrown by two people. Kevin would have joined, but he had signed himself up to give blood at the hospital in hopes of running into Mandy. He'd left a gift wrapped in leftover Christmas paper. Unsure what to get a young woman of Izzy's age, Kevin had gone through Walmart's beauty aisle and gathered what had to be one of every nail polish color and lined them up in a shoebox. If Izzy didn't like them, Josie had no qualms about helping herself to the collection.

Josie carefully picked up the lit cake and began singing the birthday song, Ben's voice chiming in to create one of the most off-key duets of all time. They needed Kevin for a solid soprano section.

As much as she tried to feign indifference to the act, Izzy couldn't fight the smile for long. She began laughing when she saw the hand-drawn whale atop the cherry chip cake. It took her a moment to blow out the candles when she couldn't get it together.

"Is that a whale?" she asked.

"Obviously. I don't know what else it would be." Josie crossed her arms over her chest and forced her most offended pose.

Izzy giggled a little harder. "It looks like a tube with a face."

Damn it. "Art isn't my strong suit. Okay? It's the best I could do."

"Well, thanks. It is kind of cute. You should go on *Nailed It.*" She dabbed her finger into the icing around the base for a sample. "Do we at least get to eat cake before you guys force me into dumb book reports?"

With a wink, Josie began cutting out a large slice, while Ben gathered the package he'd gotten Izzy and anxiously paced behind her chair once more. As much as he'd talked about giving this gift, Josie couldn't believe he hadn't met Izzy in the driveway with it. There was still the apprehension of how Izzy would respond to the proposition of going away alone with her father for the weekend, but

Ben seemed so hopeful. If Izzy declined, Josie didn't know how she'd help Ben pick up the pieces after that.

"There's a reason I want you getting your homework done now, Iz." Ben took a seat beside his daughter and twisted his chair to face her full on. "I got you something."

Izzy snatched up the package and looked it over. Ben had wrapped the getaway info, plus aquarium tickets in a small box that wouldn't fit much else. The girl had to be curious about what he could have possibly hidden in there.

"Can I open it now?" she asked.

"Yeah." He leaned forward as if to see through the wrapping and Izzy's reaction.

Izzy backed up slightly. "Why are you acting so weird?"

"I'm not."

"You literally are." She tore a small piece of the wrapping but kept her gaze on her dad. "Is this a gag gift?"

Josie couldn't help but chuckle. At least it reminded her to breathe again since she realized she'd held her breath anticipating Izzy's reaction.

"Not a gag." Ben's expression softened. "Just open it so we can discuss."

"So weird, Dad." Izzy tore off the rest of the paper and slowly opened the lid like she hadn't totally believed her father told the truth about it not being some sort of prank. Her head cocked as she studied the printed tickets in her hand. "Is this the aquarium with the belugas? The one in Chicago? Are we going?"

Her voice squeaked a little more with each rapid-fire question. Ben inched closer in his seat and cleared his throat. This was it. The big moment.

"That's the one," he said. "I know you've mentioned wanting to see those whales, and I wondered if you'd want to go away with me this weekend to see them. We'll get a hotel, visit the aquarium, and get some deep dish and Cheesecake Factory. Just kind of have a birthday weekend together."

Izzy seemed to do the math with the two tickets and turned to Josie. "Aren't you coming?"

Oh no. Ben had mentioned Izzy's attitude changing since Josie's arrival, but if Izzy's positivity switch was contingent upon Josie's presence, they could be in big trouble here.

"No, I'm not able to join you this weekend." Walking around downtown Chicago didn't sound terribly appealing at this level of pregnancy. She also had a doctor's appointment in the morning, which made for a decent enough excuse to keep from tagging along, leaving the father and daughter to bond solo. "It'll just be you and your dad."

"Oh." Izzy lowered the tickets into her lap. "Does Mom know?"

Ben swallowed hard, though he couldn't do much to hide the panic on his face. Was Izzy happy about this trip? Confused? Upset? Who freakin' knew? They needed answers! Josie bit her lip to keep the questions from flying out of her mouth.

"Yeah, we talked about it, and she said it was fine if we went." He wiped his brow where sweat was beginning to bead. "Are you, um. I mean, do you *want* to go?"

Izzy slid her chair backwards and placed the tickets gently on the table. While the action seemed to happen in slow motion, what came next went so fast that Josie thought for sure there was a glitch in the matrix somewhere. Izzy leapt into Ben's lap, throwing her arms around him. His gaze met Josie's, his surprise clear. He placed his hands gently on Izzy's back as if she were made of porcelain. His head bowed until his face practically buried in Izzy's thick black hair.

Josie's eyes welled with tears, and she snatched up a napkin from the table, trying hard not to sniffle loud enough that the sound might destroy this precious moment.

"This is the best gift ever," Izzy whispered so quietly Josie almost didn't hear it from her position.

My gosh was she glad she'd stuck around for this. She couldn't wait to tell Kevin all about it when he finally got home later.

"I'm glad you like it. It's been hard keeping it a secret," Ben said when Izzy finally pulled away.

Izzy sat back in the afterglow of receiving such a gift. "I wish you could come with us, though, Josie. Since you used to live in Chicago, you could show us around, and we could get ice cream."

"We'll just have to save our ice cream date for your next visit." During a nonpregnant phase, Josie might have jumped at the opportunity to join them. Izzy's enthusiasm was certainly contagious.

Josie reached to slice off another piece of cake for herself but felt Ben's gaze on her. He offered a quick smile and patted Izzy on the back.

"Maybe next time Josie and the baby can come along. Make it a family affair." He winked, which sent a little shiver through Josie's veins.

In these moments, she wasn't thirty years old. She didn't have an ex-husband or an unborn child, financial despair or unemployment drama. None of it. Ben's quirked little grin sent her back in time to high school. That first class of the day when she rounded the corner and saw his wonderful smile. Some days, it was the only thing that got her out of bed.

And now she lived with him. She saw him every day, helped with his daughter, wrote him silly notes on the bull sheet. Now he suggested they take their respective children and go away together. One day.

She had no words. Just a shy smile and nod. Hopefully he understood.

"So when do we leave?" Izzy's question broke through the fog and drew Josie back to reality.

Ben took a deep breath that seemed to inflate his entire body. "As soon as your book report is done, I guess."

Izzy groaned. "How am I supposed to do any homework knowing we're about to see my whales?"

Josie laughed, drying up any lingering tears in her eyes.

This beautiful interaction between father and daughter had filled the room with so much hope. In the future, she and her son have a moment like this too. Well, not exactly like this. Ben had been working so hard to mend the relationship with Izzy. These tween years were tough, which didn't make it any easier on him. But somehow, he'd gotten this far. Izzy had said yes, and that yes meant so many things at once.

"I realize now that might have been a mistake. Probably should have waited until after we did the book report." Despite his words, Ben still beamed. "Josie, we're going to need your help more than originally expected."

"I'll just have to use my teaching skills to crack the whip on the two of you." She pulled out the chair on the other side of Izzy and wrapped the girl in a side hug. "Let's eat cake, tackle these pirates, and get the two of you on the road."

31

Together Like Peanut Butter and Jelly

STARBUCKS BREWED STRONG COFFEE; teachers brewed it stronger. How else could they keep up with hundreds of bullheaded, energetic students?

"I still feel like I'm cheating somehow by being here." Ella tore open her snack cake and examined the room.

Josie chuckled. "I don't think you're breaking any rules by coming to the high school for lunch. What are they going to do? Give you detention?"

"That wouldn't be too bad today. My students are so wound up." Ella dumped the dessert from her lunch pail and hummed a delighted tune. "I'm so glad I packed an extra snack cake."

"Gave up on the diet, huh?" Josie asked.

Ella glared. "It's about moderation. I'm having two instead of three. Plus, stressful days don't count when dieting."

"Oh, right. I feel you, though. My students are nuts this week too. Gotta love that February cabin fever." Josie finished stuffing salty potato chips into her peanut butter and jelly sandwich and took the first crunchy bite. With a mouthful, she continued. "It's hell to get them to care about anything right now."

"You getting excited for the wedding?" Ella nudged Josie with her elbow.

Josie scoffed. "Why, oh, why did my brother plan his wedding in the dead of winter?"

"Least it's something to do. I've been so bored lately."

The copy machine hummed in the corner, printing off announcements and fundraising flyers. None of those were terribly exciting either. They'd reached the phase of winter where the days were long and the boredom flourished.

"Well, this should be plenty entertaining. I've heard my dad mumble on more than one occasion he's glad he doesn't have to pay for it. Roses of every color, a small orchestra for the reception, filet mignon on the menu. My bargain-bin dress may not be good enough."

"And then they're honeymooning in Belize? My Mall of America honeymoon suddenly seems so sad…"

Josie chuckled. "That's what I thought about Florida."

"You think you're going to make it?" Ella wiped her mouth with a napkin and nodded toward Josie's stomach.

"Oh, yeah. This kid is snug as a bug in there." Josie rubbed her baby bump. Her abdomen had grown harder and harder as time went on. Sometimes, she could even feel body parts sticking out. She'd spent many recent nights chasing a little heel across her belly button. "Dr. Mallory said I'm not dilated or effaced at all, and since my blood pressure hasn't gotten any higher, she said I can go if I sit around most of the time. Which is pretty much all I planned to do anyway."

"No 'Cha-Cha Slide' for you, then?" Ella asked.

"Nope. Gonna have to skip that one. Though I'm getting a little more paranoid by the day that my water is going to break in a public place. Line dancing might be the perfect way to make that happen."

Ella raised her snack cake. "I remember that feeling. Doctor had to break mine every time, though, so don't stress it too much."

"And you guys are heading up on Thursday and staying at the

hotel?" The best part of Will and Emily throwing a massive wedding was that they invited *everyone*. Since Ella practically grew up at their house through infinite sleepovers, Will thought to include her on the guest list. At least Josie wouldn't have to face the entire weekend alone.

Ella tapped her pop can on the tabletop as she sighed. "Yeah. We thought it'd be fun to stay the extra night, let the kids swim, and get away for a bit. It's been a long winter. We're all cranky."

"The kids will love that. My parents are going up early too. I think they're leaving tomorrow. I'll be there Friday afternoon. Mom insists I ride up with Aunt Cayla instead of trying to drive myself. She's going to swing through town and pick me up. Rehearsal dinner is at seven, so I'll get there about seven thirty if she's as speedy as usual." Josie chugged the last few sips of her water.

"That sounds about right." Ella chuckled. "You bringing either of the guys?"

Josie scrunched up her nose. "I'm pretty sure they can't behave themselves long enough to attend such a fancy event. Though that's not stopping them from begging to come. They want to meet my family. My fault. I've sorta portrayed them as a fun sideshow, I think."

Ella's gaze shifted to the ceiling tiles to avoid eye contact. "Maaaybe you should take Ben at least."

If Josie could eliminate the questions from her family and the awkwardness of running off with Ben alone for an entire weekend, the image of cozying up with him by the resort's fireplace or dancing with him during the reception might have made her swoon. "Yeah, what guy wouldn't want to go away for a romantic weekend with a platonic pregnant friend? I wake myself up snoring, can't tie my own shoelaces, and sometimes fart when I walk."

Ella covered her mouth to keep the soda from spewing across the table. She reached over and whacked Josie with her free hand. "She's beauty, and she's grace."

"This looks like a fun way to spend lunch," someone said from the doorway. Gale Abnor's arms crossed over her chest and a grin was plastered to her face. "I'm so sorry to interrupt, but I wanted to see if I could borrow Josie for a moment. It's your free period next, right?"

Josie nodded, though she couldn't imagine why the principal needed to speak with her. The only time she'd gotten called into the office in high school was when she pranked Kevin by sticking an open can of tuna in his locker before spring break.

So far on this round at Clarkson High, she'd subbed steadily for months, picking up maternity, vacation, and illness leaves without getting into any trouble. That paycheck had become more necessary than ever. Not only did a baby wait just around the corner, but she'd emptied her entire savings envelope to start repaying her student loans.

"Thanks for coming down for lunch, Ella. I'll text you later." Josie knew Ella would be beyond curious over what the principal wanted and would probably text incessantly until she found out.

"Please do." Ella winked.

Josie pitched her trash into the nearest bin and followed Ms. Abnor down the corridor toward her office. A bell rang overhead, signaling the end of the lunch hour. The roar of students filled the hallways as they prepared to head to their next class.

In the office, the secretary handed the principal a small stack of papers to sign and bid hello to Josie. They then proceeded into Ms. Abnor's personal office where she closed the door behind them.

"Have a seat, Josie." Ms. Abnor's freshly painted office held an assortment of colorful binders that lined the bookshelf. Her walls held documents of achievement, each meticulously placed a few inches apart. "You're not in trouble or anything. I just wanted to chat a minute."

Nothing about "chat a minute" sounded uplifting. "Chat a minute" felt more like "We need to talk" or "It's not you, it's me."

Josie forced a smile. "Sure. What's up?"

"You've been subbing for me for almost five months straight now, eight weeks of which was covering Anna Meyers's maternity leave." She pushed some papers around on her desk before folding her hands in front of her. "Do you enjoy it?"

"Absolutely. It's been a lot of fun being back in the classroom, and I feel like I'm getting to know the students better now."

Ms. Abnor leaned forward on her desk. "Do you like teaching English?"

Josie chuckled. "I felt in over my head at first, but I'm enjoying this English curriculum. It's been fun to see the students' creative sides."

And it had been. Josie had particularly loved the poems the kids presented when they'd wrapped up the poetry unit. She adored their Friday Book Share, where each student pitched a book they enjoyed in hopes of getting other students interested in reading it. She'd never been much of a reader herself, but some story lines in those books made her reopen the library account she hadn't activated since childhood.

"It's definitely a different environment than where you taught before, but it's great you're settling in. I spoke with Anna. She's planning to return next week and work to the end of the school year, but then she's going to stay home with her daughter."

"Oh." Josie didn't know what else to say.

Ms. Abnor continued. "I'm curious if you're interested in applying for that position for the next school year."

Relief washed over Josie like a tidal wave. This job would mean everything for her and her son.

"Yes, of course." Josie slid forward in her chair until the armrests collided with the desk. "A full-time teaching position?"

"I know it may not suit you with a baby of your own to plan for, but I'd love to consider you if you're willing to earn the proper credentialing."

"Yes, I am absolutely interested." Her heart pounded. She wanted to keep talking to prove her sincere interest, but nothing came out.

Teaching English at the same high school every day sounded like a dream. She'd be a building away from Ella, get to follow the same students through their high school career, have a steady income and...*benefits*.

"I'm so glad." Ms. Abnor clapped her hands together. "I'll get your application started, and we'll do the formal interviews and everything later this spring when you're back from maternity leave. I'm so excited about this possibility, Josie. I've been so pleased with the work you've done here. I even have a list of scholarships for teachers returning to school if that helps you at all."

Josie's eyes misted, but she couldn't stop smiling. "That is so sweet of you. I've loved being here," she gushed. "I'm really excited about this and will get the ball rolling on scheduling classes as soon as possible. And thank you so much."

Her mind flashed forward to sitting at the window table with Ben, their laptops open as they worked on research papers together and Kevin brought them pizza—since this job would undoubtedly shoot her right to the top of the pact's leader board.

She'd explore all of Ms. Abnor's scholarship opportunities and then some, but most of all, if she re-enrolled in school, her student loan debt would postpone until she finished her licensing requirements with no penalty. That could give her time to catch up and start paying things down when her teacher salary kicked in.

"My pleasure." Ms. Abnor reached across the desk to shake Josie's hand, and the two women stood. "You know, Josie, I've been in touch with Rich and Jill Witter a few times. It sure sounds like you've been a real support to their daughter, Hadley."

Josie rested her hand over her heart. "I've loved getting to know Hadley."

"Her parents worried about what the pregnancy might do to her schooling, but her grades have turned around in the past few weeks. I know that's because of you and the attention you've given her. We all appreciate that more than you know."

Josie couldn't hold in the tears now. She'd often prowled the hallways, keeping watch over Hadley like a protective mama bear. They'd met twice a week during a down period for tutoring and venting. Those quiet class periods had proven more rewarding than anything Josie had ever done in her teaching career.

Josie shook the principal's hand again and bid her farewell.

With her son's birth just over a month away, things were falling nicely into place for his arrival. He'd have a mom on track in her career, even if she had to work another summer at the smoothie shop. She'd have decent enough savings to provide for his needs and a bassinet in her little loft to bring him home to. His biological dad wanted to be in his life, and he had two other goofy father figures in the meantime.

32

The Egg Roll Mission

Entering her ninth month of pregnancy made painting her toenails quite the challenge. First, Josie tried lying on her back and sticking her foot in the air, but she couldn't reach that far. Next, she sat cross-legged where she *could* reach, but only managed to put polish on her biggest toe on each foot.

"This used to be easier." She straightened her legs in front of her, wiggling her two turquoise toes. "Thought I could at least have pretty feet for the wedding if I couldn't make a dress look good."

Ben dropped his folded shirt into the pile next to his laundry basket. "Do you want help?"

"Nah, I can figure it out. There has to be a way…" She shifted around again to attack the project from another angle, but each time she bent forward, it got harder to breathe when her stomach crushed her lungs. As lovely as Ben's help would be, him touching her sausage toes was just a little bit on the mortifying side.

He pushed his laundry pile away and crawled across the floor. "Ah, come on. This could be my practice for if Izzy ever wants my help."

"Seriously?" Josie clutched the polish in her hand, one eyebrow raised as she observed Ben. "I'm ticklish. I might kick you in the face."

A mischievous grin swept across his mouth as he took hold of her foot. "Sounds like a challenge to me."

"You be nice," she squealed and tried to wiggle her foot from his grasp.

"I'll behave. I promise." He stretched out a hand for the nail polish. "Let me have it."

Josie placed the turquoise paint in his palm and watched as he twisted off the top and dabbed the brush into the container a few times. He pulled her foot into his lap and pinched her second toe between his fingers. His face held the intensity of a man about to perform surgery, not simply apply some color to a toenail. At least her leggings hid that she hadn't shaved in a few days. That task, too, had become increasingly difficult.

The brush had barely touched her when Kevin's bedroom door smacked against the wall and he rounded the corner into the living room. He sank to his knees and face-planted like someone shot in the back.

Ben pulled the brush back before Kevin's thump disturbed his attempted masterpiece. "Whatcha doin', Kev? You almost ruined Josie's feet."

"She doesn't want me," Kevin moaned into the carpet.

"Who doesn't want you?" Josie rolled to her side to level herself with Kevin.

He turned his head to look at her, moving no other part of his limp body. "Mandy. She accepted my friend request, so I started talking to her here and there, but then when I asked if she wanted to meet up, she shot me down. I guess she thinks I'm into *you* since you live with me and we've pretty much blown up each other's Facebook pages. She just unfriended me again."

"She thinks you're into *me*?" Josie cringed when she recalled the number of comments they'd posted on each other's walls. Neither of them displayed appropriate social media habits, even if all in good fun. "Did you tell her we're just friends?"

"Yeah, but she didn't believe me." He closed his eyes and put his forehead to the carpet again. "Now I can't undo it because she won't even let me try."

Ben patted his friend on the back. "I'm sorry, bud."

Kevin rolled over and sighed. His hand smacked against Josie's leg when he let his arms fall beside him. "If she won't talk to me, how am I supposed to convince her we were just being stupid and that I'm absolutely not attracted to you at all?"

Ben's hand flew to his mouth to stifle a laugh. Josie just shook her head and frowned at his reaction. "Um, I don't know. Maybe I can message her or something."

"Thanks, but it's useless." Kevin rolled up and climbed to his feet. "I got my hopes up, I guess."

"Give it some more time." Ben twisted the nail-polish bottle around in his palm without looking up. "Sometimes you have to wait longer than you want to."

A flush of warmth crept up Josie's neck as she studied the threads of the carpet to avoid any chance of catching Ben's eye.

"I don't think that's the case this time." Kevin shook his head. "I missed my chance with her a long time ago."

With that, he left, returning to his room and shutting the door behind him.

"Youch." Ben winced in Kevin's wake.

"I've never seen him like that. I don't like it." In that moment, Josie wanted to do whatever she could to fix it and bring back the loud, crazy Kevin she knew. But how in the world could she force Mandy to forgive him and convince her he was trustworthy? She had to have some sort of card to play, though, if one of her concerns was that Josie meant more to Kevin than he let on... "He said Mandy works at the hospital, right?"

Ben's head snapped in her direction. "Yeah. Why?"

"I might go talk to her." She tried to formulate a plan in her head that wouldn't immediately make Mandy call for security.

"Are you serious? And say what?"

Josie froze midshrug. "I don't know. I just feel like if she's worried I'm secretly Kevin's mistress, then who better to tell her otherwise than me?" It sounded insane out loud. "But also, Kevin has done so much for me—*us*. He's pushed us both to make some seriously big life changes, and I want him to be happy too. Even if it means I have to totally embarrass myself in front of a complete stranger."

Ben tapped his finger to his jaw as he thought. "Yeah, I'm gonna come with you."

"You are?" Josie paused on her hands and knees in an attempt to stand.

He leapt to his feet and shook his arms out as if to get psyched for this adventure. "I am. We're all in this pact together, and if we can help him achieve his Number Three goal, then I say we do it. We can finish your toes later and get Chinese food from the place with the egg rolls you like."

"Oh yes, please." Josie scrambled to her feet, and she and Ben hurried to grab their coats and sneak from the house to Ben's car without alerting Kevin to their whereabouts. The moment they left the driveway, Ben queued up the *Mission Impossible* theme song and cranked it through the car speakers.

If either of them had a game plan for when they arrived, no one said a word about it. Josie had no idea what department Mandy even worked in or where to find the poor, unsuspecting woman.

When they parked, the pair entered through the main entrance and stopped at the reception desk. Josie grabbed Ben's elbow to urge him to inquire.

The elderly woman sitting behind the desk spoke first. "We usually have labor and delivery patients enter through the ER, but I'll call down a wheelchair to—"

"Oh, no. I'm not in labor." Josie squeezed harder on Ben's elbow when he chuckled under his breath. "We need to speak with one of your nurses. She's a friend of ours."

"Mandy Parker," Ben added quickly.

The woman smiled and typed away on her computer. "I apologize for assuming. Nurse Mandy is on the fourth floor in cardiology. You'll want to ask for her at the nurse's station and then please remain in the designated waiting room."

They hurried down the hallway to the elevator, the *Mission Impossible* theme still rolling through Josie's head. "What are we supposed to say to her?"

"I have no idea." The elevator door opened on the fourth floor, and Ben led the way to the nurse's station where a nurse ushered them to a waiting area.

Josie let out a sigh of relief when they found the waiting room empty. Having this discussion in the hospital wing that dealt with cases of heart attacks might have been incredibly awkward in front of a patient's worried family member. Then again, they'd come to the hospital for the sake of their friend's heart, too, so…

The door opened, and a young woman in blue scrubs entered. Josie couldn't stop her eyes from going wide. This girl was *beautiful*. She had to stand nearly six feet tall, her flawless skin and bronze curls and on-point eyeliner application making her look every bit a cover model for *Nurses On Fleek*.

The moment Mandy looked up and spotted Ben, she threw her hands in the air and reached for the doorknob.

"Mandy, wait," Ben called out and took a few steps forward. "He didn't send us, and this is not a trick or something, I swear."

"*Us?*" She paused and leaned to regard Josie standing behind Ben. "You're the girl from his Facebook page that calls him Big Poppa."

Oh hell. Josie *had* called him that.

Ben sank to his knees, burying his face in his coat sleeves as he tried to suppress his cackling. Josie's cheeks burned, but she had to keep it together. She pushed Ben over and took his place in front of Mandy.

"I have so many regrets about that right now, but I promise you, I don't call him that because we are in love. Kevin is my *friend*, and friend only." Josie tried to read Mandy's expression, but the woman held a stone-cold glare that brought on all the nerves.

"You're pregnant." Mandy crossed her arms over her chest and shifted her weight to one leg. "He refers to it as 'my baby' online."

"Yeah, I've told him to stop doing that. This is not his." Yup, this was going to be a much harder situation to talk her way out of than she'd expected. "Look. Long story short: I was married, got pregnant, caught my husband cheating, filed for divorce, and moved in with my parents. I ran into Kevin and Ben here at the fair, and we agreed to live together to catch up financially and stuff." Josie wobbled on her feet when Ben grabbed hold of her leg and began using her as a stabilizer to stand up.

His face had become a deep shade of red from trying to stifle his laughter. Surely, he'd never let Kevin live down the "Big Poppa" nickname for as long as they lived.

"That's the honest truth," Ben said. "We're all trying to get our lives together. We even have a pact on our refrigerator to prove it. Kevin's doing the best of all of us."

Josie nodded. "He really is. He's come so far, and he's trying so hard."

Mandy's jaw set as she looked to the ceiling. They needed more. Josie had to connect with this woman somehow if Kevin had any hope of winning her over again.

Ben spoke up first. "He's not the guy you remember."

That got her attention. Mandy's head tilted as she observed Ben. "No, I think he is." The fluorescent lighting in the waiting room highlighted the sheen of tears that misted in Mandy's eyes. "He's still the same outgoing, fun-loving, crazy guy I liked back then." She sucked in a big breath. "The same guy who didn't want to be tied down to one girl. To *me*. It took me a long time to get over him, and then he just comes out of nowhere talking to me again? And the first things I see on his page are interactions with another girl. What else am I supposed to think?"

Mandy turned toward the door, but Josie moved faster and placed her body between Mandy and her way out. If she meant to call security, this was the most likely moment. However, Mandy hardly appeared threatened by a pregnant woman almost a foot shorter than her.

"I'm sorry we barged in here and surprised you like this. I know we don't know each other at all, and coming out of a sucky marriage where my husband decided he didn't want to be tied down to *just me*, either, I get where you're coming from. I really do." Josie put her hand over the doorknob to steady herself. This was her last chance. "I've known Kevin since high school. He's one of my best friends, and I love him dearly. And I am so proud of how he's going after what he wants in life and encouraging us to do the same." She swallowed back the lump in her throat. "The last thing Kevin hoped to do was win over the girl he cares about most, and that's you. I wouldn't be here if I didn't think he was ready for this."

Mandy's face softened, and she turned to regard Ben, who had taken a seat to watch the scene going down between the two women.

He forced a smile. "I know this is all super weird and out of left field. Kevin would kill us if he knew we were here—"

"He seriously doesn't know you're doing this?" Mandy took a few steps back from the door.

"Nope. We snuck out." Ben patted his coat pocket. "Though my phone won't stop buzzing, so I'm guessing he's figured out we're missing."

Mandy wet her lips and sucked in a deep breath. She paced in front of the chairs for a long moment, while Josie and Ben watched in silence. Was she considering their words or just waiting for help to arrive and remove them from the building?

When she stopped moving, her gaze fell on Josie. "I don't want to go through that again," she whispered.

Josie knew that feeling all too well. Her shoulders drooped when she let go of the door handle, walked across the room, and sank into the chair closest to where Mandy stood.

"I don't blame you. I'd be scared too. I *am* scared." If they insisted on ambushing this poor nurse in such a way, Josie could at least bare her soul in solidarity. "After Grant and I filed for divorce, I thought for sure I'd be alone forever, especially since I'm pregnant. I mean, who dates a pregnant woman? And even after I have this kid, I'm still going to be a single mom barely holding things together with a messy past following me around. Kevin's the one who challenged me to keep trying. To give love another chance." Her gaze flickered up to Ben. He sat across the room, elbows rested on top of his thighs, a grin turning up the corner of his mouth. The smile grew when he dropped his head to avert his eyes.

Her heart picked up its pace, but she refocused on Mandy. "So, I guess that's all we wanted to say, really." Josie stood and pulled her coat together across her chest. "We'll let you get back to saving lives and whatever else you've got planned today."

Ben gave Mandy one last sheepish smile and held the door open for Josie. The two of them climbed into the elevator and pushed the button to the lobby. When the door closed, Ben stepped closer to wrap an arm around Josie, bringing her into a side hug.

He gave her shoulder a squeeze. "Mission accomplished."

33

Three Suppers Later...

THE DRESS BAG HIT the floor with a loud rustle, and Josie fell against the door to catch her breath. Trying to pack for a weekend away with three weeks till her due date might have been one of the craziest things she'd ever done.

"It's not too late to take me with you, you know," Kevin said from the kitchen.

Josie raised an eyebrow and righted herself. "Don't you have someplace to be?"

"I'm at my leisure, little mama." Kevin winked.

"Who goes to the gym this late at night anyway?" Josie wiped her palm across her forehead. It wasn't right that she was sweating so much when the outside temperature barely hit double digits.

"Enough people that they pay a twenty-four-hour staff, apparently." Kevin slid off the counter and grabbed his coat. "Gotta get my money's worth out of this membership and destroy some cholesterol. Plus, Louise in the mailroom made fun of me for the sounds I made when I picked up one of the boxes. Can't have that."

With a wink, he headed out into the night.

Josie shook her head as she reached for her water bottle and leaned against the kitchen counter. So far, she'd only accomplished tucking her dress into the bag it had originally come in and dragging it down the stairway without tripping on the long plastic wrap.

Why had she waited till the night before to pack? She knew it would take forever in her condition. How the heck should she know what to pack for a weekend of fawning all over her brother and his fiancée while also feeling like an overstuffed sausage?

She so did not want to go.

The dryer buzzed to indicate the finished cycle, and Ben bounded up the stairs to empty the load. He paused on the landing and peeked in through the glass window to the kitchen.

She waved, and he came inside with his full laundry basket. "Hey," he said. "Kev leave?"

"You just missed him. Off to get his abs of steel," she said.

Ben dropped his basket by the door and grabbed a water from the fridge. "He said he didn't want to fall into the 'dad bod' category once the baby comes."

She smacked her palm to her forehead. "Oh, for Pete's sake."

"That's what I said." Ben held up his water bottle to clink against Josie's. "Kind of surprised you're still up, Grandma."

She gave him the stink eye and checked the clock again. "Growing a human makes me tired. And I'm only awake *now* because I'm experiencing a severe lack of motivation at the moment." Josie shook her head and pointed toward the lonely dress bag on the floor. "I've packed one thing for my weekend away."

"And you leave when?"

"Tomorrow?" She bit her lip.

Ben laughed. "You want some help?"

Josie tried to imagine Ben delicately folding her unmentionables and placing them inside her purple suitcase with care. Certainly, her maternity bras with the extra clasps, the stretch-mark cream, and the panty liners would be a total turn-on. The underwear that came up to her belly button would make him propose on the spot.

"That's okay. I think I can handle it. Just give me…six years?" She slumped farther against the countertop.

"I don't have to pack your stuff, but at least let me carry it down the stairs for you." Ben turned to open the freezer and pull out a box of strawberry waffles. "You go get started, and I'll be up when my waffles are done. Want one?"

"Make it two." Frozen waffles had never sounded so appetizing.

"Go on then." Ben waved toward the stairwell.

She had to move fast. Ben's method of waffle making didn't take long, and the stairs seemed to have grown in number the more pregnant she'd gotten. Since the entire household only ate their waffles with butter and no syrup, she could expect to see Ben up the stairs in about five minutes tops. And her bedroom was a disaster.

Josie kicked her dirty laundry into a pile and squatted to gather handfuls for the basket in the corner of the room. She threw her comforter over the bed to hide the crumpled sheets and smashed pillows. What to do with the food wrappers?

The door at the bottom of the stairs squeaked, and Josie wadded up the trash and shoved it into her purse next to the bed. As much trash as she already had stashed in there, a few more pieces wouldn't make a big difference.

"How's it going?" Ben leaned against the doorframe, his hands loaded with two plates of buttered strawberry waffles.

Josie peeked over her shoulder, still clutching her purse. Her hair had fallen in her face as she sat there hunched over the open bag.

Ben pushed a laundry basket from the doorway with his foot. "You know we have a trash can, right?"

Caught.

"You saw nothing," Josie said.

"I'm immune to Jedi mind tricks. Here." Ben handed Josie her plate and sat on the floor next to her. "So, you're taking Kevin this weekend?"

She nearly choked on her first bite of waffle. "No, I'm not taking Kevin. Why?"

"He said you were."

"Good grief, Ben. When are you going to stop believing everything he says?" Josie licked the melted butter from her fingers. The best part.

Ben groaned. "I have no idea."

He folded a waffle in half and finished it in two bites. Josie took only slightly longer to maintain a bit of self-control. On a non-Ben-in-her-room day, she could fit a whole dang waffle in her mouth.

"So, where are we starting?" Ben pushed his plate to the side and stood. "You're only going for two nights, right?"

"Yes." Josie pulled herself up onto the mattress and rubbed her tight stomach. Her hunger hadn't dissipated in these final months, even though the doctor had told her it might. Over the past couple of days, though, food hadn't set as well. It wasn't a nausea sensation. Just…full. Not that it had stopped her from eating anything and everything she could find.

Ben pointed at a bag next to the dresser. "And what's that?"

"My hospital bag. For when the baby comes. I may be way behind on wedding prep, but I'm ready to get this kid out."

Ben shook his head. "You're brave to travel this close to D-day."

"It's still three weeks away. Doc says baby's sitting in there pretty tight, and I fully plan to keep my legs crossed for the entirety of the weekend." She winced. "And don't say I should have done that in the first place."

"Hadn't even considered it." Ben opened the top drawer of the dresser and peeked inside, then closed it quickly.

"I can pack my own underwear, if you don't mind," Josie said.

Ben held up his hands. "I'm thinking I'll stand over here and wait till you have something for me to take downstairs."

"Solid plan." Josie hobbled to her feet. By the time she reached her dresser a few steps away, all breath had left her lungs.

While she explored her underwear drawer, she felt Ben's gaze on her.

"Can I help you?" she asked.

"You gonna make it?"

Josie took stock of her position. One arm rested on top of the dresser to support her weight, while she gasped as if she'd run a marathon rather than walked a few steps across the room.

"I'm fine. Just super, super pregnant," she said.

"And sweaty. You're sweating…in February. And it's kind of cold up here."

She usually stayed quite toasty upstairs, but never enough to make her perspire. Had she put deodorant on that morning?

Ben scratched his head. "I'm not pressuring you, but do you want me to go with you this weekend?"

Yes, she wanted him to go with her, but she also didn't want to explain their relationship a thousand times over the course of the weekend. They weren't dating. He wasn't her child's father. And damn it if she didn't wish the answer to both questions was a resounding yes, which made it so much harder to say, "No."

"I can drive, watch out for your pregnant ass, and rush you to a hospital if you explode."

Josie peeked at him from over her shoulder, her elbows still propped on top of the dresser. "You're sweet, but honestly, I'll be fine. My aunt is going to drive, and I've been assured there are wonderful, fancy hospitals readily available near the resort."

"Okay, but why don't you want us to come?" Ben crossed his arms, and Josie pictured a little boy pouting to his mommy about wanting to go to his friend's house across the street.

"Why do you *want* to come?" She wiped her forehead on her sleeve. They really should turn down the heat.

He guffawed as if she'd asked the stupidest question he'd ever heard. "You said they were having prime rib, crab cakes, and filet mignon. Why would we not want to be a part of that beautiful celebration of love, Josie?"

She wadded up a couple pairs of underwear and stockings and shoved them into the internal pocket of her suitcase before Ben could get a good look. "Honestly? I would love for you to come. I'd probably have way more fun if you went. But I don't want to explain you to my entire family. If you think my mom is crazy, you should meet the rest of my relatives. There are at least two alcoholics on my dad's side and a crazy cat lady on my mom's, and my brother's best friends are painfully hipster. Plus, my grandmother is totally off her rocker. She refuses to acknowledge that Grant and I split up. She also probably thinks I'm just fat and hasn't accepted the pregnancy factor. Imagine what she'd think if I showed up with another man."

"Oh." Ben's forehead creased. "I'm so sorry you can't drink this weekend."

Josie pointed to her nose. "Bingo, my friend."

Staring into her closet, Josie grabbed the only other maternity dress she had: another simple, plaid dress she'd bought for teaching. If she paired it with a nice scarf, it might pass as a decent rehearsal dress. By her standards, at least. Emily might think otherwise.

"Besides," Josie continued, "I only recently told my parents the rest of the story with Grant. They're still trying to wrap their heads around the idea that their perfect son-in-law cheated on their daughter. It's…a lot to deal with."

"Which, again, is why you shouldn't have to do it alone." Ben sank onto the mattress and pulled Josie's pillow onto his lap.

She offered him a smile. "You've already been more than I deserve, Benjamin. Both of you guys. I wouldn't make you face my mother and her relatives like that. And Ella will be there, at least, if I really start to lose it."

Ella's family had probably arrived hours ago and now were sleeping soundly in their hotel room. Well, more like Ella probably has pulled all her hair out as her children jumped from bed to bed and Cory walked the hallways with Leland, trying to get him to fall asleep.

Why couldn't Josie simply get excited about her brother's wedding? Shouldn't she be happy for him? She loved him. He'd found the woman of his dreams. Had been successful in life. At least, if she couldn't be joyful for his sake, she could focus on other aspects. By the end of the weekend, she'd have a new sister, get the chance to catch up with family members she hadn't seen in ages, eat some top-notch food…

Her stomach flipped, and she swallowed hard, suddenly afraid she might throw up all over her closet.

"You all right?" Ben rushed over and grabbed hold of her elbow.

"I'm fine." Josie clutched her armful of clothes against her chest and rubbed at her stomach. "Not feeling so great all of a sudden. Might be the three suppers that did me in."

"Three suppers?" Ben chuckled and helped Josie to the bed with her clothing wad.

"Well, I had soup at five, then Kevin and I ate pizza pockets at eight. And, well, waffles."

Ben shook his head and did a sweeping look around the room. "You need anything else up here?"

"No, I think I'm good." She debated sitting on the mattress but knew she wouldn't get back up if she did. "Do you care if I sleep in the living room tonight?"

It might be best to stay close to the bathroom. She'd never make it down all those steps in time if anything came up.

"I was going to suggest that, actually. If my room wasn't in the basement, I'd trade you for the night." Ben zipped Josie's suitcase and snatched up her pillow to stick under his arm. "We can always kick Kevin out."

"Now we're talking," she said.

Ben took hold of her with the same arm he used to pinch her pillow against his side and helped her toward the stairs.

"You don't have to do all this, Ben."

He stopped on the second-to-the-top step and glanced up at her. "I want to."

His hand slid down from her elbow to take her hand. Josie's fingers fluttered as they skidded across his palm and wrapped around his.

"Thank you. I appreciate it, but I feel bad for making you work so hard. You really are the best." Josie eased her foot onto the first step and noticed just how much her back had started hurting. She must have moved wrong or something.

Ben walked in reverse down the steps, guiding her along. "Does that mean I'm a better roommate than Kevin?" His eyebrows waggled.

"Oh, no doubt." Her sweaty palm clutched the banister harder than usual. Her back had better settle down before the long car ride to Michigan.

Once they made it to the landing, Ben let go of her arm to put the bag next to the dress bag. He motioned for her to follow him into the living room, then slid the two beanbag chairs together, placing her pillow at one end.

"Maybe I should bring your mattress down—"

"Oh, no. This is fine. I might be able to stay more upright this way." Josie wrapped the blanket around her shoulders and stepped toward the beanbags.

She stopped when Ben intercepted, his hand outstretched once more to help lower her to the floor. Would she ever not feel like a giddy teenager every time he touched her?

Josie positioned herself between the two mounds, propping her head up with the pillow. The beanbags cradled her aching body and allowed her to recline enough to let the pressure off her back. She missed sleeping on her back and stomach and had big plans to pick that up again the moment her son popped out.

Ben went to the kitchen and returned with Josie's bottle of water.

He then grabbed a bunched-up fleece from the saucer chair and used it to cover Josie's legs and bare toes. "You care if I stick around for a bit till I know you're okay?"

She tried to answer, but the words caught in her throat as she watched him adjusting the blankets. It was well past midnight. There was a strong probability that she was dreaming Ben had asked to stay at her side and watch over her. "We can put on a show if you want."

Ben paused, his arm resting over his opposite knee as he knelt beside her. "Yeah, that sounds good."

She nodded slowly. "Late-night TV is always more fun with company."

"And it gives me an excuse not to do any more homework." Ben crawled across the floor and settled in on the other side of the beanbag chair, leaning close enough that Josie could almost feel the warmth of his skin against hers. He crunched forward, grabbed the remote, and flipped through the channels.

Neither said a word, settling on the game-show channel without needing to discuss.

Josie let out a long breath as she nestled deeper into her beanbag and pressed her head against Ben's shoulder. With her hand draped over her stomach, she began drifting off to sleep.

Until a sharp pain coursed through her stomach.

34

Do Storks Deliver Snacks Too?

BEN FELL OFF THE beanbag pillow and stumbled to his knees. The remote toppled to the floor between them, and he grabbed Josie's shoulder to better see her. "What's wrong? You okay?"

Josie held her stomach, knees drawn in. She looked at Ben with wide eyes, but said nothing.

Her son kicked against her side in his usual happy manner, but something felt off. Had he kicked a nerve? Dislodged an ovary? Punctured her spleen?

The pain subsided almost as quickly as it had come.

Josie pushed out a big breath. "I don't know what that was, but it hurt."

Ben sat back on his ankles and inched forward. He reached up to brush another long strand of Josie's hair from her face and examined her expression. In any other circumstance, she might have melted over the gesture, but now…

The game-show host called on a new contestant. Theme music cued up as the audience applauded. A lovely assistant showed a plethora of fabulous prizes. The only fabulous prize Josie wanted now was a painkiller.

"Argh." She buckled again. This time, rather than the sharp pain that had delayed her sleep, her stomach seized all over, like an unrelenting charley horse or the worst period cramps imaginable. The tension held for a long moment before subsiding.

"Are you in labor?" Ben's voice squeaked up an octave.

"I…" Holy crap! *Was* she in labor? The doctor had told her it would be a while. She still had three weeks to go. What about the wedding? Her parents were already in Michigan. Her mom was supposed to be there with her in the delivery room.

Ben's fingers coiled around Josie's forearm. "Josie?"

The possibilities flew through her mind so fast that she couldn't focus on a single thing. "I don't know what to do."

"It's okay," he said. "Just breathe. We have to breathe."

Ben took his own advice, breathing loudly and deeply as he stroked her arm and readjusted on the floor beside her.

"I'm trying." Josie bent forward and waited for the next unavoidable contraction.

"I'll take you to the hospital. It's going to be fine." He stood and ran over to turn on the lights. Next, he dashed through the dining room to grab his and Josie's coats, nearly throwing hers over her head when he returned. "What else do we need?"

"My purse? My go-bag? I want my flip-flops." Snacks? Did the hospital provide snacks?

"Here." Ben knelt behind her and wrapped his arms under hers, lifting her to her feet.

He turned her to face him, drawing her in to his chest as she tried to get her bearings.

With her head pressed to his shoulder, she caught the familiar scent of his cologne and focused on the smell. Tears lingered in her eyes, and she clutched hard on the fabric of his tattered T-shirt. "I don't know what I'm doing, Ben."

"Does anyone?" He tried to laugh as he stroked her back and held her. "It's gonna be fine, Josie."

She wrapped her arms tighter around his middle. Could she

push pause on life for a little while? Stop the pain in her stomach and breathe Ben in for a long moment. Enjoy being held for the first time in so long, even if it meant nothing more than one friend supporting another.

The front door creaked open, and Kevin crept inside, probably expecting to find the household in bed for the night.

"What are you guys doing?" He kicked off his gym shoes and froze when he spotted Josie and Ben wrapped tightly in each other's arms. "I leave for a couple hours, and you two start mackin' in the living room? What is going on here?"

"Josie's in labor, you dipshit. Put your shoes back on." Ben kept a hand on Josie's elbow as he bent to retrieve her coat from the floor and wrapped it around her.

"I'm sweaty," she whined.

"You won't be when we get outside. And you're not catching pneumonia on top of everything else," Ben said.

Kevin still stood in the doorway, unmoving. "Wait."

"Shoes, Big Poppa!" Ben shouted. "Start the car!"

"It's not time for the baby yet! The family calendar says he's due in March," he shrieked.

"Apparently the calendar is wrong!" Josie yelled.

Kevin crashed into every piece of furniture in the dining room while fumbling around for his shoes and keys. Soon, he flew out the front door to start up the car.

Josie glanced at the clock.

1:13 a.m.

How could anyone function at such an obscure hour? Especially when her back still ached and her stomach tried to turn itself inside out with every contraction.

She moved into the dining room when she had a chance. Getting anywhere when the contractions hit might not be all that possible.

"You good?" Ben asked her as he followed behind.

"This is so inconvenient," she mumbled.

"I'm not so sure you get much say otherwise." He flashed a smile, but she could see the sweat shining on his brow too.

Josie tapped her fist to her forehead. "My parents are in Michigan already."

"We'll get ahold of them. Don't worry." Ben opened the door for Kevin, whose gaze flickered between Ben and Josie.

"We ready?" Kevin asked.

"No." Josie put both hands on the doorframe, locking herself into place. "Maybe this is a false alarm. That happens, right? It'll go away. I mean, we're a few weeks early. Let's just wait it out."

"Not a chance I'm willing to take." Ben's gaze held firm with the worried lines on his forehead. "We need to get you checked out at the hospital to be sure."

"We can go in the morning. Wait until my mom gets here." Her stomach seized, and she bit her lip to hide it.

"I will carry you to the car, so help me God." Kevin pushed his wild hair away from his face and grabbed her arm from the doorframe to wrap around his shoulder.

"You will not!" Josie's voice pierced the room at the thought of being carried from a house in the middle of the night in her über-pregnant, laboring state.

Ben stepped between them. "Just calm down. Josie, breathe. Kevin, breathe. Everybody, breathe."

"My mom!" Josie cried.

"Right." Ben tugged at his shaggy hair. "Kevin, pull the car up closer to the house and call Josie's mom. Her number is…" Ben growled and rushed to the living room, kicking beanbags and throwing blankets until he found Josie's phone. "Here. I got it. Go call her parents. I got her."

Kevin snatched the phone and headed out the front door, letting the blustery winter air take over the house.

Josie burrowed into her coat, the chill catching the layer of sweat across her skin.

"Okay. We can do this." Ben rested his elbow on the high-top table by the door, his palm flat against his brow.

Josie shook her head.

"Josie." Ben leaned forward, his fingers brushing over her wrist before taking a tight hold of her hand. "It's gonna be great, okay? We'll stay with you until your mom gets there."

She looked up through her fallen hair. "I am freaking out."

"I know you are. I'm weirdly freaking out too." He squeezed her hands harder. "I was no help when Noel had Izzy. I was nineteen, and they carted me from the delivery room because I started to pass out when they brought in the epidural needle."

Josie managed a smile at the image of young Ben as an unconscious spectator.

Ben sighed. "And I don't know what to say to you now to get you out that door. Clearly, I sucked at doing this the first time around. But you're gonna be awesome. I know labor and delivery isn't specifically written on the Corn Dog Pact, but it should be. And you'll ace it."

Josie lowered her head. "Thanks."

"Pep talk over. Get in the car." Ben spun her around and hastily guided her out the front door, shutting it behind them both on the way out. Kevin had pulled the car up onto the lawn with the back door wide open. He waited at the bottom of the steps.

"Oh, Ben." Josie turned before climbing into the car. "My bags and flops. Where are they?"

"On it." Ben rushed into the house, while Josie slid into the back seat of the car and braced for the next contraction.

Kevin tapped on the steering wheel, waiting for Ben to return. He stared hard at her from the rearview mirror. "Do you need to sit on a towel or something?"

"Why?" Josie hugged her stomach.

"When does your water break?"

Oh, hell. How could she ever look either of them in the eye again if she exploded all over the back of Kevin's car?

Josie opened her door again and shouted into the nighttime abyss. "Ben!"

Ben hurried out the door with a bag and a pair of flip-flops in hand. Kevin popped the trunk, and the whole car jolted when Ben threw the bag in and slammed the trunk shut. He'd barely climbed into the front seat when he started shouting for Kevin to drive.

"What'd my mom say, Kevin?" Another contraction set in, and Josie gasped, teeth clenching.

"I, um…" The tires squealed when Kevin turned the corner. "She didn't answer. It went straight to voicemail."

"What?" She let out a howl of pain.

"I left a message. I'm sure it'll be fine." Kevin tapped his thumbs harder against the steering wheel.

Ben reached into the back seat and grabbed hold of Josie's knee. "We'll keep trying. We'll call the hotel as soon as we get to the hospital, okay?"

Josie nodded through the pain.

At that very moment, her mother slept four hours away at a resort lodge. Her phone wasn't on, and she had no idea her daughter had gone into labor on the day of her son's wedding rehearsal.

Meanwhile, Josie sat in the back seat of her friend's car and pinched her knees together, wanting to scream at Kevin to stop taking the turns so fast.

This was it. The baby was on his way.

35

Mid-Labor Coffee Run

THE MONITORS CLICKED AND hummed with heartbeats, contraction measurements, and vitals. The blood pressure cuff around Josie's arm swelled until she thought it might cut off all circulation, only to release at the last second and spare her limb.

In the hallway, nurses hustled, papers shuffled, and carts rolled. Josie sat there, propped up in her bed with nothing but a thin blue gown separating her naked body from the two wide-eyed men across the room.

Neither guy spoke. They simply watched her, as if waiting for the moment she'd erupt and produce a human child.

Somehow, they'd managed to check into the hospital, with Ben taking over the paperwork while Kevin parked the car. In that instant, relief washed over her at having both men by her side to take care of the extra things she could hardly process over the pain. But once they'd gotten into the room and the nurses instructed her to strip down, the relief had vanished.

Josie ran her finger over the IV in her wrist. She hated the feeling of a needle under her skin. She'd already been there for a couple of hours, and her contractions hadn't gotten any closer together. Her water hadn't broken, so she wouldn't have to worry about paying to detail Kevin's car or getting the guys' shoes all wet. She'd eaten about three cups of ice—the good, round kind that only the most upscale fast-food restaurants produced.

"Ben, are my socks in my bag?" Josie set her ice cup on the bedside table and shifted to sit up straighter. "My feet are kind of cold."

He hurried to grab the bag by the door, seemingly grateful for a job when there was nothing else to do. Ben unzipped the bag, froze, then turned slowly in Josie's direction. In his hands, he held a pair of black dress shoes and the decorative scarf she planned to wear to her brother's rehearsal dinner.

"You grabbed the wedding go-bag?" Josie covered her mouth to hide the grin.

"I am so sorry." He lowered the items into the bag, then smacked himself in the forehead. "I'm an idiot."

Kevin laughed loud enough to drown out the beeping monitors for a brief moment. "Good thing we don't live far away."

"I'll go see if the nurse's station has any socks." Without another look in her direction, Ben left the room.

At least after giving birth, she'd have plenty of formal wear to show off her post-baby bod in. Even better, Kevin teasing Ben about this for the rest of their lives would provide plenty of future amusement.

Another contraction took hold of her, and Josie wrapped her fingers around the bed rails. She pinched her eyes shut and hummed to herself. On the TV in the upper corner of the room, announcers argued over who might win the upcoming wrestling match. While a renovation show would inspire her any other day of the week, WWE reruns did the trick during horrific labor pains.

"Still climbing," Kevin said from across the room. He'd taken on the task of talking her through the contractions as they appeared on the monitor. She found it oddly helpful. "On the way down now."

Her breath released along with her abdomen. The nurses had

scolded her at least a dozen times for holding her breath during the contractions. They'd insisted that breathing through them worked better as pain management. No idea what they'd been smoking to get that idea.

"You know you can come closer to the bed, right?" Josie let go of the rails and folded her hands over the top of her stomach.

Kevin stiffened in his chair. "I can see the monitor fine from here."

"Whatever." As much as she appreciated their presence, having the guys on the other side of the room didn't put much of a personal spin on things. They acted as spectators, and who wanted that during childbirth?

Josie checked her phone again. She still hadn't heard from her parents. Even if they got up early and listened to their voicemails, she'd still have over four hours until anyone arrived. Could she hold on that long? She'd already texted Grant to let him know the baby was on his way and that she'd keep him posted. He hadn't responded, either, probably sound asleep in these wee morning hours, but it didn't stop her from checking for a reply from him.

Ben returned with a pair of socks and lifted the blankets to put them on Josie's feet. He cradled her heel in his hands as he wordlessly set to work, the gesture strangely intimate, considering their rather unromantic surroundings.

"Thank you. That's much better." The latest contraction had warmed her up some already, but Ben's gentle touch made the room feel downright hot.

"Sorry about the bag," he said.

Like she cared at all right now. "It's fine. Really."

A small woman in scrubs decorated with pink llamas entered the room, which sent Ben hustling to his chair beside Kevin. She smiled brightly. "Hi, Josie. I'm Daphne. I'm going to be hanging out with you for the next few hours, all right?"

Daphne scribbled her name on the whiteboard next to the door, then strolled over to the bed to check the screens. She rested a hand on Josie's knee as she examined the cuffs and fetal monitor. Pleased with the readings, she leaned down against the rails to reposition the straps over Josie's stomach.

"Did you find out what you're having?" Daphne asked. The baby's heart rate chimed louder on the monitor beside them. "I'm guessing it's a boy. The little stinker won't hold still long enough to keep track of him."

"It is a boy." Josie liked Daphne's playful demeanor already.

The nurse clapped her hands together. "Third one I've gotten right this week. Out of ten? Not so bad, eh?"

Josie started to laugh, but the next contraction settled into her stomach. She wadded up the blankets in her fists.

"And which one of you strapping gentlemen is Dad?" Daphne's hand returned to Josie's knee, giving it a good squeeze that mimicked the contraction.

Kevin and Ben looked at each other, waiting for the other to answer. Josie just moaned.

"Alrighty." Daphne straightened and turned back to her patient.

"It's complicated," Josie forced out through gritted teeth. "Can I get drugs now?"

"Hey, Daphne?" Another nurse appeared in the doorway, but it wasn't the anesthesiologist Josie had wished for. She wasn't a total stranger either. "I've got those… Oh!"

Kevin shot out of his seat, nearly dropping his phone from shock. "Mandy."

"Hi," she answered. Whatever medical device she held in her hand lowered when her arms went limp at her sides.

Daphne cleared her throat in what sounded like an attempt to keep her laughter at bay. "The complications continue, I see."

Josie bit her bottom lip. While she dreaded the onset of another contraction, it seemed the only thing that could spare her the awkwardness in the room now.

"Thanks for bringing that down on your way out, Mandy dear," Daphne continued and shuffled across the room to take the device. "Enjoy your weekend off."

The words knocked Kevin out of his stupor. "Weekend off? That's… How lovely. I—"

Ben stood and placed a hand on his friend's shoulder. "Maybe you could walk her to her car?"

"I could walk you to your car!" Kevin practically shouted.

Mandy glanced around the room, quickly meeting the gazes of those fortunate enough to watch the painful encounter. "Okay. Sure."

Kevin turned toward Josie on the bed as if suddenly remembering why he was there. "Do you care if—"

"Just go," she managed through another contraction. Any other time, her heart might have leapt for joy at this beautiful moment, but right now, her uterus was too busy leaping with agonizing spasms. Romance made for a subpar painkiller.

He took the hint and hurried from the room, Mandy close behind.

"Well, that settles it," Daphne said. "You're the most entertaining room of the night."

"Great." The contraction subsided, and Josie gasped for air. "Then my birth plan is going splendidly."

Daphne chuckled. "Well, you've got a long while to go still, dearie. Sit tight for a bit, and we'll try to keep the matchmaking to a minimum so you can rest. The doctor will be in shortly to see how far you've dilated, and we'll have a better idea of a timeline for the epidural."

At the mention of dilation, Ben stumbled from his chair. "I'm, uh, gonna go chaperone the big kids for a quick sec. Maybe get some coffees for everyone. Definitely, definitely coffee. Good luck here with…all that. K. Bye."

✑✐

Every muscle in Josie's body hurt from clenching through the contractions. She'd tried breathing, meditating, listening to music, shouting at the wrestling match, everything, but labor hurt like hell.

Dr. Mallory had stopped in to check on her at sunrise, but Josie hadn't made much progress since she'd first arrived at the hospital, even if the contractions had gotten severely more intense.

Nurse Daphne got ahold of the anesthesiologist, Dr. Nagis, to start the epidural process. She'd warned Josie to expect another full day of labor due to slow progress, which wasn't the most reassuring thing ever.

Josie inched her way toward the edge of her bed as Daphne rolled the table closer for Josie to rest her arms on. As much as the IV in her arm bugged her, a foot-long needle to the spine didn't thrill her a whole lot either. She'd suffer through it if it meant escaping the wretched contractions and not having to feel a watermelon-sized baby come out of her nether regions.

"I'm going to head out for this one too." Kevin stepped over Ben to reach for the doorknob. He took another sip of what had to be his fourth coffee since they arrived, his hand twitching so much that he could hardly get a decent drink.

Josie sat on the edge of her hospital bed, her stocking feet dangling over the side. "Are you sure?"

"It's fine. I'll be much more help to you if I'm casting good vibes from the waiting room."

Ben wouldn't look at her from his seated position, which was fine in this moment. The nurse had begun to untie her hospital gown in the back once again. She'd tried to close it so many times throughout the night, but the nurses always pulled it open again with each visit for her "comfort." What did they think was comfortable about any of this?

Josie leaned forward on the tall table, while Dr. Nagis stood behind her and prepared for the epidural. Not being able to see what he did unnerved her something awful. She desperately needed someone to hang on to, someone to ground her.

Why hadn't her mom answered the phone? She couldn't do this alone.

Dr. Nagis's gloved fingers brushed something cold over her lower spine, and she flinched.

"Easy," he said. "It's just the antiseptic. I'll let you know when it's time for the pinch."

Pinch? Please. Stabbing, maybe.

Josie tapped her fingernails on the table as another contraction seized her. She couldn't fight both the contraction pain and the fear of a yardstick needle plunging into her back. Her eyes filled with tears again. Most women had partners to hold their hands through this, wipe their brows, and speak words of comfort into their ear when the going got tough. Not that Grant would have done any of that even if he had stuck around.

Josie shut her eyes once more and grabbed hold of the table.

Warm hands encompassed her wrists and moved up to her elbows. She opened her eyes to see Ben bent low in front of her, his forehead nearly touching hers. His face appeared whiter than the bedsheets, and he gulped when he glanced behind her at what Dr. Nagis did.

Josie reached for his forearms and clutched him tightly. His fingers caressed her arms in the most reassuring way. She breathed in the faint scent of his cologne again, in and out.

Dr. Nagis placed a steady hand on her shoulder from behind. "I'm ready, Josie. I need you to hold very still now."

Ben grasped Josie's elbows, and she squeezed harder on his forearms.

"It won't last long," Ben whispered.

Breathe. In and out.

A tear slipped down her cheek when the needle pierced her skin. She winced, and Ben inched closer to bring her head against his shoulder.

The seconds passed slowly.

Josie held on to her dear roommate, afraid that he might slip away if she let go.

In. In. In…

"We're done," Dr. Nagis said. "You can go ahead and lie back."

And out.

Josie couldn't move. Ben kept one hand on hers and pushed the rolling table out from between them with the other. He moved forward and wrapped Josie in the tightest hug she'd ever felt.

"See?" he whispered into her hair. "Piece of cake."

"Thank you, Ben."

He kept hold of her until she let go first.

"I can't feel my legs," she said.

Ben chuckled. "I think that's kind of the point, right?"

Without having to ask, Ben wrapped his arm under her knees, slipped his other hand behind her back—her bare back—and spun her into position on the bed. She fought with the hem of her hospital gown to keep her bits covered. He probably couldn't see her butt from such an angle, but who knew?

"Better?" He pulled the blanket up over her legs and adjusted the pillow behind her head.

"Ben, I love you. Like, a lot." Josie said.

He grinned.

She didn't need to confess anything more than that. She just loved him. Like a friend, like family, and way beyond that if she were honest with herself.

"I'll go grab Kevin and see if he got ahold of your mom yet."

Ben reached over to give her hand a squeeze. "The hotel number was giving him fits, so he was trying to find alternates. I'll go see what he found out."

Josie nodded against the pillow. The monitors hummed beside her, and she watched the rise and fall of her contractions without feeling the intensity. She could breathe much easier now. With the slow progress, her mom had plenty of time to get there before the baby came.

Everything would be fine.

She must have drifted off with the help of the medicine, because the next thing she knew, the door swung open and smacked the door-stop, startling her awake. Daphne rounded the corner and bypassed Josie on the bed. She knelt beside the monitor without offering her usual greeting or smile.

Josie tried to wiggle upright and wipe the sleep from her eyes. What time was it? Had her contractions gotten stronger while she slept?

Daphne reached a hand up to touch Josie's knee. "Josie, it doesn't look like the baby is tolerating the contractions as well as we'd like. I'm going to call Dr. Mallory and see what she thinks, but it looks like we're going to have to get this baby out."

The world around Josie faded in and out with each breath. Daphne came and went, giving updates and spouting medical terms, but Josie barely understood any of them.

At some point, someone came and placed oxygen tubes in her nose. If they told her why, she didn't hear them.

Kevin paced near the door. He kept his phone in his hand, the screen lighting up over and over as he checked for messages. Ben leaned against the wall next to the door, watching the foot of Josie's bed, his eyes glazed over.

Neither of them said a word.

Kevin's phone rang, and he hurried out of the room. When the door shut, Ben snapped out of his stupor and took slow, labored steps toward her bed.

He gathered her hands in his. "It's going to be okay," he whispered.

Dr. Mallory stood on her other side, and Josie let her gaze follow the doctor's every movement. "We're moving you to the OR, Josie. We'll scrub up and get you prepped as fast as we can." The doctor looked up at Ben, who stood beside Josie's bed. "If you're going in with her, you'll need to scrub up too."

Ben stuttered, not truly forming a response.

Even with the extra oxygen, it grew harder to breathe.

Josie grasped at her stomach. Something had happened to her baby inside her, and she could do nothing about it.

Someone else burst into the room, and Josie looked past Ben to see Kevin return. But he wasn't alone.

"Mom," Josie sighed.

Her mother rushed over to the bedside and nearly collapsed on top of her daughter with a hug. "Hey, sweetie. Kevin told me what's happening. I'm going in with you."

"I am so glad you're here." Josie let the tears spill down her face.

From beside the bed, Ben let out a long sigh. He brought Josie's hand up to his cheek and gave it one last squeeze. "We'll be in the waiting room."

For having felt so alone, so scared, love had never surrounded her more.

"Kevin," Josie managed. "Thank you so much."

Kevin rubbed at the back of his neck. "Hang in there, JoJo."

Ben and Kevin left the room, and Daphne escorted Josie's mother away to change and prepare for the operating room.

Josie lay staring at the ceiling as they wheeled her bed from one room to the next. People fussed over her, strapped her arms into place as if preparing for a crucifixion. They moved all kinds of IVs and tubes around and pinched at her stomach.

Dr. Nagis, the anesthesiologist, returned to sit at her head.

"Ready?" Dr. Mallory asked from somewhere in the room. Josie hadn't seen her enter the OR, especially with the tentlike sheet they'd draped under her bust that blocked out 90 percent of the room.

Her mother, too, had taken up a space next to the anesthesiologist. Josie had hardly recognized her with the face mask and blue scrubs. "I'm so sorry I didn't answer right away. I still had it on silent from the rehearsal. But you've got a great group of friends looking out for you, Josie. Ella banged on my door to let me know what's going on. She and your father are in the waiting room with the guys."

Josie closed her eyes and gave thanks for the wonderful support team she had silently cheering her on. Now she just had to get her little boy to safety.

"Hang in there." Her mother brushed the hair out of Josie's eyes and stretched to see around the blue curtain. "They're moving really fast to get him out. It won't be long now."

Josie couldn't bear to open her eyes. If she looked up, she'd see red in the silver-lined light fixture hanging overhead: her insides reflected back at her.

She needed earplugs. All the beeping, the commands, the silence. What if the baby didn't cry?

What if he didn't cry?

The pressure on her stomach grew, though she couldn't feel any pain.

"Hang on." Her mother pressed her cheek to Josie's forehead.

An eternity passed.

She felt so helpless strapped into place. Josie desperately longed to rip her arms out of their hold and reach down to rescue her son. Suddenly, the pressure on her stomach vanished, and her eyes sprung open.

"It's a boy," Dr. Mallory announced. "He's okay."

At the proclamation, the faintest hint of a whine escaped tiny infant lips.

The tears poured, and Josie gasped for breath. Her son was here. He made it. *They* made it.

"Say hi to Mommy," Dr. Mallory said.

Josie's tired gaze drifted toward the large blue sheet over her stomach. There, looking back at her, was the sweetest face she'd ever seen in her life. Chubby cheeks puffed out beside pursed lips that blew spit bubbles. Blood flecked his little body, his skin holding a faint blue tint. His little wrinkly forehead frowned. He *frowned*. As if the traumatic birth that had nearly shattered his mother's heart had merely inconvenienced his tiny baby self.

All the pain of her divorce, the stress of work and money, the uncertainty of life vanished in a moment. Josie loved her little boy more than anything. And he'd been so worth all the heartache leading up to his birth.

"Hi." Josie's voice shook. "Welcome to the world."

She meant to tell him she loved him, but her voice broke as the tears fell. She would have a lifetime to remind him over and over again of that truth. And as soon as they put her together again, she'd get to hold him in her arms for the first time, kiss his chubby little cheeks, and promise him the world.

"Wow," her mother whispered and kissed Josie on the forehead.

Dr. Mallory passed the baby to Daphne, who toweled off the blood and got him ready for the scale.

"Everything looks good, Josie," Dr. Mallory assured her. "The umbilical cord was around his neck a few times, and the contractions made it tighten. I'm so glad we didn't wait to get him out."

Josie's mother dabbed at her tears with the cuff of her scrubs.

Dr. Mallory continued. "I'll finish up here, and we'll get you into recovery. Do you have a name picked out?"

"Yes," Josie said.

"You do?" Her mother placed a hand on Josie's shoulder and looked at her expectantly. After all the day had brought, Josie didn't have the energy to argue baby names. She wanted to relish in the joy that came with her new son and having her mother there at her side when she needed her most.

Josie glanced across the room at her squirming baby on the scale. "Theodore Joseph."

Her mother squeezed tighter on Josie's shoulder and rested her cheek on Josie's forehead. "I love it."

Once they had finished stitching her up, Daphne placed Theodore in Josie's arms. The hallways blurred with the passing time as they moved into the recovery wing. People talked, nurses rushed, monitors beeped. Music hummed overhead on the hallway intercoms.

Josie hardly noticed any of it.

She pressed her lips to her son's head, while her tears spilled against his tiny hospital-issued cap. His round little bottom fit perfectly in her palm, and his warm body contoured to her neck the way puzzle pieces fit together. She couldn't think about how she'd almost lost him. Surely, that thought would haunt her for the rest of her life. But she also couldn't remember how she'd ever lived without him either.

Nothing in her adult life went as planned, but somehow, she received the most beautiful gift in the midst of the chaos.

36

Plum Tree Paradise

THE FIRST MONTH HOME from the hospital had gone by in a whirl of sleepless nights and precious moments. Ben had surprised her with a recliner in the living room where she could recover from her C-section without climbing up and down the steps, and Kevin had set up the penguin bassinet for Teddy to sleep at her side. Between her mother and Ella, they had plenty of home-cooked meals to get them by while the entire Hale/Romero/Lawrence household adjusted to having a new family member.

Josie stood hunched over the sink, rinsing bottles, appreciating the fact that her shrinking stomach now allowed her to get this close to the faucet. She'd never been so happy to stand barefoot in the kitchen, washing dishes, while running on almost no sleep. Those doctors could cut her open a thousand times over if it meant she got to smell Teddy's little baby head and kiss his little chin every time she picked him up.

She shook out a bottle and glanced into the living room, unable to imagine a more perfect scene.

Ben had drifted off, propped against the beanbag chair with a sleeping Teddy sprawled across his chest, his arm draped protectively over the babe. Izzy leaned against her dad's shoulder, stretching across Ben's chest to brush Teddy's fuzzy hair with her fingers. She'd begged to spend every weekend since Teddy's arrival at their home. *Begged.*

The front door opened, and Kevin tiptoed over the threshold. Josie waved a hello.

He whispered across the room like he always did when he came home and didn't know if the baby slept or not. "You're supposed to be resting. I told you I'd handle the dishes."

"It's just the bottles, and for the hundredth time, I feel fine now. I can contribute to this household." Josie grinned and pointed toward the living room. "You might as well go join the rest of the crew in the cuddle puddle. They're watching a movie."

"Fine, but I'm calling dibs on Teddy." He rubbed his hands together as he made his way toward Ben.

When he joined the others in the living room, Josie paused her work to listen to the playful banter taking place. They often argued over whose turn it was to hold Teddy. She had to play the "mom card" just to get time with her son. It was such a lovely problem to have.

Ben's stocking feet padded through the dining room, and he placed a small stack of dishes on the counter, yawning and shaking off the drowsiness of his catnap.

He patted his stomach and stretched his arms over his head. "Does Ella want to cook for us always? We can just have her move in too."

Bless her soul. Ella's lasagna, beef stew, and baked sandwiches had been the best—and healthiest—things any of them had had in, well, maybe their entire adult lives.

Josie turned around and rested her weight on the counter ledge. "She said she's taking this week off cooking for us. Something about having to take care of her own kids or some crap."

"Ugh. Selfish," Ben scoffed.

"Mom's bringing us supper tomorrow, though."

Ben let out a quiet whoop and threw open the dishwasher door. "My mom will probably make something too. She wants to come meet the baby. I requested her homemade chicken noodle soup, 'cause it's freakin' cold outside, and that stuff is the bomb. It's perfectly seasoned. You'll love it."

Josie stood up straight and nearly dropped the bottle in her hand. "Your mom wants to meet Teddy?"

She hadn't been around Ben's parents in over a decade. He'd mentioned their disapproval of Kevin moving in, and she couldn't imagine they supported him inviting a pregnant divorcee into his life as well.

"And you. I've been sending her pictures of Ted, and she's kind of in love. She said if you're feeling up to it, she'd like to finally meet the girl I've been living with for six months." Ben winced, then side-eyed her. "If that's okay with you."

"Of course."

He wanted her to meet his mom. He'd sent his mother pictures of the baby like a proud father might do. She wet her lips and tried to bite back a smile.

She'd secured a place in Ben's life now. A life they shared.

Josie's phone buzzed in her sweatpants pocket. She slid her finger across the screen and clicked on the text from her mother: I've got a pot roast or baked mac and cheese on the menu this week. Preference? Looking forward to loving on my little guy!

Her mother's text tone no longer caused a wave of dread to wash over Josie. In fact, the new roles of mother and grandmother suited them better than anything else. Their mutual love for Teddy bonded them in a whole new way.

Ben gestured to her phone. "Grant get back to you yet about visiting?"

"Oh." Josie tapped on her phone screen again and scrolled to the newest message he'd sent. "Yeah, he's going to come up again on Sunday with his mom. He said Teddy looks like me in the last picture I sent."

"Cool. We'll get out of your hair and let you guys have some privacy then. And he's right. Ted *does* have your nose." Ben's hand flattened against the counter, his head tilting to get a better look at her. "It's cute."

"Oh, thanks." With Ben's focus locked on her, the butterflies went rampant in her stomach. Josie nearly missed her pocket when she tried to put her phone away.

Ben paused with a dirty dish in hand. "You know, it's kind of funny. Do you remember that day at the fair?"

"Um, you mean the day where I cried all over my corn dog and freaked you both out?"

"That's the one!"

Josie stuck out her tongue.

He laughed and put the plate in the dishwasher. "No, really. I was thinking about how the mention of Grant back then kind of made you spiral, but now you're just handling life like a boss."

Josie clutched her stomach to keep it together when she chuckled. "Am I, though? Doesn't feel like it if I'm being honest."

"I think you are."

"Well, I'm okay with that, I guess." Josie slid a few dishes his way. "It's hard to believe all the changes since then, you know? We're not the same people."

He lifted a bowl in praise. "Thank God."

They had grown so much in such a short amount of time. Josie planned to join Ben by enrolling in online classes and had already found great success in her scholarship searches. They'd saved a decent amount of cash for emergencies that might arise and finally learned how to make chicken and veggies in the Instant Pot. Their doctors would certainly approve of their new blood pressures and cholesterol levels.

Mandy accepted Kevin's friend request again too. The man had sung of nothing else over the past few weeks, especially after talking to her face-to-face during their wild night in the delivery room. Now that the lines of communication had reopened, he had this grand plan of attack for getting her back in his arms. Josie was pretty sure she'd see it written out and magnetized to their refrigerator any day now. He remained blissfully ignorant of Ben and Josie's undercover mission to talk to Mandy on his behalf—a day that would forever live in Josie's heart.

"I don't know if I've said it before, but thank you for all of this. If you hadn't taken me in when you did, I might have been in a wildly different situation right now." Josie didn't make eye contact or confess the desperation she'd felt all those months ago. The emotions sat too close to the surface.

"If you hadn't moved in," Ben pointed into the living room where Izzy watched the movie with Teddy's tight fist wrapped around her finger, "my daughter wouldn't have wanted to spend extra weekends with me."

Josie swallowed the lump in her throat. "Well, that's probably to Kevin's credit for initiating the Corn Dog Pact, huh?"

"Yeah, but let's not tell him. It'll go straight to his head." Ben smiled and reached under the sink for some detergent. "To be honest, I thought this pact would just be a way for him to boss us around for a year, while he sat back and watched, but he's not doing too bad on his part either."

"Even more amazing, we're all ahead of schedule on our dead-lines. He turned thirty-one a few weeks ago, so technically we made it by the earliest date option."

She regarded the piece of paper hanging from the hardware-store magnet on the fridge. Kevin had taken a red pen and scratched out the first two points of the pact, apparently deeming the household successful in their money-saving and job-seeking efforts. No one but him could touch the red pen he'd fixed to the magnet.

"Imagine how great we'll be by my birthday in June." Ben closed the dishwasher door and raised an eyebrow. "Unless you still think you need to be Miss Independent, move out, and break this beautiful life pact."

His brown eyes appeared black in the dimly lit kitchen, his hair forever sticking up on the left side of his forehead. His faded T-shirt, nearly as old as their friendship, accentuated his broad shoulders.

She studied him more intently every time he came near. "Not right away, but maybe eventually. I don't want to overstay my welcome, and I have a child now, so—"

"That baby is the most beloved member of our household," he said. "No offense."

He could not have said any sweeter words. "None taken."

"Josie." Ben stepped forward again and reached out to touch her elbow so lightly she barely felt him. "I'm being serious when I say you can stay. We'll buy a real couch and get Ted one of those funky doorway swing things. I can learn to make comfort salads instead of comfort nachos. We can take turns watching the little guy when we've got online classes. And there's plenty of space in the backyard for a vegetable garden and at least two, maybe three, plum trees."

He'd remembered the plum trees. Her knees weakened, and she grasped the counter to support herself. She'd told no one about her desire to settle in suburbia and take up gardening except for him. It was such a silly little wish, but he hadn't forgotten.

He lowered his eyes and his voice. "I want you to stay."

"I want to stay too," she whispered. "You guys are my home."

She'd craved a family of her own, always dreaming of a life-altering miracle to force it into existence with Grant. She never would have expected it to come in the form of a small house, two former classmates, an angsty tween, and a tiny baby boy.

Their lives were individual messes. But together?

"So you'll stay?" he asked.

"I'll stay."

"Good." He inched closer. "And, um. I also wanted to ask. Well, I know the doctor said you have to take it easy for a few weeks, and I've been trying to be patient. But when you're up to it, would you care if I took you out somewhere?"

Josie's heart fluttered to life in a way she hadn't experienced in so long. Her hand slid across the counter toward him, her body following slowly behind. "Like, on a *date*?"

Ben's fingers brushed her knuckles as he leaned in closer still. "I should have asked you a long time ago."

"Now works too." She read the intention in his eyes and floated forward. This was it. He was going to kiss—

"Hello?" Izzy knocked on the countertop, which sent Ben flying upright and back a few steps.

Josie's legs nearly gave out underneath her weight. He finally meant to kiss her, and it just had to get interrupted.

"You ever going to get me that hot chocolate?" she asked her father.

"Coming right up." His voice held a slight squeak.

"Thanks." Izzy's gaze trailed over both of them for a moment. She grinned wide enough to reveal cheek dimples that matched her father's, then returned to the living room.

Did Izzy know what went down in the kitchen?

"Alrighty then. Thank you, daughter of mine." Ben blushed when he looked at Josie and snatched up a packet of hot chocolate. "Can we maybe try that again after I shut her up with chocolate?"

Oh, yes, please.

"Actually…" Josie had dreamt of this moment since her sophomore year of high school. She longed for him to be a part of her life. Not just in this moment, but always. "She can wait a few more minutes. I've been waiting for fifteen *years*." Josie reached forward and grabbed a handful of Ben's shirt, tugging him forward as she rose onto her tiptoes.

He laughed as he cupped her waist with one hand and took her cheek in the other. And he pressed his lips to hers softly, his grip tightening on her hip as if to let her know how hard it was to hold back.

Behind them, someone cleared their throat. Ben stilled. The two of them peeked over his shoulder to find Kevin standing by the bar top. Baby Teddy slept on his shoulder, and Izzy stood at his side.

Kevin shook his head and marched to the fridge, where he plucked his red pen from the magnet and pulled the cap off with his teeth. He scribbled across Corn Dog Pact: Number Three and sighed. After recapping the pen, he chucked it across the room toward the trash bin, completely missing.

He then wrapped his free arm around Izzy. "Well, pretty sure I still won, but y'all played a good game."

"You won? Excuse me?" Ben kept hold of Josie's waist as he shifted toward Kevin.

Josie buried her head in his chest and giggled. Of course, Kevin declared himself the winner. And though she'd never admit it out loud, she'd buy him pizza every day for the rest of his life if he wanted it, just as a thank-you for initiating the most ridiculously named pact she'd ever heard of and creating this new world for her.

Kevin began escorting Izzy to the living room. "I'd like a stuffed-crust sausage and pepperoni." He snapped his fingers for them to get on it and left, a chuckling Izzy tucked under his wing.

Ben wrapped his arms fully around Josie. "I guess I'd better order some pizza then, huh?"

"If we feed them, they might leave us alone for a couple minutes." She shrugged.

He whipped his phone from his pocket and planted a kiss on top of Josie's head. "I like the way you think."

Kevin might have scratched out all three pact points, but Josie knew they'd never really finish the Corn Dog Pact. Every stage of life brought new challenges they'd have to overcome, but at least they'd have each other to get through it together. They'd simply set up the foundation for a life that could be truly beautiful and full of hope.

And it felt so good to dream again.

The End

If you love hilarious, heartwarming, feel-good fiction, we think you'll love Tracy Goodwin's charming story of a mother determined to teach her kids there's no place like gnome:

Available August 2, 2022
From Sourcebooks Casablanca

Chapter 1

AMELIA MARSH HALTS MIDSTEP, stricken by the laughter and squeals of a half-dozen children racing towards her.

"Incoming!" Grabbing her daughter and son, she wraps them in her arms, turning just in time to avoid the melee. One for the win column! Sure, those children appear to be sweet and innocent clad in their frilly dresses and formal ties, but she knows better. Amelia is a mom after all, and this is war—playground style. She's got the superpower of keeping her children in check. Like the Hulk/Bruce Banner, those powers come and go. Some days, Amelia is a master, while other days…well, not so much.

The playground is surrounded by trees and lush green grass; however, its pretty setting is *this* parent's nightmare. Kids of all ages shout, wrestle, and run like they're all on one heck of a sugar high. While she's scoping a group of younger boys wrestling in the kiddie play mulch underneath the jungle gym, Amelia's eldest tugs at her arm.

"Mom, can we play?" Her son, Jacob, asks, looking up at his mom with his signature bright smile. At ten years old, he is a charmer. What's worse? He knows it. One flash of his megawatt smile and he receives free cookies at his favorite bakery, or snags extra stickers at their local supermarket.

A little girl rushes past them, dressed in a pink tutu with a bunny tail that hangs haphazardly in the back. The child's faux tail bounces with every step she takes, and her bunny ears remind Amelia of their mission: today, they are attending their community Easter egg hunt and taking pictures with the Easter Bunny.

This is their first major outing since the big move back to Amelia's hometown of Houston, since her divorce, since their lives drastically changed. The last thing she wants is her children running around in the sweltering Texas sun, then taking pictures with some costumed cottontail while they sweat profusely with tangled hair or—worse yet—covered in mulch. She glances again at that same group of boys, who now have pieces of mulch stuck to their clothes and in their hair. The chances of more than one shower needed: likely. Drain-clogging potential: high. Just what Amelia's trying to avoid.

Crouching in front of her son, she ensures that her long skirt is covering her legs, then reaches for the hands of Jacob and his sister, Chloe. They're twenty-two months apart, the best of friends on most days, and bicker like nobody's business the rest of the time. "Why don't we take pictures with the Easter Bunny first, then you can run around. Deal?"

Jacob wrinkles his brow, considering his mom's offer. He's not buying what she's selling, and Amelia's glad that she didn't go all out like some other parents. Contrasting the once-pristine girls and boys wearing their best attire and ruining their special outfits, her kids are wearing clothes of their own choosing—cargo shorts and a polo shirt for Jacob, while Chloe wears leggings and her favorite ruffled shirt with a pink flamingo on it. No fancy shoes, either. Just socks and sneakers.

Picture-taking Marsh style is practical by necessity, because their family is cursed when it comes to family photos. Without fail, the better dressed her children are, the worse the picture. There could be fifty photos taken, and not one would include both of the kids smiling or looking at the camera at the same time. But, when they wear comfortable clothes—their favorite clothes—voilà! It's like a Harry Potter moment with magical smiles and happy memories.

At this community event, she seems to be the only parent with this mindset, seeing the abundance of children once dressed to impress now getting dirty, sweaty, and screaming louder than the audience at a Metallica concert.

"I promise you can play after—"

"They have cookies! Can we have cookies, Mom?" Chloe, her eight-year-old spitfire tomboy, points to a little boy eating a large cookie, then sprints toward the clubhouse, followed close behind by Jacob. When all else fails, cookies will do the trick and, thanks to a little boy covered in grass stains, a trail of cookie crumbs is leading Amelia's children away from the lure of a crowded playground.

"Save some for me!" she calls to them, walking close behind until they reach the pool clubhouse, also known as their community's "aquatic center." It's a fancy name for a small in-ground pool, and a building with bathrooms.

Their subdivision of Castle Rock is a newer one, situated in the northern suburbs of Houston in a town named Timberland, Texas. Here, in what is known as the *Lush and Livable Timberland*, where natural pine trees that were once in abundance are rare thanks to the building boom, residents pride themselves on their thick green lawns and blooming flower beds.

Under the shade of the clubhouse and its covered patio, Amelia spies tables accentuated with spring-themed tablecloths whipping in the warm breeze, upon which plates of cookies with colored icing and cups of lemonade are arranged around stuffed-animal bunnies and Easter decorations.

She's traded sweat and dirt for icing and lemonade. Given the fact that her kids used to hate any and all imaginary figures in costumes, from Santa to the Easter Bunny to their school mascot, Amelia will take whatever photos she can get. Cargo shorts? Sure. Flamingo shirt? Done. Icing turning their tongues blue like Smurfs? She'll deal.

Such is the single mom in her. Always trying to please, to make the kids happy, and to find her own sense of satisfaction. Without her ex-husband, Daniel. It was his choice to start a new life with his mistress. Did it hurt? Yes. Because he walked out on their children and because he caused them pain. Though Daniel may have wanted out, he also wanted everything that he valued—their house, their money, their investments. What he didn't value are Amelia's biggest blessings: Jacob and Chloe.

Granted, she's no pushover. With the help of a brilliant attorney, Amelia fought for what her children and she deserved. When the divorce was finalized, it was time to remove her children from the situation and give them a chance to heal—near some of Amelia's best friends.

Today, she's on her own, with her children—who are scarfing down cookies like they haven't eaten in days. "Slow down, sweeties. Let's take a break from the cookies."

Mom rule number one: never let your kids overeat and throw up. As a matter of fact, avoid vomit at all costs. Gross, but true.

"Hello there." A saccharine-sweet voice and a terse tap on Amelia's shoulder grabs her attention. "I'm Carla, from the community's management company. I don't believe we've met."

"Nope, not yet." Amelia would remember Carla, who is a sight to behold with teased red hair, full makeup, and a pristine pantsuit. How is this woman not melting in today's heat? In her light maxi dress and messy bun, Amelia is already perspiring, but Carla's heavy makeup remains flawless. Is she human or is heat endurance *her* superpower?

"Hi, Carla. I'm Amelia Marsh. These are my children, Jacob

and Chloe." Her daughter waves while her son gulps more lemonade before flashing his signature grin.

Carla narrows her eyes, staring at Amelia's children, seemingly immune to Jacob's charms. In turn, Jacob smiles wider, arching his brow. With still no response from Carla, Jacob gives up and studies his feet, while Amelia gives him a reassuring pat on his back.

"Where's the Bunny?" Chloe asks.

"He's coming. How about you line up over there?" Carla points at the seating area where four carefully arranged lawn chairs remain empty, and a line has already formed, full of flushed and disheveled children. Parents are doing their best to right the damage done by playtime. *Good luck with that.*

Amelia's children look to her for approval, and she nods. Jacob smiles, his teeth blue from the icing. "That's my boy!" Amelia encourages him with a thumbs-up.

Mom rule number…who knows, since there are so many mom rules that she's lost count, but this is one of the most important rules of all: you can only control so much. Amelia has traded the messy, sweaty, grass-stained debacle for blue teeth. The glass half full theory is that the blue might not show up in the picture.

"Keep drinking, buddy." She smiles as Jacob takes another sip of his lemonade, then she turns to Carla. "What's the difference between the HOA and the management company?"

"The Homeowners Association consists of Castle Rock residents, some of whom preside on its board of directors. The management company, for which I work, handles the logistics, enforcing the bylaws—in other words, the community rules, and—"

"Collecting the annual dues," Amelia adds with a smile. Now she understands. "I know my dues are paid for the year. I took care of that at closing."

Studying Carla, Amelia notes that the woman has a half smirk/half grin plastered on her face. Just like her makeup, it isn't moving.

"I'm sorry about the letter arriving so soon after you moved in. But rules are rules, you know."

Amelia's catches the woman's exaggerated grimace. "Letter? I'm lost. Why would I receive a letter when I paid my dues?"

"Oh, no. You haven't read it yet." Carla gasps, her hot pink nails matching her lipstick as she covers her mouth with her hands.

"Nope, I haven't received it yet. What's in this letter? It sounds ominous." Amelia's humor falls flat on the stoic-faced Carla.

"There are rules."

"Right. You've repeated that. Three times, I believe. Possibly four." Shoving her sunglasses on top of her head, Amelia refuses to break eye contact with Carla, whose expression remains serious. "Rules like what, exactly?"

Carla shifts, then whispers, "Your gnome."

"My what?" Is *gnome* some sort of code word for one of her children? Amelia's head snaps immediately to her kids. Jacob laughs while Chloe chats with him, probably reciting one of her famous knock-knock jokes. The kids are safe, so her attention returns to Carla. "Did you say my 'gnome'?"

"Your garden gnome. The one in your front yard," Carla counters.

Amelia laughs. She can't help it. Carla's mock horror that this new resident finds her comment amusing quickly fades into impatience, her eyes emanating frustration and disapproval, the lines around them deepening.

Clearing her throat allows Amelia time to keep her expression neutral, her tone calm, and her snark to a minimum. "Do you mean my tiny, hand-painted garden gnome hidden within the bushes, flowers, and mulch that comprise a small portion of my front yard? You can barely see it."

Carla scoffs. "I see everything. It's my job to inspect the front yards. I drive by intermittently, so I can ensure our community remains up to the standards set in the bylaws."

Of course she does. The fact that Carla *sees everything* is a bit alarming.

Sticking to the topic at hand, Amelia explains, "My children made me that gnome for Mother's Day last year." Before the divorce. Before their move. It was displayed prominently in the front yard of their old home. That gnome represents her children's only request when moving to Houston: that she'd place it in their new front yard. It helps them feel at home.

"You must remove it, I'm afraid. Rules are rules, and some people's trash is others' treasure, so to speak." Carla grins, seemingly oblivious to the fact that she just insulted Amelia and her beloved gnome.

"Trash?" *Carla. Did. Not. Just. Say. That.*

Carla nods. "Not that I find your troll trashy, of course. Playing devil's advocate, the truth is that you may like it, but your neighbors may find it tacky. Besides, the ban is in the bylaws."

So, this woman has called her kids' gnome *trash*, *tacky*, and a *troll*. For any mom, especially Amelia, those are fighting words. "Who bans garden gnomes that you can barely see in their bylaws?"

"Your HOA. If you don't like it, I invite you to attend your next quarterly Homeowners' Association meeting. You just missed the last one, but I'll send out an email blast to all residents, signs will be posted at the entrances to the neighborhood, and an announcement will go up on the community website approximately ten days in advance of the next meeting." Applause drowns out Carla, and Amelia turns to see the Easter Bunny waving at the kids.

"Time for pictures! Have a good day." And just like that, Carla dismisses Amelia, sauntering away to schmooze with other residents.

Amelia blinks. *What the heck?* Gnomes are off limits, but bunnies are okay? She scans her surroundings which, like most front yards in her subdivision, are decorated with colored ribbons, bunny cut-outs, and enlarged egg décor. Yeah, bunnies on full display are fine, yet one tiny, beautiful gnome—the gnome that her kids made for her—must go? The same gnome that makes their new house a *home*.

The Easter Bunny high fives Jacob and Chloe, and Amelia makes a beeline to them, just as her daughter begins hiding behind her brother. Apparently, Chloe hasn't gotten over her fear of fake bunnies after all. This one is cute, sporting a purple suit jacket, a yellow vest, and a rainbow-colored bow tie. Though this event is held weeks before Easter, beads of perspiration trickle down Amelia's spine, causing her to pity the poor soul who drew the short straw and must wear a furry costume in this heat and sticky humidity. Hopefully, his or her costume has a fan.

"Hi, Bunny!" She smiles and high fives the faux fur paw of whoever is in the costume.

Nodding and swaying to the beat of Taylor Swift's "Shake It Off", which is blasting through the pool speakers, this rabbit is in character. Amelia needs to shake Carla off, since her blood pressure is still high from the woman's lack of tact and the accompanying ban notice. Over a gnome? Really? So, Amelia takes Taylor's advice, singing and dancing with her children in line. The Easter Bunny must be a Swiftie, too, because the person in the costume dances over to the chairs before taking a seat.

When it's their turn for picture time, Amelia hands her cell to a man standing next to Carla, who will take the picture for them. Carla...ugh. The sight of her after that catty "tacky" comment makes Amelia's heartbeat pound like an anvil.

Normally, Amelia would have let Carla's comments about the letter go. Who knows? She might have even removed her gnome. But Carla insulted Jacob and Chloe's art, even after Amelia explained the importance of it.

One simple, passive-aggressive comment is all it takes for her to decide that she can't let it go. Instead, Amelia may drive the kids to

Target, Walmart, or both after they spend time at the playground and buy out their entire garden gnome department. If she's lucky, maybe they'll be on sale, and she'll display an extended gnome family on her front lawn. If the HOA wants to send her a letter, she might as well earn it.

As they approach the Bunny for their picture, Chloe hides behind Amelia's skirt while Jacob charms the fluffy cottontail immediately with a knock-knock joke. No matter which way Amelia turns, her daughter won't come out from hiding. Amelia half expects Chloe to hide *under* her skirt any minute. Every time Amelia moves, so does Chloe, taking her mom's dress with her. "Sit on my lap, Chloe. Let's take the picture together."

With Jacob on one side, and Amelia and Chloe on the other, they pose with the Bunny.

When the man holding her cell prompts them to smile, Amelia instructs her kiddos to smile, adding, "Say 'garden gnome!'"

"Garden gnome!"

It's official. The Bunny must think I've completely lost my mind.

On the bright side, the kids smiled, laughed, and took a great picture. Add to that the fact that Amelia's got a plan.

The HOA better look out, because this mom protects her gnomes at all costs.

Chapter 2

THANKS TO A BROKEN fan in Kyle Sanders's costume, he's about to suffer heat stroke by rodent impersonation. It's not exactly the way he expected to go, but hey, if you're going to sweat to death, why not do so wearing a goofy Easter Bunny costume? Go big or go home, right? Sure, it'll be humiliating, especially when it hits the local news. And it would traumatize a lot of children.

Oh man! The kids…

In an effort to hide his demise from the neighborhood children, Kyle darts into the cleaning closet of the Castle Rock community's pool house, desperate to cool off. Struggling with the top of the costume, a muffled curse word escapes his lips, as one of his pawed feet lands beside a bucket and a mop slams against his bunny forehead. It's Kyle against a cottontail costume, in a cage match, or in this case a closet match. His opponent—a bulky, furry rabbit costume—is a modern-day torture device that's currently winning.

Why did I ever volunteer for this?

Taking a step to the side, his oversized furry foot lands in the empty bucket. Still, Kyle manages to use his floppy tail to leverage himself against a wall. "The things I do for this community. Come on!"

Managing to free his face from the bunny head, Kyle tosses the thing onto a small table taking up too much space. He then rips the Velcro at his back and frees both arms, sliding the costume down to his waist. Drenched with sweat, he grabs his sports drink and takes several desperate gulps from the large bottle.

Though his foot may remain stuck, at least he won't die of dehydration. Limping over to the small table with the decapitated rabbit head, Kyle narrows his eyes, staring at the bunny's face which remains frozen in place, that wide toothy grin taunting him along with its glossy eyes and fake wire-rimmed glasses.

Kyle mutters under his breath while placing the bottle on the table before attempting to yank his enlarged rabbit's foot from the yellow bucket. It still won't budge. Kyle once considered a rabbit's foot to be good luck, but in this cleaning closet of horrors, it's anything but.

Blood-curdling, high-pitched screams cause him to jump, as his eyes dart to the closet door, which is now open. Standing in the doorway is the cute mom wearing the casual dress who has covered her daughter's eyes, gaping at Kyle as her son yells, "The Easter Bunny isn't real! He isn't real!"

"I'm sorry!" It's all Kyle can manage. Repeating it louder, over the screams, doesn't do much.

I've traumatized this woman's children! I've destroyed their inno-cence. It's all he can think as his neighbor—Kyle doesn't know her name because they've never met—leads her kids into the closet and slams the door shut in an attempt not to traumatize anyone else's children, he supposes.

"Jacob, Chloe, it's okay," she says in a soothing voice, caressing her kids' shoulders. "This is the Easter Bunny's helper. Think about it. EB can't be everywhere at once, right?"

She wipes her little girl's tears as her son surveys Kyle with a skeptical expression. "You're the Bunny's helper?"

Sure, why not? Right now, Kyle would agree to anything that will calm the kids. "Yes, I am." He glances to their mom, who nods at him, as if encouraging Kyle to elaborate. "Your mom is right. The Bunny is busy painting eggs, making baskets, buying candy—"

"He buys candy? From where?" This little boy asks a lot of questions.

Kyle shrugs. "A candy store."

"What does he pay you?" the kid asks him.

"Not enough." It's the first thing that comes to mind. In truth, Kyle doesn't make a dime for this. He's a volunteer, donating his time so the community can save money as opposed to hiring a professional hare. He's also the community's Santa. Multitasking is his thing. Along with running his own business, he is the acting HOA board president, also on a volunteer basis, which means residents yell at him about the cost of their annual dues (in spite of the fact that the cost of dues hasn't risen once in Kyle's four years as president), letters they receive from the management company prohibiting decorations in their front yards and criticizing the height of their lawns, and all other concerns. Meanwhile, he sweats in a rodent costume on an eighty-plus-degree day for kids who don't belong to him. It's a thankless task. One he was reelected for, because no one was willing to run against him. There's only one poor sap in Castle Rock willing to torture himself, and he is currently being interrogated by a kid.

The boy scratches his head. "I want to drive a Ford F-250 when I grow up, have a Mercedes transit van, and a Tesla. My mom says I need to make a lot of money to pay for all of it."

Talk about a change of subject. "That's ambitious. You'll figure it out, though. You've got time." Kyle winks at him, hoping he's appeased the little boy's curiosity.

All he wanted was to cool off in a cleaning closet. Now Kyle is giving advice on a kid's future career path and vehicle ownership. This is way too much. Especially since it's cramped with the four of them in the tiny space, and the walls seem to be closing in. Or it could be Kyle's claustrophobia. Fun times.

"What's your name?" the boy asks Kyle, jerking him from his concerns regarding the confined quarters and heavy costume still covering the lower half of his body.

"My name?" That's an easy one. "Kyle Sanders. What's yours?"

"I'm Jacob Marsh and this is my mom, Amelia Marsh. My sister, Chloe Marsh, is there," he points at the little girl, whose red cheeks are tear-streaked.

She nods. "Yeah, I'm Chloe Marsh and this is my mom and brother."

"Got it." Chloe, Jacob, and Amelia. *Amelia Marsh.* A brunette with a killer smile, Amelia is luminescent, wearing minimal makeup and exuding a natural glow. Her dress is sleeveless and floor length, but when the breeze blows in the right direction, sandals that lace around her ankles attract Kyle's attention. She's left him breathless, or maybe it's the lack of oxygen in the cramped closet.

About the Author

Stephanie Eding specializes in humorous women's fiction about the struggles of adulthood in the twenty-first century. She works as a freelance editor, cleans when stressed, and hates cooking but loves to eat. Away from her desk, she's a wife, mother, expert napper, and leader of a cat horde.